EPIPHANY

EPIPHANY
Paul Harrington

For Denise, Paul and Will.
The Magi had one star to guide them.
I'm fortunate enough to have three.

PROLOGUE

*Pariyatra Parvata Mountains, high above the Salang Pass,
Northeastern Arabia, in the days of the Saba Empire*

S*crunkch. Scrunkch Sccccrunnnkch.* The men painfully ascended the twisting mountain path, their tedious passage marked by the sounds of their inadequately shod feet punching through the ice-covered snow.

Scrunkch. Scrunkch.

The wind whirled and wailed in protest at their ascent, and tried to push them back. They were two men — common, decent folk of the soil who scraped out a living a thousand feet below on the slopes of the mountain. They were breeders and traders of goats. And this was the time of year they sent their flocks up the mountain to feast on the fresh green grasses growing in meadowy nooks of their mountain. At least, that was the way it had always been, doing as their fathers had done before them for centuries. But this year was different, and it felt wrong.

"Ateeq, my feet! I can't feel them — I think they're starting to freeze!" shouted Muhsin at the hunched and snow-caked back of his companion leading the way. "I can't go much farther!" Muhsin whined, trying to make himself heard over the wail of the wind.

Ateeq turned to face him. "He's my son; he's all alone up there with the flock. I'm sure he won't leave the goats to die, so we have to go help him. It's not much farther, my friend. Come on!" The older man, with determination glowing in his eyes, reached out a hand and pulled Muhsin to walk alongside him.

Scrunkch. Scrunkch.

"It's never snowed this late. This is an unholy storm, I tell you!" shouted the superstitious Muhsin, making the ancient camel's head gesture to ward off evil spirits.

Ateeq could only nod and agree. A shiver ran up his spine to accompany the shivers already running through his slowly freezing extremities. His heart agreed with Muhsin: the snows had melted months ago, and the mountain had been deemed more than safe enough for the annual ritual of taking the goats high to graze. His son, on the cusp of becoming a man, had taken the family flock up to fatten the goats on the rich grasses fed by the melted runoff.

But soon after his son left, the freak snowstorm had fallen on the upper half of the peak, dumping deep snow and freezing rain onto its summit. From below, Ateeq could tell all was not right, but he had no grasp of how treacherous the situation was until he'd started to make his own way up to help his son bring down the flock.

"Just up here is the good place I told him to take the flock, the one with the spring to the side, you know?" Ateeq asked; Muhsin nodded mutely and stumbled on.

They rounded a sharp bend in the path and looked down into an open area that should have been an emerald meadow full of bleating goats and a snoozing shepherd. Instead, it was a scene of absolute horror.

The snowy floor of the meadow was splattered with blood, the crimson fluid melting through the crust, leaving ghastly steaming red pockets in the snow. Half-devoured, fully savaged goat carcasses littered the meadow floor. A howling cry rose above the shriek of the wind, emitted from the authors of the horrific landscape.

Three powerfully built, large wolves were busy feasting on their prey, and howling in pleasure at the kill. To Ateeq's eyes, they looked too big, bigger than any wolf he'd ever encountered. Their thick, coarse coats were as black as ink, sinister silhouettes against the snow-bleached meadow. The falling snow seemed unable to find a purchase on their darkly glistening fur, and a sickly steam rose and evaporated in the turbulent air.

Ateeq's mind raced as he tried to process the horrific scene. The wolves he'd encountered before now were cowards, thieves who snuck in and stole away silently. Not these. He felt an evil purpose at work, an unbridled savagery in them that paid little heed to how wolves would normally behave.

Ateeq's brain told him that this—all of this—wasn't right. Too many things didn't add up: the freak snowstorm this late in the year, wolves hunting brazenly in the daylight, slaughtering an entire flock, and their gigantic size. None of it made any sense. Everything was...twisted. He felt fear seize his heart.

"Save us," whispered Muhsin as he came alongside Ateeq and laid his eyes upon the slaughter.

The force of the wind shifted, and the change betrayed the men's presence to the chewing wolves. One of the wolves lifted its nose into the air and snuffled at the scent of the men. It pivoted its head to look at them and released a blood-chilling howl to its brethren. Gore dripped sloppily from its open jaws, and it fixed its eyes upon the newfound prey, yellow, glowing eyes that betrayed a sinister, unearthly power at work behind them.

Discovered, Muhsin's last shred of courage whistled away on the wind and he shrieked in terror. The other two wolves forgot the fresh kill at their feet and began to advance upon the men. Muhsin made to bolt, but Ateeq's hand stayed him, for across the meadow, sheltering the last of the flock with his arms spread wide, was Ateeq's terror-stricken son. "Waziri!" the father exclaimed under his breath. "He's alive."

The wolves spread out into a triangular attack pattern,

employing their inbred pack mentality to try to encircle the men on the ridge above them. They were just 30 paces from their new meals.

"Muhsin! Muhsin!" While there was still time to act, Ateeq shook his companion back to reality. Muhsin slowly peeled his wide eyes from the ghastly scene to Ateeq's face.

"I'll draw off the wolves. You get the boy and run. Don't stop—run until you're far away. Save my boy, and don't come back!" Ateeq spat the commands hurriedly, sensing that he had only moments to lure the creature off.

Ateeq began flailing his arms and shouting at the top of his lungs as he bounded down the snow bank and onto the blood-splattered floor of the clearing.

"Heyya! Over here! Come on, you dogs! Get me!"

The wolves swung their heads to fix a bead on the man foolish enough to draw their attention a second time. Ateeq ran deliberately away from his trapped son, forcing the beasts to turn their back to the boy and the remaining goats. With hungry snarls, the wolves redirected and padded across the snowy floor towards Ateeq.

Muhsin, to his credit, did come down into the meadow's open space, but only moved a few paces into the clearing. He gestured to the boy, calling to him in a whispered shout, "Waziri! Come! Come quickly!"

But the wolves sensed the ruse and froze. One twisted its head and blew long streams of steam from its snout as its shimmering yellow orbs spied the unfortunate Muhsin.

With silky speed, the wolf spun and loped to cover the space between it and Muhsin in the blink of an eye. The poor man stood rooted to his place. Urine spilled from his loins. His heart stopped beating, his arms became limp and useless, and he drew his last, sad breath. As Muhsin feared, the wolf lunged forward and sank its fangs into the soft tissue of Muhsin's throat, its heavy paws pummeling his chest and throwing him backward.

"Glurg!" Muhsin tried to scream, yet only managed to

blurt out a wet explosion of pain from his punctured throat as the wolf took him down. Beneath the heavy collision of the wolf, Muhsin's body fell like a wet sack, and a dark red cloud of blood immediately began to seep out into the snow beneath him. The beast was easily his match in size, and more than his better in strength and ferocity. Muhsin's frame convulsed as the wolf tore open his jugular vein, shredding the life from his body. Muhsin's heels kicked at the snow in vain as he was murdered. The last sight Muhsin's eyes beheld were the iridescent yellow eyeballs of the sneering wolf.

The other two predators had paused to witness their brother's success. Ateeq used the distraction wisely and stealthily moved to his son's position. The remaining goats had scattered, and Waziri held only a small kid in his arms, the last of his flock. Waziri's young face was petrified in horror at all he'd seen, and Ateeq could see that his son was incapable of speech. Ateeq smiled grimly at the boy, proud that he'd held his place and determined that they wouldn't meet the same fate as poor Muhsin.

The two wolves resumed the hunt for Ateeq, annoyed that the man had tried to sneak away but finding him easily in the swirling snow nonetheless. The added bonus of the boy and the baby goat just fueled their supernatural bloodlust. They advanced.

Ateeq felt his fear groping to paralyze him, to take control and fix him to a similar fate as Muhsin. They were trapped, he knew it, and their options were nil. His son looked at up him with eyes that begged for hope, but he had none offer.

The two wolves advanced as the third ravaged Muhsin's corpse across the meadow. The pair of hunters slunk silently across the snow, dark shadows of doom that crept steadily towards their quarry with unblinking amber eyes. Long strands of sanguine drool swung from their open, panting maws. The wind seemed to quiet in anticipation of their strike.

Ateeq's heart quailed, and he prepared for the inevitable.

CHAPTER ONE

Mountains of Panjakent, eastern Arabia

The ancient ways were dying, violently vanishing beneath the turbulent waves of time, never to return. For the new world to exist, the old world had to perish. And it was to be a brutal end.

These were turbulent times, very different from today. Disputes were solved with the sword. Kings jealousy guarded their thrones, suspicious of even their own bloodlines. Diplomacy was simply a prelude to war, and conquest was the ultimate objective of even the most meager of despots. Blood was cheap compared with gold, and gold a pittance when compared to the soil of an adjoining neighbor.

But there was another way that the ancient world differed: the old world was ripe with raw power. Energy and magic, unbridled, flowed through everyday events and objects, fuel for the tales so easily dismissed as mere legend from the comfort of safe, predictable, contemporary lives.

In every heart, stone, and breath of wind lay the promise of the impossible. Those who could harness and apply their mystical talents became leaders, wielders of influence and achievers of stature. Those who had none, the majority of mortals, became the serving class on whose backs empires were built and mighty mystics rested their feet.

Yet the polarities of life and nature held true even then, and they remain as steadfast as ever, for good and evil are eternal and cannot be changed by the sands of time. What was different in the ancient world was the clarity of each extreme, and the defined spaces in which men lived between the light and dark. One's actions were more easily read. The pure hearted were proclaimed heroes and immortalized, while those who practiced dark deeds performed them without apology or remorse. Those were the alien times and circumstances, the crucible for the violent cataclysm that would erase the old world.

Arabia. In ancient times, it was a vast region, and it encompassed mountain and field, hillside and heath, oasis and desert. It was an immense land, running from Egypt in the west to the Gulf of Persia in the east, from Mesopotamia in the north to the shores of the Sea of Arabia in the south. For many years, since the passing of the occupation by Alexander and his Persians, the land had known everything from peace and prosperity to strife and savagery. It was said that Arabia was in fact not a land, but a lover whose moods changed with the shifting of her sands.

There were many regional factions and rulers in a land this diverse, but chief among them was Melchior, who became a king at his father's death and eventually unified most of Arabia under his rule. Powerful and a bit mystical, Melchior was nonetheless pleasant and generous of spirit, and thus loved by his subjects as he took up the throne.

Melchior made his kingdom in the mountains far to the east in Arabia that bordered on the stifling desert that rolled westward. Situated on a lofty, terraced mountain slope where eagles, falcons, and phoenix swooped and soared just out of bow shot, the palace of Melchior overlooked a narrow swath of fertile land that gave way reluctantly to the great sprawling carpet of sand.

The palace's ornate spires shot to the sun, and the multi-colored onion domes inspired many a weary traveler to climb the final few hundred feet to enter its gilded gates. The stones that formed the palace's walls were set as tight as skin to flesh. Even the most skillfully fired arrow would find no passage through its formidable frontage, and its battlements had never been breached. In all, it was a mountaintop fortress to inspire fear in the hearts of its enemies and song in the hearts of those who called it home.

As majestic as its outer visage was, the true magic of the palace lay within its walls. In the great hall, magicians, or magi, as they were called in those days, routinely arced great bolts of lightning through the air, and conjurers passed sharpened swords through the taut, bare waists of slender, veiled girls without drawing a drop of blood. Debates of Aristotelian magnitude were hotly argued back and forth by learned scribes, and tales of Sophoclean tragedy were spun upon the lyres of balladeers from lands far away. Dreams were read, sacrifices were studied, and minds were expanded within the four walls of the palace's great hall. These, and many other feats of wonder were part and parcel of everyday life in Melchior's realm.

Melchior was already a man, old enough to have drawn his first blood, yet wise enough to regret it and learn to stay his sword. Melchior appeared younger than his years. He was fit for a man just shy of two score years, tall and lean, but the first speckles of gray in his beard, and the edges of his dark hair gave a truer reckoning of how he'd spent his years.

His eyes were cerulean blue, and they softly gazed out from beneath his dark heavy brow and lent an air of sad wisdom to his weathered visage. His face was angular and tanned, and he bore the carriage of a man who was weary from his trek, yet ready to push on for a good many miles.

Melchior possessed the gift of the supernatural and was a magus as well as a king. It was as powerful a combination as any under the sun, but he chose to wield both of these gifts quietly.

Melchior had no queen and desired none. Certainly, he had concubines in plenitude and never wanted for a silken girl to bring him icy delights as he reclined in contemplation of the landscape. But Melchior's existence was restless, and he waited impatiently for an event, a challenge, that always seemed shadowed in the future, just beyond his vision or grasp. He was...unfulfilled.

In appearance, Melchior looked no more like a king than his stewards did. He favored the simple dress of the common man; light, billowy pants tied at the ankle and a short vest of azure blue over a woven shirt. He traveled the halls and fields in simple sandals, often with neither sword nor staff nor crown. But even as he adopted the look and genial attitude of the everyday man, an unearthly glow of comfortable attraction emanated from him, drawing others to him as the moth to the flame.

Counselors he had in the hundreds. The palace itself, considered the center of learning for the entire kingdom of ancient Arabia, was home to most of the magi of the land — sorcerers, scientists, astronomers, astrologers, prophets, soothsayers, and priests. The magi held great symposia a few times a year, and Melchior's reign was considered an era of enlightenment.

Yet with all this at hand, Melchior chose to remain an introverted figure. He dispensed justice, war, peace, and generosity all with the same even-handed uncertainty. Melchior had everything a man could desire yet he remained incomplete. In his heart, he was doubtful of himself and his abilities. Something was coming, though Melchior knew not what. He sensed an event of incredible magnitude on the horizon, an event, it seemed, for which he'd waited all his life. And yet it never arrived. So he waited. And watched.

Melchior received the request for council on a bright, cloudless morning. Shafiq, Melchior's Magus Primus and one of the few men he considered a true friend with no ulterior motives, delivered the appeal.

Melchior had spent his morning considering the role water, or want of it, played in the overtures of the world's empires. All too often, an empire and its armies were laid waste by no foe mightier than thirst.

Melchior knew that the desert is a covetous mistress who doesn't often share her precious riches with interloping armies and their beasts of burden. Most generals relied on the two most conventional means of watering their men and beasts; by carrying water in clay jugs and animal skin bags, and by planning their marches to include as many villages with wells as possible. But since many places didn't welcome large groups of heavily armed men with joy and open arms, getting that village's water usually meant laying siege, which was never a military objective in the first place. So, water was a problem.

Melchior decided that there had to be a much smarter and easier way to quench one's thirst under the desert sun. At first, he'd tried a variety of spells, spices, and commands to make a vase full of sand spout water. After a few hours, he'd succeeded only in melting the sand into a lump of rock. No one ever said being a member of the magi was easy.

Then Melchior turned down a more promising path; making the air above the desert so heavy with rain that it would fall at his command. The king conjured a small storm cloud in his bedchamber, roiling with tiny bursts of lightning and thunder, but he grew more and more frustrated when he couldn't control the downpour. All about the cavernous royal chamber, spontaneous cloudbursts zipped hither and yon, soaking his Persian carpets quite thoroughly. But not a drop had fallen as commanded by Melchior into the bowl he'd set to collect it.

Shafiq had entered during one of these renegade deluges, and a miniature thunderhead sought him out and set to work. Shafiq was soaked immediately. Waving away the diminutive storm clouds, Melchior laughed good-naturedly as the older man grumbled while wringing water from his beard.

Yet Shafiq's countenance betrayed that this was no ordinary visit. His eyes were dark; they looked as though one of the court artisans had carved them even more deeply into his skull. Melchior closed his eyes as he dismissed the last remaining storm cloud, which zipped through the open doors of his balcony and out into a beautiful sunny day.

"More than one courtesan will get a drenching as you just did, with no idea why," Melchior said with a smile. He made a mental note to figure out a way to get the standing water out of the bedchamber later.

"A thousand pardons for the intrusion, my king. But I bring dire news and a prediction of great turmoil," Shafiq said gravely.

The old man had a flair for theatricality in speech, but dressed the part of the humble servant. He wore light gray robes that perfectly matched his long, stiff, pointed beard, yet his moody dress was a sharp contrast to the mighty power and insightful spirit it clothed. With Melchior, Shafiq normally started off formally. It usually took five to ten minutes for him to shake off his royal respect and speak to Melchior casually. But when his opening gambit was this gloomy, both mentor and king put aside the pleasantries.

"Shafiq," Melchior carefully replied, nodding while committing himself to nothing.

"My liege," Shafiq said while bowing his head in respect, "the signs portend great catastrophe. I know of no other way to say it. Many fellow magi concur; dark tidings are at hand, and we wish to convene an assembly as soon as possible."

Melchior wasn't caught completely off guard. He'd seen the same coming wave in the heavens for years and felt it in his bones. Perhaps the event he'd waited for was finally at hand. Unfortunately, if these were the times Melchior had spent his life waiting for, they seemed to be larger and darker than he'd ever anticipated.

CHAPTER TWO

The council of magi convened after the noon meal. The great hall was cleared, not a minor task, and the council members gathered. From the gallery above, it sounded to Melchior's ears more like a marketplace than a meeting of minds. Squawks and squeals intermingled with shouts and shrieks. There was an atmosphere of agitation in the room, with a touch of panic.

As Melchior descended the stairs into the vast chamber, the clamor faded. He wasn't a king who relied on pomp and royalty to command respect; he earned it by looking people in the eye and giving them his attention when they spoke. The assembled council of magi sat in a grand circle, in no particular order and with no one superior to another. Men sat or reclined on broad cushions of bright silk, with a few showing off by levitating a hand span above the floor. To be heard, one had only to rise and enter the circle.

In the center of the circle was a massive, hand-hammered bronze brazier that stood as tall as a man's chest, and yawned wider than the same man's outstretched arms. The mammoth basin was held upright by black wrought iron legs that peeled back into gentle curls near the lip of the container. A supernatural fire flickered quietly within its confines, blue and orange flames that hungrily lapped the sides of the giant metal bowl and strained to escape its confines. Standing off a pace to one side of the fiery cauldron was a standing matching bronze urn filled with a glittering magenta powder.

All rose and silence fell as Melchior and his gigantic bodyguard Barir reached the circle. Melchior sat and gestured for everyone to do so. Barir protectively stationed himself with crossed arms a step behind Melchior's shoulder. Gauzy curtains billowed and flapped in the crisp mountain breeze blowing through the hall. It was a rather amiable environment for such a dismal discussion.

Shafiq was the first to enter the circle. He was his usual blunt, formal, and rigid self. "Fellow magi, we haven't met in such a fashion, nor under such dire circumstances, since Phillip of Macedon, and then his son Alexander, brought his armies to our lands. Then, as I'm sure we will now, we sought and found the answers we needed, guided by our king. There's compelling evidence of a change in the forces that shape our world. I call upon all who would speak to present what they've discovered or witnessed."

At first the silence was so perfect, one could have heard a feather drop. Then conversation rumbled into being, almost as if on cue, and the circle came to life. Conversations, shouts, protestations, and laments flew through the air and around the ring.

Perhaps it was testimony to the freedom that Melchior gave his subjects, or perhaps it was evidence that he may have given them a bit too much latitude and say, but no one seemed particularly concerned with what the king thought on the matter. Melchior decided to hold his tongue and counsel until all had had their time in the circle. It promised to be a long afternoon, indeed, but also be quite entertaining at times.

On the floor before him, Melchior spied a trio of tiny red ants spindling their way across the marble tiles on their slender legs. They linearly wound their way, as if searching for something on the many-colored tiles that made up both their world and the floor beneath the king's world. He absently reminded himself to monitor their progress during the session.

Melchior looked up to find that Naji, a young magus of one of the newest and lowest orders in the palace, had rather courageously taken the center of the circle. He met as many jeers as shouts of encouragement.

"Ugh," quietly grumbled a magus sitting next to Melchior, "a novice." Shafiq cleared his throat loudly, and the circle became as mute as a smoke ring, and just as hard to read.

"Gr-greetings, my masters. I am Naji," he started rather shakily, and then gained speed and confidence. "A magus of humble means who still has much to learn and do."

Not bad, thought Melchior, *taking the I-am-so-humble approach*. Many of the elder magi allowed him satisfied grunts, but their minds were as impatient as ever.

Someone said, "Get on with it then."

Naji swept an arm toward his fellows. "I—we—study the clouds, the winds, the zephyrs, the breath of the heavens that brings the spring rains and the winter snows. And in the clouds lately, we...I...have seen grave things."

For a magus of the winds, he was well appointed. Naji was fresh in his manhood, plump about the face and waist. He wore his hair long, and Melchior imagined it whipping about his face or fanned out against a mountain slope as he lay day and night, gazing at the clouds. He wore a long, silky robe of soft blue that, were he to stand on a summit on a clear day, would melt right into the sky and make him appear as just a head, floating in the air. And with such a prodigious head, that would be a sight to behold.

Naji hesitantly stepped to the urn and pinched a small amount of the powder from the urn. He cast the powder into the indigo flames of the brazier, and a billowing cloud of white floated from the fire with a hissing sound and began to take shape just above the murmuring flames.

20

"Habb, lord of the winds, is telling us something. For nigh on twenty passes of the sun, I've witnessed such awful signs that I feared for my life," he said. "A cloud in the form of a djinn appeared from the north, and the cloud actually *became* a horrible djinn of fire, spouting flames from its mouth, and its eyes were *looking at me.*"

The white cloud contorted its diaphanous shape to add testimony to Naji's report. A djinn, an evil genie, appeared in as a gossamer visage with eyes that flickered like lightening storms. Orange flames belched forth from the cruel smile that cracked the misty djinn, and it zoomed around the periphery of the brazier until it exploded with a dramatic *poof!* After evaporating, the air above the brazier returned to it formerly placid state with just a few remnants of the vision wafting on the breeze.

Zoth, who was a seer of the dark arts and Melchior's nemesis cousin, interrupted. "Indeed, little one," he intoned, "had you encountered a real djinn, as I have, you would have experienced much more than…fear…from the genie. You wouldn't he standing there like a fool, for example. You'd be…" he paused for effect, "quite dead. And burnt."

Chuckles arose, and even Naji knew that his bombast was ill placed. Still, the young magus continued. "And just yesterday, I saw a galloping horse in the sky, too, bearing down on me so close I could feel its hooves pounding the walls of the palace. It was as white as the new winter snow and seemed intent on destroying the palace. Then it turned and rode, I mean flew, to the west."

He quickly snatched up a handful of the scarlet powder and threw it onto the fire. A majestic white stallion, the most noble man has ever set eyes on, galloped out of the hastily conjured misty cloud above the cobalt flames. The stallion reared, spouting small plumes of white breath from its nostrils, and then cantered away into the wind and dissolved.

This bit of news and the accompanying vision sobered up the circle in a hurry. A djinn was one thing. False reports of genie sightings were as common as avalanches here in the mountains above Arabia. But while the djinn was easily dismissed, the phantom steed piqued Melchior's interest. It was an uncommon sighting, and clearly a symbol. What did the horse mean? For whom was it meant?

Cutting him off, Shafiq rose.

"Well done, Naji, very well done," said Shafiq, standing and walking to the center to place a hand on Naji's shoulder. "You've given us much to consider. I'm certain you have much more to contribute, but I beg you to yield the floor to another. We're here to paint a picture, and many are the colors and brushes that will contribute to the finished work." Naji bowed his head and left as the fellows of his order stood and nodded their approval.

A commotion in a corridor outside the assembly chamber drew silence and everyone's attention. Shafiq went to the chamber's massive entrance where a phalanx of royal guards prevented someone from entering the council. After a quiet discussion, the guards stood aside and Shafiq ushered in a young boy, a peasant by all looks, who was as nervous as the assembly was curious.

"Go ahead, speak. You have nothing to fear here," said Shafiq soothingly to the young man. "You're among friends."

The young man pulled a sheepskin cap from his head and held it before him. Remembering himself, his tried his best to perform a courteous bow to Melchior, which drew quiet chuckles from the circle.

The boy, who had the look of one about to become a man, was ashen faced and stupefied into place. He didn't utter a word.

Melchior said kindly, "Tell me, what's your name?"

"Wa-wa-waziri, King Melchior," stammered the boy.

Melchior continued to try to put the lad at ease. "And good Waziri, what news do you bring? Your king would be mightily in your debt if you would share what you know with the rest of this assembly."

The rosy flush of excitement drained from the boy's face as he remembered what had brought him here, all this way, to the royal palace.

"My lord, my father has sent me with news for you and your army. My father, Ateeq, a good man, a simple goatherd like me, sends these tidings," and the boy began to recite his message he'd clearly committed to memory.

"King Melchior the Kind, I send tidings of great woe. My son, um, that's me, and I barely escaped death in the mountain passes. Wolves attacked us in broad daylight during a storm that came unnaturally late. Something is very wrong here in Arabia," Waziri faithfully relayed the message as he'd been instructed, but he could not help but add his own interjections and colorful commentary. "They were monsters, my lord! Their eyes glowed, and they were huge, and they killed my entire flock!"

The circle of magi murmured at the news, for it was clear that the boy was faithfully telling all he knew. Shafiq walked quietly up to the boy and softly placed a hand upon his shoulder. Shafiq bowed his head in concentration, and took the two steps to the urn. He scooped a small amount of the red powder up and tipped it into the fire. Waziri's eyes widened as a billowy image of the scene high in the mountain pass appeared and floated above the flames. The stormy scene was replaced by an image of a wolf, supernaturally large with flashing yellow eyes and massive fangs.

Waziri was petrified at the image, and could not speak. Melchior spoke soothingly to him.

"Fear not, young one. This is but an image of what you speak, an echo of that which you saw. Shafiq has pulled it from your memory. It cannot hurt you, or any here. Please, tell us all you know."

Melchior smiled, and saw the relief wash over the young shepherd's face, only to be replaced at wonderment at the ghostly enchantment as it hovered in the air.

Emboldened, Waziri continued with his father's message.

"Evil was at work that day, in both the storm and the wolves. They claimed the life of my traveling companion, Muhsin, and devoured an entire flock of goats. And they almost got me and my son."

As Waziri recounted the tale, the story visually unfurled above the flames. Two wolves advanced on a man and a boy who was holding a baby sheep. They looked hopelessly outmatched. But the father reached down and scooped up a handful of snow and hurled a snowball into the face of a wolf. The wolf was stunned, more a product of surprise than any real pain. But the effect was enough to encourage the man. He snatched up fistfuls of snow and threw the chilly projectiles with uncanny accuracy, pelting the beasts repeatedly.

The magi watched in impressed silence as the image of the father yelled to the boy, and each began to hurl snowballs at the snouts and ears of the wolves. And amazingly, it worked. The wolves retreated from the barrage, skulking off to vanish into the snowstorm as mysteriously as they had appeared. The vision above the flames swirled into a tiny maelstrom of white snowflakes and fell back into the fire.

"We drove them off and were able to flee, but we didn't kill them. They're still out there, my lord. I fear all this is an omen of great evil. As a loyal subject, I felt it was my duty to tell you. Respectfully, your servant, Ateeq, son of Quasim, father of Waziri." They boy paused in his narration and added his own note of clarification, saying, "My father throws a hard snowball, King Melchior. He saved my life."

Although the boy's spontaneous interjections should have brought many guffaws from the assembled magi, they didn't laugh. The circle was nervous.

Melchior thought for a moment, troubled, and then remembered his audience and smiled again. "You've done well, Waziri. And I wouldn't want to face your father in a snowstorm. His quick thinking, and bravery, saved you.

Perhaps, saved all of us. The Assembly of Magi will take your information to heart and use it to guide us. And a hunting party will be sent out to find and destroy the wolves. Tell your father: he should be proud."

"Yes milord," answered the boy shyly, his head bowing, "I must return to help him and my family."

"Then you mustn't return empty handed. Barir!" Melchior leaned backward and to address his captain, Barir. "Feed young Waziri here, and see that he goes home with some gold in his pocket and a fresh flock of goats to guide."

Shafiq, on cue, tossed a few granules of the ember powder into the flames, and the cloudy form of a goat appeared and bleated. With a smile and a wave, Shafiq dismissed the apparition and the air grew still.

The boy's eyes glowed with thanks, and he smiled widely. Melchior returned it, and with a nod to Barir, the shepherd boy was led away.

Muted conversation bubbled up at the addition of this even more disturbing news. An air of doom began to creep over the assembly.

Then without warning, Zoth rose. For the sorcerer to lend his voice here only confirmed Melchior's belief that times were dire indeed. With a grimace, Shafiq yielded the circle to the dark magus. Barir scowled over Melchior's shoulder and a low growl boiled in the bottom of the guard's throat.

With a supernatural show of strength, Zoth began to create sickly lavender images above the brazier without touching the powder. The violet images turned inward and upon each other in grotesque contortions to emphasize the speech of the dark necromancer.

"Not since the plagues of Egypt, when Pharaoh and his army were drowned and utterly destroyed in the Sea of Red, have we seen such pestilence," he began, filling the hollow silence of the hall with his baritone whisper. "The fields far below us are barren, and no milk flows from the withered teats of our beasts. Not since Jason of the Golden Fleece sailed the waters have I heard of such carnage, creatures, and war. Not since the demise of the dread Persians have I smelled such fear among the people of our lands."

Melchior noted sourly that the magi around the circle were utterly transfixed with Zoth's delivery and the purple pantomime of his sad story and dire predictions.

And why not? Melchior marveled sadly at his kin, and silently reminisced about the cold distance between them.

With skin as white as the sands of the Western Sea, Zoth appeared translucent. Yet pale as he was, darkness vibrated from him, only physically apparent around his eyes. They were dark caverns with tiny white specks at the bottom. Tall and threatening, despite the wasted quality of his skin, and swathed in robes of black satin edged with lavender, he cut a formidable figure. His left hand always gripped the hilt of a long, crooked dagger tucked into his purple sash. That evil blade had creased the neck of more than one reckless adversary.

Zoth was a truly powerful magus, choosing to focus his energies on the dark arts and the magic of the night. His power was quiet, deadly, leaving enemies cold and stiff in their beds, killed as much by fright as any potion or weapon. Needless to say, Zoth never had trouble finding a seat at the table or a path through a crowd. He was, however, horribly addicted to power, and never had enough of it to suit his taste, which explained his everlasting enmity toward his cousin the king. Today, Zoth focused his dark strength within the circle. He needed the knowledge that many eyes could provide and would use it as leverage in his lifelong pursuit of dethroning Melchior.

Hatred of Melchior drove Zoth. Their fathers had been brothers, fraternal twins, and bitter rivals since their first breath. Melchior's father, the first to come into the world, was the heir. Zoth's father was forever the spare, a prince without a realm. Eventually, despairing of his secondary role, Melchior's uncle renounced all connections to the throne and killed himself by throwing himself from a precipice into a chasm without end. All mourned the loss of the prince, none more so than Melchior's father, who eventually became King of Arabia in his own right.

Thus Zoth became the king's ward, and he'd shown the boy love. But Zoth's jealousy had poisoned his heart long ago, and he'd gravitated toward the dark arts to succor his pain. In the soft murmuring of incantations, in the cleverly laid plans designed to disrupt the peace, Zoth found the power he craved. He had a natural inclination toward the darker side of magic, and once at home there, wielded his sorcery ruthlessly. Revenge became his destiny.

Since Melchior had taken the throne at the passing of his father, Zoth had despised him. Shafiq and others had advised Melchior to have him banished or executed, but the king couldn't. Melchior, an only child, longed for the brother Zoth could have been.

Yet that was never to be. Zoth's hatred was an odd combination of his lust for power and his none-too-secret disapproval of how Melchior ruled the land. Since they were boys, Zoth had known the dark fear of hesitation in Melchior's heart, the dreaded anticipation of some unforeseen dire event. He knew how this paralyzing uncertainty kept Melchior from expanding his mountain kingdom into a greater empire. As the two became men and argued over the fate of the kingdom, Melchior reasoned that if calamity could be avoided by accepting the gifts they already had, the gods might take pity on them all and spare the kingdom.

Zoth considered Melchior's acceptance of peace and prosperity, and approach of caution and care, the greatest crimes a king could commit. For Zoth, power was an absolute weapon to be wielded and since Melchior would not do so, they were forever to be mortal enemies. And now that things were beginning to unravel, Zoth saw his opportunity to gloat.

Melchior's wandering mind returned to the present as

Zoth continued to fill the air with his perilous prophecies.

"Flocks are laid waste. Crops burn and wither, or they're demolished by driving rain and pelting hail. Babes are born without eyes, arms, and ears. And constant storms sweep the land and mountains," Zoth continued, scanning the circle with his eyes. The horrific images he conjured disturbed his audience greatly, but they were unable to peel their eyes from the unwinding tale of misery.

"I've traveled near and far, from the icy plains of the north to the searing jungles of the south. The lands, seas, and people, all are in turmoil and chaos. Something approaches. Even I don't know what. Yet this I do know. We cannot fathom its power, and it will bring down even the...mightiest...amongst us." As he finished, his eyes met Melchior's in an intense scrutiny. With a dramatic flair, he waved his arm and dismissed the image of a melting, crumbling lavender mountain that eerily resembled the one upon which they all stood. Silence filled the room.

The king didn't avoid Zoth's gaze; instead, he met it with a slight smile and nod. The alabaster sorcerer slid magically and effortlessly around the periphery of the circle and resumed his seat in silence. Zoth felt he had as much right to the throne as Melchior, and he made it no secret. Melchior, for his part, indulged his power plays and court antics, and in return Zoth took his place in the council, biding his time. Melchior took his warning solemnly, but couldn't help noticing how much Zoth enjoyed being the bearer of such ill tidings.

And there was more, much more, to that fateful council. Suffice it to say that many a beast's entrails were poured out steaming onto the floor and studied with interest. Some argued over charts, others over stars, both aligned and misaligned. Balls of crystal were consulted, spirits appealed to, and visions related. As the orange sphere of the sun dipped its way back into the earth, Shafiq raised his hands and called for an end to the assembly.

28

He rose wearily, his knees crackling with stiffness. "Much has been said here. We could go on for an eternity. In fact, someone make certain we haven't. The time has come for King Melchior to speak his mind."

Melchior rose quietly, and only took a small step into the circle. Instead of going to the center, he paced just inside the periphery, his head bowed in thought, a hand on his thinly bearded chin and another at the small of his back. He paced for a while, lost in thought. When Melchior stopped and raised his head, he was standing opposite Zoth. Melchior gave a small smile while Zoth merely sneered.

"We've heard much today, but what have we truly learned? We see, we hear, we *smell*." Melchior stepped over a gutted sheep "Dream, and foretell great distress. Yet we do not know what comes, or whom. We don't even know when," he said bitterly, but without condemnation. "Clearly, a great evil is upon our land. It's as if a djinn opened his bottle and poured out trouble upon us. Shall I raise an army? If so, where will I send it? Shall I reinforce the palace and call in the herds and villagers? If yes, who comes to threaten my gate? Shall I sit and taste the treats brought by the palace girls and ignore these warnings? Then what shall I do when the beast darkens my doorstep?"

Melchior paused and seemed to make up his mind. "No, I choose to wait. Patience, I think. We must understand. We must first have the knowledge we need. We want—I want," he added softly, "a true sign. This council is concluded, thank you all."

With that and a few sighs of disgust, the circle began breaking up. Zoth shot his pinpoint eyes at Melchior briefly, whirled in a swirl of black smoke, and vanished rather spectacularly. A throng of magi crowded around Melchior and Shafiq with scrolls, chickens, and a plethora of gesticulating hands, begging for a private audience.

He nodded patiently and signaled to Barir that it was time to beat a hasty retreat. Palace guards with meaty arms and long poniards stepped in and formed a path for Melchior to ascend the stairwell.

As he left, Melchior looked down to see the squashed remains of the tiny red ants. They'd gambled everything to try crossing the vast circle, only to be crushed by a power far mightier than they. Briefly, the king pitied them, yet admired their courage all the same.

Melchior took the stairs slowly, pausing near the top to survey the pandemonium below. He felt like a coward, that he had failed to provide direction because of his own failings of doubt and insecurity. The arguments and discussions continued. He shook his head sadly, as befuddled as those below, and slowly climbed the last few marble steps to his tower sanctuary.

CHAPTER THREE

That night Melchior lay in his bed, unable to sleep. His mind kept turning to the undeniable truths unveiled at the council. After fruitless hours of wandering thoughts and shifting positions, he rose to prowl the palace. With a wave of his hand, the guards outside his door fell fast asleep and slumped against the wall. He descended alone.

It was late, and no one else moved about. Melchior made his way to the cooking pits and found a skin of wine. If nothing else, he'd drink himself to sleep. The magus took a long draw and let the rich, heady liquid roll about his mouth before he swallowed it. Then, slinging its thong over his shoulder and across his chest, he continued his prowl through the palace. He'd already dismissed his personal guards as he often did when his mind was plagued with discontent.

In a courtyard set off to one side of the palace near the armory, Melchior found he wasn't as solitary as he'd thought. The full dish of the moon illuminated the plantings and flagstones as if it were midday, but with that eerie, magical luminescence that only Apollo could create. In the middle of a glittery reflecting pool that mirrored a perfect image of the moon, a large natural rock of white marble seemed to be absorbing the lunar power.

Melchior had spent many an evening here considering

the heavens, searching for answers and direction from the gods. It truly was an enchanted place. What gave him pause this evening, however, was the woman perched upon the marble outcropping. With a blanket wrapped around her slight shoulders, she peered with relentless intensity at the sky. Moonlight cast her face in silver and added sheen to her long jet hair. Melchior didn't know her, but that wasn't uncommon in the palace. That the king would find a stranger sitting on a rock in the middle of his favorite pool in the middle of night was.

"E-hem." He cleared his throat as royally as he could, feeling a bit light-headed from the wine and the intoxicating effect of the moon.

She jerked her gaze his way and promptly slid from her precarious perch to splash into the pool, erasing the picture-perfect reflection of the glowing orb. She leapt up into a crouch and swung toward the king, arms cocked and fingers crooked in a rather menacing fashion.

"Peace now! My apologies, my apologies!" Melchior said earnestly. Then, unable to maintain his clenched jaw and stomach muscles, he released a grin. With all that occupied the king's mind at the time, that alone was a small miracle.

She found no humor in the moment, however, and waded through the water to see whom the intruder was. A few feet from the stony lip of the pool, she halted, recognizing Melchior at last. Concern registered for only a second, replaced again by the anger he'd already witnessed. She pulled her wet, scraggly hair out of her face, revealing a perfectly sculptured Arabic face with almond-shaped eyes, and snatched her drenched blanket from the pool.

Melchior offered her a hand, which, after a moment of reflection, she reluctantly accepted. He tried to hide his grin and hoped the darkness hid it. One thing not hidden was the shapely form that emerged from the water, curved in all the ways Melchior found appealing.

She stood a bit defiantly and looked at him as she wrung

out her blanket, and he decided a bit of good-natured magic was in order. Melchior held out his left hand, palm upturned, and blew along the face of it in her direction. A warm gust of wind rose from the gesture, moving the branches of the bushes and rippling the surface of the water, once again disturbing the moon's narcissistic contemplation. The breeze dried her almost instantly, and the sight of her raven hair blowing from her chiseled face touched the heart of Melchior.

Her dense eyebrows sheltered large, sparkling emerald eyes in a long, yet perfectly proportioned face. She had a razor-straight nose that lent her a regal bearing, perfectly in keeping with her facial angles. Her small mouth opened a bit in sheer enjoyment as the warm breeze replaced the cool air that had been goose-pimpling her velvety skin, now revealed to be a rich copper color without the reflective effect of the moon. She was stunning. "A thousand thanks, my liege," she said rather saucily, once the gust had subsided.

"It's the least I can do, after causing your unplanned swim. I see that I'm not the only one unable to find sleep this evening. I'm sorry to have disturbed you." Melchior paused for a moment, then decided to stay and speak with her. "But I must ask, what are you doing out here?"

He gestured to a squat stone bench beside the pool, and took a seat upon it. She sat on the opposite end of the bench from Melchior. Then both, as if on cue, turned their eyes skyward.

She began, "For the past few evenings I've been out here studying the skies. And after what I heard about the council today, I felt sure that I'd see something out here. But…" She trailed off, lost in thought.

Melchior pivoted slightly and looked at her, and her eyes slowly dropped to meet his.

"What have you seen?" he asked.

"Much, and yet nothing."

"Explain yourself," Melchior said, playing his royal

trump card.

"Well," she began, "it's as you said today. There's something happening. Evil is abroad and strange omens are all around, but I haven't figured it out yet. But the stars, they're, well, they're…*moving*." She whispered the last word.

Melchior's head snapped skyward, and instantly he knew she was right. They were, almost imperceptibly, *crawling*. He watched for a few moments. At a point high and to the west, there seemed to be fewer stars. A void was forming there, a small, inky hole in the firmament that grew by a hairbreadth every few moments.

"You're right. They move in this direction." He gestured east with his hand.

"I don't know why, my lord. The constellations retain their form, but they move to the side as if…*to make room for another*. It's almost as if, as if a new celestial power comes to take a place in the night skies. Do you think that's what's happening, what all the signs and omens indicate?" she almost pleaded, as if seeking reassurance that this was indeed the answer they sought.

Melchior searched his heart, his mind, his bones, and he knew this was still not the solution to the puzzle. It was a piece of it, no doubt, and this woman he didn't know had offered more than all the jesters he'd suffered through earlier in the day.

"No," he replied, "but this is an important thread in the tapestry unfurling before us. I, too, felt that something was coming in the skies. And always, the signals point west."

Melchior fell silent. He was frustrated that he couldn't deduce what lay before them. It was his duty, his *destiny*, to protect the kingdom from whatever danger the future held. He curled his hands into fists and thumped them like rocks on his thighs. Melchior turned to her, released a gasp of built-up tension, and smiled.

"You should have been at the council today. This is important, and you should be recognized for having learned that which others did not. Who are you?" he asked.

She smiled, a bit ashamed, and said, "The circle isn't always the most…um, comfortable…place for a woman to enter. It wasn't my place to do so."

"Well, we'll do something about that," Melchior murmured.

"My name, King Melchior, is Nur. I study the night skies, and look for secrets in the stars. Tonight, I think, I found one. Don't you?" She smiled slyly. "Now if I may ask, what brings the king out so late in the evening? Trouble sleeping?"

Melchior was astonished at her audacity. It was one thing to find a mysterious movement in the stars, but it was another thing altogether to question the king's sleeping habits. Still, he rather liked the taunting tone of her voice.

"You might say that," he answered as coolly and regally as he could. Melchior wasn't accustomed to saucy taunts from bold, beautiful astrologers. He hadn't met many women with the composure to stand up to him. His subjects usually groveled, and concubines either giggled or cowered.

Being a king has its responsibilities. Kings who are generally unloved take those responsibilities lightly. Melchior was always keenly aware that people would do whatever he asked, simply because he did ask or because they wanted to court royal favor. And Melchior despised that falsehood. It isolated him from most of life's true love, true friendship, true anything.

This was different; a meeting of peers and minds, and Melchior liked it. He felt a warm jolt go through his body as he realized that this woman might actually have a genuine interest in him.

"Well," she said abruptly, rising from the bench, "some more of that wine and one of your slave girls should take care of that sleeping problem. With your leave, I shall retire."

Melchior felt as if he'd been the one dunked in the reflecting pool. He nodded mutely, and she turned and left the courtyard. Yet, still…he caught her sneaking a glance at him as she walked away. Melchior decided right then that he needed to make more late night trips to the pool.

"Yes," Melchior agreed loudly, bluffing as only an injured male can, "perhaps a few slave girls!" But she was already gone, and he only sounded stupid. He walked the opposite way toward his chambers, but paused a few steps into the dark hallway to peer back into the courtyard.

Nur returned to the edge of the pool and stepped out onto the water. She walked delicately across the surface of the water, never penetrating it and barely disturbing it, and clambered back up on the white rock.

A simple feat, any magus or even an apprentice could do the same. Then why did a chill run up Melchior's spine, and why did his hand clench the wineskin so tightly that it dribbled a ruby pool of wine at his feet? He knew he'd seen a sign, a portent, of something. And it was disturbing.

Melchior went back to bed more troubled than when he'd left it.

A few days later, Melchior was no closer to understanding what waited around fate's corner.

Shafiq and Melchior went horseback riding, an exercise they both loved. Because Shafiq was thirty years Melchior's senior, the king often rode ahead and circled back once Melchior's stallion had run hard enough to create a white lather along his proud neck. Melchior knew that somewhere in the distance Barir shadowed him protectively, allowing his king to think he was actually free to roam.

They left the palace gates and rode at an easy pace down to the plains and, eventually, the desert. The two discussed the normal situations at court, the mystery of the symbols, and a variety of other topics. Finally Melchior mustered the courage to ask as dispassionately as he could about Nur.

"Oh, I see, yes, I see. Met her, have you? Quite a witch, that one. Not bad, mind you, no, no, but powerful. Her father was a strong magus from the north . . . an alchemist, if I remember right. Caught your eye, did she?" Shafiq asked with a wry smile.

Obviously, Melchior's inquiry wasn't dispassionate enough to dupe the old man. Maintaining the air of nonchalance, however, Melchior persevered, "She's discovered something of interest, that's all." And he described the moving stars. Melchior didn't, however, tell him of the trepidation he'd felt when he watched Nur walk on the water.

Shafiq's brow furrowed as he mulled over the king's words. This latest revelation seemed to worry him as much as it did Melchior. Shafiq, of course, had noted the bizarre movement of the firmament. And like the king, he had no idea what it all meant.

"I'm afraid that we have more questions than answers, my liege," said the old man, "I'm at a loss to explain or grasp it."

Melchior decided to give in to his frustration and let his horse have some rein. "I'm going to let him run. Back in a bit," he said, and the horse and rider bolted off.

Rider and beast became one as they galloped along. The rich greens of the hinterlands quickly changed to the dull grasses of the steppe, which in turn became the soft brown padding of the desert beneath his hooves. Melchior leaned low and felt the horse's mane lickety-whip his face, reveling in the howl of the wind and the heat of the noonday sun. Before him, the desert lay outstretched like a carpet that knew no end. With the sun high overhead, and had he not known the mountains lay behind him, he could easily lose himself and ride on forever.

Then Melchior spied a black speck on the horizon and knew where the horse was heading. Even before the horse slowed to a canter and then a trot, Melchior knew who it was; Zoth, of course, standing there like some kind of burned totem on the sand. And still white as a ghost. Zoth didn't turn his head or lift his eyes to acknowledge the king, an offense that could have earned him a month in shackles if Melchior had the heart for such things.

Melchior's horse stilled and stood, puffing and blowing moist snorts, eventually wandering over to the meager shade offered by a modest dune. He slid down easily and stood beside the dark magus. He breathed hard himself for a few moments, letting the silence of the sand wash over him and the uncomfortable situation.

Finally, Melchior spoke. "Been waiting here long, I hope?"

In his familiar poisonous, hollow tone, Zoth replied, "Not long. We must speak, and without that fool Shafiq dogging your every step."

"I find it odd that you wish to speak to me out here in the middle of nowhere," Melchior said suspiciously yet playfully. "You could just as easily meet me in the palace. Are you sure you're not more interested in sliding a blade between my ribs?"

Looking out at the sea of sand before them, Zoth intoned, "Brave words for a man who must surely see that his time is at an end. Can you not see the signs for yourself? Your reign, it seems, is over. Death and destruction are at hand. Uncertainty and fear have become the masters of your soul—we can all see it in your eyes, in your delays and cowering indecision. It's disgusting . . . I came here merely to see how you felt about it. I must say, I'm rather enjoying it." He finally turned his black eyes to the king.

Melchior knew that he should have felt rage at the insolence, but he couldn't. Zoth was right; he was worried that disastrous days lay ahead, and his own heart was shadowed. But all the doom and gloom seemed, oddly enough, bigger than just the king. "You know, Zoth, I wish it were all just for me, that this were all just my problem. I truly do. A terrible storm is coming, I fear, and the world may well be destroyed when it strikes. And that includes even you."

It always gave Melchior a thrill to shock Zoth. He looked

palpably stricken when Melchior finished, as if he'd heard the truth in his cousin's words.

Then the old defense mechanisms kicked in. "Curse you," Zoth muttered, "and your damned crown. Ominous times are afoot, surely, and your house shall be trampled beneath them. Not I. Your kingdom is already lost to you. In the end, I'll ultimately have everything, and you'll have nothing. Your weakness . . . shall be my victory."

Agitated because he suspected his dark reflection might be right, Melchior walked to his horse, which nickered in appreciation of the imminent departure. Mounting, he wheeled the stallion to retort to Zoth, but the dark figure had already wisped away with the wind. Melchior squeezed his heels into the horse's sides, and they slowly cantered back toward the mountains. Only this time, the ride seemed longer than ever before.

CHAPTER FOUR

For a fortnight, the Arabian king visited the pool to look for her. But she never returned. Instead, he regarded the stars as they rolled backward, creating a hole in the darkness. Still, he waited.

The snows continued to fall and melt. The sands shifted and smoothed themselves, creating and erasing a new façade every moment. Birds flew, crops grew, and winds blew. And while on the surface it appeared that nothing changed, everything seemed wrong.

And still Melchior waited and watched.

Then one evening, just at dusk, a knock came at Melchior's door. He opened it, and there she stood. Nur.

It took courage. Guards, not to mention a few spells, protected the king's chamber to prevent an ambitious magus from creating a shortcut to the throne, so she couldn't just stroll in. Yet Nur had found her way to the door with relative ease. Two catatonic guards stood like statues against the stonewalled corridor outside his chamber. Melchior made a mental note to review his security protocols.

"Ah—Nur! Come in, please, come in. I've, ah, looked for you...I mean, I wondered where you got to...you know, haven't seen you around much...and..." He stammered around a mouthful of squab as she crossed the threshold. He did his solid best to look as disinterested as he could. But he suspected that it didn't work.

"Have you — sorry — should I come back?" She hesitated when she saw that Melchior was in the middle of a meal, but he gestured that she remain and continue. With a wave of his hand, he magically commanded a mallet to strike on the little gong that sat on the stone floor. He told the servers who appeared to bring more food and another silver plate. They left bowing, and Nur settled upon a ruby-red cushion a few paces from the king.

She cut right to the chase. "Have you seen? The stars — they've stopped moving!" She said it almost breathlessly, as if she had run there from the pool right after discovering the conclusion of the astral progression.

Servant boys interrupted the conversation by bringing enough food and wine to feed all of Arabia. When they bowed and departed, Nur and Melchior finally had the room to themselves. Her plate would remain untouched for the entire evening. She had more pressing matters on her mind.

Nur wore a silken shift similar to the one she'd worn fortnights before, girded about the waist with a simple gold rope that dangled down to her feet. She wore no jewelry or decoration, and its absence made him wonder if she had neither the time nor inclination for such vanity. Besides, her simple beauty needed no adornment.

"Yes," he said, forcing his eyes to snap from her to the goblet of wine he held out with both hands. "I've noticed. Last night they had slowed almost to a full stop, and they left a sizable void in the west, almost the width of my hand when I held it up. What, ah, what do you make of it?"

There was tension in the air. Certainly, part of it was sexual in nature, but the uncertainty of the celestial march overhead lent an air of apprehension as well.

She began slowly. "Wel-l-l-l-l, that's why I came, to see — I mean, to *ask* you." Her self-conscious stumble actually eased the strain. Nur lifted her goblet and sipped from it.

Melchior visibly relaxed, smiled and decided to open up to her. "I wonder, is tonight a turning point? All day, my skin's felt…tight…against my flesh. My head's been light, and I haven't been able to concentrate on anything. At first I thought it was because I was thinking of…" He paused, and she looked down in embarrassment but smiled nonetheless. He eased even more, sensing that the attraction was mutual.

"But it's more than that." He sighed and looked off into the distance. "I feel that that's all I've been saying; it's more than that. But it is. Whatever's coming, it's big. Bigger than me, than this palace, than even this kingdom. I'm concerned for all of us." Melchior's candor surprised even himself; it wasn't a royal admission to make, but with her, he felt he had nothing to hide. It turned out, he didn't.

"Yes," she said. "After meeting you and seeing the stars shift, I thought it was a sign perhaps that I should leave and search out an answer. So I went to the land of my birth, far in the mountains to the north. But the elders there had no solutions. My mother told me that I couldn't solve my troubles by turning away. So I returned. And…" She paused. "Came to see you." She smiled weakly, and with the admission, the ice of formality melted between them.

They continued to talk and drink, and after the servants cleared the meal, they rose and walked to the chamber's balcony. It looked out over the courtyard and the main gate of the palace, and provided a breathtaking view of the heavens. Only the last crescent of the sun was visible as the velvety cover of night slid over the land. They gazed skyward, waiting for the stars to peek through the firmament.

Emboldened by the ease of their conversation and a few goblets of strong wine, Melchior turned and gently pulled Nur's body against his. She didn't resist. He smelled the rich natural perfume of her hair, felt the curves of her soft body find the hollow points of his, and the sensations he dreamed about became reality.

Naturally, their mouths met in a kiss that needed no

spell to make magic. His tongue tasted her being, reveling in the captivating mixture of seductive berries and jolting sparks that were Nur's inner being. The kisses ended as their bodies shifted to a strong embrace.

"So." She ventured to his close ear in a nonchalant voice that was anything but, "Just how many concubines do you have?"

Sliding away and leaning on the railing to idly watch the frozen night sky, he replied. "Oh, I don't know. I've lost count over the years…a hundred, at least."

"So sad," Nur said with a sigh, not taking the bait for an instant and instead reeling in a man. "All that practice, and you've never learned what it is to be with a real woman."

Later that night, Melchior lay with Nur in his massive bed, her lithe form entwined in his legs and cradled in an arm. Silken sheets twisted about their cooling bodies, all sense of modesty and decorum abandoned hours ago. Their quietly breathing bodies silently enjoyed the comfort of the soft mattress beneath them, overstuffed with cotton from faraway Egypt, a kingly luxury indeed.

Melchior, on his back with his other arm crooked behind his head, peered up at the bed canopy that gently undulated overhead in response to the evening breeze blowing in from the open terrace doors. The woven fabric, which he'd studied so many times before, held new meaning for him tonight. Magic had been woven in with the linen fibers of the canopy, so the pictures within it would animate and tell small chapters of legend and lore. Symbols of good fortune and power, captured in vivid green, scarlet, and ochre threads, throbbed and glowed to protect him as he slept.

Married with these symbols were embroideries of triumph on the sacred fields of battle. Prisoners were won and taken, armies slaughtered, and fortunes reaped over and over again. Scattered throughout the tapestry were talismans to ward off evil and magical beasts such as savage griffins, clever satyrs, three-headed snarling chimera, incendiary dragons and voluptuous mermaids. Many a night, he'd lain here and felt overwhelmed by everything the future held in store for him as the tapestry unraveled its mysteries in the night.

But not this night. Now, thanks to the woman who had just shared the most precious gift of her soul with him, it was all starting to make sense. Maybe he could master himself and the days ahead, and maybe, just maybe, there wasn't so much to worry about after all. Perhaps this was what the future held in store for him. If so, it was a good future indeed.

He smiled to himself. Even though he'd bragged and teased about his sexual exploits with Nur, the truth was much more chaste. Melchior had always been tentative and nervous in the few private encounters he'd had with women, which he could, sadly, count on one hand. It wasn't that he didn't *like* women — quite the contrary — but that it had never felt like they'd been the *right woman*...another symptom of the indecisive melancholy that had plagued him his entire life. But this woman, this indeed *seemed right*. He felt a sense of peace and resolution in his heart, and savored a confidence he'd never tasted before.

Then Melchior heard the call.

It first filled his ears as a roar, like that of a lion, and it made him sit bolt upright in the bed as a chill waved across his flesh. The sound then transformed seamlessly into a kind of celestial music. It was a tinkling, plinking, sparkling song that no man or instrument could ever mimic. The sound wasn't loud, but not a song to be dismissed, either. It beckoned him.

Melchior felt an irresistible pull. He was like the snake that can't resist the song of the charmer; the lover who can't help but pause and listen to the strum of the lyre; and the sailor who can't help but sail upon the rocks following the siren's call.

He was like the servant who can't help but heed the

king's command. Melchior was helpless.

Yet he was in no trance. No fog filled his brain or addled his senses. On the contrary, Melchior had never felt so alive and liberated to act in his life. It was a powerful feeling—it had to be, to lure him from that bed.

The song had no discernable words, but nonetheless whispered to him, *Come, and you shall see. Look, and you shall learn. Follow, and you shall believe.*

The magi king rose from the bed and took what oddly felt like a last, lingering look at Nur. He wrapped a light black robe about his shivering torso and walked barefoot on the cold stones into the center of the bedchamber. The curtains to the terrace, suddenly snapping and curling, were alive with energy. He hesitantly walked over and threw them aside. Instantly, the purest light to ever touch the face of the earth blasted him and enveloped Melchior in dazzling energy.

The star.

More beautiful than any could imagine, more awful than any could appreciate, the star hung perfectly centered in the western void of the darkened sky. Beams of crystalline power shot from its white-hot center, creating an astral light show that cheapened the most precious gemstone and diminished the moon's incandescence. Indeed, later Melchior couldn't recall seeing the moon at all, even though he knew it was almost full that night.

His heart beat against his ribs as a horse's hoof pounds the desert sand, and hot, unbidden tears fell onto his exposed chest. He flung his arms out from his sides and fell to his knees, trying with every inch of his being to soak up, to comprehend the power of the celestial magic. As he looked at the star, his face bathed in its glow. Its extraterrestrial summoning filled Melchior's mind.

Come, it sang to him in his head and yet seemed to fill the night air, too.

"Where?" he asked aloud.

Come, it sang.

"To whom?" he cried. "When? Why?" he begged.

Come.

The once-mighty king crumbled lower on his knees, unable to shut out the star's music, answer its summons, or resist its pull. Melchior's capitulation was instantaneous. He surrendered and yielded his soul to the star. Melchior knew he was powerless to deny it, had he even the inclination to do so.

Hours passed. Melchior still knelt back on his haunches, transfixed, awash in the radiance, mesmerized by the song, beauty, and majesty of the star.

Behind him, Nur stepped quietly out onto the terrace. She, too, had slipped on a silk robe of white, more for warmth than any sense of modesty. Her concerned look shifted to relief when she found her lover, but changed back to alarm when she discerned that he was on his knees looking out into the sky.

Bathed as she was in the light of the star, she was even more breathtakingly beautiful. She looked not at the star, but at Melchior, and her face openly betrayed her worry. "Melchior, what is it? You look...odd. Your eyes—why, you're crying..." She stepped closer to place her fingertips on his face and searched his eyes.

He grudgingly pried his eyes from the lightshow to look at her.

"The star, Nur. It's what I've—we've—been waiting for. It's finally here. And it's calling us!" he replied, his voice cracking with the blend of fear and hope that boiled from within him.

"Star? What star? What are you talking about?" More distress creased her face. She quickly looked to the sky and her eyes searched back and forth. "I don't see a thing. Just the hole in the heavens. Why? What do you see, Melchior?"

He turned his head and looked west, and the star shone on. Its music continued to fill his head, and he sadly realized that the star didn't sing to her. He knew then instantly in his heart that it was his special destiny to follow its call. And it was a bittersweet realization. It seemed especially cruel to Melchior that Nur be taunted with the movement of the other stars, only to be denied the vision of the true marvel.

He turned his head to see her more clearly. Looking at Nur's face, her lovely face limned in the light of the star, he slowly began to understand. The star's summons was a challenge; it demanded sacrifice, the sacrifice of power, of everything to heed its call. He'd been dared to accept the challenge.

"It's here. The sign. It's—it's a star. A star like no one's ever seen before," he whispered as he rose and moved closer to her. Melchior tried to put words to the intangible pull he felt drawing him away. "I'm sorry…so sorry…you can't see it, can you?" She looked at him helplessly, and he concluded, "No, of course you can't. It's here for me. And… and I have to follow it."

"Where you go, I follow, my king," she said instantly. Melchior saw her pure strength then, unfettered and proud, a match to any who would dare question it. He suddenly found himself uncomfortably trapped between the power of the star and the power of a woman.

Her will of spirit was washing away the blissful fog of the star. He knew he had a problem to address, so he stalled.

"Well," he said, looking away and avoiding her eyes, "we'll see."

Melchior noted the shadows darkening and turned to see that the star was fading, relinquishing its reign as rosy-hued dawn began pulling himself up in the east. The music slowly faded in his mind as well, but he knew he would witness it again.

Nur could tell that the vision had passed from the reaction on his face. She lowered her head, and he sensed her hurt. She believed Melchior, and felt robbed of something she had long awaited. He couldn't help her. He led her back to the bed where she sobbed into his chest, envious of the vision only he had beheld. But somewhere in the remainder of that night, she forgave him his vision of the star and all that it entailed.

CHAPTER FIVE

Chengdu, China

Lazily, the child looked at the two leather cords and thought that, if they were strummed, they'd probably make a low, interesting sound. Each of the cords was attached on one end to a wooden beam high overhead and tied about the largest toes of each of his master's feet at the other. It was the strangest triangle the child had ever seen.

Suspended a few arm-lengths from the bamboo mat-covered floor of the monastery, the master's face was as placid as the surface of water just before a pebble wrinkles it. The master held his palms pressed together, fingertips lightly touching, elbows and forearms perpendicular to the floor beneath him. He held his legs immobile, impossibly scissored out. One stretched straight forward and the other backward, pressing his rather lean muscles and tendons against the dark green silk pants he favored. He looked like a runner frozen in mid-leap over an invisible hurdle who had decided to pray.

The only visible manifestation of his intense effort was a sheen of sweat on his brow and upper lip—and a single sweat droplet that bobbed up and down on the very tip of one of the thick, white hairs in his long, whip-like moustache.

Everything was frozen in time; the master, the leather cords, the sweat droplet, life. It was easily one of the most boring hours the child had ever spent, at least since being sent here eight years ago to serve, and possibly one day even become, a high priest of the land. The fact that no one really knew what the crazy old man did up here in his hill-top monastery didn't seem to matter. Since being orphaned, the child had served as the master's servant and potential apprentice. Even now, after more than a year in the master's service, the child was still waiting, cautious of what the future held.

One week into servitude, Shin-shin had the first chance to flee, like a grouse from the rushes. For some reason, the child remained. But at times like these, Shin-shin questioned that decision.

Shin-shin quickly stifled a yawn, thankful not to disturb the master's meditation, which looked a lot like torture to Shin-shin's 10-year-old mind. The child's sleepy eyes wandered back down to the scroll page of assigned reading, a mathematical treatise on how to lift a large rock with a slender stick. The crispy page of xuan zhi paper was filled with the delicate strokes of ink that danced and coalesced together to illustrate the mechanical principle. And the child couldn't care less. This time, the yawn couldn't be stifled.

It was then that Shin-shin noticed an extraordinarily fat, black-and-green fly land with a *click* and begin crawling over the strokes of black ink on the thick paper. Mesmerized, the child watched as the bug *ratta-tap-tapped* its way back and forth with its tiny bug feet, its wings transparent and shiny at the same time. *Finally, something fascinating,* Shin-shin thought. *I could study it. I could pluck one or both of its wings and alter its fate forever. I could try to catch it in my hand.* But, as the child was tired of looking at the open scroll anyway, Shin-shin impetuously decided to slam a hand down upon the page and see what kind of interesting smear the fly would add to the awful algebraic symbols, slashes, and strokes.

Whap! smacked the child's hand upon the hand-painted page.

"*Erk!*" said the startled master as he flipped upside

down, his concentration shattered and his toes practically plucked from his feet.

Plap! plopped the drop of sweat as it landed somewhere on the matted floor.

Brrrzzz! taunted the untouched insect as it orbited Shin-shin's head once and began its flight to freedom.

The silence that had commanded the room resumed, interrupted only by the leathery creak of the thongs as the master swung back and forth like a bizarre, inverted reed in the wind. His head swung past his apprentice's, but he didn't look at the child. His legs were still outstretched back and forward, as the interruption had only resulted in flipping his position.

At last, slowly, he turned his head and looked at the child sternly. "Shin-shin," he scolded. Then he made a clucking noise in his throat and cheeks that assured Shin-shin that there would be many unpleasant chores to make amends for the interruption.

Shin-shin learned long ago that excuses, apologies, and speech in general were useless in situations like these. Shin-shin's head hung in true shame, because the intent was never really to get in trouble; Shin-shin just seemed exceedingly good at it.

"Did you at least catch the fly?" the master asked, and the child's head fell even farther.

"Shin-shin. When will you learn to concentrate? Perhaps never." He turned his head away from the child and closed his pale green, almond-shaped eyes.

Folding his hands together, the still inverted master pressed his lips together in a hard line and wrinkled his brow. After a moment, he effortlessly performed a perfect flip and returned to his former upright position. Then, ever so slowly, he brought his feet together and himself to a standing position, the leather thongs creaking in protest.

He showed no pain, gave no evidence of exertion. Shin-shin was sure the master's toes would be ripped grotesquely from their joints, but they didn't. The pupil's mouth hung open in awe. Then, like a monkey in green silk, the master easily clambered up the thongs hand over hand until he reached the beam to which they were attached, untied them, and dropped cat-quiet to the floor.

Shin-shin rose and stood before the master, ready for the real lecture to begin. Instead, the master only raised the child's head with one hand and held out the other. He opened his fist to reveal the fly, walking on his palm.

"Concentrate," he said.

The master, Balthazar, was a hermit of sorts, revered and feared by the inhabitants of the village at the foot of the rolling hills where he lived. They recognized him as the mystic leader of the land, for there was no true ruler in this remote part of ancient China. When the child's parents, simple farmers, fell victim to a terrible sickness that had devoured village after village, the survivors brought the toddler Shin-shin to the priest as a servant and offering.

Balthazar was slight of stature and frame, always clothed in loose silken, pajama-like pants and shirts of dark emerald green. On his feet, he wore simple black Tai Chi slippers, and his head was often adorned in a traditional soft black skullcap fitted tightly over the single braid of hair hanging down his back.

Balthazar's face was an ageless plane of taut flesh, one of those faces that could be as old as the hills or as young as the bamboo shoot. Only his gray hair and long, wispy moustache hinted that he was older than he appeared.

He was a hodgepodge of a man, part priest, part alchemist, part mystic, part astronomer, part wise man, and part simpleton. He could remember all the names of all the birds in the sky, but couldn't remember to eat. He could rub together a few rocks and make a purple flame, but stood like a fool for hours admiring the sun as it broke through the clouds.

Balthazar could stand on one foot and balance a pot, a brick, a cat, a feather, and a large rock at once on his other foot, hands, head and nose, but seemed unable to fetch a bucket of water. He was both warm and distant, teacher and student. He *taught* Shin-shin little, actually, expecting rather that the child soak up experience by simply following Balthazar's example.

Shin-shin slept on a mat of woven bamboo leaves on the floor in a corner. Dressed as simply as the master, Shin-shin wore dark pants and tunic with no embroidery or ornamentation, hair tucked beneath a cap like Balthazar's. Shin-shin cooked simple meals, swept the dust from the doorway, and performed the tedious chores that were supposed to build character and patience.

The two actually spoke little, except when something captured the interest of Balthazar; then he went to great lengths to explain it, as much to himself as to the child. Lately, though, Shin-shin had noticed that Balthazar was more distracted and impatient than usual. He spent hour upon hour in cramped, twisted positions, and meditated furiously. He spent many a night consulting the stars, scribbling complex computations on large sheaves of xuan zhi paper. He never shared his thoughts with Shin-shin, but it was clear that something was bothering him.

One day, without warning, Balthazar rose from sitting on the floor and strode quietly out the door. Shin-shin scrambled to catch up and soon deduced that they were walking the mile or so down the vegetation-shrouded hill to the village below. Such trips were rare.

The master walked quickly down a path overhung with the dense, moist foliage that covered most of the countryside. Shin-shin trotted behind him, trying to avoid the big green leaves as they slapped and whipped in the master's hasty wake. Soon they reached the outskirts of the village.

The residents here eked out a humble existence, growing only as much food as they needed to eat or trade. Dirty pigs ran squealing around bamboo-thatched huts, usually chased by a gang of similarly dirty, squealing children. A chicken or two strutted about. Most of the village inhabitants paused to stare at the duo as they walked past.

Due to his role as hermit/high priest, the merchants of the village would warily give the strange couple a sampling of their wares as an offering to ward off the unseen gui, or demons, whom many felt followed the master. The gifts were accepted without a word of acknowledgement or thanks from the master. It was Shin-shin's job to thank them and carry everything back. Sometimes, mostly out of pity, the child would be slipped a mouthful of sweet stuff to suck on for the return journey. Therefore, Shin-shin rather liked these unplanned jaunts. They broke up the monotony of monastic life and sometimes tasted good.

Shin-shin ran head-on into the master's back as he stopped short. The child took a few steps around him and turned to look at the object of Balthazar's intent stare: a mother sitting in a doorway, rocking back and forth with a newborn infant in her arms. She didn't notice Balthazar and Shin-shin at first, as the babe held her attention.

Finally, the master spoke. "Many pardons. The child, yours?"

The woman looked up, startled, then shocked as she realized the crazy old hermit from the mountain was addressing her. "Yes," she replied rather proudly, "my son." She was pretty, with a soft oval face framed by long, dark, shining hair. The babe was blessed with her beauty, already sporting a tuft of dark hair atop his head and a ruby purse of a mouth that searched for his mother's milk.

"Master," Shin-shin asked him, "why are we stopping? Have you never seen a baby before?"

"Of course I have," he replied, as if in a dream.

A chill ran up the old man's spine, an unfamiliar sensation to the seasoned enchanter. The supernatural was no stranger to Balthazar, so why should an infant give him such cause for concern?

"Is the baby special?" Shin-shin whispered, intrigued and yet fearful, returning the daydreaming Balthazar to the present. "Is the baby...evil?"

"Shin-shin," Balthazar sighed, without breaking his study of mother and child, "do not be silly. I cannot tell you why this sight gives me pause. It simply does. But I do know that you ask too many questions. Sometimes there are no immediate answers. Sometimes, to look and listen is enough."

And he sped off. They spent the rest of the day collecting supplies, observing and studying the world around them, but Balthazar was unusually quiet. They returned home in the late afternoon, Shin-shin heavy with bundles and Balthazar heavy with some dark secret he couldn't share or put words to.

CHAPTER SIX

Shin-shin struggled through a troubled sleep. The child tossed and turned, dreaming that an angry mob of men and women came and wanted to drag a noble, bloody and sad-looking man away.

Then the vision shifted. Shin-shin saw a boat with two fishermen, but their hair was lighter and unbraided so they didn't look like anyone Shin-shin had ever met. Their faces were longer and their skin darker as well. They hauled in a net full of fish.

Shin-shin shivered, deep in sleep, as images of wicked men, soldiers dressed in odd clothing, tossed dice and argued.

Shin-shin screamed, still deep in the thrall of sleep, as a massive stone was rolled across a cave entrance, trapping Shin-shin inside.

The child awoke washed in cold sweat, panicky. As Shin-shin's nerves calmed and lungs sucked in the warm, sweet night air, the student saw, framed in the entryway of the hut's entrance, the master's silhouette. He stood with his back to Shin-shin, feet apart and hands clasped at his back, staring at the night sky. Shin-shin watched him for a few moments.

He acknowledged his pupil without ever looking back. "You feel it too, Shin-shin. Something is coming. We wait.

We watch. We study. We listen."

Head heavy, eyelids heavier, Shin-shin struggled as sleep fought to reclaim the child.

"Rest," Balthazar said, "for soon we shall need it."

And the child succumbed to sleep.

The next day was odder still. A cold front swept in, layering the land in a heavy coat of fog that moistened everything. Fronds dripped, the air was thick and made breathing labored, and clothing stuck to the body as an uncomfortable second skin. At the master's request, Shin-shin wrapped dried meats and fruits in leaves, poured dry grains of rice into small sacks, and bundled a faggot of wood with a string, a series of tasks the wet atmosphere made even more difficult. Most important, Balthazar instructed, was acquiring drink. Shin-shin thought they could suck water from the moist air, but obediently made the long trek to the nearby stream and filled two medium-sized porcelain jugs with water, balancing each from the ends of a long bamboo pole. Preparations were made, but for what? wondered the child.

As the sun sank, Balthazar sat Shin-shin down on the floor of their small hut opposite him, and together they took a modest meal. Shin-shin was exhausted from the day's labors, but Balthazar was his usual pensive self until he set down his bowl of rice, methodically rested his chopsticks on the rim, and looked at his apprentice closely.

"You spoke in your dreams last night, Shin-shin," he said, "but your words weren't for me. So tell me now, what visions did your dreams reveal to you last night?"

Defensively, Shin-shin demurred, saying, "No, master, I had no visions, just bad dreams from eating too much yesterday in the village."

Balthazar smiled kindly, a rare vision itself. "No, my pupil, you had visions last night, prophecies of what is yet to come. I had them, too, but they were of a different nature than yours, I believe. I'll tell you what I dreamt, then, perhaps you'll tell me what you saw.

"I saw the end of the world. I saw armies of death marching. I saw a man, a kind man, crying. I saw him hanging dead, nailed to a set of wooden boards. And I saw millions of people weeping for this man. I don't comprehend the meaning of all this — who he was, why he was killed. The images lead me to conclude that he was murdered, or executed, or both. But he, or something, calls to me. To us, I believe," he finished and looked at the child patiently. "If I may…"

Balthazar reached out and placed his hand gently on Shin-shin's cheek. With an eerie realization and shudder, Shin-shin felt Balthazar magically slipping into Shin-shin's head, searching the child's mind and thoughts. The sensation wasn't altogether *unpleasant*, but there was no denying how odd it felt; like unseen, gentle fingers probing the soft tissues of Shin-shin's brain.

Shin-shin knew the master possessed supernatural powers, although Balthazar utilized them reluctantly and sparingly. Taming a beast so it could be studied, lowering a heady stream for a drier traverse — those were the displays of power Shin-shin had witnessed first-hand, but they weren't topics for query or discussion. No, the power Balthazar valued most, and pressed upon Shin-shin constantly, was the power of the mind. Magic, enchantments, and the like were almost cheating to Balthazar, a shortcut, a last resort, to be employed only when absolutely necessary; and apparently, this was one of those occasions.

Surrendering to the master's power, Shin-shin began recalling the dreams in no particular order because they were foggy and jumbled. The images played out again, haunting and removed, yet personal and heart wrenching all the same. When Balthazar finished, he frowned and looked at the mat-covered floor between them, no doubt trying to decipher the secrets the dreams held. Shin-shin sat quietly a few moments, yet another rare vision on this day of wonders, until the master looked up somberly.

"A riddle," Balthazar said. "A mystery. A puzzle for which I think we don't hold all the pieces. Yet. But I suspect that soon we may meet others who may hold the pieces we need. Do you not agree, Shin-shin?"

Shin-shin nodded. It was a rhetorical question, of course, but the child knew nothing, except that it was quickly becoming time to get really scared. Shin-shin was the first to admit to cowardice, as a healthy respect for danger and the occult had served the child well so far. And that cowardice was about to be sorely tested. In the weeks to come, Shin-shin would give anything to be only as frightened as that dark night in the hut when the visions first appeared.

Hours later, Shin-shin heard a voice singing, beckoning the child to rise and come. Shin-shin was shocked; Balthazar had never so much as hummed, or whistled, let alone sung a song like this. Could the voice Shin-shin heard be that of the master? No, the pupil quickly concluded as the last wisps of sleep cleared the child's mind. The voice held echoes of the orphan's long-lost parents and friends, and thousands of other voices calling out in unison. And something more, something breathtakingly beautiful.

Shin-shin stumbled out into the night that should have been dark and quiet, as it was the hour that comes just before the dawn. Yet Shin-shin was forced to squint, not because it was dark, but because it was so brilliant outside the hut. Fear gripped the child. Was this still a dream? Was the world coming to an end, right then, right there?

Shin-shin lurched down a frond-framed path that opened onto a clearing at the apex of their hill, a space hacked wide by the forces of nature from the very skin of the hilltop. The promontory overlooked the lush jungle panorama below. Shin-shin came here often to find solitude.

The student wasn't surprised to find the master also standing on the granite ledge, hands resting at the small of his back, peering upward. He nodded slightly, as if he'd expected the child at precisely that moment.

Shin-shin, frozen with fear at the light and voices in the night, didn't look up. But finally, summoning an unknown reservoir of courage, the apprentice stepped forward, mindful to stay a respectful step to one side and behind the master.

"Look up, Shin-shin," he whispered in a voice the child had never heard him use before, a voice filled with awe and reverence. "Look up and behold the most beautiful sight your eyes will ever see."

The shining star overwhelmed Shin-shin. Tears streamed down the child's cheeks as Shin-shin's eyes fought to take in so much power, so much beauty. The starlight reflected in the tracks the tears made, becoming tiny rivers of ethereal silver spilling out. "I can hear it, too, master. Do you? Can you hear it?"

"Yes," he said. "What does it say to you?"

"It calls to me. It tells me to come," Shin-shin whispered.

"Yes. It calls to me as well. And it marks something, or more precisely, someone. It's what I've been expecting. My astronomical calculations have shown it. My meditations have felt it. Our dreams have foretold it," Balthazar said.

"What does it mean?" Shin-shin asked, abandoning protocol and boldly taking a step forward to turn and face him. Shin-shin searched the master's face for a hint of what he meant, but Balthazar's countenance revealed nothing, awash as it was in the heavenly glow from the star.

"A bright star can herald many things. War. Revelation. Death. Birth. Here, I suspect…a birth. Yes. It has certain logic to it. And surely a star this powerful symbolizes that he or she will be a powerful being. This child comes to rule us all, perhaps. Destroy us, perhaps. But we're to go to him or her. Yes. We're summoned," he concluded simply.

"What? Where? Why me?" Shin-shin asked in rapid-fire succession as fear won control of the pupil's emotions. Shin-shin's slow life, and boring existence, was at least somewhat comfortable and familiar. Servitude in the name of some death-dealing baby-king sounded about as poor a lifestyle choice as Shin-shin could imagine. Shin-shin envisioned wiping smelly filth from the behind of an infant with an impish crown on its head. He was laughing; Shin-shin wasn't.

Oblivious to his apprentice's dismay, Balthazar continued. "I know not where or wherefore. The star is to serve as our guide, of that I'm sure. All will be revealed in its time, of that you can be certain."

"So that's why you had me prepare everything," Shin-shin said in slow realization and with a bit of accusation. "You knew we'd be leaving."

"Yes, but I don't know our destination. My studies show it will be warm where we're going, and that a long journey lies before us. We shall see lands and peoples the like of which we've never beheld. I think you'd call it an *adventure*."

Now for Shin-shin, an adventure was another thing altogether. An *adventure* was an opportunity to get out of this one-room hovel existence and see the world, travel, get rich, and be free.

Balthazar finally pried his eyes from the star and looked at the child with a sly grin creasing his thin lips. "Are you willing to undertake such a journey? It will be difficult. You'll face danger and many challenges. You may never return here; in fact, you may perish. Are you prepared for this, Shin-shin?" he quietly challenged.

After pausing for a moment to weigh the pros and cons, Shin-shin committed. "Yes, master," the apprentice replied simply. The star's song and light had penetrated Shin-shin's heart and left little room for choice. And although the pupil would never admit it, Shin-shin loved Balthazar like a father and would follow him anywhere. Quite simply, Balthazar was all that Shin-shin had.

They returned to the monastery and gathered their scant belongings. Earlier, Shin-shin had transferred the water into skin bags that they now slung over their shoulders. Packed up but not loaded down, the duo stopped at the door of the modest hut and surveyed it one last time. The departure had an air of finality about it.

"We shall travel at night, following the star. During the day, we shall rest and gather food and water. We must make haste, for I feel that time is precious to us, and the star will not wait," Balthazar said.

Thus he walked from the hut that had been his home for years without so much as a glance backward. Shin-shin lingered for a moment, touching a scroll or two and drinking in the room's familiarity. Bidding this life a silent farewell, the apprentice trotted off to catch up with the master.

Starlight caught the broad leaves of the dense jungle they walked through and created a shimmering world of phosphorescent white and vivid green. The foliage seemed to give way as they followed a path illuminated by the star.

"Our path is to the west, Shin-shin," stated the master as he walked quickly and deliberately through the undergrowth. "To the west lie many strange lands, with strange peoples. Most are barbarians who would just as soon eat you as speak with you. We must take care and keep to ourselves, rely on our wits and our training. Everything you've learned will be tested."

The child's eyes went wide at the mention of child-eating barbarians, but Shin-shin knew enough not to voice the fear — for now.

Oddly enough, even though they'd been walking for hours and had already covered many miles, Shin-shin wasn't winded. And for long stretches at a time, Shin-shin could only recall looking at the star rather than watching the path ahead. But neither traveler ever stumbled, fell, nor slackened their pace. The star provided the strength necessary to follow it. But talk of barbarians feasting on Shin-shin eventually brought the child back to earth. "People who eat other... people? Like...me?" Shin-shin asked fearfully.

"Oh yes," Balthazar answered without looking back.

"Especially you. A small child such as you would be quite a delicacy. Quite tender."

Shin-shin thought about this for a moment. "How — how do they eat you?"

"Raw, mostly," he said as if discussing how a bean sprouts or a swallow flies, "but I've read that there are many ways to cook a child. Slow roasting is quite popular in Babylon, I understand. Boiling, while producing a meal less tasty, is often the choice of the traveling nomad. Quite succulent, I'm told. But don't worry," he finished, "You're so small and skinny, they would probably not find you very appetizing."

Whether this was his clever way of getting the child to ration the food supplies or of keeping his pupil from getting eaten alive, Shin-shin wasn't sure. But either way, it worked.

They traveled far into the night, weaving their way through the hilly terrain toward the star. As its light began to dim, Shin-shin felt waves of exhaustion suddenly arrive.

Then, like an oil lamp being snuffed out, the star vanished. The night sky replaced it, but it had already begun surrendering its dominion to the interloping sun. A void of silence in Shin-shin's ears slowly gave way to the sounds of the receding evening: tree frogs croaking, peepers peeping, hooters cooing.

Balthazar stopped dead in mid-stride when the star vanished. "Well," he exclaimed, "that appears to be all for tonight."

"Am I tired!" Shin-shin exclaimed, collapsing on the ground.

"Indeed," said Balthazar. He was a bit bent and stiff. "But this isn't where we shall make camp. Come, let us find a quieter place off the beaten path."

But Shin-shin was already asleep. Balthazar scooped the slumbering child up and wound through the dense underbrush until he found a small clearing. He gently laid Shin-shin on the ground, gathered a few stray sticks, and after whispering an incantation, produced a small fire to warm their weary bones.

Then he hung their packs from the lowest branches of a stout tree to foil any scavenging beasts. Sitting deliberately against its spreading trunk, he let out a quiet, but satisfied sigh. At last, Balthazar lay down on the smooth brown ground, folded his hands on his chest, and closed his eyes.

But he hadn't quite earned his respite yet. "How —" asked Shin-shin sleepily, interrupted by an unstoppable yawn " —far do you think we journeyed tonight, master?" Sleep slurred the student's speech.

"Hmmm...difficult to gauge, considering we traveled at a speed beyond our normal ability. Supernatural forces are quite obviously at work here. Still, when you add in the uneven terrain, the density of the undergrowth, and the rather novel means by which we're navigating, I estimate that we've traversed a great distance indeed. How shall we calculate this? Let us postulate..."

His drone lulled the child back into the embrace of slumber, and Shin-shin heard no more.

Chapter Seven

Danakil Desert, Ethiopia

K*rinngg!!*
Schnack-Krinngg!!

After a forearm-shuddering parry, his opponent's blade swiped out and missed the warrior's throat by the span of a child's finger. The attempt slashed open the black shroud that covered the warrior's face and throat, and he could feel fresh air reaching in to stroke his sweaty neck.

His overmatched opponent's thrust failed, leaving the man vulnerable. It was the final error the doomed man would make in his twenty some-odd years of life.

Pirouetting and crouching slightly, the warrior whirled his immense scimitar around, raising a sanguine cloud of Ethiopian soil into the air with his feet. More impressive than the spin move was the aura of energy that mystically emanated and enveloped the warrior. Streaking bands of translucent crimson outlined and echoed the dark warrior's movements, softly whispering a low hum of might. The warrior's opponent saw the magical power and dread filled his heart.

As the scarlet-charged scimitar descended upon its target, time slowed in its wielder's mind and he wondered, was this a good or evil man? Did he have a woman somewhere worrying about him? Had he a son to carry on his name? Were his affairs in order? What would his friends say of him afterward? Was he afraid now? One ponders these things in mortal combat, especially before making the deliberate decision to take another's life when there's an opportunity to spare it.

Schwooop!

Decision made. As he committed all his strength to that final blow, the dark warrior deftly swung wide and pulled the handle of the humming scimitar across his chest. The move had its desired effect. A long, wet slash appeared in the young combatant's gut. Telltale blood blossomed, then gushed. Liberated from the confines of his flesh, the once young man's innards splurted out and landed with a plop on the dusty ground of the tribal center where they fought. A howl of anguished pain and defeat burst from the victim as well, which then yielded to immobile shock on the dying man's face as he saw his life come to such a quick and unsightly end. Then his knees buckled, unfortunately pitching him face-first into the quivering heap of his own abdominal contents.

The ebony fighter paused, bowing his head slightly to thank his deities for another victory, and spared a moment to consider his beaten foe. The dead man's last sight would have been of himself standing over him, dressed in the billowing black tunic and trousers of the warrior's homeland, shod in black goatskin boots and blocking the brutal rays of the African sun with a swirled black turban.

The victor of the contest stood tall among mere mortals, wore a tattered dark shroud that covered all but his eyes, and wielded the massive, bloody weapon. Considering his heavy, gore-spattered visage, the warrior looked like Death incarnate. And that was precisely how he felt.

Gaspar. Lord of the Ethiopia. Warrior king. Dispenser of death. Arbiter of justice. Wielder of magic. Possessor of strength beyond the measure of other men. And alone: aged well beyond his thirty-odd passes of the seasons — in Ethiopia, there are really only two, hot and hotter — and battle-hardened to a lonely, bitter position of solitary authority. Gaspar was alone as a man can be, his solitude wrapped about him as a last defense against both blade and regret.

But the dark reaper of men didn't have time to dwell on any of this. Two other combatants howled tonsil-tearing war cries and rushed to take their fallen comrade's place. Fools.

The skirmish through which the warrior waded was of the routine, tribal sort. A group of adventurous and rather foolhardy fighters from the south, darker of skin and heart than his people, had overrun this village on the southern outskirts of Gaspar's lands. The village had little value in terms of strategic placement or plunder; the foray was merely the ploy of a faraway and arrogant chieftain who hungered for more than his fair share.

Gaspar's assemblage of warriors, loosely organized but swift and powerful all the same, rode at daybreak into this square in the center of the village, which was, like most places in Ethiopia, a collection of meager huts centered around a perpetually dried-out well. The sun cooked the earth to a copper dust that coated everything, from tongues to turbans and crops to camels, in a thin, rusty layer.

The village already showed the ravages of the invaders' visit. Some corpses hung, flayed, from a gnarled tree, examples to discourage the rest from resistance, Gaspar suspected. A few of the huts were nothing more than burning embers. And the villagers' few beasts had been herded together to one side for the trip back to the conquering horde's home. The beasts never left their home fences. Silently, Gaspar's men quickly and efficiently dispatched the two dozy sentinels left to guard against just such a reprisal.

The invaders, unprepared for Gaspar's arrival, nevertheless made themselves so with surprising alacrity. Within moments, forty men came streaming out of every door, window, and nook in the huts. Though outnumbered more than two to one, Gaspar and his company dismounted and went man to man — a fair fight, given that Gaspar and his men were more experienced warriors and, more important, fully awake.

The man Gaspar had just disemboweled seemed to be someone of importance, judging by the reaction of the two crazed men approaching him. In a single fluid motion, Gaspar slipped a short-bladed dagger from the black cloth belt he wore around his waist and flipped the knife into the soft hollow of one man's throat, bringing him to his knees, gagging on blood. The other, after a few feeble swipes of his blade, lost the use of his right hand forever as Gaspar severed it above the wrist with his own sword. This was bad luck, as it was also the hand he used to wield his weapon. The doomed man looked at his amputated arm, dumbfounded, as Gaspar scimitared his head from his neck.

The Ethiopian lord's blood charged through his veins, and power roared in his ears and temples. As he always did, Gaspar knew he wouldn't taste defeat this day, and perhaps any other, because of his special powers. He'd always had them — greater strength, speed, and skill with a blade than any other — and they were part of the legend that kept him alone at the head of his people and tribe.

The other part of the legend was his supernatural command of men and nature. Gaspar had an aura about him, a mystical field of strength — both literal and spiritual, so powerful that it willed men to his side as effectively as it killed those he opposed. This unearthly power flowed through his limbs and weapons, too. No blow he dealt was ever untrue, and no objective ever unrealized.

And so Gaspar, magus of war, whipped his weapon above his head and sought another kill.

Gaspar had no difficulty finding one. His tribesmen dressed alike. From head to toe, they draped themselves in customary black to shield themselves from the prying eyes of the sun and strangers. Only visible were their brown eyes and the rich ebony skin of their hands. Gaspar's people weren't prone to adornment, mostly because such riches were rare and considered a waste. In fact, they considered a skin of water thrice as precious as any shiny bauble, and a healthy horse thrice again as valuable as the water. Yet what they valued most was honor in battle, and the honor of the family. The Ethiopians may have been a loose clan, roaming the baked earth and cracked stretches of their homeland, but they were fiercely loyal to each other.

So identifying another adversary was relatively easy for Gaspar, even though their numbers were dwindling swiftly. Many were deserting rather than fighting, and the brave few who stayed soon regretted the decision. By the time the sun was high, the last man stood, bloodied but unrepentant, encircled by the magus' black-robed brethren.

Gaspar walked up to the group, and the circle parted to allow him entrance. The last opponent turned and nervously addressed Gaspar with his nicked and ruddy blade. His eyes darted back and forth to the other men surrounding him, suspecting a less than honorable approach from the rear. He had no need to.

"Lay down your blade. Your comrades, those who still breathe, have abandoned you. Surrender to your fate, and you may yet see the sun rise again," Gaspar intoned plainly and quietly, with an authority that victory in battle always lends.

"Wh-wh-who are you t-to tell me what to do?" he challenged. He had courage, foolhardy as it was. His eyes were wide with fear. He'd seen too many of his countrymen executed in too many horrible ways that morning.

Gaspar smiled mirthlessly beneath his tattered shroud. "I'm Gaspar, lord of this land which you and your kinsmen made the mistake of entering when you thought to take this village."

Gaspar removed his black mask and revealed his equally black face to the gathering and the heat of the noonday sun. He slid his scimitar into his belt and crossed his arms as he assessed the prisoner: medium build, medium skin color, and medium fighting skill. Gaspar correctly ascertained that he was most likely a hired mercenary; a thug for hire who'd made a rather poor career choice of late. The fact that he'd lasted this long through the slaughter was a bit of a surprise. Regardless, the question was, Gaspar asked himself, what to do with him now?

"To which bastard lord of the south do you pay homage?" Gaspar asked.

"Thinlobuttu," he said, adding painfully, "the mighty" as he dropped his sword, accepting the hopelessness of his situation.

"I'm unfamiliar with Thinlobuttu. Until now. But you can be sure my men and I won't forget him. And you are — ?"

He answered meekly, "Mowbli."

"You fought well, Mowbli, and stayed when others ran. For this, today you live. But I'm not done with you. Go to your master, this Thinlobuttu, and tell him Gaspar is displeased and demands tribute. Ten horses and twenty goats are to be brought here to this village within a fortnight or my riders, tenfold of what you see now, will visit Thinlobuttu in the night and slit his throat, and the throats of his wives and children. This, I promise you." Gaspar uttered the final words with severity.

"Should we cut off his hands?" one of the men in the circle suggested. Whether in jest or not, Gaspar was unsure.

"No," Gaspar responded to the great relief of Mowbli. "Let him go as he is. And Mowbli, should you ever tire of serving a chief who thinks little of slaying the innocent, we would always welcome a man with courage such as yours."

Gaspar spun on his heel and walked away. The other members of the Ethiopian tribe immediately accepted Mowbli into said tribe and embraced him with many kisses, slaps on the shoulder, and signs of affection. It wasn't the kind of reception the poor survivor had in mind. But he called out to Gaspar, "Master, how shall I find you?" Gaspar didn't pause or reply but strode away in silence.

"Ha! Ha-ha-ha!" The circle of tribesmen laughed good-naturedly at the question.

An elder tribesman whispered to Mowbli, "You don't find him, our enchanter. He vanishes like the shadow! He comes and goes with the shadows. No, you don't find Lord Gaspar…he finds you."

Chapter Eight

Later, Gaspar realized he'd received a light wound in the fight, a clean gash on his upper left arm that was sure to fester if left untended. Bowing his head, the magus concentrated his will upon the wound. Invisible fingers of magic stitched the flesh together, almost erasing the injury and leaving only a thin scar line as a reminder to be more careful next time.

Gaspar was a day's ride out of the village. He'd journeyed north and left the hard lands behind for the outer edges of the great desert. It was here that he felt most comfortable. From the far brown ribbon of the Nile to the west, to the azure ripples of the Arabian Sea to the east, Gaspar and his nomadic people called this vast span of earth their home.

Although the acknowledged ruler of the Ethiopian people, Gaspar hardly led the life of a king. No palaces or thrones for him. He'd become leader by killing or besting everyone else who wanted the job and impressing everyone who watched with his supernatural powers. But in truth, Gaspar was king of a land of roamers, nomads whose homes were nothing more than a tent, a camel ride, and the few belongings necessary to survive. True, more verdant lands lay to the south and east, where spices and crops flourished, and it was there they turned for trading and barter. But here, in the lands of the sun, was where they chose to roam.

Gaspar's people were a hardy lot, baked tough, wiry, and black by the unforgiving sun. Quiet by nature, merciless when angered, they kept mostly to their extended families and moved only when urge, misfortune, or weather motivated them. A stranger was as likely to be staked alive to burn in the sun as he was to be welcomed into a tent and fed figs by half-naked women. What determined one's fate was usually pure whimsy.

He'd been riding hard after the skirmish. Gaspar had no doubt that the tribute he'd demanded would be paid, mostly to ensure that the ravaged village had a chance to rebuild and survive. His fighting force had disbanded, fracturing into tiny groups, as was their wont. Gaspar had split off by himself as usual, this time surrendering to the internal, relentless tugging that would give him no peace. It had started a few days ago, a restlessness that kept Gaspar scanning the horizon day and night. A warning? Good fortune? Or a summons of a sort, a mystical call he'd never experienced before? He couldn't identify it, but the urge pestered at the corners of his consciousness.

His stallion's haunches glistened with a crunchy layer of dried sweat and sand that had cooled in the dying sunlight. A horse was a precious commodity in these lands. The one Gaspar rode, in fact, had been taken in a raid on a marauding caravan from the east. Word had reached Gaspar, who was fortunately nearby, that a band of bloodletting thieves were cutting their way across Ethiopia with no regard for any others but themselves. Gaspar, alone, attacked in the dead of night and slit many a snoring throat. He'd found the dark stallion, which he later named Makeda, tied up and bearing evidence of brutal beatings at the hands of the marauders. The man Gaspar had found sleeping with the bloody whip next to him had felt its sting more than a few times before he was finally dispatched.

Gaspar claimed the horse as was his right, and he left the

remainder of the marauder's ill-gotten gains for the locals to take away as reparations for the hurt they'd suffered.

Both rider and ride were jet as the night, and they cut an inky silhouette as they galloped across the light sands. Gaspar rode north, still a long ride from any village or oasis. He was usually a nocturnal traveler, choosing to lie low during the hottest parts of the day. Gaspar would start just as the sun would start to sink and would ride far into the night, bivouacking among the dunes only when exhaustion would let him go no farther.

Gaspar was riding up a rather large dune in the heart of the night when it appeared unannounced. The star.

Its light exploded upon him, almost throwing him from the saddle. Makeda reared, terrified by the brilliance. Sounds, music like he never experienced before, battered his eardrums. And for the first time in Gaspar's life, he felt *fear*. Submission. Awe. His heart stopped, and he struggled to keep his seat, but his eyes never left the iridescent vision in the western skies.

More beautiful and real than a shimmering mirage in the desert, the rising star's radiant beams pierced Gaspar to the soul. Brighter than a dozen stars poured into one, it illuminated the entire desert before him. Music, sound, voices that he felt he could reach out and touch, swirled about and through him like a million tiny shafts of life. He gazed at it for what seemed like an eternity, drinking in its beauty and majesty completely.

Certainly, this was what he'd been waiting for. It was clear, simple, and undeniable. Gaspar had no doubt in which direction the fates were pointing him, calling him, and commanding him.

Without hesitation, the dark lord of Ethiopia dug his heels hard into the sides of his mount, turned his back on his homeland without a passing thought, and rode northwest, following the path illuminated by the star.

CHAPTER NINE

The palace of Melchior buzzed with anticipation. No one else had seen the star, it seemed, but many sensed that a threshold had been crossed. As in autumn, one day arrives when all of nature feels the first hint of winter and begins the preparations for the hardships to come.

Shafiq and the rest of the elder magi, therefore, were relatively hesitant in their objections when Melchior called his advisors together for an impromptu meeting to announce that he was departing the palace that very evening for a long journey with an indeterminate conclusion.

A striding Melchior led a small procession through the hallways and stairways of the stone palace. The immense royal structure was composed of vast blocks of greenish, bluish granite, hewn from the heart of mountain upon which it sat. The palace's airy chambers were linked by corridors labyrinthine and dark, lit only with sputtering torches held by enchanted iron hands attached to the walls. The torches would burst into revealing flame as walkers strode by, the hands moving to help illuminate their path as they passed. The stone walls and floors sparkled in the firelight, creating an unearthly, cave-like ambiance until the torches snuffed themselves out again after the travelers had passed.

The assorted sorcerers, scribes, soldiers, and servants hustled to match Melchior's pace, occasionally peeling off once a duty was assigned. "I want a small but well-armed force to travel with me. Fifty men, no more, no less," Melchior barked, not knowing where he was getting these figures or ideas. They just seemed to flow from somewhere around his stomach.

"King Melchior, where are you going?" queried Master-at-Arms Barir, the large, brown-haired colossus of a man whose kindly, fatherly face belied his prowess on the battlefield and his devotion as the king's bodyguard. An expert soldier and swordsman and veteran of many a siege, Barir never moved without his massive blade and an assortment of short daggers with leather-wrapped hilts on his person. His concern was genuine, as was his loyalty. On a dark night in dismal circumstances, Barir was the man you wanted at your side.

Melchior stopped dead in his tracks, hesitated for only a second, and said with confidence, "West." He instantly started off again, leaving the slack-jawed crowd, still sorting itself out from the pileup the king had just created, to run and catch up.

"That's it? West? Nothing a little firmer than that?" Shafiq asked with a trace of kindhearted sarcasm.

"Yes," replied Melchior with a confidence he didn't really possess. There are times when a man knows only in his own heart what course of action he must undertake, and it's a lonely feeling. Rarely can he communicate why he feels this way or provide a rational explanation for that course of action. Today was one of those times, and if he'd not had the support of the throne behind him, Melchior would have felt like a fool acting this way.

"How far will you travel, my liege?" queried one magus.

"What will you take with you, my lord?" asked another.

"How long will this journey last?" inquired a soldier.

"And...when will you return?" a fourth voice sweetly yet defiantly demanded from a doorway. Melchior skidded to another stop at the sound of the voice and turned to find

Nur's eyes boring into his.

He stood rooted to the spot, spellbound, the men behind him murmuring strained apologies as they stumbled into each other again at the sudden stop.

"I don't know," he answered quietly and honestly. Sheepishly, he nodded to her and picked up his parade again, leaving her in the glow of the torches with arms crossed and brow puckered.

Barir, sensing that the king couldn't explain himself to everyone's collective satisfaction, took the lead in the conversation and stepped forward to speak with Melchior as they walked. "With your leave, I will hand-select a contingent of my best soldiers to ride with us and outfit a caravan of horses and camels with supplies to last a few weeks' ride. Is this satisfactory, my lord?" he asked.

Breathing a hard sigh of relief, Melchior slowed his pace. "Yes. Many thanks, Barir."

As they entered the main courtyard filled with sunlight and a gentle breeze, Melchior stopped and turned to address the group. "Look, I can't tell you what this is all about, where we're going, or who we are to meet, simply because I don't know. Yet. I can tell you, however, that I've heard a call and I'll lead us to a destination — or event, or person, or *something* — that will decide all our fates. I feel it wise that we be prepared for the best, as well as for the worst. That means wine as well as weapons. Gold as well as grains. We pack light for fast travel, nonetheless. For tonight, at nightfall, we ride."

With the orange glow of dusk beginning to cover them, the caravan assembled in the open yard just within the gates of the palace. From his high balcony above the palace courtyard, Melchior observed pure chaos.

Camels and camel drivers were having their historical differences of opinion. Horses pranced in anticipation, their eyes wide with fear of the many newly lit torches that passed so close to their heads. Footmen yelled, gestured, pointed, yelled, packed, unpacked, yelled again, and generally tried to fit four weeks of supplies into two-week packs. Soldiers loudly scraped swords across stones. Wives, children, and loved ones hugged and wept. The scene had all the hallmarks of a departure for war, noted the magus king.

In his chamber, however, Nur stood dry-eyed and grim, no candidate for sappy farewells.

"There's no good reason for me not to go with you," she argued. "What harm will one more do? I can carry my own. I can use a weapon…I'll be of more use to you than most of the buffoons down there!"

"This feels…right," he countered, knowing it sounded as weak in her ears as it did in his. "Who's the king here, anyway? You must remain, and that's the end of it. Besides…" He paused. "I'll need a good reason to return, won't I?"

That attempt at flattery fell flatter than his shadow on the marble floor. She merely scowled at him and turned to face a tapestry on the wall, which ironically depicted the last leg of Alexander's final journey, his sad journey home from his failure in India.

Melchior clinked up behind her and placed his hands on her shoulders. He'd chosen to wear his light battle gear for the evening's departure, which consisted of a light shirt of shiny mail and similarly light guards on his shins and forearms. He'd not yet donned the helmet that was half metal and half turban, and it sat on the top of a stone chest at the foot of his bed. Hammered onto its brow was the royal crest, a relief in gold of a mountain stag with its head bent for battle.

Melchior gently turned her to face him and looked for what he feared could well be the final time into her eyes. He was worried. Her proximity made him question his decision to leave her behind, but ultimately his fear of the unknown was stronger, and he wouldn't put her in harm's way. "Even now," he whispered and confessed, "I can hear it call to me.

If I don't answer, I'll go mad."

Straightening, his hands still on her shoulders, Melchior said, "Look. I've faced screaming armies, bloodied with anger and outnumbering us one hundred to one, and yet I felt no fear. I drove my sword into the breast of the chimera, felt his claws rip my flesh, and I didn't cry out. I've even faced down that monster Zoth and lived to tell about it." He smiled weakly. "But now, leaving you, I feel my heart quake. I fear I'll never see you, hold you, and taste you again. That I'll die, alone, naked on the sand, and another will hold you as you sleep. But I mustn't let those fears shake me from this calling...my destiny...you mustn't. I need to know that you'll be here, waiting for me."

The tears finally broke from her eyes, as pure and sweet as the mountain streams that appear when the sun strokes the snows. He touched his fingertip to one and pressed it to his lips. The salty sensation strengthened him. "In the days to come," Melchior murmured, "I'll call upon these tears to bear me through. I thank you for them, and...love you for them." At last, he'd finally said it.

She smiled and surrendered. "I love you too. Come back soon, for without you here, I'm slowly dying."

He made no bold departure, or proud exclamation of certain victory. That wasn't who Melchior was. The king simply stood there and wept himself, looking at her and trying to convince his heart that this journey was a brief interlude, nothing more.

The tiny rivulets of tears stung Melchior's eyes as he pulled away. Scooping up the helmet he left without turning around, afraid that a final look at her would weaken him even further. He paused on the steps on the way down to gather himself, wiping his eyes. They weren't the last tears to be shed.

In the palace courtyard, chaos had given way to a semblance of order, and Melchior suspected the firm hand

and loud voice of Barir lay behind that. The sounds of preparation had quieted, with only the occasional snort of a horse and the sizzling of torches filling the air. In the cooling night air, the smell was almost overpowering, a mixture of sulfur, sweat, and animal excrement.

The camels knelt to one side, all chewing with the same labored rhythm and looking about slowly with heavy-lidded eyes. Their drivers sat atop them surrounded by an impossible number of packs wrapped in white linen. They didn't appear any more active than their mounts.

The king's horsemen stood beside their steeds, holding their reins. Bright eyes shone in lined, suntanned faces, many mustachioed or bearded, and all bearing the same grim countenance. Most wore white cotton shirts beneath their mail to protect them as much from the heat of the sun as from the chill of the night, and each was armed with a curved sword, the saif. Each mount bore a spear, holstered upright toward the rear flank just behind the light saddle, and each carried a light pack and a large skin of water high on its rump.

Shafiq stood near the gate, holding the reins of his horse and the king's, looking mildly amused by the melee of the preparation. Melchior initially had reservations about bringing a man of Shafiq's age along, but ultimately the older magus argued convincingly that his knowledge and experience would be invaluable in the days to come.

Ancient Shafiq was the only other magus accompanying Melchior. When he'd announced that decision early in the afternoon, Melchior had to suffer a long line of intrepid magi to his throne, all quite willing to risk their neck on the chopping block of fate for the chance to join the journey. But Melchior was firm. The same voice that commanded Melchior to leave his terraced palace also guided him in choosing who would go on the journey and who would not.

"Well," Melchior said, stopping a pace away from Shafiq and Barir, the duo he'd come to rely on and trust like no other. "Let's get on with it then. Is all ready?"

Barir replied quite formally in the tradition of the kingdom, "The caravan is yours, King Melchior. Lead, and we follow."

Shafiq just smiled and nodded. His eyes revealed his concern, but he was determined to put on the brave face. Melchior appreciated the façade.

The Arabian king mounted his dark stallion, Ejaz, in a single, smooth motion and gently pulled the reins against his neck to turn him to face the group. Melchior raised his right hand even with his head, giving the signal to the caravan to mount up.

As one, the camels rose from their knees to stand on their spindly legs. Riders performed rolling mounts onto the backs of their horses, and instantly the caravan was ready. Melchior stole one quick glance at his balcony, but darkness hid the face he knew looked down on him. He nodded nonetheless, wheeled his horse about, and reared Ejaz onto his two hind feet, completing the ceremonial start of the war cavalcade.

"Gate," Melchior said quietly under his breath, motioning his hand and with an impressive display of power, moving the palace's massive iron web of a gate to the left and right. Normally, Melchior would lead them out like the qibli, the sirocco, on a tear, but that didn't feel appropriate. Instead, he clapped his hand on his sword in its leather and gold scabbard at his hip and gestured slightly with the other. Nickering softly to his horse, he led the caravan quietly and deliberately through the opening into the quiet night.

As the procession filed out, only the occasional animal snuffle or human cough broke the quiet. Then without looking back, Melchior shut the gates with another wave of his hand, and their *cling-clang* rang loud and harsh, violating the stillness.

The train of man and beast rode in silence, single file

down from the palace's perch high atop the mountain, with only the hooves *clip-clopping* on the path worn hard by years of travel. Per custom, Melchior rode first, followed by Barir, then Shafiq and the rest of the caravan.

As they descended, the rugged highland landscape of stone and cliff began to yield to grassy slopes and short vegetation, all dimly silhouetted in what soft light the night provided. After a while, the men began to loosen up and speak quietly to each other, the conversations layered and occasionally peppered with laughter and good-hearted curses. For Melchior it was good to hear that the men were of sound hearts and spirits. But rounding a sharp bend in the path where the mountains just ended, he drew up and lifted his left hand to halt the caravan.

Zoth waited there, sitting astride a massive black horse as if he knew exactly when they would arrive. He wore a slight smile, a dark slice in his ghastly-white face, and sarcastically tilted his head in acknowledgement. "Melchior."

"*King* Melchior," Barir corrected with a growl. Behind him, the men had fallen silent, their good moods instantly shattered. Non-magical persons of the kingdom dreaded Zoth and looked upon him as a curse or a wraith — or both. Even the horses whinnied their annoyance.

"Lord Zoth," Melchior answered flatly, trying to disguise the fact that he was taken aback by this unexpected and somewhat frightful appearance in the darkness.

Zoth's intention was perfectly clear. He was inviting himself on the pilgrimage. And although his head advised Melchior of the foolhardiness of bringing his most dire enemy on a journey to points unknown, the inexplicable voice within his heart told him this was as it should be. It felt…right.

"Good of you to join us. We were worried you wouldn't make it. In fact, I thought you might've had second thoughts. Have you?" asked Melchior, unable to resist baiting his relative. Zoth merely scowled, now unsure if his surprise appearance had created the drama he'd planned.

"Please, take your place and let us continue," Melchior said amiably, anticipating the part the unexpected would play in the days to come. Melchior's invitation elicited gasps from the rest of the caravan, however, and quite a few invoked their personal gods.

"I don't believe this," muttered Barir, but Shafiq silenced him with a sharp glance.

"Shafiq," acknowledged Zoth as he fell in beside the elder magus.

"Zoth," replied Shafiq just as coolly, staring straight ahead as the caravan began moving again.

"This," Melchior said grimly to no one in particular, "is getting interesting."

Though waning, the lonely moon still emitted a steady light, and the few stars that remained with it in the sky seemed willing to let the satellite have its time to shine. As the caravan rode out past the last of the dying grass onto the first puddles of desert sand, silence had again overtaken them. They walked for a few hundred lengths on the sand, letting the animals become accustomed to the new footing, eventually picking up the pace to an easy canter for the horses, an ungainly trot-lope for the camels.

Melchior craned his head upwards. But the star wasn't there.

Night had completely fallen hours ago, yet the star hadn't taken its place in the blue-black void in the west. Immediately, Melchior's life-long companion, doubt, made its presence known. Melchior started playing out in his mind how to tell the caravan that all this was a waste, a monumental mistake, and that they were turning around for the palace. "This was just a test of your readiness," he tried on himself, then unconvincingly tried "I've changed my mind." Both sounded as dreary and foolish as a child's excuse for misbehaving.

Melchior's horse sensed his hesitation, and it broke from its canter into a jerky trot, eventually slowing to walk and a halt. The king didn't even seem to notice as all his attention was focused on the night sky. The wind whistled and prickled over the sands, the only sound in the night. Melchior's eyes looked as if they'd pop from their orbits as he strained to see what was not there. He leaned so far forward he almost fell from his saddle. This isn't good, he thought. Not good.

"This isn't good," echoed Zoth from the darkness behind him. "Our king and guide seems a bit...confused. And we've been riding for what, hours? Perhaps we're...lost?"

While scathing, his chiding was on target, thought Melchior. Barir wasn't as sympathetic. "So help me, sorcerer, I'll cut that insolent tongue from your mouth without blinking. Hold it or—"

A yelp cut him off.

Standing high in his stirrups, Melchior held out his right arm, pointing toward what he'd been so desperately searching—the star.

With perhaps an even greater luminosity, it shone like a beacon in the western void, slathering the desert with its brilliance. Its rays touched the horizon in all directions. And its music—oh, its beautiful music—rang off the sand and filled the air with euphony.

Those in the caravan, however, looked at Melchior as if he were mad, sand-crazed without having seen a single day in the sun.

"It's here!" Melchior proclaimed proudly, gesturing with the vindication of man who has proven his sanity. But the rest of the caravan looked back him with the blank stares of the unenlightened, even Zoth.

The king twisted and looked at them in disbelief. "Do you not see it? Can you not hear it? It calls to us!"

Barir looked down, embarrassed for his king. Zoth smiled his wicked little grin. And Shafiq regarded Melchior from across the few yards separating them with skepticism in his eyes. Yet to Melchior's eyes, its light coated their faces. Its song reverberated off them, the horses, the camels, the sand itself! How could they be so deaf and dumb?

Melchior turned and slumped back into his saddle, feeling frustrated and stupid. He looked up again at the vision, which, he was beginning to fear, was a vision that only his own demented mind could perceive. He commanded it quietly, "Star, reveal yourself!" but nothing happened.

Melchior called upon all his power to bend the star to his will "Reveal!" he commanded loudly, arms outstretched, his fingers curled into powerful claws.

"Reveal!" he bellowed again. Uselessly.

He sat alone in the star's brilliance, and the caravan began to get a little restless. Horses stamped their hooves impatiently, camels chewed loudly on their cud, rides shifted uncomfortably in their saddles.

"Please," he whispered. He begged and hung his head down in utter despair. Then...

"By all that is holy — "

"Save us!"

"Gods!"

Melchior's head popped up like a hare from its hole. The star remained unchanged, but the caravan had not. They *saw*. They saw the star.

Many of the soldiers had either fallen from their horses in fright, been thrown by a frightened horse, or were trying to calm a frightened mount. The camels, with their perpetual nonchalance, chewed on unperturbed. Their drivers, however, cowered in the star's majesty and covered their faces.

Barir drew his sword by force of instinct. Shafiq slid from his horse and stood on the sand, staring hypnotically into the star's white-hot center. Zoth just sat there, occasionally glancing upward, yet looking disappointed that things were taking a decidedly exciting turn for the better for his cousin the king.

"You see? You see!" Melchior exclaimed, like an idiot who has only just grasped the most simple of concepts. Of course they saw it. But he was so relieved—overjoyed, in fact—that he was not, in fact, mad as a mountain goat. Simpleton sentences like "You see!" were just about all the mighty king of Arabia could stammer out.

After a while, the rest of the caravan realized that there was little to fear and even less they could do about the appearance of the star. Its appearance provided a somewhat comforting validation of their king. They all sat or stood there rather dumbly, admiring the star's beauty and listening to its song.

"It speaks to me," said a soldier in the rear. "Can you hear it?"

"I can't bear to look at it...but I can't look away! Aiyeee!" screamed another.

Those around him mumbled their assent. Another voice, Melchior thought it was Barir's, asked, "Where? Where does it want us to come?"

"I don't know where it'll lead us," Melchior answered loudly, turning to face the assembly. Slowly, most of the glistening faces looked at him and waited for the magus to continue. "But now, at last, you understand. How can we not heed its summons? I call on you all, now, to pledge with me to follow it until we reach wherever it leads us. Decide not to, and there will be no shame or punishment. I want no one to be uncertain of this journey. All, or nothing—there can be no in between. Are you with me?" he challenged.

Normally, when a king ventures a dare like that to his horde, the response is quite...enthusiastic. Tonight, though, faced with a dread power the likes of which none had ever encountered; the response was a bit more modest. The men thought for a moment or two.

Then Barir replaced his weapon with a flourish and nudged his steed forward a step. "I'm with you, my lord.

I'm with you. Always," he pledged.

"Well, of course, we're with you." Shafiq smiled and slowly climbed aboard his horse with his usual lack of grace.

The rest of the men nodded and soberly pledged as well.

Finally Zoth spoke up. "Well, then, stop wasting my time and let's be off."

The dark magus' tacit agreement to continue didn't shock the Melchior. For clearly, this was where the action was. And Zoth sensed, as did Melchior, that he belonged there, at least for now. What fate held in store for the two of them, perhaps only the star truly knew.

Come, beckoned the shining star. And they obeyed.

"West!" Melchior shouted and wheeled his mount to ride in that direction. And finally they whipped into form and whirled off in a cloud of sand toward the burning, distant point in the carbon sky.

CHAPTER TEN

The irony of the star lay in the fact that, although it heralded the end of an age for everyone on the planet, few actually witnessed it.

Melchior, king, sorcerer, perhaps the most magically powerful of the three Magi, saw the star and answered its call. Melchior's caravan saw the star.

Balthazar, scientist, astronomer, enchanter, numerologist, came from the Far East when the star beckoned. Shin-shin, apprentice to Balthazar, saw the star.

Gaspar, warrior, chieftain, loner, mystic, witnessed the star and followed it.

Others saw the star, but didn't comprehend its significance.

Half a world away, an Olmec priest stood atop a ziggurat in the heart of a dense jungle and held aloft the still warm and pulsating heart of a victim, one of the hundreds of human offerings made that day to the new star god.

A contingent of Japanese soldiers readied themselves, at the behest of their tribal warlord, to defend against the imminent invasion the star certainly signified. Since no one else would ever see the star, the warlord was forced to perform seppuku and gut himself in shame.

A cabal of Druids gathered in the meeting place, a circle of standing stones erected by the gods eons before. The circle's meaning was finally made clear when the star appeared, illuminating a large stone in the center of the circle. A shaft of starlight pierced the heart of the stone and shattered it, foretelling the coming of another.

Walking across the icy tundra, an Inuit hunter looked up, smiled bloodily at the twinkling star, and continued to feast on his seal blubber.

In Rome, even mighty Caesar Augustus, also called Octavian, god, emperor of the civilized world, ruler of the mightiest host ever gathered, stood on one of his seven hills, watched the star's rising, and felt his blood run cold.

On the Hill of Vaus in the far reaches of the desert, twelve astronomers, Watchers, who'd waited a lifetime for just such a revelation, saw the star and fell to their knees, fulfilled. The Watchers *saw*.

For hundreds of years before the star's appearance, on the very same Hill of Vaus, Balaam, an old priest of the order of Madian whose life fire was burning to its final embers, stood stargazing. He witnessed a star more magnificent than any he or any other mortal man ever beheld. Revealed in the star was a vision, and Balaam made a prophecy based upon what he saw. He gathered twelve of the wisest men and astronomers to hear the prophecy.

Balaam foretold, "A star shall spring forth out of Jacob, and a man shall rise upon Israel and shall be lord of all folk."

Thereupon Balaam charged the twelve men to keep vigil upon the Hill of Vaus for the rising of the star that he had foretold. And over the centuries, these same twelve of astronomers land kept watch on the Hill of Vaus, looking for the star that heralded the coming of the king. And they waited. And waited.

Then at last, the star appeared, and the Watchers of Vaus recalled the prophecy of Balaam and knew that somewhere, in the bosom of the desert, a king would be born.

In the meantime, the three Magi made their way toward a destination they couldn't divine. Balthazar, who had the farthest to come, traveled quickly. Once he and Shin-shin had left the foothills of their homeland in the Orient, they bartered an elephant from a ruby-skinned Indian merchant, and the duo made excellent time as they followed the star south and west.

Gaspar, unencumbered, rode like a bird on the wing from the lands of Ethiopia. His horse Makeda gobbled up the leagues of sand as a parched man gulps down water. The black magus made his way quickly north and westward.

Melchior and his retinue, having the shortest path to travel yet moving at the slowest pace due to the size of their party, continued on a path almost due west.

CHAPTER ELEVEN

The star was leading them to Judaea, a small and rather unremarkable stretch of arid land that ran from Syria in the north to Beersheba in the south, and bordered to the west by the Mediterranean Sea and to the east by the River Jordan. However, the path to Judaea the Magi followed was anything but a straight line. The star, and the power behind it, had some challenges for the Magi to meet along the way.

The fates and paths of the Magi were being manipulated by the unseen hand of a powerful force, and thus it was no accident that, soon after the star first appeared, the three Magi were within a few leagues of each other, unaware of each other's presence or calling. As they each approached Judaea, they were able to take advantage of the ancient Persian roads, constructed long ago by the engineers of Alexander of Macedon. The three roads intersected at a rather ordinary spot in the middle of the desert, a modest watering hole with a few scraggly date trees that had served as a meeting and rest spot for centuries. Sandal-shod armies had marched through it on campaigns eastward and retreats westward. Vagabonds, traders, mercenaries, emperors, kings, queens, pharaohs, pilgrims, caravans, families, minstrels, priests, and a few ghosts had passed this way as well, leaving little to mark their visit as they did.

Later, the Magi would realize that, until they met,

the star's appearance was as individual as the wise men themselves. It controlled the direction of each man's path, and the duration of its appearance, to bring the three Magi together at this innocent watering hole in the middle of nowhere.

Deep into the night, the star shone, and Melchior and his group pursued it, galloping along the hard-packed road with conviction that what they sought lay just over the next rise.

The journey so far had been uneventful. There'd been no more overt "signs." They'd encountered no dangers or other travelers. Supplies and water were well rationed. There was little cause for concern except, of course, for Zoth, but many a wary eye kept watch on the pale figure shrouded in black and lavender.

Melchior, fixated on the shimmering beacon, rode first and fastest. He gave little thought to the others in the group, but perhaps he should have. While he had his most steadfast allies and trustworthy friends with him, he had his most dire enemy and a few strangers in his retinue, as well.

Everyone seemed to share the same conviction. The star, the mysterious and powerful star, was leading him to an unknown appointment with destiny. And until they'd realized that destiny, there seemed little else to do but follow where it led.

Conversation was nonexistent. But one thing everyone seemed to realize was that the journey, and the traveling in general, seemed effortless.

"My lord, do you know that we've traveled over a thousand leagues in just a few short days?" Barir had asked around a roaring fire a few days earlier.

"Ah...hmmm. Well, now that you mention it, no," Melchior replied as realization flowed over him. The star had mesmerized him into a lemming, blinding him to the passage of time, their journey over the sand, even life itself.

The call of the star overrode everything.

"And have you also noticed," Shafiq said to his lord, "the star doesn't shine uniformly each night? Tonight, for example, its light vanished long before the break of dawn. But last night, it shone until the sun's rays peeked over the eastern horizon."

"There's deliberate purpose to its course, that I grant you," said Melchior, "but I trust its light, its…nature. It's, well, alive. I think we're being led to something great, and that it's up to us to do something equally as great. Like Jason, with the fleece. Or Hercules, with his labors. But, I'm…I'm at a loss. Anyone have any ideas, any feelings? And where is Zoth?"

This met ominous silence. Zoth, as usual, had disappeared as soon as the star hid itself. He slept, ate — everyone assumed he ate, although no one knew for certain — and generally existed apart from the group except when traveling and even then, he kept a buffer of about thirty paces between himself and the nearest rider.

Tonight Melchior felt compelled to search out the warlock. Leaving the establishment of the camp to the others, he moved away from the fires and felt his way toward the blackest hole in the night. There, a few dunes away, he found Zoth supine on the sand, his eyes wide open. If Melchior didn't know better, he would have thought he'd stumbled upon a corpse.

"Why are you bothering me, Melchior? Is there something you desire, my…king?" he asked sarcastically, twisting the last word cruelly on his tongue. He propped himself up on an elbow and looked hard at Melchior, who seated himself a respectful few paces away on the side of another dune.

"I came to ask one of my subjects and counselors," Melchior began slowly, ignoring the jibe, "what he thinks of our journey. Of the star. Is this all…folly?"

Zoth seemed genuinely taken aback for a moment. He then lay back down on the sand and stared at the starry firmament, studying its bizarre redeployment of the constellations. His voice lost some, but not much, of its edge. "I don't know as yet. There's nothing in the world I desire as much as to see you fail miserably on this silly jaunt of yours. You'd be laughed out of court. I'd be rightfully placed on the throne. I'd have your foolish head cut off right in front of everyone…including that witch Nur," he said.

Melchior flinched, as much at the idea of being disgraced and beheaded as for the revelation that Zoth knew how he felt about Nur.

"But still…" continued the necromancer, "there's more at work here than your misguided imagination. I, too, see the star. I think, though, that it's summoning you to your doom. A uniquely grisly one, I believe."

"I don't think so, cousin," replied Melchior. "You pretend to be different from me, and think differently, but you're not. You hear the same song. You're just a darker reflection of me.

"It's leading us to a new beginning, I grant you that—" Melchior said, but Zoth cut him off.

"Any new beginning means the end for you, Melchior," he hissed. "Never forget, I know the fear that lurks inside you."

"Perhaps," Melchior admitted, "but what is it, do you think? I, for one, think…hope…a new day has dawned, the like of which we haven't seen since the Persians. Perhaps, a new power comes to rule the world."

"I think it's these Romans we keep hearing about," Zoth said. "Their emperor is summoning us to pay fealty to him. Don't, and he'll lop off your head. Do, and he'll follow you home to squash you. Either way, it destroys you, and probably your kingdom. Like it or not, you've at last stuck your head out of your shell only to find the knife at your throat. It's what you've always feared. And I relish it."

The two men fell quiet, each realizing that, despite the threats, this was the longest conversation they'd had in years, since they were children.

"Maybe. Maybe, but I don't think so. This feels…greater than that. I guess the only other question is, will you beat this new king to the task and kill me for him?" asked Melchior, watching for the dark mage's reaction.

"Well, I'd sleep with one eye open if I were you," replied Zoth, crossing his arms on his chest and closing his eyes as a signal that the discussion was over.

Melchior stood and brushed sand from his bottom. He paused, then said, "Sound advice for both of us, I'd say."

Walking away, he resisted the temptation to look back and check the sorcerer's eyelids. But before he'd moved out of earshot, he heard Zoth's soft words carried magically on the wind: "I mean it. I *will* be there when you face your death. I've foreseen it. "

Dead tired, Melchior trudged back toward the campfire that glowed in the distance. Halfway there, he realized that Barir had accompanied him on his nocturnal visit to Zoth. Ever the protective and paternal soldier, he'd stayed a few dunes away and waited, ready to intervene if things got nasty.

Falling into step alongside his king, Barir let out a small sigh of exhaustion. Melchior realized that it took quite a bit of effort for the man to sit in the darkness and wait as he had.

Barir was troubled. He'd overheard the conversation between his king and Zoth, and more than once he'd moved his hand to his sword. But what bothered him was doubt. Melchior was obviously unsure where they were going, and why. Not a good position for the leader of a caravan in the middle of the hottest, most dangerous desert in the world to find himself in.

Even more troubling was the acknowledgement by both Melchior, a man Barir would gladly give his life to save, and Zoth, a man Barir would gladly give his life to slice open from head to toe, that they had no idea what was going on, what the star meant. Bravery was one thing; foolhardiness was quite another.

"How much of that did you hear?" Melchior asked him quietly as their boots made soft holes in the silent sand.

"My lord," Barir paused. "All of it. I'm sorry, but—"

"No, no, it's alright. Don't lose hope in me yet, Barir. I think…I think this journey's a test of our courage, of our faith in each other," said Melchior, and his voice sounded certain.

The light was coming on strong in the east as the two men reached the dying fire. Each went to his bedroll and wrapped up for slumber, protected from the searching beams of the desert sun. Barir noticed that Melchior, no doubt heeding Zoth's advice, slept with one eye open and one hand on his sword.

Soon, the star would be in the heavens again, beckoning them onward.

Balthazar and Shin-shin were making excellent progress from the Far East. More and more, Shin-shin was coming to realize that there was more to Balthazar than met the eye. How else could he know so much about so many strange lands?

They'd traveled mainly in the twilight, following the path highlighted by the star. But Balthazar usually roused the great gray beast and Shin-shin before it appeared, and the little troupe was usually well underway when the star made its appearance. And without fault, they were invariably heading in the right direction, southwest. When the star winked out for the evening, the old man usually pushed them on for another league or so.

Along the way, Balthazar pointed out the beasts, birds, people, plants, and everything else they passed, and later quizzed Shin-shin on what the child had learned. The results varied. Even in the heart of night, the world was alive with life, but the teacher-pupil relationship seemed never to change.

Shin-shin felt relatively safe atop the giant elephant. It would take a rather impressive feat of cannibalism to climb the great pachyderm and feast on the rider. Still, the pupil kept a watchful eye on the underbrush for savages with bones through their noses and bloody hatchets in their hands. Much to Shin-shin's relief, the dense foliage gradually gave way as they moved toward the warmer climes, and cannibal hiding places became fewer and fewer.

Mostly, though, the two discussed the meaning of the dreams and signs they had seen. Balthazar didn't understand the significance of Shin-shin's dreams of being buried alive in the tomb, the gambling soldiers, or the fortunate fishermen. And Shin-shin could add nothing to Balthazar's vision of the newborn babe. The only thing they agreed upon was that the star was leading them to the answers to all their questions.

"Who do you think the baby is?" asked Shin-shin for the fourteenth time.

"The identity of the child hasn't been revealed to me since you asked last, which I believe was only an hour ago," replied Balthazar with a touch of annoyance.

"I was only thinking out loud," Shin-shin countered.

"Please think quietly then," said the master. "I have my own thoughts to contend with."

But then he indulged Shin-shin. It seemed the question his young apprentice had asked was precisely the one he'd been asking himself. "One may suppose that the star leads us to the child, which logically dictates that the child is guarded over by an entity of incredible power. But why would we be summoned by such a power?" Balthazar mused.

Shin-shin said in a hopeful tone, "Anything that powerful should be able to clean up after a little baby. They don't need us."

The elephant let out a trumpet, signifying her agreement. Shin-shin laughed, and even Balthazar smiled a bit.

The two continued on until they'd left the mountains and greenery far behind. The brown, sandy desert rolled out before them. Shin-shin had never seen such a desolate place and was ready to deny the star and its calling. But once it rose again in the west, the two travelers couldn't turn away. Urging on their massive mount, they took up the next phase of their trek and rode out onto the vast, empty plain.

A few compass points to the south, and a hundred or so leagues away, Gaspar galloped alone toward the shining star like an arrow launched from a bow.

CHAPTER TWELVE

In the middle of nowhere in the middle of the desert sat a nondescript three-way junction of caravan paths.

Melchior and his group reached the crossroads first, deep in the night. Like the roads themselves, the land around the intersection had been packed hard by the footfalls of the many who'd made camp there, and tonight would be no exception. For as soon as the group of riders reached the point where the roads joined, the star's light was snuffed out, as if someone had thrown a cloak over it.

The star had shown its fickle nature before, and the group resigned itself to making camp here until the guiding light reappeared. Barir set up the camp, as usual, and posted a light ring of sentinels out in the sandy dunes and along the roads. A few campfires sprang up, and soon food was roasting on spits as the travelers pitched their tents for the remainder of the evening and the next day.

Melchior, his senses alive with an expectation similar to that which he'd felt prior to the unveiling of the star, retired to his white tent to meditate.

One of the sentinels ran into camp, searching for Barir. Had the circumstances of their journey not already tested the limits of what he thought possible, Barir would have thought the guard had fallen asleep and dreamed at his post. But since things were already pretty odd, the incredible sighting the guard reported came as no surprise.

Pushing aside the fabric door of Melchior's tent, Barir entered and interrupted the dinner discussion between Shafiq and Melchior. "My lord, chief magus," Barir said. "A guard reports the approach of a...ah, beast...or monster, on the eastern road. Two strange people ride atop it. They move quickly and will be here within the hour. I've already roused the men; we'll circle behind them and—"

"Wait," said Melchior. "Don't do anything rash, Barir. Stand down the riders."

Barir and Shafiq both looked at Melchior as if he'd lost his mind. Barir, recalling Melchior's doubt of a few nights before, saw folly in not preparing to meet an obvious threat. Shafiq, less militant though no less vigilant, quirked a brow as though wondering what the king was thinking.

"Who comes?" asked the old magician.

"I'm not sure...but my heart tells me it's a friend. Pilgrims, like us, following the star, I think." said Melchior. He closed his eyes and consulted some interior source of information, then said, "Prepare places for guests to join us in a meal."

Barir left to summon servants. He also ordered a small detachment of soldiers to go out and shadow the approaching "pilgrims."

Inside the king's tent, Shafiq looked at Melchior. "What's this all about?" he asked.

"No idea," replied Melchior, meeting his gaze. "Perhaps this will provide the answers we're seeking. All I know is that we're no longer in my kingdom. The star led us here; the best we can do is wait and see who comes, and why."

For a while, Balthazar had been aware that someone was trailing them. Since they'd made no threatening moves, he was content to follow the star's passage with Shin-shin riding on the elephant behind him. The star had vanished an hour or so ago, but he pushed on, listening to his inner compass.

As the duo rounded a curve in the road, small dots of light on the desert floor extinguished night's darkness — campfires and a group of heavily armed soldiers to tend them.

Shin-shin, predictably, went right into panic mode. "Cannibals!" the child shrieked, clawing at Balthazar's shoulders.

"No," said Balthazar patiently, "I think not. They've been aware of our approach for a while now, and if we were to be the main course at yonder feast, you would already be roasting over one of those fires.

"We're meant to meet up with these people here. They share our purpose, our path. Let us go and meet them. Keep quiet, and for once, behave," commanded Balthazar.

The commotion conjured by two Asians astride a hulking, sand-encrusted elephant distracted everyone in the encampment from the southern road, where Gaspar flew in pursuit of the ever-elusive star.

Until it vanished from view.

Melchior walked out of his tent, leaving his sword and armor behind. He found a place at the center of the circle that was naturally forming around the juncture of the three roadways. He looked up at the empty sky quizzically, and wondered silently why the star had chosen to hide itself.

Moving on, he came upon a sight he'd never forget. Lumbering up from his left was a beast that seemed to come right out of a madman's worst dream, a huge monster with a long nose, gray, wrinkled skin, and a tiny tail. Two fair-skinned people dressed in oddly colored pajamas and small black shoes rode atop it — one an older man and the other seemingly only a boy. The beast took a few last steps, its dark eyes reflecting the flames of the fires, and stopped just outside the circle of Melchior's men. Only the crack and spittle of the burning fires greeted their arrival.

On Melchior's right, a lone, black-skinned rider in black atop a black horse galloped toward the camp. Only the firelight reflecting off the handle of the rider's huge blade marked his passage until the rider reined in his steed, and the giant stallion reared with a whinny to come to a stamping halt on the opposite side of the circle from the great gray creature.

No one spoke; how could they? Melchior and his retinue spoke the tongue of the Arabians, Balthazar and Shin-shin of the Orient knew only their native language, and Gaspar the Ethiope spoke in the dialect of his fathers.

The old man and the child slid from their high mount and walked into the circle. The black man dismounted as well and let his horse wander freely as he too entered the circle, his face shrouded in black with only the whites of his eyes to give him away. The silence was becoming painful; everyone eyed everyone else.

The older man introduced himself and the child to Melchior, who stared dumbly and tried to decipher the gibberish. Shrugging, Melchior turned to the man in black and said that he couldn't understand them; the massive man in black stared blankly. Silence again filled the void.

The soldiers looked in awe at the monstrous beast. The monstrous beast looked in fear at the fires. Melchior looked at the old man. The old man looked at the black man. The black man looked at Melchior. The child looked at everyone as if waiting to be eaten. And from the edge of the group, Zoth looked on the gathering with intense interest.

Suddenly the star exploded into the dark sky overhead with a *ploof!* and a *pop!* It showered the assembly with a light the intensity of which they'd not seen before. It seemed to actually permeate their skin, bones, and hearts. Every eye was turned upward toward the light. It hummed and vibrated throughout each of them, uniting them as no other force could.

"It's...even more beautiful," murmured Melchior.

"Yes; beauty supreme. Power absolute," agreed the old man, his emerald eyes never leaving the star.

"I've followed it for leagues upon leagues," whispered the black man.

Slowly, realization washed over the group. They were conversing. The miraculous power of the star once again had changed them forever, giving them the ability to speak to each other with ease.

For a brief moment, there was nothing but the star. It melded everyone in the gathering together. Its silvery sheen painted everyone and everything in shades of gray and black. Then, as suddenly as it had appeared, the star blasted away, vanishing as its task for the night was completed.

As one, they all let out a collective sigh, touched with sadness. It was as if a mother's breast had been pulled away before the babe had finished feeding. There followed a short moment of embarrassment, wherein each of the three groups didn't know what to do next.

Melchior, assuming the role of host, spoke up first. "Well. Well...well, welcome. You are all welcome. I suspect that we've all traveled far. And, it seems, for the same reason. At least, I think so. We've been brought together here, that much is clear. And now that the star has empowered us to understand each other, we've much to talk about. So let's eat, as well. Tonight is a special night. Don't you agree?"

"Special, indeed," said the old man, stepping forward and bowing. "I'm Balthazar, of the Orient far away to the east. My apprentice, Shin-shin, and I have traveled long and hard to meet you here. We humbly thank you for your offer of hospitality."

With a long stride, the black man joined them. When he unwrapped the veil of black that shrouded his face to speak, Shin-shin gasped, as did many of the soldiers of Melchior's group. They'd never seen a man with skin as black or as beautiful as his.

Nodding slightly, the man gruffly addressed the two. "Gaspar, lord of Ethiopia. I've traveled alone following the star. I accept your offer of food and counsel."

Melchior smiled, a big wide grin, and felt a burden lifted from his soul. He wasn't alone anymore. While he'd had his caravan with him, he'd still felt a solitary bond with the star. But now the star had summoned others, much like him. He felt an immediate kinship with these two men, even though they couldn't be more different than he. He bowed low to them and said, "You are welcome, my friends and brothers of the star. My name is Melchior, and I'm from the lands and mountains not too far to the northeast in Arabia. These are my men, and you may count them among your most loyal subjects and allies. I fear we haven't traveled as far or hard as you both have, but our calling was just as strong and compelling."

Melchior gestured toward his tent. "We've already seen some powerful magic this evening; I think much more lies before us. But come join me in my tent. My men will see to your beasts." He paused for a moment, glancing uncertainly at Balthazar's mount. "Or better yet, you can show them how you want them stabled. Then we eat, for I think the star is finished for the evening."

Gaspar and Balthazar nodded, and the circle broke up as everyone went about their duties. Gaspar wordlessly handed the reins of Makeda to a soldier, who led it to drink from a trough that sat near the watering hole. Balthazar gave Shin-shin some quiet instructions regarding the elephant, and turned to join Gaspar and Melchior in the white fluttering tent.

Shin-shin, suddenly surrounded by strangers who could still very well be sizing the child up for the impending feast, stood beside the giant elephant. Then Barir walked up and slapped a heavy hand onto the youth's shoulder, almost knocking Shin-shin over. Barir, sensing Shin-shin's apprehension, smiled kindly. "What do you call this . . .

thing?" he asked.

"An elephant, my lord," Shin-shin meekly replied.

"What does it eat?" asked Barir.

"Water, grass, things like that. She won't harm you, if that's what you're worried about." The child's courage was growing.

As if on cue, the elephant's trunk snaked out and began searching and sniffing Barir for food. Barir, at first a bit nervous, laughed as the moist nostrils tickled him on the neck and under his ears. "Alright, alright! She's hungry. You men, get some feed for this thing before it eats me whole!"

Shin-shin, still half-expecting to be eaten, smiled nervously and patted the elephant's trunk.

The three Magi sat on a square, ornate rug spread on the floor inside Melchior's tent. The nature of his journey had allowed only scant appointments. Off to one side, Melchior's armor and blade were tied to a line that hung from one of the tent's poles. Opposite the armor, a small bedroll had already been unwrapped. In the center of the tent, a small oil lamp provided surprisingly bright illumination.

The camp's cook, a wiry old man with a wiry beard to match, delivered a pot of stew and a stack of thin slabs of warm mountain bread. With many bows and apologies, he backed out of the tent.

With a slight smile, Melchior said, "Our provisions are humble, but I promise that you'll find Alieh's cooking satisfying." He paused while Balthazar began ladling some of the stew into a bowl, then added, "At least, it hasn't killed any of us yet."

Balthazar looked up, sensed a joke, smiled, and continued. "One would hope that his cooking is the most dangerous thing we encounter on this journey," he replied.

"I think not," Gaspar interjected soberly.

They ate in silence, unsure of where to begin. Surprisingly, it was Gaspar who spoke first.

"I'm a man of few words. Deeds speak louder where I

come from. I'm a warrior first, second to none. And I'm accustomed to operating alone, choosing my own path and companions. In this, taking up with you, I'm…uncomfortable." He hesitated, searching for the right words. "But I feel I have little choice in the matter. We are, I guess, joined together." Anger flickered across his smooth face as he grimly spoke the last few words.

Melchior and Balthazar sat and drank in his declaration. The tall, strong man was an imposing character. They found it a bit disconcerting to hear him say that he was less than thrilled to be in their company. But Melchior rose to the challenge.

"My friend, I think all three of us have other places, and other people…" An image of Nur bubbled to the surface of his mind, "We'd rather be with. But we're called on a quest with a higher purpose. Just what that purpose is, I still don't know."

"I'm sensing that we each hold a small piece of the star's puzzle. Once we assemble the pieces, our course and actions will be clear. Do you agree?" asked Balthazar after tearing off and swallowing a small mouthful of bread.

The other two Magi assented with silent nods. They then each took turns retelling their respective stories, describing the events that led them to their present location. As the night wore on, it became clear that they had much in common, not the least of which was their respective supernatural ability. While many questions remained, and although there were still symbols and signs whose meanings were unclear, they were able to ascertain a few facts.

Science, logic, and analysis were clearly a few of Balthazar's strong points. He took the lead.

"So…" He paused and closed his eyes briefly to collect his thoughts. "We're in agreement on a few things. The star appeared to all three of us less than a week ago, give or take a few nights. The circumstances of each appearance differed, as has its position and duration in the sky each evening hence. This is logical, as it seems the star intentionally led us all to this very point from diverse locations. Everyone here has actually witnessed the star. I suspect the star shall reveal soon whether others are coming or not. For if more travelers are to come, it will lead us no farther tomorrow night.

"However," continued the slight man, "we disagree on what the star's actual meaning is. Shin-shin, my apprentice, and I have seen symbols and signs indicating that the appearance of the star heralds a birth, perhaps of a mighty king. My lord Melchior has seen signs and dreamed that the star portends doom and the possible ruin of his kingdom and people. And my lonely lord Gaspar hears and feels nothing but the compelling call of a master perhaps even mightier than he."

Outside the tent, the diminishing fire crackled loudly, filling the hole in Balthazar's one-sided conversation. He sighed and said, "I fear I cannot reconcile these different interpretations of the star's relevance. Perhaps it will continue to offer a different meaning to everyone who beholds it."

"Yes, I think you're right," murmured Melchior. Gaspar, as was to be his wont for their journey together, remained stoically mute.

Standing and stretching, his joints popping in protest, Melchior signaled an end to the council. "It's late...or early, depending on your point of view," he said, smiling. Outside, the sun was already pulling itself from its bed to begin its fiery assault on the small gathering on the sand. "I offer you whatever comforts I can. All that I have brought here, consider your own."

"Many thanks, King Melchior," responded Balthazar, "but you've already offered more than I would've expected, here in the middle of the desert. The tents, the food, all are quite...opulent. I shall sleep well."

"I require nothing," said Gaspar. He spun and made it all the way to the tent opening before mumbling a word of thanks. "I shall meet with you later, when the sun falls." And with that, he slid through the flaps and vanished into the brightening morning.

"He's an...angry...man," suggested Balthazar, "but I sense in him a supernatural strength that we shall rely on in the near future. No?"

"I agree," replied Melchior, and the two men bade each other a pleasant rest.

Melchior settled onto his bedroll, pondering his newfound traveling companions. He rolled onto his back, and noted that the sun's first rays were just reaching the pinnacle of his tent. A slight gap in the fabric allowed a beam through, which in turn painted a faint, white beam on the tent's side. It was the last image his eyes beheld before exhaustion claimed his eyelids.

CHAPTER THIRTEEN

The encampment scrambled to life just as the next day ended. The travelers hadn't become accustomed to sleeping the day away and journeying by night, and they always found the sight of the fiery red orb dropping like a stone below the western horizon a bit disconcerting. But as soon as the sun vanished, the star of wonder appeared in the still-glowing sky, obliterating the vestiges of the solar presence. With it came the sing-song call of the star, beckoning the travelers to make haste.

The beauty of this particular moment wasn't lost on the entourage. The shimmering white light made even an elephant and a camel herder both a little more elegant than the daylight ever could.

Exiting his tent, completely refreshed and surprisingly eager to journey even farther, Balthazar paused and crossed his arms to contemplate the mysterious star that was re-routing the life paths of so many. He wasn't surprised to learn that others had been called to the same journey he and Shin-shin had undertaken. Who they were, and their nature, however, he found rather amazing.

Melchior was a man—a king, Balthazar reminded himself—who seemed to embody that which was most noble and attractive in a leader. Balthazar was perfectly comfortable relinquishing leadership of the quest to such a man.

Certainly he had doubts and unanswered questions about Melchior. Balthazar suspected that troubled waters roiled beneath that handsome, weathered countenance. But he was the natural, logical head of the expedition.

Which, of course, wasn't at all ideal for the mysterious ebony warrior. What lay beneath Gaspar's exterior was hidden from all but Gaspar himself. While Balthazar could employ his powers to read the man's thoughts if he wanted to, he'd avoided looking too deeply for fear of arousing further doubt in Gaspar's already suspicious mind. A warrior, no doubt, an excellent and ruthless one, at that, and a loner, his role in the future of the journey could spell trouble and danger as easily as it could protection and security. The overriding question was, how would Gaspar deal with playing second sitar to Melchior?

As for Balthazar himself, he was content to let the fates spin on for now. Soon, he would attempt to divine what the future held in store for them, recognizing the horrible and immutable responsibilities such knowledge required as payment.

Even before the appearance of the star over his simple hut many nights ago, his heart had troubled him. Balthazar sensed that his role would be crucial in the days to come, but not the central one. He also felt in his heart that his days were numbered.

Shin-shin's role truly perplexed Balthazar. Why had Shin-shin been summoned? What role would the child play? Intelligent, gifted Shin-shin would someday make an excellent philosopher, perhaps even a magus like he. But for now, "apprentice" was even a bit of a stretch. Yet adolescence already had Shin-shin firmly in its grasp, and all too soon the child would face the world as an adult. All too soon.

On cue, Shin-shin's head popped through the flaps of the tent and hung as if mounted there. The apprentice looked around, making sure no child-eating creatures lurked nearby. Satisfied, Shin-shin called, "Master, is it time to leave this place and continue on our way?"

Frowning, Balthazar replied, "Collect your belongings and come. We travel from here onward with King Melchior, Chief Gaspar, and the rest. Chop-chop!"

Distracted from the fear of becoming an early evening repast, Shin-shin bolted out of the tent and stood before the master. "We don't need any help or other people to slow us down. Let's go our own way, before something terrible happens!" urged Shin-shin.

"Search your heart, Shin-shin. Does it not tell you that this is what was meant to be and that you can put your faith in these companions? Did you not sleep soundly? Is your head still attached to your rather skinny and unappetizing torso? And did you not feel the community that arose when the star appeared to all of us last night upon our arrival?" queried the Asian magus.

"Well," mumbled his humbled apprentice, "I guess so. But when are you going to tell me what's going on here? Who are these people? Where are we going?"

"Gather our gear. We travel on foot from now on, and the elephant will share the load of the other pack animals. If you're fortunate, perhaps someone will offer you a ride. The rest you shall learn as it becomes relevant," Balthazar finished. Dejected, Shin-shin shuffled back into the tent to pack.

Balthazar made his way to the glowing embers of the camp's main fire. Gaspar stood beside it, gazing intently into the rosy chunks of fire. He appeared as he had last night, evidencing neither a good nor a poor night's rest.

"Balthazar," remarked the tall warrior without looking up.

"Gaspar," he replied, bowing slightly, noting that an air of informality had been unconsciously adopted between them. "You slept well, I trust."

"I'm a man, and therefore require rest as much as any other. I prefer to sleep upon the sand so I can feel the footstep of an assailant before he strikes. A tent keeps out the wind and cold, but does not slow the stroke of the blade much," noted Gaspar in a mocking, but not unkind, tone.

Balthazar smiled, folding his hands before him. "Yes, yes, but what of the scorpion?"

"There are much more dangerous things hidden in the sand than scorpions, Balthazar." His eyes scanned to the left and right, assessing his newfound colleagues.

Melchior interrupted the discussion by striding up and joining them. But before he could speak, Gaspar's and Balthazar's eyes met for a moment in mutual assent, forming a tenuous bond of trust. They turned to address their host, who was full of vigor and excitement.

"My friends!" exclaimed the king. "We're about ready. Balthazar, the large...um, elephant...is a great help in distributing our burdens. I offer you my own steed in thanks."

"That won't be necessary, King Melchior. I shall walk and contemplate for a while, and perhaps ride later on," answered Balthazar.

"Let us be off then," said Gaspar, giving voice to the urgency energizing the blood in their veins. "The star calls."

Just then, Zoth made his first appearance to the newcomers. The three Magi swung their heads in unison to look at the figure that still, despite the darkness, managed to carve a dark hole in the night. Zoth paused, looked at the trio, and laughed aloud. He strode from the top of the dune he had appeared upon to stand before them. Crossing his arms, he laughed again. "Well, well!" he sneered contemptuously, "Three *kings* and not a crown among them. I see that more than one royal line will end with the passing of this star, and if you two are as...impotent...as Melchior, all the better."

Melchior glared, shamed. Balthazar, as was his custom, smiled infuriatingly back at the sorcerer. Gaspar, though doubtless used to twisting off the heads of insolent rogues like this, took his cue from Melchior and stayed his hand.

He did, however, draw himself up and take a threatening step toward Zoth. The sorcerer fell an involuntary step backward.

They could have been two sides of the same coin. Both dressed in black. Zoth was pale as the sand, Gaspar as dark as the night.

"Your purpose on this journey," whispered Gaspar, "is a mystery to me. Perhaps it's only to satisfy my sword's call for hot blood. Yet I warn you now, fool. My patience is shorter than your king's."

Visibly shaken, Zoth took another step back. Yet he resumed his bravado almost instantly and walked away with a low chuckle and whisk of his cloak.

"He's a problem," said Gaspar to the others as he watched the night swallow up Zoth. He mused softly, "Maybe I was mistaken about the scorpion . . ."

Balthazar quietly assented.

Melchior offered almost apologetically, "He's my... cousin. And yes, he's more trouble than he's worth. Still, he's seen and heard the star. He belongs here with us. I just try to keep an eye on him all the time, that's all."

"Leave that to me," growled Gaspar, turning to face the other two again. And they kicked sand into the hissing fire.

The caravan heaved itself to life quickly after that, with the three Magi taking the lead behind the ever-vigilant Barir. Balthazar had been persuaded to ride by Melchior. The master-at-arms cut an imposing figure, armored and glistening in the starlight. His eyes constantly surveyed the landscape, searching out the unseen dangers that his instincts and gut told him were there.

Sporadic conversation passed between the new traveling companions as they tried to sort out the mysteries confronting them. Just within earshot rode Zoth, a black blot that always hovered just within the peripheral gaze of Gaspar. Following at a few respectful paces were Shafiq and the rest of the soldiers and pack animals. Bringing up the rear was the heavy reinforcement, the elephant. Shin-shin, on an appropriated donkey, floated between the various groups, never really fitting in anywhere.

The caravan reached a row of undulating dunes that seemed to flow out before them forever. It was a sea of sand, silhouetted by the icy light of the glimmering star overhead.

Barir found himself riding beside Shin-shin. The slender child was looking at him, so Barir started a conversation.

"How's your, ah, backside doing? That donkey appears to be a little bouncy," Barir tried to ask seriously, but he felt the corners of his hard mouth turning up.

"My backside," replied Shin-shin, "is none of your business. Besides, I've been trained by my master to overcome all sorts of physical pain and distractions through concentration. This is nothing." Shin-shin's audacity was none too convincing. Barir saw the youngster wince as the donkey semi-trotted to keep pace with the large stallion Barir rode.

Barir offered kindly, "Perhaps later on, you could ride behind me for a while...that is, when you want to give your concentration a rest, and your behind, as well."

Shin-shin, knew a good deal when it came along. The child replied a little too enthusiastically, "Oh yes, good idea. Perhaps now—"

But the swift slash of Barir's hand silenced the donkey jockey as he halted the group. His stallion's neck stiffened, the horse's nose flared and *snoofed*, and its ears stood at attention. What the animal's and Barir's keen senses had already picked up was soon apparent to everyone in the caravan. The stale, gut-clenching smell of blood and carrion carried toward them over the sand on the cool night breeze.

CHAPTER FOURTEEN

Barir directed Shin-shin to stay behind and, to his surprise, the child obeyed. Barir signaled Melchior to stay put and told two guards to accompany him over the next dune.

Shingles of crusty sand slid down the glowing face of the dune as they rode up and out of sight of the caravan. The rest of the animals in the entourage sensed that trouble was near and stamped nervously. Balthazar turned and walked a few paces to stand between Melchior and Gaspar, and initiated a quiet council.

"It can't be good, whatever it is," muttered Gaspar. "I've seen my share of death, and that's exactly what this feels like."

"I agree," concurred the Asian magus, "but I think it important that we three acknowledge that we're no longer the masters of our own destinies. If we encounter someone, or something, on this quest, we must assume that it plays some crucial role, one that perhaps we cannot fathom at first."

"Yes," said Melchior, "and if we—"

He never finished his thought, for Barir had returned to view atop the foremost dune. His stiff silhouette and bearing signaled to Melchior that what he'd discovered was indeed, not good at all.

The entourage shuffled back into motion, the previous air of enthusiasm noticeably absent. Melchior's mind raced ahead of his horse, knowing already from the smell that something gruesome awaited them, sensing that this wouldn't be their only encounter with death. Overhead, the star radiated.

Gaspar spoke under his breath to Balthazar. "Perhaps it would be wise to shield the child from this."

Balthazar, not looking up from his study of the churned-up sand as it passed beneath his horse's feet, replied, "I appreciate your concern. But I think it's time that Shin-shin comes face to face with the reality of our situation. Perhaps a child walks up this side of the dune, and an adult walks down the other."

Once again, Melchior was amazed at the wisdom the small old man possessed and tossed out so casually. Gaspar grunted his acknowledgement of the decision and said no more.

As they rode up the dune, the horses and camels huffing with the exertion, the putrid smell grew stronger. Melchior, Balthazar, and Gaspar were in the lead, and paused as they reached Barir. The scene below was enough to make them all stop.

"Gruesome" wasn't a strong enough word to describe the scene, thought Melchior. Horrific was close, but no word could communicate what he saw.

A ring of larger dunes surrounded a shallow open space. Every inch of the arena's sandy floor was chopped up, a stark contrast to the smooth surface the rest of the desert presented. Whatever had happened here, it had been quick. Two lines of tracks came in, one single file from the north, the other a wide swath from the east. They ended at the circle, and that's where many of the track's creators still lay.

The caravan proceeded down into the circle of dunes, silently and apprehensively. The rigid hairs on the necks of the battle-seasoned soldiers told them that this was a dangerous place, too easy to stage an ambush. From the looks of it, that's precisely what had happened.

116

Melchior and Gaspar dismounted to join Balthazar on foot as Barir quickly set guards and stations around the periphery of the area. Shafiq joined the Magi as they walked grimly to assess the scene. Shin-shin, quiet with shock, followed a pace or two behind the group.

"I'd say about twelve bodies, my lord," a captain standing near a cluster of corpses quietly reported to Melchior.

"How...how can you tell?" muttered the king in reply, noting that most of the bodies had been hacked beyond all recognition. All were men. And almost every corpse was missing something, usually a head.

It looked as though the party had put up a fight, but from the confused state of the sand and the fact that most of them were grouped within a few feet of each other, the battle hadn't lasted long. Some hands still held swords or daggers, but not many with arms still attached. The thirsty sand had drunk in the spilled blood, but a dark, crusty stain marked each entry point. Insects of all sorts writhed and worked furiously on the leather-tough flesh. Bone glinted white in the starlight from dried, open gashes.

"A slaughter," said Gaspar, hunkering down to assess a dead man. His attitude was detached, matter-of-fact. "Some kind of scouting party, coming in from the north, there. Perhaps looking for water. They were lightly armed, not prepared for a confrontation. Not much armor, see?" he asked, turning and addressing Barir, the other battle veteran in the small group.

Barir grunted his agreement and squatted beside the Ethiopian. "Their horses were killed, too," he said. "So not thieves. But I've never seen men like this before. Their skin is dark, but not black like yours. And their dress is odd, too. Are you familiar with it?"

"No," answered Gaspar.

"Master-at-Arms!" hollered a soldier from atop one of the farthermost dunes. He pointed beyond the circle to something that clearly disturbed him just outside the circle of the slaughter.

"There's more," stated Balthazar with unnerving equanimity.

They ran up the slight dune, the sand cascading beneath the pounding feet. Atop it, they all paused again. Melchior wondered how many other surprises awaited them over the other dunes that stretched in all directions to the horizon.

On top of a lesser sand dune were three crucified bodies. The beautiful light of the star transformed the scene into a kind of ghastly portrait.

The Magi slowly skidded down to the dune. The wooden posts on which the men hung were roughly hewn and approximately ten feet tall with cross beams five feet wide. Crude spikes had been driven through their hands and feet, and it appeared that swords or spears had been run through other parts of their bodies, as well.

Balthazar said, "I've had a vision of this, or something similar. I don't know what it means."

Melchior was the first to notice. "By the gods, the one in the center. He's alive!"

And it was true. The man's chest moved almost imperceptibly, but he was breathing nonetheless. Melchior motioned for some soldiers to hack down the cross, which they did as quickly as they could with swords and battle-axes. Another group caught the cross as it teetered downward and jolted with a sickening thud. The man managed a brief moan, the only acknowledgement that his situation had changed.

Melchior knelt and poured some water from his flask onto the man's lips. His face had been baked into a cracked, black mask of death that was as stiff as stone. The corners of his mouth and eyes were red sores that once had bled, but now were just evil rips in his face. Melchior thought that once, this man had been noble and handsome. Now he was just a cruel wound.

The man's eyes fluttered open and seemed to behold for

118

the first time the shining star glistening overhead. He let out a tiny gasp of awe. He took a moment to savor it, then turned to Melchior and uttered his last word, wrapped in his last breath. "Rome..."

CHAPTER FIFTEEN

The star winked out with the crucified man's last wheeze, as did the man's life. Dawn was still a few hours off, so the travelers took advantage of the break to create a funeral pyre for the dead.

Soldiers dragged the bodies of the three tortured men to the rest of the corpses, then poured precious lamp oil onto the huge pile and ignited it. The desiccated bodies and the fuel conspired quickly to create an enormous bonfire, the smell of which trumped even the earlier foul scent of death.

While everyone was busy readying the gruesome task, Zoth silently floated over the sand and bent over an unattended corpse. He grasped the dead man's forearm and wrenched a stiffened hand from the hilt of a sword with a series of soft cracks and snaps. Drawing his crooked dagger from within his inky robes, he quickly severed the claw-like hand. Blackened, syrupy blood sluiced from the stump, but the black magician paid it no heed. He stashed the hand in an unseen fold of his robes, stood, and disappeared behind the dunes.

The hunter within Gaspar knew that the fire would send a signal plume leagues high and surely alert the party who'd done this deed that their butchery had been discovered. He also knew that was precisely what they wanted. Why else would they go to the trouble of crucifying their victims unless it was to make an example for others? Trouble was, Gaspar wasn't so sure the lesson was intended for them.

Their grisly work done and a moment of silent prayer noted the caravan pushed westward. After an hour of riding, the Magi agreed that they'd put enough distance between themselves the scene of the massacre. On cue, the star fizzled into a speck of light and vanished. Exhaustion immediately set in, and the travelers stopped to rest. With an enemy afoot, Barir took great pains in selecting a stretch of sand that provided a clear view of any oncoming danger. Tents and lean-tos popped up, and soon the camp settled down.

The three Magi, however, had pressing matters on their minds and almost unconsciously met inside Melchior's tent. After a few moments, Barir and Shafiq joined them. The last member of the impromptu council, Zoth, who'd been mysteriously quiet regarding from the massacre site earlier in the evening, flowed darkly into the tent and stood silent as a statue at the rear of the tent.

Melchior took a moment to look around at the group. *What an odd gathering of souls,* he thought. Barir glared at Zoth, who glared at Gaspar, who studied the backs of his eyelids. Balthazar, with a smirk, nodded gently to Melchior to begin, acknowledging his role as leader and host of the uncomfortable assembly.

"My friends," began the king and faltered even there. "Right. Let's not fool ourselves. We're...ah, traveling partners, at best. Associates, at worst. But we're in this together, as seems to have been preordained by a higher power than any who sit here tonight."

That earned him a glower from Zoth. *Too bad, Zoth,* he thought. *Even you're outclassed by the miracle of the star.*

He continued. "But before we discuss what to do next, let's see where we are. Barir, the state of the caravan."

"My lord, there's fear and dissension, as we should expect. To some, this journey has felt like a fool's errand from the start, even after the star appeared. The camel men in particular are grumbling. They see the star as an evil omen…a warning that even some in this tent, I believe, share."

Barir shifted uncomfortably. Melchior suspected he felt not only uncomfortable in front of so many, but also disloyal in discussing such matters. Still, he continued.

"But they're herders, not soldiers, and we shouldn't expect them to become fighters, should we encounter an enemy. For now, they're fairly loyal. As for the soldiers, they remain true, but they're a superstitious lot. And finding a bunch of slaughtered strangers in the desert doesn't help much. I think some good news, or even direction, would greatly help everyone's morale."

Shafiq cleared his ancient throat quietly and said, "Your request is quite normal. Our situation, I fear, is not. I've spent many hours in contemplation of the star, of our quest, of our purpose…and I still know little on all three accounts."

"I agree," said Balthazar. "I, too, have focused my thoughts on the song of the star, yet its meaning I'm unable to penetrate. It's clearly leading us, but I don't know where. It's chosen us, but I don't know how. We were meant to find these unfortunate souls this evening, but I don't know why."

Melchior sat and ruminated on the discussion. Then, the obvious occurred to him. Sitting upright he shared his inspiration. "We've got to pool our resources — act as one instead of acting as individuals. If we concentrate our power, perhaps the answers will become clear!"

A noticeable quiet met this suggestion. But Melchior suspected that he was onto something and wouldn't relent. Choosing the small fire in the tent as a focal point, the magus raised his hands, palms forward, and focused his concentration at the center of the circle in which they sat. The fire flared in intensity and size, then turned a soft blue in color. Small beads of perspiration formed on his brow, but the heat of the fire didn't spawn them.

Gaspar watched Melchior, then pressed his hands together with his elbows jutting sideways and his two long index fingers pointing toward the top of the tent. His face was set sternly, as if he were scolding an impudent child. Soon a small rivulet of sweat wound down his ebony cheek. The fire, in response, turned to a conflagration of reds and blues.

All eyes then turned to Balthazar of the east, sitting cross-legged on the floor. His hands rested casually on his thighs. The forefinger and thumb of each hand were pressed lightly together, forming small loops of flesh. Eyes slightly glazed, he gazed into the blazing fire, green flames danced in harmony with the blue and red ones, then with a flash, melded together into the effervescent white light of the mysterious star. Instantly, the song of the star emanated softly from within the center of the supernatural blaze.

Zoth closed his eyes and sought entrance into the triumvirate of the Magi, but to no avail. The invitations to this séance had been issued and returned, and there were no more seats at the party. Frustrated, he folded his arms in indignant protest and watched the situation unfold. He knew that he had other, darker resources to turn to later.

Shafiq, no stranger to magic and displays of power, was nonetheless impressed by the collaborative effort. He could feel the supernatural waves flowing over his skin, raising the hair on his arms and neck, keying in on his own humbler powers. Enraptured, he leaned forward to see what the Magi's efforts would yield.

Barir, a man of mundane stuff, nervously watched the pyrotechnic display. If you could touch it, eat it, kiss it, or kill it, it was real. He wasn't comfortable in this environment. It took a lot to spook him, but Barir knew his limitations, and knew he was straining them.

Snooping in from under a loose corner in the tent, Shin-shin hadn't breathed in over a minute and had to remember to consciously suck in some air. This was probably the greatest thing the small, shivering orphan had ever witnessed.

Then the wonder truly began.

The song of the star, clear in the light, spoke. *Make haste. Tarry not. Thy journey hath only just begun. Thy task is still at hand. Follow.*

The Magi sat entranced, fixated on the fiery light, fully absorbed — or was it controlled? Hypnotized? — by the unearthly power. They could neither query nor respond.

Shafiq, sensing the vacuum in leadership, addressed the entity within the pallid inferno. "What is our task? What's your bidding?"

Follow, beckoned the star, maddeningly.

"Where? What do you ask of us?" asked the frail old man, trembling with fear, frustration, and anticipation.

The fire roared, then grew eerily silent. The voice then whispered, *To Judaea you travel, to the City of David. There you find what you seek. Let no one, no thing, prevent you from reaching your destination. Time grows short…*

And with that the fire snuffed itself out in a flash of brilliant light and a sharp *crack-powf!*

The witnesses all blinked at the hot spots the tiny explosion had left on their eyes, clearly distinct even when they shut their eyes and rubbed them.

The Magi slumped like dead men, all semblance of life sucked from them by the power within the silver fire. Slowly, they blinked back into the real world, regaining their strength and wits. Everyone looked a little shaken by the experience, most of all Melchior, Balthazar, and Gaspar. The others eyed them warily.

"Well, I've never done that before!" Melchior laughed nervously as he spoke, still feeling the electrical charges of his experience running up and down his arms and into his fingertips. He held out his right hand and white-hot sparks crackled in the air just beyond his fingers.

Whatever just happened to Melchior, and presumably to his two counterparts, was the most powerful and yet frightening experience he'd ever had. He'd shared a communion with his fellow travelers, an intimacy that left a warm glow upon his heart for the other two men.

Melchior's spirit, mind, and muscles had been completely under the control of what was presumably the force, nay, surely now the *god*, behind the star. For only a god could exert that kind of influence over him.

During the trance, he'd been part of the stellar power, yet apart, as well; both a witness and a participant. He heard and absorbed what was said, but he felt changed — stronger, yet more humble; determined, but even more curious than before; destined, yet all the more certain that a dangerous, unknown fate awaited him. His thoughts strayed briefly to Nur and the potentially comfortable life he'd left behind.

Zoth, Barir, and Shafiq stared at them wide-eyed. Shin-shin, still undetected in the rear of the tent, had forgotten again to breathe a few minutes ago and finally gulped sulfurous air into screaming lungs. The child's hands wouldn't stop shaking.

Balthazar gave voice to the thoughts that danced between Melchior's ears. "Well, that was interesting."

Gaspar asked, "Judaea? Where's that? Who is this David?" and looked down at his own hands to see the electrical pulses shimmering around his knuckles.

"Judaea," said Zoth with air of boredom, "is a small, inconsequential land north and west of here, across the Sea of Blood."

A trace of a smile played across Melchior's lips as he realized Zoth had dropped his guard to join in the discussion. *The star's magic is having an effect on everyone*, he thought. Then Zoth seemed to catch himself and straightened indignantly.

Barir mused aloud, "My grandfather told me of David. He was a great king in the lands to the west centuries ago. He slew a giant to become lord of his people. He was wise, as was his son who followed him, Solomon. I learned this at his knee as a child."

Gaspar said, "This is all well and good, but we know as little now as we did before."

"I disagree," Balthazar responded. "We now have a destination, and when that is known, only the path has to be chosen. And for that, the star will make its intentions known. We must simply follow and comply."

The dialogue continued another hour or so, but it was Shin-shin's snoring that told everyone it was time to repair to their own tents and catch some valuable sleep. Barir, as if feeling some sort of ownership of the slumbering youth, carried the child to Balthazar's tent. Zoth vanished into the darkness, as was his nature. Shafiq walked out slowly, stroking his ancient beard, deep in thought.

The Magi, alone for a moment, looked at each other almost shyly. They'd shared a personal bond wherein their very spirits had touched and intermingled. And each felt changed within. With no words spoken, they nodded to each other and went their separate ways.

Soon Melchior was lying on his back with one arm crooked beneath his head, the other held aloft as he watched the tiny sparks fly between his fingers. It was not long before he fell asleep, and the same silvery stars shot beneath his eyelids as he dreamed.

In the inky darkness, a few dunes away from the encampment, Zoth sought to reenact the previous scene. A small fire caught and crackled. Chanting and whispering commands only he and his dark spirits knew, he fed particular elements into the blaze: a small, oily, and quite dead snake he'd captured a few days ago; a black powder produced magically from within his robes that ignited and sent sparks shooting into the air; a thick lock of his gray-black hair. And the black, putrid, amputated hand of the dead soldier.

The fire roared, seemingly furious at being forced to do Zoth's bidding. When it changed to dark silver, Zoth bent over the blaze and said with venom, "Reveal to me the secrets of the star, so I may slay Melchior and his fools. This, I command."

The fire, though, reacted unexpectedly. A solid, white-hot beam of energy licked out and froze Zoth's head in its grasp. He stiffened, unable to control his body, certain that his life was at its end. His imprisoned head and body were pulled closer to the licking, silver flames.

You have been chosen, dark one, to fulfill our wishes. Your will is not your own. Yet you will face a moment where two paths lie before you. Choose well, lest you lose your soul forever, hissed the flames.

The fire shot up into the air and vanished with a flash. Zoth was tossed backwards and fell unconscious to the sand. Only after a while did he move and feel the blood flowing through his body again. He struggled to sit upright and turned his sooty face toward the charred embers of the fire.

The skeletal remains of the hand were there, frosty white in the dark night. Suddenly, the small bones withered and dissolved to dust before him.

Fearful for the first time in his life, Zoth rose and backed away from the fire. Unlike Melchior, he wouldn't sleep for the rest of the night, or for the long, hot day that was just cresting the horizon.

CHAPTER SIXTEEN

The following days and nights passed uneventfully, if a large caravan chasing a burning star across a sea of sand could be called uneventful.

The routine began with rising at sunset, breaking camp, and tearing off at breakneck speed as soon as the glorious star shimmered into view. The wind whipped at their faces and wrung tears from their eyes as the incongruous cold of the desert night froze the sweat in their shirts and beards.

At last, they'd collapse into increasingly cruder campsites as soon as the star snapped out its guiding light. They'd sleep fitfully, soaked again with sweat as the noonday sun beat on their tents and bodies with fists of fire; and rise just as the heat began to abate to take up the journey again.

The men began to feel the strain. Their spirits withered under the sun, the star, and the stress. The water supply shrank as well, as the leagues of parched sand seemed only to grow longer. And the animals began to drop, drained by the uncompromising pace of the journey.

All this Melchior noted in his heart. And he feared that, should they fail to reach their destination soon, all might be lost. Yet his inner voice urged him not to relent from the pursuit of the star. So he pushed them on as fast as their remaining mounts would carry them.

Eventually they left the undulating dunes of the desert

and rode out onto a flat plain of heartless sand that stretched before them farther than the eye could see. Sunlight danced off the glistening grains, refracting and piercing their eyeballs with shards of painful light. This new slice of the desert was harder, coarser, meaner than they'd see before. It was a most unwelcome sight.

Shafiq dropped back to ride with Melchior and Gaspar. The pace was still swift, but not overly so. Exhaustion, frustration, and dehydration were all taking their toll, moment by moment, on the party's progress.

For an old man, Shafiq held a pretty good seat, Melchior thought, as he watched the magus maneuver deftly to ride beside his king and Balthazar. Gaspar rode at the vanguard with Barir, keeping a keen and ever-vigilant eye on the landscape unfurling around them. Shin-shin rode behind Barir, desperately holding onto his shoulders or shirt when the ride became especially bumpy. The pair had a tacit understanding that Barir would be Shin-shin's guardian, and they both seemed pleased with the arrangement.

Shafiq and the two Magi quietly discussed the journey, the status of supplies, and the growing concern among the herders and soldiers that they were lost and looking like fools. Fortunately, no one had died or suffered severe injury on the trip. So far.

"But that can't last for long, my lords, and when our good fortune ends, we'll have trouble on our hands," warned Shafiq.

Fortune seemed to have been paying careful attention, because at that very moment, Gaspar shot his ebony arm into the cool night sky and reined his horse to a wheeling halt. The party ground to a stop, with lots of camel noses jamming into the flanks of the camel before them, and a few riders ending up on their own flanks, unceremoniously dumped to the sand.

Once the caravan was stopped, everyone noticed that something was wrong. Eerily wrong. The desert, while always quiet by nature, was dead silent. To be certain, the sing-song of the star was there in the backs of their minds, but something else was missing. It took Melchior a moment to figure it out—the wind. There was no wind, no breeze, and no movement at all. It was as if everything had come to a complete halt, including time itself.

Gaspar was off his horse, kneeling on the ground. He sniffed at the air, and placed his hands on the sand. Shin-shin, a few paces behind Barir, began to ask him a question, but Gaspar silenced the child with a dark glance. Head cocked slightly, prone on the floor of the desert sea, he looked almost comical. But with the tension he emitted, and the void that filled everyone's ears, no one laughed.

Suddenly he leaped to his feet. Even thirty paces away, Melchior could see the concern in his eyes. "Sandstorm!" he bellowed at the top of his lungs. The moment, dramatic as it was, froze everyone in mid-step.

For the inexperienced in the party, the weather report was a minor irritation, adding to the *Now what?* list of hindrances. But those with an inkling of what lay ahead, such as Melchior, shuddered and cast a wary eye to the horizon for the telltale dark cloud.

The veteran desert nomads among them, such as Gaspar, wasted no time looking for what was surely to come. He began issuing commands even as he began wrapping and hiding his face in a long trailing tail of the turban he always wore for just this possibility.

Balthazar and Shin-shin, newcomers to the arid land of the Sahara, wondered aloud at all the fuss.

"What's the problem?" Shin-shin asked innocently.

"Can we not weather out this storm?" asked Balthazar.

"Are you mad?" yelled Gaspar. "Quickly, everyone, listen to me," he instructed.

But panic had already set in. Horses and riders, camels and herders, and the poor lonely elephant, already moved in a hundred different directions. Gaspar and Barir, along with a few levelheaded soldiers, shouted directions to those who would listen.

"Dismount, circle, and tie mounts to each other, get them to kneel if possible, and for the gods' sake, cover your mouths and noses with a piece of cloth!" screamed Barir above the din.

Then a shout from the left made everyone stop in mid-motion and follow the caller's outstretched hand. A curtain of black, darker and more sinister than the night itself, swept toward them from the south. Small at first, it swelled and extended as it came closer until it stretched from horizon to horizon. It moved with impossible speed. The granular storm, dark against the black night, was alive. It was an embodiment of evil.

A wave…it looks like a black wave, thought Melchior as it hovered for a moment, ready to engulf them.

"Too late!" squealed Shafiq as the first sounds of the wind reached their ears. It was animal in nature, bestial in its fury. The force of the wind and sand was tangible, a true blow that toppled those unwise enough to have try to withstand its striking power on their own two feet.

Shin-shin screamed, but the wind tore the feeble cry away. Barir wrapped his arm around Shin-shin, and the pair fell to the ground beside Barir's prostrate horse.

The stinging wave of sand that lay within the wind washed over them and began peppering their eyes, cheeks, hands, feet, ankles, scalps, fingers, nostrils, ears, tongues, and every other conceivable inch of exposed and even un-exposed flesh on their bodies.

Overhead, even the beams of the true star were hidden from view, masked by the shade of the storm. Looking up, Melchior felt his hope slip when he saw that his beacon was gone.

Then the true vigor of the storm hit them.

Melchior looked to his right and saw a man—he knew not whom, nor ever would—in a semi-crouch simply lifted into the air by a swirling hand of sandy wind and disappear. Somehow, above the howling din of the storm, Melchior could make out his horrified scream as it dwindled away.

A few meters away, another man, a camel herder, was leaning into the wind and pulling on the reins of his beast, searching vainly for a refuge from the onslaught of wind and sand. After a few feeble paces, he and the camel collapsed against a dune, defeated. The swirling sand, in search of any crevice to fill, soon buried them alive, filling their mouths with sand even as it stifled their futile screams and bellows for help.

Each person struggled to breathe, as the sand seemed to fill too much of the air. They were suffocating.

Balthazar saw a man, a soldier, struggle to return to the leeward side of his camel and being struck by an exceptionally strong buffet of wind. The soldier successfully made one step, then another, and then was shredded alive by the razor-like slash of the wind. His skin and flesh were peeled and flayed in ugly tears, and he hurled a pitiable scream with his last breath as the storm took his life.

Zoth sensed an opportunity amidst the chaos. He stole up next to the prone Melchior and drew his wicked, crooked blade from his robes.

Was the storm a creation of Zoth's? Did he summon the tidal sands that threatened not only their lives, but also the very purpose for which they all had been chosen? Was he a conspirator in this assault, and if so, was he willing to perish himself just to destroy his nemesis?

These were the questions that would bother Melchior later, for Zoth was unsuccessful in his attempt. Just as Melchior turned to see the raised blade about to begin its lethal descent into his heart, a crazed camel came hurtling between the two combatants, directionless and panicked in the dark sandstorm, dragging some unfortunate herder by his stirrup-cuffed ankle.

The storm snatched Zoth's anguished gurgle over the

lost chance and delivered it to a disappointed dark force somewhere in the realm of the supernatural. Zoth, chastened but not yet defeated, evaporated into the storm to search out his own survival.

Choking, wheezing, and close to suffocating, Melchior blindly crawled away to where he thought he'd last seen Gaspar. The gamble was significant. By leaving the shelter of his horse, he exposed himself to the fury of the storm.

The gamble paid off. After a few moments of panicked groping, his hands found the steely flesh of Gaspar's calf. Pulling himself up, Melchior pressed his shrouded face against the similarly encased face of the ebony magus.

"Can't last! Losing men! We'll die!" he hoarsely barked through the flying bits grainy sand.

Then a third body pressed in close, and the voice of Balthazar cut through the wind and the sand and spoke to them within their minds. *We must act. And act together. Just as we did with the fire.*

Sand was piling over their bodies; death seemed just grains of time away. Somewhere in the maelstrom, another man howled in protest as the ferocious storm stippled his life away.

Understanding, and purpose, gripped each of the Magi, and they crouched together. Linking arms, they slowly stood, wobbling against the silicon sirocco.

The storm was not an insensate combustion of wind gusts, pressures, and weather patterns, but a creation of the black powers, one of the many playing pieces on the board pitted against the Magi. The evil entity sensed a rebellion within its heart, and the frenzy of sand and wind increased twofold. Clothing was shredded, blood was drawn, and muscles were bruised as the three men withstood the assault, holding their ground.

Joining hands and holding them aloft, the Magi fought back. The power manifested in the fire the other night came to bear. Pure bolts of energy were released from within the

Magi. Coursing upward, the shafts of emerald, cobalt and ruby light met overhead and coalesced into a single glowing orb of power. The globe of energy grew, and in moments soon enveloped the three men. Within its protective periphery, the storm's potency weakened, and they could breathe.

Their eyes rolled back into their heads so only the whites shone in the darkness. The Magi poured their life force into the effort. Soon sweat streamed down their foreheads, and grimaces contorted each face. But the circle of sanctuary continued to grow.

Around the edges of the energy field, the wind and sand pounded with renewed ferocity. Where the two forces met, the air flickered, shimmered, and crackled in a supernatural stalemate, the eventual winner of which would lay claim to the lives of the wanderers.

Soon the dome of safety reached its limit, and stretching it farther risked violating its integrity. The men who were fortunate enough to be inside its periphery breathed again, coughing and hacking up bits of blood-soaked sand and lung.

Barir and a few of the hardier souls braved leaving the shelter the Magi had created to drag in the limp or semi-buried bodies of men they could see through the energy envelope. A few stray souls wandered in by sheer fortune, or perhaps because above the protected area, the magnificent star shone once again and helped guide them to the haven. Even a few of the beasts, including the wayward pachyderm, seemed to instinctively home in on the security of the Magi. The elephant jammed its massive head into the periphery of the energy dome, and let loose a trumpet of relief.

The intensity of the storm seemed to increase and focus on the shell of energy in response to the Magi's efforts. The whine of wind increased, and the sand became flying silicate blades of doom. One poor soul, drawn by an inner directive, crawled on his hands and knees toward the safety of the shield. But the sinister storm would yield no more lives; the wind and sand shredded the skin and flesh from his bones before the horrified eyes of those protected within the dome of protection. Sand poured up to cover the still shrieking man, filling his mouth even as his last cries were carried away on the winds.

For hours the storm continued, pummeling the group. They huddled together, kneeling or lying at the feet of their saviors, anxiously waiting for the bubble to burst and the storm to descend upon them for one final, stifling blow. But the Magi persisted, empowered by the unearthly force that had set them on their journey. That day, they wouldn't perish.

At last, the storm surrendered and departed as quickly as it had come. The vacuum that had preceded it returned, and the black cloud of destruction spun into a gigantic cyclonic column. With a giant sucking sound it shot straight up into the heavens, not to be seen again. It was an awesome sight, and proof to those who witnessed its departure through sand-caked eyelashes that it was indeed a storm of malignant nature.

With the threat gone, the travelers could hear and feel the crackle of the energy emanating from the three Magi. It tingled over their skin, crawling on them like a million tiny sand lice. But with the onslaught vanquished, the electrical show ended as well, snapping off with an explosive *pop!*

Melchior, with little cognition of what he'd been doing for the past few hours, buckled at the knees and fell face first into the sand. Gaspar and Balthazar collapsed as well.

Gaspar, though, before the swirling darkness of fatigue overtook him, said aloud to no one in particular, "Did you see that? The power. It was incred—" and blacked out.

And on that note, the star of the west vanished for the evening, and Apollo rode his chariot over the horizon, heralding the beginning of another hot, dry, and deadly day in the desert.

CHAPTER SEVENTEEN

Melchior peered up through the gaps between the fingers of his outstretched hand. The scorching midday sun, as ferocious in its own right as the storm of the previous evening, took no pity on the party that lay beneath its rays.

He couldn't believe so many, many things: how hot and parched he was; the fact that he was still alive; that a storm of such magnitude could come out of nowhere and pummel them as it had; that so many of them had been buried, shredded, swept away, and simply murdered by the storm, which clearly had a life and purpose of its own.

And how damn hot it was.

Pushing himself to a sitting position, he squinted at the wreckage around him. Bodies, many he couldn't identify, were strewn haphazardly in a rough circle of thirty paces or so. Some were obviously dead, their faces and heads buried in soft pillows of silica. But some, most, had to be alive. Had to be.

Melchior tried to call out, but only managed a croak. That was enough to rouse Balthazar, who lay curled up a few paces away. The Asian magus sat up, crossed his legs, and shook the sand from his cap and head. Melchior sensed him reaching out mentally for Shin-shin's life force before turning to look at Melchior and forcing a wan smile through lips caked black with blood.

Reaching up to explore his own face, Melchior realized that blood had flowed freely from his nose during the night's supernatural battle, the vestiges forming a mustache of dried blood. He wiped a sleeve across his face, hoping and failing to eradicate the evidence of their efforts.

"It would appear that exhibitions of power such as those we partook don't come without a price. But the price is a small one. On the whole, I'm unharmed. And you?" inquired Balthazar.

"I'm dry as a bone, but alright, I guess. I can barely move my arms and shoulders, though," Melchior responded hoarsely.

"I," whispered Gaspar, slowly sitting up, then standing to survey the damage. "I feel like I wrestled with a lion. And the lion won."

The humor, grim though it was, revealed a new facet of the warrior. As the strain of the journey stripped away his veneers of formality, Melchior came to like and trust him more and more.

"If you could see how you look, Gaspar," said Balthazar, "you would think the lion ate you and spit you back out."

Gaspar's face, crusty with blood-caked sand, cracked open to reveal a wide, ivory grin, a startling contrast to his usual grim visage. He looked down and assessed his state, then nodded agreement. "The least the beast could have done was lick me clean first."

The levity, while refreshing, was fleeting. Slowly, the bodies that lay about stirred to life like mummies reanimating and rising to walk the earth.

Barir rose to his hands and knees, revealing Shin-shin asleep in a small hollow the soldier had carved out and shielded with his body. Ever the leader and stalwart friend, Barir stood and moved about, taking the count. Many of the bodies he shook would never move again, and many were the eyes he softly pushed closed, never to see again.

A little more than half their number remained, the

majority soldiers. Hardier than the herders and support personnel, they knew when to cover up and weather a beating.

Melchior sized up the remainder of the caravan. He knew they were in a dire situation. Only a few of the camels survived the storm with their supply packs intact. A handful of horses lived, but the price for watering them and keeping them so would be high and would soon threaten human lives. The sand had destroyed or stolen much of the food. And, of course, there wasn't an oasis or settlement in sight.

Shafiq was alive, but barely. A soldier helped him walk to a camel, where he slumped down in a daze. Zoth, as ever, hovered on the periphery, but even he seemed diminished by the unholy storm.

Barir assembled the group into crude formation and turned to await instructions from the Magi. Balthazar and Gaspar turned to look at Melchior.

Melchior, feeling the weight of responsibility settling on his shoulders, turned and searched the horizon. Here in the middle of the day, the cause seemed hopeless. No star to guide them, no hope in their strides. Feebly, he lifted his arm and pointed westward. He wordlessly climbed onto his horse and prodded the beast into motion. The caravan lumbered after the slouched figures of the Magi as they continued to a destination they knew only as David's City.

Try as he might, Barir couldn't ration the water as well as he would've liked. Some, like ancient Shafiq, would perish within hours if the life-sustaining liquid didn't pass his lips regularly. Shin-shin needed regular hydration, as well. The child had risen from a hot, dark sleep only to receive a few small sips before blacking out again.

Slowly weaving his horse among the soldiers who walked ankle-deep in the burning sand, Barir found a place beside Gaspar and spoke quietly to him. "My lord, we're in a bad way here."

"Water?" Gaspar asked.

"Yes. Enough for a day, perhaps two. And we can't continue to travel by day. It's too taxing," said Barir, his tongue thick and dry, hampering his efforts at speech.

"We must keep moving. If we stop, we die," Gaspar predicted with absolute conviction.

Barir, his nature darker than usual, muttered as he pulled up to drop back farther in the line, "We die either way."

They found little relief when the last edge of the sun's glowing plate finally inched beneath the horizon. The weakened caravan was easy prey for the icy claws of the desert night as it stole upon them. A cruel wind blew from the west into their faces, slowing their progress and chilling their bones.

The star still beckoned them, though. At its rising, Melchior and the rest felt a small glimmer of hope. At least the star hasn't abandoned us, each thought. It was not much to go on. But enough.

Another night of travel left them beyond exhausted, and they collapsed where they stood once the star's white light vanished. Seeking shelter or setting up a camp was beyond any of them now.

Melchior lay on his back and stared at the glow growing in the east, heralding another day of heat and pain. He recalled his cool mountain bedchamber, where he'd tried unsuccessfully to create and control the rain cloud. He lacked the energy or will to even muster up a raindrop and knew that saving the party from the desert was beyond his skill, and now beyond even the collective powers of the Magi. He shivered as he slipped off into sleep.

The next day brought more of the same miserable, unrelenting heat. The water was gone. Food was a distant, taunting memory. They hunkered down next to their dying beasts to hide from the pelting beams from the sun. Slowly and surely their number began to dwindle as the heat took them.

The caravan crawled at a sloth's pace when the star appeared, despite its insistent call. That night, they lost another horse, two camels, and two men.

Each had a different breaking point. When one man reached his, he simply took a final seat on the sand. An unspoken rule of dignity prevented the stronger ones from trying to coax the exhausted ones to their feet. Old friends simply nodded their goodbyes and prayed that they would have the strength to avoid a similar fate.

And still they journeyed on.

More animals and men died during the next day, and even the strongest among them couldn't rise at sunset. With a soft trumpet, the elephant had finally crumbled beneath the burden of the heat. The mighty creature had dwindled to a skeletal shadow of its former self without water. Balthazar whispered soothing words of magic and stroked its head as it perished. The astronomer was thankful that Shin-shin was unconscious and unable to witness its sad passing. Balthazar knew it wouldn't be long for the rest of them either. Death's messenger had found them; his master wasn't far away.

Gaspar and some men utilized the dying beasts of burden as best they could. As experienced desert nomads, they know that within the carcasses were organs that held precious water that could sustain them, if even for a while. Rending open the guts of the camels, Gaspar opened the camel's stomachs and found the sacs that contained the liquid. But the punishing heat had taken its toll on these stores as well, and he was not able to squeeze much life from the dead beasts. Eventually, he gave up, as he feared he was using more of his precious bodily fluids than he was gaining.

Gaspar led his stallion, Makeda, away from the group. The proud horse still held its head high, but Gaspar could see that it was close to perishing. Makeda's ribs were clearly outlined in the starlight, and his haunches were gaunt. Stroking the beast's neck, he removed the bridle and light saddle.

"I set you free, my brother. Ride on the wind and save yourself," he whispered into the night as the horse nuzzled him. "I thank you."

Gaspar clapped the horse hard on the rump and sent it off to seek its fate among the dunes.

The group, now down to less than a score, had collapsed on the edges of a rocky plain. The sand seemed to have little foothold here, sliding and slipping across the craggy surface to gather and pool in the shallow places. Still, this new landscape offered nothing more than a harder place to lie down and die, offering no shelter from the sweltering rays of the sun.

Balthazar found Melchior resting his arms on his knees in utter defeat and exhaustion. Without looking up, Melchior said, "I cannot believe the star led us here to die like this. It's so...senseless."

As Balthazar sat beside him, he looked at Barir as the gentle giant cradled Shin-shin's head. The slight child, tongue swollen, reeling in heat-addled confusion, hadn't spoken for a day. Melchior watched helplessly as a single tear welled from the soldier's eye, only to evaporate before it hit the dry rock beneath him.

"I can't reconcile it in my mind, either," Balthazar replied. "The signs, my calculations — all had me convinced we were meant for more...I know not what. But not...this..." His voice trailed off.

The sun continued to crisp them. Soon the burning orb would declare victory and collect their souls as bounty.

CHAPTER EIGHTEEN

The sun, however, hadn't vanquished one man, not yet. Drawing up and wrapping his dark robes tightly about him, he surveyed the party as they lay dying under the ruthless solar assault.

Individuals lay where they had fallen, strewn as though flung by a giant's careless hand. The surviving beasts lay panting on their sides. Some weren't moving at all and never would again. The same held true for many of the men.

Shedding all but the most essential traveling necessities — his weapon, of course — he set off, leaving behind those he had come to think of as dear to him, not just companions on a journey.

Gaspar felt the heat and exhaustion as much as the others did but, accustomed to the perils of the desert, he had a tiny reservoir of strength left to draw upon. Doing so would either save them all or destroy him, leaving his friends as a feast for the vultures already circling overhead.

Seeing no sense in turning back, Gaspar made his way due west into the setting sun, a course easily set even without the guiding star. The terrain underfoot got firmer, rockier, and steeper, but it remained lifeless, offering no sustenance and little hope.

Zoth awoke by himself. Not an unusual situation, to be

sure. But precisely *where* and *how* he woke up was the point of interest here: half buried in sand, with a rather nasty-looking, not to mention hungry, vulture perched on a rock only a pace away from his foot.

Zoth silently wondered who was more startled, the impending dinner or the would-be diner, but the result was decidedly in dinner's favor. With a loud cry, the huge creature hauled itself into the air, its wings curling to grasp at the thin desert air.

Too weak to defend himself, Zoth was thankful for the reprieve. Conjure as he might, he couldn't wring even a droplet of water from the arid sky. He called upon his dark masters, but it was in vain; he'd been abandoned to live or die on his own.

He knew he had to find water, which meant finding the others. He pulled himself from his sandy grave and stumbled to his feet. Within a few moments, he located the rest of the party lying on the other side of the craggy hill where he'd passed out.

He found the motionless form of Melchior. Sensing that life hadn't quite left his loathed cousin, Zoth bent to pick up a rock to crush his skull. The bending, however, exhausted the last bit of energy the black sorcerer had left, and the effort only resulted in depositing his form alongside Melchior's. The irony wasn't lost on Zoth. To die here beside his sworn enemy wasn't the reward he'd expected for his years of obedience to the forces of darkness.

"So," whispered Melchior, apparently aware of Zoth's intentions all along, yet powerless to stop them, "here it ends. Not really what you'd hoped for, eh?"

Zoth only breathed in response.

"Cousin," Melchior hoarsely continued, "you, too, saw the star. Felt its draw...its power. Could you not feel its innate goodness as well?"

Zoth's head scratched over the sandy rock as he turned it to meet Melchior's eye. He imagined he looked much like his nemesis: parched, sunburned skin drawn taut over protruding cheekbones, lips hideously swollen and covered with sores. He responded and heard the resignation in his voice. "I can...no more understand...why the powers to which I've devoted my...entire...life have left me here to die, than why your star led you to a similar fate. So, I surrender. I welcome whatever powers reside here to take me. I don't care anymore. Dark, light—all the same, I think. All that will be left are two dry sets of bones."

Melchior sounded surprised when he said, "Old Zoth, I believe you're having a change of heart." He turned his head away and squinted up at the azure, cloudless sky above. "But my heart tells me we're not quite done yet. Something's coming...a life after death, perhaps. Maybe that's the meaning of the star."

"You're...still a fool, Melchior," choked Zoth, "but I'm done. Done fighting you. However, I think I'll wait around just long enough to see you go first."

But Melchior had already passed out, exhausted from the effort of conversation. Zoth stared at him for a long time, trying to recall why he had hated him all these years. The throne, in fact, was nothing but a headache and not really that desirable. Power, he'd actually always had. So why had he lived the life that was about to end? But what was he thinking? It must have been the heat...because he almost felt sympathy for the cousin dying beside him.

Slowly, Zoth crawled away over a dune to perish in peace, apart from Melchior and his fool's quest. Collapsing, he rolled over onto his back. His brain, its juices almost boiling in the heat, shut down and everything went black.

Barir laid Shin-shin's head on the sand. It wouldn't be long. Barir rolled over and came face to face with Shafiq.

The kind old man looked at the soldier and smiled. "We've seen much, no?" he croaked. "It's not such a bad way to die, serving your king."

Barir said, "I'd slit my wrists if I thought my blood would sustain you, master. But I've failed you and Lord Melchior. And Shin-shin. The boy I promised to protect is dying in my arms. But I'll give him a warrior's burial."

Shafiq smiled what would be his last smile, drew what would be his last breath, and pronounced his last prediction. "I think that life has a few more surprises in store for you, my friend. I'll miss you. Tell Melchior…I'm sorry."

And Barir, who'd witnessed too many deaths of too many friends, bid the ancient magus farewell.

Balthazar simply lay on the sand and conserved his energy. Of those who could still raise their heads, most considered him deader than dead. But his corporeal body was in stasis, as his mind reached out to contemplate fate, formulae, fortunes, and futures.

CHAPTER NINETEEN

Gaspar leaned heavily on the scimitar in his hand and watched the beads of sweat that slid from his brow drop with tiny *plip-plips* onto the sun-hardened dirt below him. He was amazed that his body could still produce it. He'd made admirable progress considering his state, but moving uphill over such rugged terrain was taking its toll.

Straightening, he took two quick steps forward. Too quick, in fact. The heat stole up on him and delivered its punch, and he pitched forward in a swoon that took him completely by surprise. Gaspar lifted his face from the ground, shook his head to clear it, and pushed himself up by his arms. He immediately collapsed again. His inner reservoirs were spent. He was done.

Hours or days had passed, he wasn't sure. Time and its passage became irrelevant. He came to a few times, started crawling, and collapsed again in a crumpled black heap. He was done. Really, really done.

And utterly defenseless. This was never more apparent than when two sets of legs appeared in his line of sight, with his sixth sense informing him of another set behind him.

Rolling to his knees, Gaspar gripped his weapon and made as if to wield it. It *janged* on the rock as gravity bested his muscles.

"Easy there, friend," a foreign voice said. "Would you

move to strike those who would save your life?"

"Is that the plan then?" asked another. "These hills are crawling with Romans. How do you know he's not one of them? Besides, you know the law—no outsiders."

"Rani, the decision's mine," the last voice said with authority from behind Gaspar. "My heart tells me that mercy is best. Besides, if he's a spy, which I highly doubt, because I've never seen a man with such black skin, let alone a Roman with black skin, we'll learn it soon enough and use it to our advantage. He comes with us."

"Wait," wheezed Gaspar as his arms were placed around strange shoulders. "There are others…"

Gaspar awoke a few hours later, face down again, draped rather unceremoniously across the rump of a coarse-haired camel. With each ponderous step of the lumbering beast, the Ethiope's field of vision bobbed up and down. If there'd been any food in his belly, he would have pitched it out his throat.

But his captors knew enough about the desert not to give a man in his condition anything more than a tiny mouthful of water. Just a few sips could send even the strongest man into convulsions that, in such a weakened state, would be fatal.

Groaning, Gaspar rolled slightly to one side to see who was steering the camel and promptly slid off the animal's hind end, landing hard on his own hind end. Certainly, now he was awake.

The two camel riders pulled up and turned to survey the toppled magus. Wry smiles turned up the corners of their mouths.

"Well, that looked like it hurt," surmised the rider of the other camel. The rider of Gaspar's former transportation simply continued to display a slight smile, and Gaspar noted how he deferred to the other.

Pushing himself to his hands and knees, Gaspar slowly

wobbled to his feet. He had little strength, but after the display he'd already put on for these two—weren't there three, he wondered?—he was shamed enough to muster the muscle to stand. Proudly, he hoped, he faced the riders and assessed them.

They seemed strangely familiar, and it took a moment before Gaspar realized that their faces and attire resembled those of the men his party had found nailed to the crosses in the desert so many days ago. Dark skinned, yet not nearly so dark as he, with jet hair and warm brown eyes, they were an attractive people. Yet in those eyes, Gaspar thought he recognized the frenzied look a caged animal has as it realizes the trap has closed.

"I thank you for your kindness. You've saved my life, and I'm indebted to you," said Gaspar. He thought that a little flattery was a good way to open a conversation with strangers who were armed, mounted, and many times stronger than he was. He continued. "But I'm not alone. I was traveling with a party going…" He reconsidered. He didn't know these men or what their plans were. He became suddenly vague. "A party going across the desert. We suffered numerous calamities, and I went in search of help. If we hurry—"

"Relax, man," said the leader. "In your delirium you told us of their plight. We've already sent for others to go and find them. With some luck, they'll bring back more than vulture-picked bones."

Goading his camel around, the man maneuvered it to within a pace of Gaspar. He stretched down his long brown arm and extended an open hand. "My name is Omar. You're my guest, and I'll take you to my father's home, where he's the head magistrate. It's not far from here. He'll decide what to do with you. If you're lucky, you may even be reunited with your companions."

Gaspar thought for a moment. Having few options at present, he accepted the arm and was hauled up behind Omar.

From his closer vantage point, Gaspar realized that his benefactor was younger than he appeared. Sun and sand, not age, had worn deep troughs at the corners of his eyes and mouth. He was strong as well, and comfortable with himself even in the presence of a black stranger. As he had noticed earlier, the pair wore loose tunics girded with rope belts, and simple sandals. Each also wore a curved sword in the style of desert nomads, and Gaspar noted that each weapon bore heavy nicks, chinks, and streaks from use.

Rather formally, the other rider said to Gaspar, "And I'm Badaat, sworn to protect the back of Omar. What are you called?"

"Gaspar." The magus chose the streamlined approach, deciding that giving away too much gained him nothing at the present.

Omar sensed his reluctance, but smiled nonetheless. "Well then, Gaspar, I'm afraid I must make a demand of you. The entrance to our home is secret, and our enemies are many. Therefore, we must bind and blind you until we reach our destination."

Gaspar thought, *how much worse can this day get?* Still, he nodded, and suffered the indignity with as much pride as a half-dead, fully dehydrated warrior could muster. Badaat tied a cloth about his head, veiling his entire face, then firmly bound Gaspar's hands behind his back with a thin leather cord.

As the camels began moving, Gaspar clung with all the strength in his legs to keep from falling off again. Then he heard Omar's voice quietly say, "Lean against me, my friend. I won't let you fall."

They rode on. Gaspar dropped in and out of consciousness. At last he sensed that they'd reached a turning point in their journey. Omar shifted in his saddle and said to him, "We've entered the secret passage to our home. Do I have your word that you will honor its secrets and traditions?"

Gaspar nodded in acknowledgement, and Omar said,

"Then I'll take off that blindfold. You must be dying in there."

The fresh air hit Gaspar's face like a slap, and his senses snapped awake in response. Omar produced a knife and cut through the cord binding his hands.

Omar and Badaat rode single file deep within a towering ravine, narrower and steeper than a canyon, and no wider than the breadth of four men. Far overhead, the sky was an azure ribbon that seemed to float beyond reach. The sun wasn't visible, and Gaspar couldn't tell the time of day.

But the ravine itself took his breath away. The path twisted, visible for only a few hundred feet ahead, between walls made of the most beautiful stone Gaspar had ever seen. The smooth, rose-colored stone looked as hard as marble and hinted at the long-evaporated waters that once cut and polished the walls and left this path in their wake. Gaspar guessed that, were he to reverse direction and follow the channel out to its genesis, he would find a mere crack in the desert that only the most skilled tracker could find twice in a lifetime.

Omar watched as Gaspar swiveled his head around, taking in the beautiful mysteries of the chasm. "Breathtaking, isn't it? Even had we not covered your eyes, I doubt you could find this passage again. And in case you were wondering, a handful of my soldiers have been pacing us from above. So it's both breathtaking and deadly, no?"

Gaspar craned his head upward, but could detect no one there. Whether they were there or not was not the point. That Omar was in total command of the situation was. Still, he didn't seem threatening. Just factual.

"How are you feeling?" Badaat asked.

"Better," replied Gaspar, still not himself, but more like himself than he'd been a few short hours ago.

"Good!" said Omar. "You're about to experience a thrill like no other! Hold tight!" With that, he gave his camel's hindquarters an enthusiastic swat, and the beast shot off with speed that astonished the black warrior.

"*Yeeee-yi-yi-yi!*" screamed Omar as the two camels galloped through the twisting, turning crevasse. The walls flew by in swaths of red, brown, and gray. Walls appeared before them, but the riders, anticipating them, guided their steeds expertly into openings that appeared just in the nick of time.

If Gaspar had any urine in him, it would have streamed out his pant leg. But after a few moments, he began to revel in the adrenaline rush of the ride, learning to shift his weight with Omar and duck when Omar did. The wind whipped back his clothes and refreshed him. For the first time in a long while, Gaspar felt *alive*. Something moved within his chest, something buried long ago and only found now as stood on the dark ledge of death. At last, it rose out of him, and he let out a laugh as he had not since the days of his childhood.

CHAPTER TWENTY

Balthazar awoke lying on his back. It was dark, but not quite the pitch black he expected in the afterlife. Did he believe in an afterlife? He must meditate more on that. Later.

He lifted his hand and touched stone just inches from his face. *Well,* he thought soberly, *they've buried me alive.*

He'd not felt panic since his childhood, when he was lost in the bamboo maze of his faraway homeland. But he felt it now. He swallowed his initial fear and forced his rational mind to contemplate the reality of the situation. He was alive, not dead. He could breathe. And he was stark naked. Nudity, he philosophized, was probably not a desirable state for one who has left the corporeal world. Why bother leaving if you're going to be naked, cold, and, well, naked? Yes, he was definitely not dead; but if anyone found him in this state, he might wish he were.

As he shook off the webs of sleep, his eyes slowly adjusted to the darkness, and he could make out a few details. A soft light to his side provided just enough illumination. Balthazar realized that he lay on a cool slab of stone in a nook of a small chamber. The rock above him was a low overhang of a natural stone wall; in fact, he was in a room made entirely of stone colored a beautiful pale shade of reddish-pink, a room seemingly hollowed out and made habitable by a force other than the hands of man. It was small yet comfortable, lit by a single candle nestled in a niche by the doorway. Beyond that smoothed opening was utter darkness.

Rolling out to a sitting position, he assessed his physical condition. His hands and forearms had been burned an ugly scarlet by the sun, and a quick examination of his face with his fingertips confirmed his suspicion that it was covered with sun blisters. His lips felt crusty, his cheeks taut, burned, and carved by the events of the past weeks. Considering the alternative, he was satisfied with his overall status. What's more, his blisters had some sweet-smelling unguent on them, and they hurt far less than he would have expected.

As he prepared to slide off the ledge, a question popped into his mind: where was Shin-shin? The last image Balthazar could recall was not a hopeful one. The child's life was his responsibility, and Balthazar feared he had been quite reckless with it so far. There was no doubt the child had a role to play in their undertaking, but was that role to be a sacrifice to the powers that controlled them? The prospect sickened him.

A simple white shift with a rope to belt it waited on a low stool made entirely of the rosy stone. Painfully, he pulled the garment over his head and cinched it high around his waist. If felt strangely comfortable and natural to wear.

Balthazar's tongue was still thick and swollen, and he needed something to slake his overwhelming thirst. Still giddy from his brush with death, he fantasized about how nice a cup of cool rice wine would be. He decided to find some drink, and his companions, if they lived.

Taking up the candle, Balthazar held it aloft and walked through the opening. He found himself at the end of a corridor of stone and followed it to its beginning, where he almost ran head-first into a grim pair of silent guards, practically invisible in the darkness. Gesturing, one brusquely led Balthazar at a good clip down another rose-colored passage, with the other guard following closely.

After a few turns, Balthazar was completely disoriented. He would not have found his way back had he wanted to. He was fairly certain that this maze-like route was intentional.

His guards remained mute, communicating through gestures and body language. He finally figured out what was nagging at him. He'd seen men like these before, slaughtered out in the desert. He kept the fact to himself and maintained his silence, mostly out of dry necessity, but also out of a fear that the crucified men in the desert would be a sore point of discussion.

He shuffled along, head down, until they emerged into a large hall, where the bustling activity jolted him to attention. The hall itself measured three hundred paces across, Balthazar calculated, and three times that in length. Fiery torches set in wall brackets lit the room with a warm umber light that danced and glimmered off the polished walls of rosy stone.

The hall, while certainly regal enough, had an air of commerce to it. Small pockets of people stood chattering all around the chamber. Men gestured wildly, and voices rose above the din only to be smothered by a competing argument, discussion, or display a few feet away. The men, and a few women, wore what Balthazar would learn were traditional Bedouin garments, loose, draped clothing worn with the desert in mind, turbans and other assorted headwear, and all kinds of swords, staffs, knives, and other vicious-looking weapons tucked into belts and sashes.

But what struck him most wasn't their attire, but their faces: shaped and streamlined by the wind and the sun, with hawkish noses and sparkling eyes recessed into cavernous orbital pits. Polished cheekbones rose high and sharp. Heavy brows, set in seemingly eternal frowns of suspicion, lifted with the broad, white smiles that came so easily in their conversations. Balthazar found himself admiring the strangers, these people who had formed a symbiotic truce with their harsh homeland. And he filed away the observation that this loose collection of sand-hardened strangers could be valuable allies or formidable foes.

Balthazar, a bit overwhelmed by the sound and activity, followed the two guards as they wove through the crowd toward the far end of the room. There, elevated between two large stanchions holding pots of flame that brightened the immediate area, an older man Balthazar couldn't quite make out waited.

"Balthazar!" exclaimed a familiar voice to his right, and the astronomer turned to see who addressed him.

Gaspar, his black skin radiant against the off-white robe he wore, rushed forward and scooped the smaller man up in a hug that threatened to do more damage than the sun had. "I'm...glad," whispered the warrior into his ear and gently lowered Balthazar to his feet.

Balthazar took a step back and assessed Gaspar. He noted a change; in the other man's eyes he saw more life, perhaps even joy, where before he had beheld only quiet, ruthless determination. "You've been out in the sun too long, I believe," deadpanned Balthazar.

Gaspar bent his head back and let out a howling laugh. Balthazar's eyes widened.

Melchior, burned almost as badly as Balthazar imagined himself to be, stepped forward and placed a firm hand the Asian magus' shoulder, a gesture Balthazar once would have shunned, but now welcomed. Their brush with death had altered them all, it seemed.

"It's good to see you alive, my friend," said Melchior. "We feared the worst when you weren't here at first. Answers and details are a bit scarce. But one thing I can tell you is that our dark friend here is not the same man we left out in the desert. He's gone quite mad."

Gaspar laughed his throaty laugh again, smiled at them, and clamped a huge hand on each of their shoulders. He looked each in the eye and said earnestly, "Perhaps you're right. I'm not the same. But I'm…better." And he smiled cryptically again.

Balthazar, in his usual way, shrugged and accepted the new man with aplomb. But his curiosity was far from satisfied. Melchior handed him a goblet of water, and he slurped it down in a single draught. His throat loosened up, and he forced his swollen tongue to spit out questions. "But where are we? Whom have we lost? And Shin-shin, have you seen Shin-shin?" He spoke with a bit of a slur, but Melchior understood and opened his mouth to reply.

But a Bedouin approached, cutting off Melchior before he could answer.

Gaspar said, "Ah, good! This is Omar, and I consider him a friend. He saved my life." He narrowed his eyes and looked keenly at the other two. "And yours, too."

Omar bowed slightly and seemed a bit embarrassed by the compliment. He addressed Gaspar. "My father will see you now. He has much to ask you. And I think you may have a few questions for him, as well. Please follow me."

As they covered the last hundred paces to the dais Balthazar had spotted earlier, Gaspar filled them in on recent history. He described how Omar had rescued him and how the Bedouin had sent out a search party for the others. Sadly, he revealed that only a handful of the caravan had survived. Gaspar dropped his voice to add that he had kept his identity and the reason for their pilgrimage to himself.

Melchior reeled as he counted the cost in human lives. He looked relieved when he learned that Barir was alive, along with some of his guards. But all the beasts had perished, and only a few of their loads had been saved from the devouring sands of the desert.

"And Shin-shin?" asked Balthazar again, his voice heavy with emotion that betrayed to the other Magi just how much he cared and feared for the youngster.

"Alive!" Gaspar grinned as he watched the relief unfold across Balthazar's face. "But I haven't seen Shin-shin yet.

Very, very close to death. The healers here haven't let me visit."

Melchior was happy to hear that Balthazar's ward was safe. But inside, his sense of doom hardened even more. He would gladly have given his own life to save the others. *What are the odds that the three of us would survive when so many others didn't?* he thought. *What – who – is watching over us?* What was the final price he would pay? What was the purpose of the star? Were they to be whittled away to the last, killed slowly to appease some cruel power?

He deeply mourned the hard death of his friend and mentor, Shafiq. Since childhood, Shafiq had been there for him. And even though he'd been old, men like Shafiq lived to twice his age in Melchior's kingdom. He was gone, taken by an untimely, unbearable death. The loss was heavy, a thick scar on his heart that would never truly heal.

"Oh yes, and that dog Zoth's dead too, apparently. They never even found the old snake's skin," added Gaspar.

A feeling, a voice deep and bidding at the back of his mind, told Melchior that they hadn't seen the last of Zoth.

"Incredible," said Balthazar. "There's a force of control, of predestination at work here. There's no doubt of it. Those who live now were meant to. Their purpose has not been served."

"Well, it's bizarre, if you ask me," injected Gaspar. Then he brightened. "But we're alive. We can't forget that. Luck, providence, powers — I don't really care. I'm just glad to see you two! Although," he added wickedly, "you do look horrible with those blisters all over your face. Makes me glad to be an Ethiopian. We sun better."

Melchior and Balthazar looked incredulously at Gaspar. Who was this lunatic? But before either could reply, the little entourage came to a halt before the elevated chair. The man sitting in it was neither majestic nor powerful, neither handsome nor ugly. He just looked tired.

Omar turned and spoke to the three Magi. "May I present

the magistrate, and my father, Sheik Um-Kawak Shareef."

The three Magi found themselves in an unfamiliar position, bowing before what appeared to be an elected official.

"Well," muttered Balthazar under his breath, "well, well, well."

CHAPTER TWENTY-ONE

Zoth lived. Survival was foremost on his sun-scorched mind, and it gave him a small dose of strength to pull himself to his hands and knees and begin crawling. He'd probably not traversed more than a few hundred yards when he came face to face with what he was sure was a mirage, the dusty, dark hoof of a horse.

Peering upward, he saw that the horse was in fact fitted for battle and ornamented in bronze and fabric that, although dusty, was impressive. Finally, he saw the silhouette of a soldier framed by the blazing sun. Unable to make out any detail, Zoth decided some warrior god had come to take him to his palace in the underworld of night.

Then the warrior barked out to an unseen companion, "Go tell the legate I've got a live one, here."

And so it was that Zoth was saved from the desert by the legions of Caesar Augustus. In the following days, he would wonder which was more preferable, death or Rome?

CHAPTER TWENTY-TWO

"My liege," began Melchior, who once again assumed leadership of the party.

"No, no," countered Sheik Shareef. "I'm no royal. Heh-heh. Ah, no, no! Although I suspect that you and your companions may be, hmmm? I'm only the head magistrate, a simple businessman, like everyone else here. Titles, crowns, empires, we leave those at the door; here in the chamber, the laws of the Bedouin govern. Which is to say, heh-heh, we have very few laws here."

Melchior rose, looked around, and saw the truth in the magistrate's words. All about him, traders bickered, haggled, gestured, shouted, and laughed in a great cacophony of commerce. What he'd assumed was a council chamber was, in fact, an underground market square. The only things missing were the chickens, spices, silks, metals, jewels, breads, and water being bartered. And from the smell of the hall, he could tell that the products waited somewhere nearby.

Shareef continued. "Welcome to Petra, our home, and the heart of what once was the mighty Nabataean Empire. Then, our cities spread throughout the desert, and traders visited here freely. Now all that remains is Petra. Heh-heh. Smaller, yes. But just as strong, I think, no? You stand in the Khazneh, our sacred meeting place, where every man may speak freely. But of all this and that, we'll speak later. First, we feast."

He swept his arm toward a smaller entryway, and then stout Shareef jumped down from his chair with surprising energy and led the way with a few quick, bouncy strides. Balthazar, Melchior, and Gaspar followed him, as did Omar and few of the men who'd been in discussion with the sheik.

They entered a generous room of smoothed walls and greater opulence than any the Magi had yet encountered in Petra. Torches cast a warm glow and provided a snapping, crackling backdrop to conversation. Magnificent woven carpets, animal skins, and overstuffed pillows surrounded a low stone table. Shareef plopped himself down at the head of the table and gestured that the Magi should sit wherever they pleased.

Veiled women emerged from other openings in the walls, bearing platters of tantalizing foods. Small bowls of salty broth began the feast, which soon gave way to spit after spit of roasted meats, still sizzling and producing tendrils of smoke to tease the nostrils of the diners. Piles of flat, wheaty breads, with crusty exteriors and downy soft interiors complemented the foods. Wine, herbed drinks of unknown origin, and other fermented concoctions flowed, loosening the tongues of everyone around the table.

Melchior paused from time to time to survey the scene and sample the conversations. Omar and Gaspar were engaged in a loud, boisterous conversation, friendly yet combative as they exchanged war stories and tales of somewhat exaggerated valor. More than once the facts were challenged, and more than a few grains of salt taken as well.

Balthazar was in a deep philosophical discussion with a pair of long-bearded men who, by their dress and demeanor, seemed to be members of a religious order. The trio was at times animated and at others pensive, and they often gestured in the smoky air. Melchior couldn't make out their conversation, but he assumed that they were discussing recent omens and their portents.

As for himself, Melchior seemed to have found a new blood brother in Shareef. The plump fellow profusely offered his home, food, sons, daughters, and beasts to the magus. Melchior politely declined the generous offers, and gently steered the conversation away from earthly desires to his intellectual cravings.

"My sheik, I've traveled far, and seen many things. But I've never seen a place such as your Petra, nor such an . . . unusual...collection of people. Share with me the story of your people."

Now, there are two things you can ask of a Bedouin that will make him happy beyond belief. One is, "What would you want for that trinket?" because the Bedou love to trade. The other is, "Tell me a little about yourself and your family!" because the Bedou love to talk even more than they love to trade.

The sheik offered a greasy grin and made himself comfortable. Around bites of flesh eagerly torn from the roasted leg of some animal, he told Melchior everything he could possibly ever want to know. But nestled in the rambling tale were nuggets of information that would shape the Magi's decisions in the days to come.

"Petra," chewed Shareef, "is like a dark, beautiful woman, no? Smooth, soft curves. Warm and glowing. Dark, dangerous places. And in the end, more a mystery than an answer. Heh-heh. No? Ah Petra…"

He paused for moment to swallow loudly, then continued. "Long before we found her, Petra was carved by the gods with wind, water, and magic. There's only one way in, and it's secret, very secret indeed. To reveal it means death in the desert with your tongue cut out and only the blood from your mouth to drink."

He became gravely serious, and his eyes fixed narrowly on Melchior, along with the eyes of the others in the small group who'd been listening to the sheik.

162

He immediately swung the conversation around the other way. "But why must we dwell on such things? Heh-heh. You and your friends are as safe as if you were in your mother's bosom! Many have searched for us, for our Petra. All have failed. We know this because we find their corpses in the sand. Very sad."

He paused to slurp up a bowl of dark liquid. "But we don't hide here in the darkness. No. We're a restless people, the Bedou, and we cannot stay in one place for long. Petra is our sanctuary, our place for joining and trading. As we speak, many, many Bedou caravans are traveling beneath the stars. Spices, of course. And bitumen."

Melchior asked, "Bitumen?"

"It's a gift from the gods beneath the Great Sea. It's their excrement. When they, ah, 'go,' it floats to the surface, and we collect it. Powerful stuff. Precious. To the west, the Egyptians use it to mummify their dead loved ones. Here, and to the east, it's burned to light the darkness." Shareef gestured to an oily black indentation in the table where a gob of bitumen burned, giving off a thick, acrid plume of smoke.

Omar added, "It's for our bitumen supplies, our reserves of water we collect in our cisterns, our gold and spices, and our strategic position here in the desert that so many wish to know and hold Petra in their own grasp. Like the cursed Romans." He spat the last words.

Melchior found himself at a spiritual crossroads. He could reveal what he knew to Shareef or keep the silence he'd maintained so far. But, he rationalized, there were no secrets here. These people, while fierce, had saved them. Truth was the course he always favored. So Melchior gambled.

"My friend," Melchior began slowly, "I bring you sad tidings. Days ago, a few days' ride from here, we came upon some of your brothers in the desert."

Shareef sobered at his grim tone. "Then they were dead. Because no Petran would be found unless he wanted to be.

Tell me," he commanded.

Melchior said, "Indeed, all but one were dead when we found them. There'd been a great battle. From the tracks in the sand, your brothers were greatly outnumbered. They must have died bravely. There…there was only one set of tracks leading away."

"However," Melchior continued, "as I said, one man was still alive. We didn't learn his name. He only said one word before he passed to the afterlife: Rome."

This met silence. Those at the table had turned to listen to Melchior. The only sound filling the gaps in his monologue was the muttering bitumen flame. Shareef's head was bowed. His salty tears fell to the tabletop.

Gaspar interjected in his deep voice that carried the gravity of the moment, "We burned their bodies and offered prayers. They died like warriors, and we treated them so."

"I thank you for that," Shareef said softly. "We had given them up for dead. My youngest son, Samir, was among them. They were on patrol. How many days away would you say they were?"

Shareef was already getting down to business. There would be time for mourning later. His son and the others had perished protecting the secret of Petra. Despite his soft appearance, Melchior realized, the sheik was a man who wouldn't take such a sacrifice for granted.

"Three days by horse, perhaps more," said Gaspar quietly.

"They're getting close," worried a tall, thin man who sat to Shareef's right, an advisor, Melchior surmised. He looked perpetually worried, but a man with that disposition had his place at a table like this.

"I'm Nabil. I doubt not your words. And you're welcome in our house, as is our custom. But the question is, who has followed you here? The dogs? The Romans would like nothing better than to have Petra as a stronghold. They want our water. Our belongings. Our trade. Petra would be their launching post to the east."

The rest of the Petrans seemed to agree with his assessment, and murmured so. Nabil continued.

"What we haven't learned is what you are doing here. Why were you in the desert? Who are you? We welcome you as guests, and will die protecting you. But I, for one, must know who I'm dying for!"

Every set of eyes swiveled from Nabil to Melchior. Melchior looked to Gaspar, who shrugged, and to Balthazar, who nodded.

"We are," Melchior began slowly, trying to put into words the odd aligning of forces and quests that had bound them together, "searchers. We-we follow a...sign we've seen. We've been called to follow it. My companions and I met in the desert. We all had the same calling. We've seen many...wondrous...and terrible things. I don't really know our destination. The journey has been, well, costly. Already, too many lives have been lost..." His voice trailed off as he recalled Shafiq.

He left unvoiced his feeling that many more lives would be lost before the journey ended. Instead he struggled to find the words that would put meaning into their wanderings.

"The star," crowed a tiny, ancient voice from the darkness far from the table.

The Magi jumped, for they hadn't noticed her before now, and the sound of her voice sent chills up the spine of everyone in the room. A serving girl shrieked and dropped her pitcher with a crash.

Omar murmured gravely, "The Crone. She rarely speaks. Or visits. The winds of the desert whisper in her ears. She has visions."

"The star, you follow the star," sang the Crone again in her creaky voice. She shuffled forward, a wraith in dirty rags impossibly bound together into a single garment, her two useless, claw-like hands held before her.

Melchior, startled as much by her appearing as her appearance, wondered how she could have been in the room for so long without being noticed. A dark, dirty shawl wrapped the Crone's head, making it difficult to see her face. But her eyes shone out, rivaling the ferocity of any other Bedouin in the room.

"Yes," answered Melchior, rising and bowing to her. The acknowledgement of her stature within the group seemed wise, and it proved to be so.

"Not all eyes that see can perceive it. Its power is strong, its song is irresistible. Can you tell us about it?" asked Balthazar, rising from his cushions and offering his hand to the scary old hag.

The Crone, ignoring him, sat with surprising ease at the table, and the hush that followed left little doubt that she was now in control of the conversation.

"A quest. You're on a quest. A holy one, at that. To the home of the Hebrew David you must go. To Judaea. Follow the star there. But beware," she intoned.

"Why, old woman? What do we face?" demanded Gaspar.

She laughed a coarse, scratchy laugh, like an old reed being crumbled into dust. Her shrouded head pivoted to address Gaspar. "What good will your weapon do you, warrior, when you face a power unlike any other on earth?"

She nodded to Balthazar. "You, stargazer. Can you contemplate the end of everything?"

"And you, king," she almost hissed at Melchior. "When your earthly realm and riches and loves are ripped bloody from your hands, will you weep? Or rejoice?"

The room was silent. Even the fire seemed to have been subdued by her predictions. The Magi, stoic, held their ground. But in their hearts, they quailed. They knew the Crone could see into their hearts, and that their worst fears were coming to bear.

"But know this. You have been chosen. Are you sacrifices to a greater power?" She paused and seemed to consult an inner source. "It's dark to me. Your purpose is unclear. But follow it, you must. The lives of everyone depend on what you do. Fail, and you fail us all."

She rose from the table, accepting Balthazar's outstretched arm then pushing it angrily away once she'd gained her feet. Suddenly, oddly, she reached down and snatched a fig from the tabletop.

"Well, I've got to eat, haven't I?" she sputtered and shuffled out of the room.

"That was," said Melchior, "quite possibly the most bizarre meal I've ever had."

The discussion and group had broken up after the Crone's abrupt departure. Little was left to say, and the Petrans were more than happy to sleep. Melchior and the others took their word for it that it was indeed nighttime, and left to hunt down their bedchambers.

Soon, with help from others they came upon in their wanderings, they gathered in Melchior's chamber, similar to Balthazar's in its bare yet comfortable atmosphere. The Magi regarded each other silently for a moment. Still strangers, in effect, they'd been thrown together on a journey that had all the hallmarks of being their first and last. The cryptic, haunting words of the Crone rang in their ears.

Gaspar spoke. "Omar says that this…Judaea…is a few days' journey north and east of here. He'll outfit us with men, mounts, and supplies, and we can leave soon. Those not well enough to travel with us are welcome to remain. He's promised their safety to me as a brother."

"Their generosity is appreciated," said the weary Melchior, and he winced as he lay on the slab that was his bed, still feeling the sting from his burns and troubles. "But I feel like we've lost valuable time here. Our lives have been saved, but the urge to continue is strong, right?"

The other Magi nodded and bid their goodnights. It wouldn't be an easy sleep for any of them.

CHAPTER TWENTY-THREE

Later that night explosions, mighty sounds, and a burning in his head jerked Gaspar awake. Disoriented by the cacophony in his ears, he looked about for a second, unsure of where he was. Then he leapt to his feet and dashed out into the passageway, naked to the waist.

And right into Balthazar, who sprinted down the darkened tunnel with a bitumen torch in his hand.

"You feel it too, my dark friend?" asked the slight Asian. "Makes it difficult to sleep, no?"

"Indeed," Gaspar growled dryly.

Trotting down the hall, they encountered Melchior. "It's the star," he said, telling them what they already suspected. "We need to get outside."

Gaspar led the way, the sheen of sweat on his muscular torso glimmering in the shaky light. One of his strides was easily two of the other men's, but the urgency they sensed commanded that they all move quickly.

Soon they entered the cavernous Khazneh, but it was eerily silent. A few sentinels stood guard in the shadows, their shifting the only movement. Then, over in a shadowed doorway, a small, bent figure appeared. The Crone.

"Of course," said Balthazar softly.

"That old woman...I *do not* like her," muttered Gaspar.

But he, like the other Magi, knew that they were no

longer in control of their destinies. Events such as this were preordained. Single file, they walked the hundred paces to the beckoning woman.

"Restless wanderers, aren't we? Sense something, do you?" she gently mocked them.

Gaspar's hands curled. Had he been carrying his scimitar, it might have found her head. Or at least her tongue.

"Crone," accused Balthazar, "you seem to have little trouble belittling us and our mission. Yet, I think you're as afraid as any of us, perhaps even more. You hide your fear well, but not as well as you think."

A gap cracked her face, as if she were actually smiling. "I *like* you, little man!" she proclaimed, then gestured for them to follow her. Shaking their heads, but anxious to get underway, the Magi followed the old woman as she scurried off into the darkness.

The Crone led them to a winding, narrow crevasse, a natural rift in the rosy rock into which rough steps had been hewn centuries before. Dust, spider webs, and stale, dank air met them as they climbed.

"This way is ancient," puffed the old seer, her raggedy skirts hoisted up her stick legs in one fist so her bare feet could climb the stairs. "Many have forgotten that it even exists. I was…a young girl…the last time I climbed this way. It was long ago, indeed."

"Eons, I'd venture," muttered Gaspar.

As the group moved higher, the air got fresher. "We must have traveled hundreds and hundreds of steps almost straight up," Melchior said through heavy breaths, his battered body not ready for such a physical test.

Gaspar nodded. He heard the mishmash of sounds that had woken him earlier gaining clarity and strength. Soon, the melody in his head reverberated throughout his whole body. His skin felt prickly, and his heart beat faster. His body seemed to anticipate something his mind couldn't fathom.

They hurried up the last few rocky steps, passing and

leaving the Crone behind. Leaping up two, three steps at a time, the Magi fought their way up toward the open air. A large boulder partially covered the opening at the top of the stairwell. Melchior raised his hand without slowing his pace, whispered some words, and the mammoth boulder rolled aside. They burst through into the open air of the rocky plateau that hid Petra beneath it, and their world was transformed in a heartbeat.

The heavens were afire. The inky sky, for weeks practically devoid of any light save the one guiding star, was lit with lavender flames tipped with orange. The fires, magnificent and mighty, licked the sky like waves lapping a shore. All around them, multicolored lights burst forth in both miniscule and gigantic explosions.

Celestial beings darted and danced through the air, showing and showering pure joy. The Magi had never seen their like. Milky white and radiant, in all shapes and sizes, they seemed to have all the normal human elements, but they were somehow more... majestic. Powerful. Prodigious wings beat the air as they zipped to and fro, pure energy that darted up and down, moving to the music of the heavens that filled the sky and the hearts of the Magi.

The vision was almost too much to behold. Their eyes stretched wide to take in all they saw.

In a corner of the sky, leading the orchestra of sound, sights, and might, the star pulsated with the power of the heavens. It was the fixed point around which all the other activity seemed to gyre.

Behind them, the Crone finally finished the steps and escaped into the evening air. She gasped her disbelief. She crumpled to the ground and hid her eyes. The Magi, in sharp contrast, stood in amazement.

"By...the...gods!" stammered Melchior, as if forcing the words from his chest.

"NAY, NOT THE GODS, MELCHIOR, BUT THE GOD."

A single being took precedence before the others. A face,

sexless yet powerful, boiled to the surface of the white-hot entity. Powerful shafts of crimson light shot from behind its head, illuminating it and adding a new dimension to its majesty. Its right hand held a flaming sword of blue; its left it held out in a soft gesture with the palm toward the heavens. Gently beating wings, soft, feathery, and yet insubstantial as well, and twice as large as the being itself, held it aloft. Flowing garments of effervescent light snapped in the night. It was the most wondrous, breathtaking sight they'd ever beheld.

"THE KING OF KINGS. THE LORD OF HEAVEN AND EARTH. THE ONE AND TRUE GOD. KNEEL, AND HEARKEN."

Without even thinking, the Magi sank to their knees.

"FEAR NOT, FOR BEHOLD, I BRING YOU TIDINGS OF GREAT JOY, WHICH SHALL BE TO ALL PEOPLE." Turning its burning blue eyes to the heavens, the being continued. "FOR UNTO YOU IS BORN THIS DAY IN THE CITY OF DAVID A SAVIOR, WHICH IS CHRIST THE LORD."

Flicks of magenta, sea green, and silver, lavender, tangerine, and the deepest ebony painted the upturned faces of the Magi. Tears of mixed fear and joy streamed down their cheeks.

"AND THIS SHALL BE A SIGN UNTO YOU. YOU SHALL FIND THE BABE WRAPPED IN SWADDLING CLOTHES, LYING IN A MANGER. SEEK HIM, PRAISE HIM."

A legion of similar entities joined the being, forming a mighty chorus of song that shook the bones of the Magi. The sky exploded with renewed energy, threatening to destroy the very fabric of the world.

"GLORY TO GOD IN THE HIGHEST. AND ON EARTH, PEACE. GOOD WILL TOWARD MEN."

And with that, there was nothing. The beings vanished, the sounds silenced, and the waves of fire disappeared. The sky was empty but for the beating of the single, suddenly lonely star.

The audience of three collapsed like puppets after the performance. Filling his lungs with the cool, crisp air, Gaspar wondered silently if he'd dared to breathe during the... vision?

Looking around at his panting companions and noting the huddled ball of rags that was the Crone, Gaspar summed up what each of them was already thinking.

"If-if—" He swallowed loudly "If I'm supposed to be so joyous, why am I shaking?"

CHAPTER TWENTY-FOUR

So *these are Romans,* he thought. *They certainly have style.*
Even for a prisoner, life wasn't so horrible. You got an occasional drink. Even the bowl of unidentifiable slop they made you eat like a dog because your hands and feet were bound — even that wasn't too bad. And best of all, they kept you closely guarded *inside* their flapping scarlet tents.

Anyone who treats prisoners like this can't be all *bad,* Zoth concluded. Which, of course, led him to speculate with surprising accuracy that this was an empire that wouldn't last and would crumble from the weaknesses within it rather than from any outside threats.

The first day of his captivity was nothing less than a hot nightmare. He could call up fleeting memories of rough hands finding him, and questions barked in the harsh garble of the Roman centurions. Then he'd awakened like this half a day ago, broken but not beaten. He had already started to summon the dark energies required for getting himself out of a predicament like this.

Then, perhaps a few hours ago, it occurred to him that perhaps he was here for a reason. That there was a purpose behind the sparing of his life. While these Romans intended to use him, maybe the tables could be turned…

Bound and gagged, Zoth sat on the floor with his back against a tent pole. The canopied campaign tent could barely hold back the relentless heat of the sun, and the air inside the tent felt dead and lifeless. Flies tormented him and sand lice feasted. The backs of his hands and his face, although hidden from his personal perspective, were in plain view of the bugs that found his cracked, exposed flesh a tasty repast.

Though still garbed in his own sand-encrusted black robes, he'd lost or been deprived of his weapons and belongings. And the tent held little in the way of weaponry, should he decide to employ some black magic to his bonds. Instead, he watched, waited, and regained his shadowy strength.

Later, Zoth was rewarded with a visit from the Roman in charge of the legion. Clad in the armor that identified him as a soldier of Rome, he had the regal bearing and intensity endemic to the sons and daughters of Romulus and Remus.

"Get the dog to his feet," the officer said tiredly to the two guards with him. While the officer was unarmed, those he commanded each held a Roman gladius, the standard issue short swords of the legions. With their free hands, they hauled Zoth to his feet.

Zoth felt the blood again flowing into his cramped feet and legs, and gave silent thanks. He assessed his adversary. The purple fabric of his tunic and his prominent features evidenced his noble lineage. The proud nose, square chin, and olive skin looked like they could adorn a Roman coin. Intimidating, but manageable.

"Remove his gag," said the officer, then, "Speak."

Grunting to loosen his unused vocal chords, Zoth adopted a groveling demeanor and whimpered, "My lord, I wish to thank you for saving your humble servant's life. I only hope that I may repay your kindness."

"A good start," said the officer. "A seat, for Caesar's sake!"

Not for Zoth. Within seconds, a soldier rushed in with a leather and wood campaign stool, and the officer slumped onto it. He appeared to Zoth distracted and irritated by the time being wasted here.

"Just how would you repay me? What's your name, barbarian?"

"My name? Why, I'm Zoth. I came in search of you and your legions. I have…information…that you'll find useful. Consider it my, ah, payment for saving me from the sands."

"And you think that what you would tell me will repay your life-debt?" asked the officer.

"Many times over," replied Zoth with forced gravity.

That got the officer's attention. "Really?" He sat up a bit in the creaking leather chair, focusing his attention on Zoth. "Another chair. And some water. Release his hands."

"Legatus," said the soldiers in acknowledgement, and soon Zoth was slurping from a copper tankard, savoring the metallic-tasting water flowing down his throat. Then, rubbing his hands, he fixed his beady eyes on the soldier before him. *Trap: baited.*

"Speak, for my kindness wanes with time," demanded the Roman. "I've spent too many months chasing vermin like you out here in the desert. My patience ran out long, long ago."

"My lord…" started Zoth.

"Legate Pilate," corrected the soldier.

Zoth transitioned smoothly. "Legate Pilate, I know whom you seek. In my travels, I came upon some of your …enemies…quite dead…in the desert. In fact, I was the prisoner of a band of rogues who intended to raise an army against the Roman legions. They kept me around — ahmmm, alive because of my unique gifts," lied Zoth.

"What do you mean? You're some kind of sorcerer?" asked the skeptical Pilate.

"In so many words, yes," replied Zoth, not quite able to hide his discomfort with such a base description. "You see, I have *the sight.*"

Pilate tried to appear nonchalant, but failed. The two guards looked at each other and took an involuntary step backward.

Pilate said, "Well, well...you're either a good liar, or my luck has finally turned in this hellhole of a land. Or both. Either way, I don't care. Show me what will happen tomorrow."

"Good Pilate, it doesn't work like that. These things take...time. Strength. Thought and preparation. I'm weakened now, and tired. Perhaps with some rest and food, I can help you," Zoth replied.

Pilate, nobody's fool, smiled darkly. "I see. Later, then. After something to eat, of course. But I promise you this. Disappoint me, and your shoulders will be wanting for a head. And your tongue will be eaten by the first vulture to find it." He rose and headed for the tent flaps, then paused.

"Feed him. And double his guard. Until later, then?" asked the legate as he turned on his heel and exited.

Bait: taken.

From snatches of conversations, Zoth soon learned what this army was doing out in the middle of nowhere. Pilate was the legate in command of a Roman legion stationed in Judaea, a Roman province. A nobleman of middle rank, he was working his way up the Roman food chain through military service. The task for Pilate and his men was nothing less than the subjugation of all the peoples in Judaea proper and many surrounding regions; plus the gathering of taxes and troops for service to the emperor, Caesar Augustus.

Of late, the Roman troops had been in rabid pursuit of the Nabataeans of Petra, and in search of their hidden sanctuary. Keepers of the ancient trade routes to the east and south, the Nabataeans were an affront to Augustus' authority and, more important, were keeping riches from the vaults of Rome. Rome's orders were clear. Keep the gold flowing. The Nabataeans were a clot in that flow.

So they'd put a handpicked lackey—Pilate—in control of sixty-odd centuries composed of soldiers, some cavalry, archers, and support staff, and told him to wipe out the resistance and be back by sunset.

Months later, they were still here. The Nabataeans were a sneaky bunch, and the Romans had wasted a lot of good sandal leather chasing them around, all to no avail. Every morning brought dead soldiers, their throats slit in the night by unseen assassins. Hot trails in the sand suddenly went cold. And the locals, even when "encouraged" with various forms of torture, were no help whatsoever.

Things seemed to be going better when the Romans surprised an armed party of Nabataeans in the desert almost a week ago. They hadn't really talked, but when their leaders were nailed to the crucifixes to die slowly in the sun, one's delirium had indicated at least a direction in which to head. Between screams, he begged to face northward so his spirit could see its way home.

The dirty business done, and with more casualties than professional soldiers such as he should have incurred, Pilate marched his men north. A scouting patrol had found the half-dead Zoth, as well as signs that he'd not been alone. The other trail, of course, had been wiped clean by the sands.

Fate, it seemed, had united the two forces.

Later that night, Zoth was escorted to Pilate's tent. He looked up to see the star, still maddeningly pulsating, mocking him with each step. Zoth spit at it.

Pilate's tent was a lushly appointed, portable Roman apartment, a stark contrast to Zoth's accommodations. The golden pitchers, miniature statues of Roman deities, bust of Augustus, and screened partitions that adorned the tent must have required the toil of a number of beasts to transport them. Zoth was impressed again. The Romans knew how to travel in comfort.

"Enter, Zoth," said Pilate as his prisoner paused between the guards at the entrance. Armorless yet no less auspicious, the commander reclined on a sofa. A fire burned in an urn in the center of the tent, and several servants waited in its darker recesses. A few officers were scattered about on stools or pillows. Some held goblets of red wine, some munched on bits of succulent food. All watched him with expressions of anticipated amusement.

The fools, thought Zoth before addressing them in an unctuous tone. "My noble lords, I'm indebted to you. For my life. For this meeting. For this opportunity to serve great Caesar."

"Yes, yes, get on with it! Let's have some tricks!" blurted an officer more wine than patience in him. Scattered laughter followed, and Pilate smirked.

"It's the Circus Minimus!" catcalled another, earning even more laughs.

"Those whom you seek, and those whom I seek, are one and the same," intoned the dark lord. His tone and appearance put a stop to the laughter. Zoth had everyone's attention.

Sweeping silently to the center of the gathering, Zoth assessed each man, finishing on Pilate. He drew himself up, and with a flourish of his black and lavender robes, spun his web. Fixing his eyes on the Roman commander, Zoth said, "Allow me to reveal that which you would know."

He crossed to one of the dividers and removed a decorative shield that hung there. The highly polished circle of bronze had served as a mirror. But its smooth, reflective face would soon show more than Pilate's stubbled visage.

Zoth turned the shield to face the now-attentive group of Romans, then released it. It hung in the air as if on an invisible hook, shining ominously. Murmurs of awe, appreciation, and some apprehension came from the men.

Zoth turned to face the shield. Those men to the side could see him whispering soft, wicked words to it. Then he blew a stream of hot breath onto its surface. Stepping back and to the side, Zoth closed his eyes and folded his arms. Quietly, hoarsely, he breathed the words, "Now, behold…"

The audience leaned forward.

The sorcerer's breath had fogged the mirrored surface. Instead of clearing in the warm evening air, the fog became a three-dimensional, cumulous mist that lifted and swirled over the face of the shield. As it swirled it grew, and a hole, a tiny eye, opened in the storm brewing there. Larger and larger the cloudy tempest grew until it framed the edge of the shield. The opening at its center grew as well, all the way to the edge of the shield, and to the amazement of all watching, images appeared and moved over the silvery surface.

Sand, leagues and leagues of moving, blowing sand, flickered into view. The watchers gasped. Forgotten goblets fell from awestruck hands, their contents pooling unnoticed on the carpet of the tent's floor.

The men watching were transported in their minds to the scene unfolding before them. It was as if they were traveling over the sand itself, moving with the speed of a hundred horses, eating up the distances as if covering them with the steps of a giant. Chunks of rock rose in the distance, resolved into a cliff face worn with crags and fissures. Slowly, a reddish glow appeared, revealing a secret opening in the rock, the hidden entrance to the Nabataean fortress of Petra.

The image flashed, and a new sequence began. A dizzying, bird's-eye view of a large Roman army appeared. The panorama offered the rapt audience what looked like a play, with performers bustling about. Then the perspective changed, swooping in to an army engaged in battle, although the word "battle" barely applied. Blood-frenzied Romans slaughtered thousands of Petran citizens who had emerged to do battle on the sandy plain outside their sanctuary. The thick, oily smoke of war hung like a grim canopy over the carnage.

The tent's audience could smell the familiar, mingled aromas of death and war. Their eyes beheld victory. Nabataean warriors were being gored and sliced open by Roman swords and spears.

The scene shifted again, taking those watching inside the city that had been hidden from them for so long. Now the Romans were making the most of the undefended caves. Laughing centurions raped the women of Petra before setting them afire; small children were held up by their hair, their screams of terror cut short as Roman daggers slit ugly red gashes across their throats.

The soldiers witnessing the carnage on the shield were a bit sickened by the scene, even if it was accurate. But the view that followed heartened them — huge coffers of gold, fat rolls of silk, dark jars of spices, flaming piles of bitumen, and other riches.

The view shifted again to a rocky overlook to reveal Pilate, proud and regal, surveying the scene. But as his image grew to fill the mirrored surface, his expression changed from arrogant confidence to horror. The Pilate in the mirror looked down to see blood flowing freely from wounds in his palms and feet. Then he collapsed to his knees and howled in fury at the sky.

Sweat beaded on Zoth's face and his eyes rolled back into his head so that only the whites were visible. He'd invested all he had in the shield's spell, but it had spun beyond his control and answered to a higher power.

Still the spectacle unfurled. The surface clouded for an instant, and suddenly the Seven Hills of Rome filled it. And Rome was burning. Crumbling. Lost. Fleeing crowds vacated the temples, blood filled the fountains and baths, armies lay dead and dying in the streets, and the Senate itself was aflame.

With a *kraannng!* the shield fell from its invisible harness and rang with a death knell as it hit the floor of the tent. Everyone awoke from their dreamy state with a start, unsure of what they had just seen. Even Zoth, who had thought himself in control of the show, was shaken by the last vision and how a power greater than he had manipulated him so easily.

The small group, at first sobered by what they'd seen, suddenly burst into an angry chorus of shouts, condemnations, questions, and accusations. A shout from Pilate, now standing and quaking with anger, silenced them.

"What is this you would show us, dark one? Our victory or our death? For surely that was Rome in peril! Speak! Who would threaten our fatherland?" screamed Pilate.

"I...I..." Zoth stammered, but only for a moment. Quickly gathering his composure, the snake began again to spew his venomous lies.

"I can only open the window to the future, as one who holds aside the curtain. The interpretation is yours to make. However...I would suggest that what we saw were, ah, pathways. One clearly led to the defeat of your enemy, and the other to the downfall of Rome. Think of what you saw as possible courses of action."

None too certain that what he was saying was at all true, Zoth nevertheless achieved his goal. The military commanders agreed that the army would mobilize in the morning, execute a stealth march to the hidden fortress, and eliminate the apparent threat to Rome.

As the group began to break up, Pilate took Zoth aside and asked him icily, "Are you certain you can lead us to them?"

"Absolutely, my lord. It's a day's march, two at the most. And they'll be taken completely by surprise," assured Zoth.

"They'd better be. Or your head will be taken by surprise, by my own sword." The legate turned on his heel and left a shaken Zoth.

No matter, Zoth mused as he walked slowly back to his tent between his two guards. *I could care less what becomes of you, your ridiculous army, and your sad little empire. I know that Melchior lives, and I only need you to deliver him to me.*

CHAPTER TWENTY-FIVE

The twelve Watchers on the Hill of Vaus were no longer watching.

The star had appeared at last. The prophecy was made reality. The archangels visited and pronounced the coming of the king. And they told the Watchers what to do.

So the keepers of the holy star left their post atop the Hill of Vaus. Clad in their white, hooded robes, they made their way slowly down the hill, took up the packs prepared months before, and filed down to the shore of their lonely isle. They entered their longboats and began to row westward.

CHAPTER TWENTY-SIX

Early in the morning following the celestial vision above Petra, the Magi met in private. They agreed that there was a new sense of urgency and that any further time spent in Petra was wasted at best, disastrous at worst.

At least now, they knew some key facts. The star they'd beheld in the west was indeed a herald. A powerful king had been born, a god, mightier than any other on earth. They had to make their way to a place called the City of David, in the kingdom of Judaea to the northwest. And if they didn't get there soon, they were done for.

The song of the star, playing in the backs of their minds like a soft tune, hadn't lost any of its urgency. If anything, it sounded stronger. Each of the Magi knew in his heart that their task was incomplete. However, they still didn't understand why they had been chosen or what role they were to fulfill.

Gaspar and Balthazar left to find Barir, Shin-shin, and the remainder of their party. Melchior went to find Sheik Shareef to thank him and secure supplies for what he presumed would be the final leg of their journey.

Not surprisingly, they found Barir practicing close-quarters combat with some of the Nabataean soldiers in one of the open-air square in the heart of Petra. The combatants used blunt wooden practice weapons and had worked up a fine, dust-encrusted sweat. Balthazar left to find Shin-shin, and Gaspar walked up to address the men.

"My lord," said Barir between heavy pants, "I've just been showing our hosts some of the finer points of defensive combat here."

The lesson looked to be well taught. Two of Barir's adversaries sat on their backsides, stunned. The third seemed a reluctant student.

As the leader of a warrior tribe where the strong were rewarded and the weak were killed, Gaspar was impressed. Barir was the kind of fighter he knew he could count on in a fight. He made a mental note of this fact.

"Come," said the magus, "we leave today. Balthazar and Melchior have gone to find Shin-shin and the sheik. Let us find the rest of your party and assemble in the main hall."

Barir bowed low to his opposition, who nervously returned the gesture without taking their eyes off him.

"Good!" Barir laughed. "You're learning. Fight well, my brothers."

Balthazar found Shin-shin playing with a throng of Petra's olive-skinned children, chasing a ball constructed from an inflated goat's stomach. Watching quietly from an alcove above, Balthazar could see no rule or reason to the game. The ball was simply being kicked and chased about by the horde, whose members laughed with glee.

For a moment, Balthazar considered leaving Shin-shin here. The child could do little to aid them on their journey. Here, Shin-shin would be safe to heal, to grow . . . to survive. But in his heart, Balthazar knew that Shin-shin had been chosen, just as he had been. And like it or not, the child had a destiny to fulfill.

Balthazar hadn't quite descended all the stone stairs to the floor of the chamber when a squeal of "Master!" reached his ears. Shin-shin leapt into his arms with surprising familiarity. Balthazar was at once shocked and touched. He understood, finally, how life altering their encounter with the desert, and with death, had been for all of them. And holding the child against his chest, he renewed his vow to safeguard Shin-shin from whatever lay ahead.

Melchior found the sheik with his retinue of advisors. They sat in council together in the small antechamber off the main hall. His son Omar was there as well, and he nodded in greeting as two guards led Melchior in.

"Ah, Lord Melchior, we were just discussing you and your companions. Enter. You are welcome. You are welcome!" said the jolly chieftain of Petra.

"Thank you. Ah, gracious hosts, as I'm sure you've heard by now, much was revealed to us last night." Melchior paused for a moment. He wasn't sure just how much the Crone had conveyed or how much she had actually taken in, but once again, Melchior felt that sharing as little as possible about the journey was best for all involved.

"You've been kind hosts, and verily, saved our lives. But I must beg for two last favors. Your leave to depart your fair city and supplies to take us farther on our quest," said Melchior. "Once our mission is complete, you shall be repaid threefold by me. On this, I give my word."

"Of course, of course," Shareef said hurriedly, as if Melchior were asking him to pass the bread. "I now know you to be true brothers of the Bedouin, and that you would guard the secrets of our home as if it were your own. Blindfolded, you were led in; with open eyes you shall depart. And we shall outfit you with whatever you require—food, water, beasts, servants—"

There was a commotion in the other doorway. A badly scraped, dirty youth stumbled in, gasping for air, and fell into the arms of Omar.

Omar looked up quickly. "He's a sentry from the southern outskirts, a watcher guarding our hidden entrance," he told Melchior. He reached for a skin of water and poured some into the youth's mouth. The sentry coughed hoarsely, but he seemed to gather the strength to speak.

Before he could, however, there came a coarse laugh from a darkened corner. The Crone was in a fit, her body contorting with every vulture-like guffaw. Everyone stared at her, waiting for her to deliver her gloomy prediction. Shareef had a troubled look on his face, as if seeing the Crone so many times in such a short period of time couldn't be a good thing.

There was no need for the sentry to speak. She'd already absorbed the knowledge he carried. The Crone swiveled her gnarled head, sweeping her beady eyes over the group. "They're coming!" she hissed.

"The Romans," muttered Omar with deadly resignation.

Melchior's head snapped up. Instantly, a visage appeared in his mind, and with the clarity of conviction, under his breath, he quietly cursed, "Zoth!"

CHAPTER TWENTY-SEVEN

The Khazneh, if it was indeed possible, was in an even greater state of chaos. The large hall, last seen by the Magi as a marketplace, had been transformed into a giant staging area for war.

Infantry, archers, and cavalry now milled about where traders, vendors, and middlemen once did. In fact, many of the faces were the same, but their roles had changed, their demeanor now displaying the heavy burden of their future confrontation with quiet resolve.

Watching the scene below from a naturally formed parapet in the stone, Melchior was saddened. The once joyous, bustling place now was muted by impending death. Rationally, he mused, *this place, this secret Petra, couldn't remain secret forever.* Melchior suspected that the betrayal of Petra's location was Zoth's doing, and it confirmed his nagging suspicion that even the desert sun couldn't kill his twisted kin. That betrayal, and the inevitable onslaught of the legions of Rome, was a palpable turning point. Another layer of the old world was peeling back to reveal the wet, pink flesh of a newer, more vulnerable reality.

Walking down and through the throngs, he saw husbands kissing wives, mothers stroking thatches of dark hair from the eyes of their sons, young women and old grimly taking their place in line to fight, and brothers giving a final playful push to those too young yet to die on the field of battle. The atmosphere was morose, thick with muffled sobs and forced smiles.

Melchior searched, then wove his way to his party. Barir and Gaspar, surveying the horses they'd secured from the sheik, were in the middle of a discussion about the division of the load between the beasts when a loud cry erupted a few paces behind them. Turning on his heel, Melchior saw the blur of Shin-shin flying to encircle Barir's waist. The guardian and the guarded seemed quite pleased to see each other, and although he couldn't make out the words, he sensed Barir's pride in the youth's recovery.

Although the reunion of master and apprentice had already occurred, a more formal recognition of the resumption of their roles was evidently necessary. Balthazar followed quietly behind Shin-shin, his soft, cat-walking-on-eggshells gait as familiar to Melchior now as it was strange. Embarrassed, Shin-shin stood apart from Barir and bowed deeply in honor of Balthazar, murmuring softly, "Master."

Balthazar acknowledged his student with a barely noticeable bend at the waist, but a smile flickered beneath his long, wispy moustache. The child had recovered miraculously in such a short span of time, and Balthazar suspected that he had the power of the star to thank for that.

The rest of their entourage, some twelve men in all, seemed an island of optimism in the ocean of sorrow surrounding them. Gathering together, the three wise men held council to one side of the group. Though anxious to resume their quest and filled with anticipation for what lay ahead, the reality of the Petran's situation didn't elude them.

"It'll be like reaping wheat...a sickle through a blade of dry grass," intoned Gaspar as he surveyed with obvious disappointment the Nabataean "army's" preparations. "They're no match for a battle-hardened unit, let alone a legion of Roman foot soldiers."

"Fight or flee? The fates of empires have been decided on

such a choice. However, I suspect that even the addition of our few knives wouldn't turn the tide of such a battle—even given our considerable…advantages," stated the Asian magus.

"I don't run from any fight," pronounced Gaspar.

"But, my friend, this isn't your fight," said Omar, who came up to the three with Barir. "I admit, I don't understand your purpose or even know your destination, but our paths part here. You have a calling; we have a responsibility. Neither takes precedence. You must go."

Omar looked nobler. Clad in the light, sun-beaten armor and dark robes of his people, he stood a bit taller and looked even more defiant and handsome. His eyes glinted with determination.

Perhaps they're not lost after all, thought Melchior. "We must leave," he agreed, but his voice held no conviction. "Someday, we'll repay you and your people for the kindness you've shown us. We owe you our lives."

"Aha, but you mustn't leave empty-handed, my friends!" bellowed the portly Sheik Shareef. He bustled through the crowd, parting it with his girth. A line of servants followed him.

"My Sheik Shareef, you're gracious indeed to see your unworthy guests off. Such an honor was unnecessary," said Balthazar, bowing low in respect.

"Psha! It's I who has been honored by your presence. I only wish that our parting…" He paused and swiveled his head sadly to take in the war preparations around them, "Was under…happier…circumstances.

"But we're traders here, and no one leaves Petra empty-handed!" He clapped his hands, and the servants stepped forward, each bearing a small wooden box intricately carved and clasped and bound in bronze.

"My lord Balthazar," Shareef said solemnly, "I sense that you're a man of intelligence, inner strength, and peace. As my people say, *Your sands hold many secrets*. I think you'll be called upon by the gods to sacrifice something great and dear to you. May it be this gift I give to you."

Shareef opened the first box and hooked a finger into the syrupy liquid within. He sniffed the finger delicately, then flicked it, launching thick droplets into the air. Every nostril for hundreds of paces around drank in the heady scent.

"A gift of frankincense," Shareef continued, "a thing dear to Petrans and many others in lands far and near. Petra is one of the few places where it can be found. Its scent may heal your aches, or it may have more mercantile uses in the world beyond our city."

Balthazar bowed again. "Sheik Shareef, your gift is too great. But I accept it, with lesser grace than that with which it was given. I'm familiar with its powers, and I thank you."

Turning to Gaspar, Omar said with a smile, "My dark friend, you were nearly dead when you came to us. But your inner fire is too great a flame to be snuffed by the mere sun. So I give you the gift of myrrh, the perfumed oil treasured by Egyptians and other noble peoples. Those you anoint with it will be blessed by the gods, and their lives will be strengthened."

The servant holding the box of myrrh opened its lid. Shareef dipped his fingertip into the unguent and gestured for Gaspar to lower his head. Rising to his tiptoes, the sheik smeared it on the magus' brow, below his turban.

Gaspar's face was stern. "I've learned much from you, Sheik, and your family. May the gods of war smile on you today," was all he could say, but his voice betrayed deep emotion.

Shareef only nodded, grinning. He turned to Melchior. "And last, King Melchior. Yes, your noble bearing betrays you, good king, and even the hidden city of Petra has heard of the wonders of your Arabian kingdom." He smiled slyly. "I'd dearly love to see it with my own eyes. Heh-heh, yes, I would."

Bowing, Melchior said, "Sheik, you'd be a most welcome guest there. It would be an honor to repay your kindness to us."

Shareef again offered his slightly giddy smile, pleased by the formal invitation. "But what gift have I that's fit to give a king?" he said. "There's much that's valuable here, certainly. So I give you two things: a hundred talents of gold to serve you on your journey and ensure you travel as a king should, and the oath of the Bedouin, who promise to come when you call."

Humbled, Melchior inclined his head. "Indeed, I'm in your debt. The people of Petra are in good hands in these troubled times. Many thanks, Sheik Shareef." He extended his hand, which Shareef used to pull Melchior into a bear hug. Gaspar laughed. Balthazar looked on in mild amusement.

Releasing Melchior, Shareef said loudly, "Now you must be off before the sun sits too high in the sky. Travel at night, and avoid the main passes, for Caesar's troops are everywhere."

They all embraced in the Bedouin custom, even Gaspar, then the Magi and those few soldiers and servants who had survived the desert took their mounts. With waves and a few backward glances, they and the Petran guides who would see them safely on their way swept out into the winding ravine that led to the outside world.

Shin-shin, galloping alongside Barir on a small Arabian pony, darkly assessed the Petrans' chances against a Roman army. "Will they...?" Shin-shin shouted to Barir above the echoing din.

Barir avoided the child's eye and didn't answer.

They rode at a steady pace for a little over an hour. The early morning sun was not yet too hot for riding hard and fast.

But the sun had a new companion in the sky, the star. It now burned brightly night and day, its supernatural glow rivaling the sun's fire. The star's prominence haunted the Magi. They knew that time was now more precious than ever.

That's why, making their way north and west, the Magi were torn between the duty left behind and the responsibility that lay before them.

Gaspar, in the lead, suddenly pulled up, wheeled his mount fiercely about, and brought the entourage to an abrupt halt.

"What is it?" asked an alarmed Melchior.

"I'm going back. To fight. To save the lives of those who saved mine. Star or no star, I know what's right, and I'm tired of running." With those words, he drove his heels into the already steaming, streaming sides of his horse and galloped back toward Petra.

Barir said, "He's right, you know."

Melchior nodded somberly. He sighed, resigned already to the fact that they were going back, and said what was on everyone's mind as he glanced at the sky.

"I know...but we keep getting delayed."

CHAPTER TWENTY-EIGHT

Sixteen strong, the pitiful little force retraced its steps, galloping back toward Petra.

It was one of the desert's dead days; no wind whipped the waves of sand, and the sun scorched with steady severity. Even those creatures that normally existed in the sands lay listlessly, peering from whatever shady nook they could locate. It was a fitting environment for what would come to pass.

They made the journey back in almost half the time. Peering ahead, Melchior saw Gaspar, leading by twenty horse lengths, rein in his horse at the edge of the plateau. Pulling his own steed in beside Gaspar's, Melchior looked down into the small, cliff-ringed canyon that served as the courtyard for the entrance to Petra and caught his breath.

They witnessed what seemed a bizarre choreography performed to some grotesque piece of music. Paired up in macabre dances, combatants moved with a fury minimized by the distance from which they were viewed. It was, nonetheless, complete carnage. The battle had begun.

The Petrans, it seemed, had decided to take the fight to the Romans outside the hidden city in the large open canyon that held the secret passage in its walls. Below the Magi, on the left, small groups of Nabataean infantry and cavalry, if the lightly armed and even more lightly armored men and boys could be described as such, were still entering the fray.

Looking to his right, Melchior assessed the situation. Hundreds upon hundreds of Roman soldiers queued up in a narrow, twisting ravine leading to the open area that was now the theater of war. The small number of Petrans versus the overwhelming number of Romans waiting to take their turn in the bloodbath forecast the outcome with a grim certainty.

Gaspar flashed his ivory smile as he turned to look at his comrades. "Well," he said with a steely irony in his voice, "at last, we fight!"

He vaulted from his horse and dashed toward the narrow, twisting path gouged down the cliff wall into the canyon. It was too narrow to accommodate the mounts. Anyone brave enough to enter the fray was also smart enough not to try riding down the path. Why risk dying en route and missing the joy of being butchered alive?

The rest of the caravan watched Gaspar disappear over the cliff's edge, then dismounted and chased after him, with the exception of a few attendants who hung back to tend the animals.

Taking charge in this martial situation came naturally to Gaspar. Melchior and Balthazar unconsciously followed his lead. As they picked their way down the treacherous path, Gaspar shouted commands over his shoulder, formulating an extemporaneous battle plan.

"Try to stay together! We'll make our way to the entrance. The Petrans have to retreat soon. They won't be able to hold long against the Romans out here. The real fight starts in there!"

"The *real* fight?" murmured Balthazar, eyeing the battle, which was suddenly not so small and removed.

"And watch each other's backs!" shouted Gaspar, then, reaching the floor of the canyon, ignored his own advice and tore off into the heart of the battle.

Melchior, a few men behind Gaspar, turned to Balthazar.

"Stay with me. Barir and I will get you and Shin-shin safely to the entrance, and then we'll go help with the fighting!" he shouted above the din.

Balthazar mutely nodded his thanks, then turned to nod at Shin-Shin behind him. Hard on the heels of Shin-Shin, Barir drew his blade.

As Melchior reached the foot of the path, the battle overwhelmed his senses. The sickly sweet smell of burning flesh, the soot of oily fires, the stench of urine and vomit, the rank odor of disemboweled organs, the clouds of boot-stirred dust all blended in a unique, disgusting, gut-wrenching stench. It was a smell that, once in your nostrils, would never leave your memory. Here, for Melchior, it sprang to life again.

A few of their group had dashed off after Gaspar as rear guard. The remainder gathered at the bottom of the pathway, a hundred or so yards away from the fighting. The ring of metal on metal, the shouts of victors and the screams of victims, the pounding of so many hearts being pushed beyond their limits, deafened them.

"My liege!" shouted Barir, assuming leadership of the group. "We should skirt around, avoid engagement until the child and Lord Balthazar are safely back in the fortress!"

"Make it so!" Melchior replied, earning himself scornful looks from said child and lord.

"We need no protection," Balthazar retorted mildly, and Shin-shin added a saucy "Hmmpf!" for good measure.

Archers, Melchior observed as they worked their way along the battle's periphery, and he saw the Romans lying on the ground with shafts embedded in their chests, throats, legs, and heads. *They held the high ground for a while.*

His eyes scanned the walls above, replaying in his mind's eye what he suspected had already taken place. He knew many of the Petran archers were mere boys and a few girls. They'd have hidden themselves among the rocky crags and boulders and shallow clefts that made up the canyon's walls, waiting until the Roman advance guard were well within range. Then the air must have been thick with arrows, trapping the Roman soldiers in their rainstorm of death.

But the Romans, many of them seasoned veterans with a few such surprise attacks under their belts, soon regrouped and covered themselves with their curved shields. The shields turned the arrows and soon the Petrans had exhausted their aerial arsenal and were reduced to flinging their bows in vain. They'd killed many, but they'd merely inflicted a flesh wound on the hulking beast of Rome.

Then the Roman archers would have come up through the dark orifice that was the mouth of the ravine, Melchior guessed, as they passed Petran bodies pierced with Iberian shafts. They'd taken their time, until those remaining amongst the rocks fled. Soon the points of the legion's swords, spears and javelins faced the entrance to Petra, not more than three hundred paces away. There was no escape, save through the wall of Rome.

High on a hastily raised platform in the rear, safely out of range of both arrow and sword thrust, the legate Pilate surveyed the battle with irritation and disgust. The plan was simple, yet hideously efficient. After an inevitable skirmish, great fires would be set at the mouth of the cavern city, and the inhabitants would either be suffocated in a sooty blanket of death or starved by weeks of siege.

Same old siege story. Or was it? Why was this taking so long?

He issued orders to runners, who dashed through the lines to deliver them to the centurions, who in turn screamed what was hopefully an accurate description of infantry strategy to the foot soldiers. He could see that the bizarre canyon in which the legion found itself was confusing the normally excellent tactical expertise of the troops.

"Arrrrgh! By the blood of Mars, this—is—madness!"

screamed Pilate, hammering his fist on the wooden rail of his platform. Shouting to no one in particular and everyone in general, he bellowed, "They're not staying in formation! Idiots! Stay together!"

A tribune answered him after a moment. "It matters not, my lord. They are rabble...uncivilized brutes. They're no match for our strength. It'll just take a little longer to crush them against the wall."

On cue, thirty or so yards from where they watched, a Roman legionnaire crossed swords with an older, bearded Petran. Displaying a fluidity the Roman didn't possess, the Petran parried a blow and spun in a tight circle to relieve the Roman of his head with a slash of his blade. The head thudded to the ground, a look of confusion frozen for eternity on its face.

Turning, Pilate grabbed the tribune and screamed in his face, "Longer? It's going to take weeks at this rate! Get down there and fight, you coward. Show Rome that you're good for more than filling my ears with your nonsense!" He shoved the man off the platform.

The tribune fell the few feet to the ground and looked up at the platform with a mixture of horror and resentment.

"Bring me back ten heads for every Roman that falls!" shouted Pilate, and the tribune melted away into the frenzy of battle.

Crossing to the rear of the platform, Pilate cried down to the centurion below, the leader of one of the many centuries of men held in reserve, "Commit the rest! Get in there! *Wipe them out!*"

"Patience, my lord," murmured Zoth, placing his alabaster hand on the shoulder of the legate, "Patience."

Pilate cringed back as if an icy blast had hit him, and took a step away from the dark sorcerer. He shrugged Zoth's hand away as if it pained him.

Pilate was still uncomfortable with his new aide-de-camp, and as his men were being butchered, the thought occurred to him that Zoth had set him up for defeat. Pilate was just about to have him dragged away and cut to pieces when a shout from below drew his attention.

"Legate, reinforcements arrive!" cried one of the platform sentries, following the pointing hands of the guards below.

And indeed, to one side of the melee, a group of men were making their way down the side of the canyon via a pathway hidden to Roman eyes.

"Melchior!" cursed Zoth under his breath.

"They aren't many, my lord; perhaps a score at best... but how many more will come?" the sentry cried in anguish.

Pilate looked at the group first with renewed frustration, then a bit of skepticism. They didn't look like...reinforcements.

Taking Pilate aside, Zoth spoke again, his tone supplicating. "These...barbarians are of no concern to you or Rome. They pose no immediate threat. They are, however, of some concern to me. They left me to die. Their deaths, well, would mean much to me. And I would be...grateful to you."

Pilate eyed him warily and said, "If they aren't killed in the battle, you may do with them as you please."

Zoth nodded and bent his eyes and his will on finding Melchior in the fracas, for he and the rest of the caravan had vanished from view.

Their plan to stay on the fringe of the fighting worked well for a while, until an unfortunate finger of rock jutting out from the side of the canyon wall forced the group into the heart of the battle.

Melchior and Balthazar still couldn't see Gaspar. They could, however, see the flash of red tunics and iron armor that marked the Romans all around them. They ran, then came up short, suddenly surrounded by an entire century of Romans, half on horseback, who were moving forward to reinforce the front line.

Who was more surprised, the caravan, quickly thrust

into the heat of battle, or the Romans, who turned to find an unexpected enemy force in their midst?

Who attacked first, however, was easy to tell: Barir, brandishing his blade, drove forward shouting "Arabia!" and clashed with the nearest mounted Roman.

Like a gigantic bonfire suddenly ignited, the hearts of the caravan members were filled with bloodlust. Swinging his own sword, Melchior joined in the fight, hewing away at the foot soldiers swarming around him. Balthazar had also surprisingly produced a sword, a slender shaft of bright steel that he'd carried within his bedroll. He gracefully arced and sliced at the occasional Roman who penetrated the circle the remainder of the caravan held to protect them.

Anarchy reigned. Swords glinted as they hacked and thrust. Blood splattered; errant limbs flew through the air. They were surrounded and outmatched.

Balthazar sent a silent summons with his mind: *Gaspar – we need you!*

A few hundred paces away, the bloodlust was upon Gaspar, too. He faced off against a duo of Roman soldiers. Familiar red motes of energy orbited and spiraled around Gaspar's form as he unleashed his warrior might.

The soldier on his right, assuming an overmatch, thrust his sword straight toward Gaspar's chest. Parrying the thrust outward, Gaspar spun in a tight circle and hewed the man's sword arm off just above the elbow. Screaming in agony, the man fell to his knees. Gaspar kicked him backward and leapt over him toward the second soldier. He sliced open that man's chest with two crisscross slashes.

"Araahhhh!" Gaspar bellowed, finishing him off with a swing of his blade across the man's throat.

Romans within ten feet of him fell back, reassessing their opponent with newfound respect and fear.

As he eyed his adversaries, Gaspar heard Balthazar's call. With a final glare, he turned and hacked his way toward his comrades.

Enemies pressed all around, separating those of the caravan into small islands in a sea of carnage. Melchior and a few men had waded farther into the throng of Romans. Using a combination of magic and metal, Melchior held his ground.

A line of soldiers, fresh from the rear and six men across, charged Melchior. Summoning his strength, Melchior waved his arm across their path. The men flew backward, slamming into another line of advancing troops.

The old Petran fighting alongside Melchior shouted, "Why don't you just knock them all down?"

Melchior leaned on his sword, panting heavily. "Too many...too hard," he wheezed. "Too many —"

And he swung his sword as another soldier rushed up and engaged him, with a hundred more coming up behind.

Not far away, though it seemed leagues, Barir led Balthazar and Shin-shin toward the entrance to Petra. Their trek was laborious and circuitous, and the press of combatants was only getting thicker.

Then they burst into an open space. It was a bit too open. It seemed as if the sea of fighters had parted before them. Barir, his arms and sides already burning with exhaustion, swiveled his head to see why.

Two gargantuan Romans, centurions by their garb, stood before the group. Shining with sweat and spattered with blood, they dwarfed even Barir. One held a ruddy sword in his left hand, and a decapitated head by the hair in his other. The other Roman twisted and jerked his spear from the gut of a fallen Petran and, hefting it, pointed its gore covered tip menacingly at Barir.

Barir sidestepped to place himself between the Romans and his charges. Planting his feet, he swung his broad Arabian sword in an arc. "No..." he said dangerously, bracing himself for attack.

Sizing up Barir, the two Romans chuckled and stepped forward.

"Aiii-ya!" Shin-shin screamed and somersaulted through the air, landing lightly in front of Barir and facing the two brutes.

Balthazar vaulted over Barir's shoulder. He struck a martial pose beside Shin-shin, his long, slender sword re-sheathed on his back. Hands poised, he held his position, facing a man thrice his size.

The two soldiers stopped short at the appearance of a child and a skinny old man, then laughed outright.

Balthazar warned, "Please stand down. We don't wish to hurt you. Lay down your arms, and leave in peace."

"Oh, that's good!" said the Roman with the spear.

"What's next, babies and old women?" the centurion with the sword asked the other, laughing hideously. He swiped at Shin-shin's head with his sword, knocking the child's cap to the ground.

A pile of thick, beautiful jet-black hair came tumbling down, framing the deadly serious face of Shin-shin, a young...girl?

"Oh, this just keeps getting better!" howled the soldier with the spear. "It's a little girl!"

"Girl? *Girl*?!" snarled Shin-shin through gritted teeth, with a ferocity that gave the two Romans pause. "I am a warrior of Chengdu," she threatened.

Barir, his mouth agape, scrambled to translate the scene. First, his mind registered anger at Balthazar and Shin-shin's stepping into harm's way. Then, *Shin-shin is a...girl?*

The situation then exploded with lightening-quick speed. Shin-shin crouched, whipped out a leg and jammed her heel into the sword carrier's groin. The Roman doubled over with a loud moan. With equal speed, Balthazar stepped toward the other centurion and deftly grasped the shaft of the spear the soldier was jabbing at Balthazar's chest. The Roman tried to tug it back, or thrust the spear point into his enemy, but Balthazar refused to release it. The massive Roman simply was not strong enough to wrest his weapon from the grip of the tiny man from China. Instead of releasing the shaft, Balthazar effortlessly jammed it backward three times, driving the butt end of the spear into the Roman's face. Blood spurted from the soldier's smashed nose, and his head swayed drunkenly, like a cobra bewitched by the music of a flute.

Balthazar twisted the spear, disarming the man. Holding it at its center, he cudgeled the soldier about the face and neck with both ends of the spear, finishing him off with a wicked spin and a backhand blow with the butt of the shaft. The Roman fell flat on his back, unconscious.

Meanwhile, Shin-shin waited for the other Roman to straighten up before renewing her attack. Quick as a blink, she leapt forward and took two steps up the Roman's chest. Pirouetting around, she locked her thin but iron-strong legs around the behemoth's neck and pummeled his face with a flurry of chops, slaps, and punches. He staggered backward under the attack, swatting at her as he would a fly, but somehow Shin-shin maintained her hold. She then flipped backward off the man, landing lightly and still facing her opponent.

Enraged and embarrassed, the Roman spun to address her and charged, brandishing his sword. The little girl leapt vertically into the air, cried "Aiii-yaa!" again, and lashed a leg out as she spun a tight orbit. The blow caught the Roman cleanly on the jaw, and he collapsed in heap, as unconscious as his comrade lying beside him. Everyone witnessing the lopsided fight stood paralyzed with amazement.

"Tut-tut," the master chided the girl poised above the fallen soldier. "You are overly dramatic. Too…showy. You give far too many opportunities to your opponent. Remember and learn—quick like the tongue of the frog, not slow like the swallow of the snake."

"Yes, master," Shin-shin replied, looking humbled and disappointed.

The centurion who'd fallen to Balthazar groaned and struggled to rise. Without looking, the master whipped out with his foot and smartly struck the soldier in the face. The centurion's head crunched back onto the sand.

Without pausing, Balthazar finished his assessment of his pupil's efforts. "But it was effective. I am…pleased."

The little girl beamed and bent to pick up her cap. But before she could, another hand passed it to her. In that isolated moment in time, Barir looked at Shin-shin with new eyes. "You're, you're, a gi—" he stuttered.

"A woman, you mean?" she said proudly, and shook her hair back in a statement of feminine strength. "Yes. Will that be a problem?"

"Uh, no…" Barir shook his head, still staring. As if the clouds were clearing, he realized why he had always felt so protective of her.

"Come. No time now for introductions. We must make for the entrance," said Balthazar, suddenly in command. Barir looked at him with new wonder as well, amazed at the strength and skill the seemingly old man had shown. Was nothing as it seemed, these days?

"No, it's not," answered the magus, reading his thoughts. And together, the three dashed off.

When Melchior and Gaspar finally met, each bore scratches, slices, and layers of gore, the badges of the battles they'd waged. Both were breathing heavily.

"This is hopeless, my friend," said Melchior, panting.

"I know," Gaspar replied dourly. "We've got to get the Petrans to retreat to the caves. We'll all be slaughtered out here!"

He looked at Melchior. "I'm sorry I made you come back, my friend."

Melchior smiled weakly but bravely back at him. He replied, "I'm not."

Out of nowhere, Omar charged up to them, with more Petrans on his heels. "My lords! I am so very, very honored to see you. We need every sword!" he shouted, smiling through the grime that covered his noble face.

"Omar, you must fall back and try to hold the entrance. The Romans are overwhelming us," Gaspar said, cutting short the reunion.

"Yes, but we'll never hold it. They are too many. They'll take Petra," said Omar grimly.

Omar knew he was on a suicide mission, and that he and his soldiers had come to fight, not to defend. They wanted only to take as many Romans down with them as they could.

"But...what if they couldn't get in?" mused Melchior, an idea beginning to glow in his mind. "How long could your people last in there?"

"Well, forever, I guess," replied Omar. "We have cisterns full of water and food to last for months and months. But how —"

Not waiting for an answer, Melchior dashed off toward the entrance to the hidden city.

"Leave that to him. Let us get back to work," Gaspar said darkly. Gripping his dripping scimitar, he led Omar and the others back into the heart of the battle.

There was less fighting near the entrance as Melchior ran through the fissure in the rock. The Romans hadn't penetrated that deep yet, although they weren't far away. Stopping at a point where the ravine squeezed to its narrowest width, Melchior looked up at the towering walls of rock. Sheathing his sword, he paced back and forth, all the while looking upward at the gap above. Every few moments a wounded Petran would be dragged past him, back into the city, but Melchior barely noticed.

It would take days to build a barricade, even with magic...and crumbling the upper walls in to block the path was too risky. Once the power to do so was unleashed, there was no telling how much more damage it would do within the city. Besides, it would take massive boulders to fill the gap, and there might be fissures.

Melchior was at a loss. He dropped hands to his sides in despair. Seeking inspiration, he peered back up to the sky where somewhere, he knew, that star still pulsed. He drew security from the thought, and a sensation flowed through him, a feeling that he'd really never truly experienced before.

Faith. Thinking of the star, its light, his mission, and all that had been sacrificed to bring him to this challenge, this moment, he found a hidden wellspring of hope within his chest. And an idea.

Melchior knelt on the sandy floor and scooped a small bit of sand into his cupped hands. Staring at it intently, he let it slide down to pile in a small cone before him. Bowing his head, he held his hands over the pile. He sat thus for a seeming eternity. Sweat beaded on his brow and dripped down to form dark round blots on the sand.

"Help me," he begged the star.

The grains of sand in the tiny pile began to move. They quivered and trembled, as if each one had come alive. An azure glow filled the space, electrifying the air. The sliding and shifting of the granules made a soft hissing sound, like the bellies of a thousand snakes slithering over the sand.

Around the pile on the floor of the chasm, almost imperceptibly, a grain at a time, the tiny cubes of silica tottered, and then began creeping toward the cone. They climbed its slanted sides, adding to its mass. Soon all the sand on the floor for twenty feet was shifting and sliding toward the pile, which grew with geometric progression. The cone stood two hands high, then, within moments, twice that.

Leaping to a rock outcropping along the side of the entrance tunnel, Melchior looked back and forth to see a river of sand flowing toward the cone on a wave of cerulean blue. The hissing had grown to a coarse grinding sound as the sand coursed toward the ever-growing wall. As he moved backward toward the open ravine, Melchior saw sand shifting and sliding from all over, struggling to fill the void and fulfill the command of the magus.

Melchior turned to head back to the battle, then paused, exhausted, and leaned on a boulder to catch his breath. He looked into the dark tunnel to see the sand now twenty feet high, bonded by magic, forming an impregnable wall that would bury any who tried to dig their way through. He said a silent prayer for the Petrans he had entombed, and for those he was forced to leave outside to defend.

He staggered with fatigue. He knew he had little of anything left to defend himself. It would be a quick end. But he'd keep the Romans from sacking Petra. Not today.

And indeed, he had. Rome wouldn't take the ancient Nabataean city, or its inhabitants, that day. The Petrans had more than one secret route out of the city, including the old stairway the Magi had climbed only a night before.

But Petra's location was secret no more, thanks to Zoth's treachery. And Rome would take what she wanted, regardless of the cost in human lives. On another day, with another army, the Romans would finally breach and sack the city, kill its people, drain its aquifers, and destroy a civilization that had lived and traded there for a thousand years.

Earning a few cuts and bruises for the effort, Melchior made his way back to the remainder of his party. Finally, using the last of his strength, he blasted a path through the Romans with another invisible stroke of his power and dashed through the corridor of tumbling soldiers to rejoin his friends.

Yet even as he did, the tide of battle shifted for the last time, and the Roman force, sensing victory, fought with renewed relish and viciousness. Circled, trapped, all but done for, the Magi, Shin-shin, Barir, Omar, and the last few Petrans knew they'd be fighting to the finish.

Melchior shouted to Gaspar and Omar as blades and blood flew, "It's done—blocked it up tight. No way in or out!" Gaspar nodded. Omar flashed a grin, confounded yet relieved that his city was safe. The knowledge allowed them all to concentrate on dying with glory.

Omar battled two adversaries at once, but fatigue, and the conviction that the end was nigh finally took their toll. Parrying the blow of one, he left his back exposed a moment too long, and a Roman sword slid on its deadly course between his ribs and through his chest. Blood blossomed and spread across his shirt around the point of the blade. The victor drew his blade out with a cry of triumph, only to be cut down by Gaspar's avenging blade.

Omar collapsed to his knees, and Gaspar dropped to his to cradle the dying man in his arms. "They won't take Petra today, my brother."

"I guess...dragging you out of the desert wasn't such a bad idea then, was it?" Omar whispered and smiled faintly. As he did, a thin trickle of blood issued from his mouth, and he died.

Gaspar howled his rage. Rising, he smote the shield of the Roman nearest him, cleaving it in two. Another stroke fell, this time cleaving the man's head.

A few feet away, Balthazar and Shin-shin and Barir battled twice their number. Feet, hands, and swords swung with deadly accuracy, and brave indeed was the Roman who engaged them—brave and foolhardy. But they, too, were tiring, and the standoff couldn't last.

All this Melchior saw and felt as he swung his sword wearily but valiantly, holding a few men at bay and striking the odd one once every few strokes. He got lucky when a stray arrow found the throat of one of his assailants. Crumpling to his knees, the man squawked and held his bleeding neck with his hands, then fell like a pillar of stone to the ground. The two remaining men squared off against Melchior. One got greedy and overextended. Melchior swiped his blade sideways with a backhand stroke and sliced the man across the stomach. He collapsed beside his fallen comrade.

Breathing heavily, Melchior adjusted his grip on his blade. The hilt was sticky in his hand, its weight almost more than he could hold. The Roman facing him was fresher, younger, bigger, and meaner. The Roman feinted left, then brought his sword down in an arc with all his strength. Melchior parried the blow, but at the cost of his weapon. The mighty sword of Arabia, handed down from generation to generation, snapped in half.

The parry was enough, however. The soldier staggered backward, buying Melchior a moment to think. Then, seeing Melchior weaponless, the Roman screamed a cry and charged the magus head-on, following the point of his blade.

Summoning the last of his might, Melchior ducked at the last moment and drove the broken blade with both hands into the gut of the charging man. The Roman, a surprised look gracing his already dead face, swayed for a moment, then toppled forward.

Melchior fell to his knees, spent. Sweat, dirt, and blood streaked his grim countenance. He gasped for air. Looking up, he searched the hot sky for one last glimpse of the star, the force that had led them to this bitter end. Yet even that was denied him; the scorching shield of the sun obliterated everything.

In the rear, Pilate still raged. He'd abandoned the platform to survey the battle from the ground. He didn't yet know that the prize had just been denied him, but he did know that this "skirmish," as his tribunes insisted on calling the bloodbath, had lasted far too long, cost far too many Roman lives, and was far too damned depressing. The finest fighting force in the world, reduced to fighting toe-to-toe with uncivilized brutes armed with little better than sticks, stones, and teeth. Pitiful.

In some sections, however, the mop-up had begun. The Petrans, overwhelmed by the sheer number of Roman bodies thrown at them, succumbed to exhaustion, to be skewered by Roman spears or swords without even putting up a final fight. Grateful for the end, no doubt. It was an…unsatisfying way to win a battle, thought Pilate. It lacked *gloria*.

Pilate walked over to Zoth, who stood scanning the remaining combatants. The dark mystic stood transfixed, his attention focused on a spot a few hundred paces away. Pilate followed his line of sight to a particularly fierce bit of fighting between his troops and some rather out-of-place adversaries.

"I take it, Zoth, that those are the ones you spoke of. I'll send men to take them—dead, I presume?" mocked Pilate.

"You could send one hundred men and never take one of them," replied Zoth darkly, never straying from his concentration. "They're more dangerous to you and your empire than you can imagine. However," he added, "I know their weakness."

Breaking his burning gaze from the distant group, Zoth strode over to crouch beside a soldier who had been dragged back from the fighting, only to bleed to death on the ground, unattended. Pilate blanched as he watched the sorcerer dig his long, bony hand into the deep stomach gash that had ended the soldier's life. He drew out a small, ruddy, fatty hunk of flesh. Standing, Zoth packed it tightly in his two hands. Gore dripped between his fingers. He bowed his head and muttered softly and wickedly to it.

Then, returning his gaze to the far group, he opened his hands. On his palms rested a thin, wet, red dart, magically transformed from the still warm flesh into a weapon pulsating with its own deadly life force. It writhed like a crimson snake on his hand, with a sharp and deadly point where the head would be. Hot, sickly steam spewed from Zoth's mouth as he blew the dart into the air, and it lifted much like a strange serpentine bird being released from captivity. It sailed off into the air, zipping tight circles in the air above the men's heads as it searched for the target its master had selected.

Was it the wicked whistle of the deadly projectile? A sixth sense that alerted him to the presence of the airborne evil? Instinct made Barir swing his sword high above his head in a defensive arc. Too late. Barir sliced the dart in half in mid-flight, but no mere mortal could stop it from finding a mark.

With a thwip! and a light thwop! half of the dart buried itself into the unsuspecting Shin-shin's slender neck. Clapping her hand to her throat, she cried out in pain and fell immediately to the ground, still as death. The other half of the dark missile smoked, hissed, and melted into a dark, evil stain on the canyon floor,

"Shin-shin!" shouted Barir, running to the girl's body. Scooping her into his arms, he rocked her like a baby, his tears clearing two paths down his dirty cheeks.

A trumpet blared; men shouted. The Romans halted their attack. Balthazar bent to examine the girl, concern furrowing his brow. He examined the wound in her neck, but the projectile was gone. It had worked its way into her flesh and was now slowly poisoning her from within. Gaspar leaned heavily on his scimitar, gathering his strength for a final fight. But it was not to be.

A path cleared, and a Roman legate approached, leading an entourage of other officers. Untouched by battle, the Roman's brilliant sneer matched his shimmering armor and frosty white garments. He stopped a few safe paces away and looked at the group with mild disgust.

"Surrender...and live. It's that simple. Or I'll have my men hack you to pieces so small, even the scorpions won't be interested in the meat you leave behind," he said matter-of-factly.

"Draw your own sword, coward, and I'll make sure the scorpions have a feast on your account," threatened Gaspar.

A look of amusement flashed across the legate's face, but it lasted only a second. He turned to give the order to his tribune when someone stepped out from the throng behind him.

"Zoth!" cried the astonished Melchior.

"Traitor," Gaspar said under his breath, hefting his blade and taking a step toward the dark figure.

Firmly in control and demonstrating the cold patience that came with this knowledge, Zoth calmly raised his hand to stop the warrior. "If you want the child to live, lay down your arms. For I alone can save...her?" He looked down at Shin-shin, still cradled in Barir's arms. He mused aloud to himself, "How strange."

Balthazar said calmly, "He's right, of course. There's a dark poison working its way through her, and I am unable to stop it." Looking into Gaspar's eyes, he said, "She must not die, Gaspar."

Knowing that this was a fight that couldn't be won, Gaspar nodded and reluctantly dropped his sword to the sand. Balthazar followed suit, laying his slender blade on Gaspar's and adding Barir's as well.

Last, Melchior came forward and tossed the gladius he'd found on the pile without taking his eyes off Zoth. "You'll never wash this from your hands, Zoth," he spat quietly.

"Spare me the speeches. This end was inevitable. You're weak, Melchior, like your idiot friends here. Your doom was sealed the day you left on this ridiculous quest. Now you pay for your foolishness—and I'm here to collect," retorted Zoth, gleeful in his victory. "You lose."

Turning and walking a few steps to the legate, Zoth said more soberly, "Legate Pilate, as we agreed, they're mine. Petra is yours. If you'll tie them up and leave them to me, I'll be on my way."

Pilate had watched the exchange between Zoth and Melchior with interest. He looked back and forth, as if noting the undeniable likeness between the two men, though Zoth seemed more a dark semblance of the other.

A runner came up, breathing heavily. "My lord, we cannot get in. They've blocked the way in with sand, all the way up. We don't know how they did it. Two men were just buried alive trying to dig through."

Zoth shot a glance at Melchior, who smiled and shrugged.

With a tone suggesting that enough was enough, Pilate turned to Zoth. Heavy sarcasm laced his words. "Somehow, this news doesn't surprise me. Not a bit. Arrrgh! This isn't quite the picture you painted with your little mirror trick, is it? Where's the glorious victory, Zoth? The gold for Rome? The tributes?" Zoth didn't react or respond.

Pilate paused for a second, fuming, clearly struggling for control of his anger and inner demons. Gaining a modicum of control, he shot at Zoth, "Now the deal changes. I didn't give up all these men for nothing. Men, soldiers, and horses — all this costs Rome dearly. What have I left? This!" He gestured to the Magi. "If they mean so much to you, perhaps they'll mean as much to the king in Jerusalem. Maybe they can be ransomed...is that it? Is that why you want them?" He looked for an answer in the sorcerer's dark face.

Finding none, he turned to his troops and barked out orders. "Secure them. And separate them. And..." he paused and glanced at Zoth. "Bind him, too."

"You make a grave mistake, Pilate," intoned Zoth, scowling in humiliation as the soldiers moved to tie him up.

"Not my last, to be sure," the legate replied sarcastically. "But it just feels so...right."

"My lord, what about this one?" asked a soldier, gesturing to Shin-shin's lifeless form.

"She's with us," said Barir. "As a fellow soldier, I ask you let us take our comrade."

Pilate sneered his frustration. "Very well. Have a physician look at her. If she lives, fine. I care not. Take them!" And with a disgusted flourish, Pilate and his retinue strode away to assess the devastation.

All around, Roman soldiers prowled the bodies, occasionally thrusting their swords into those that still breathed. Dark smoke and soft moans filled the air as the sun, mercifully, began setting on the canyon.

Chapter Twenty-Nine

And thus, the Magi fell beneath the yoke of Rome.

Pilate was just an over decorated thug, an aristocrat turned solider who did Rome's bidding. It was the Emperor of Rome's chief thug, the Governor King of Judaea, who passed down the bidding to smaller thugs like Pilate.

Handpicked by Caesar, the governor enforced Caesar's wishes, collected taxes, put down revolts, and kept the peace. Part of Rome's strategy was to keep some locals in places of authority to quell unrest, but they were really just puppets manipulated by the emperor.

This particular governor, Herod, was lord over more than one land, so he would move from city to city as the need arose. So it fell that, while the Magi pursued the star, Herod was in Jerusalem, the capital city of Judaea.

The line of Herod was cursed. This particular Herod was called Herod the Great, although he was hardly that. A friend to Marc Antony, Herod earned the throne of Judaea through marriage, by currying the favor of Rome, by enlisting dubious religious leaders of Jerusalem, the Pharisees, and finally by murdering all his family members until he alone could claim it. He ruled Judaea ruthlessly, driven by paranoia, and slaughtered anyone and everyone he imagined a threat, including his own sons. His evil was without question. But the star had other plans for Herod.

The prisoners were divided into two groups thrown into wooden and iron cages atop carts, and hauled like beasts through the desert under the melting sun. The cages, originally made to hold wild animals the soldiers captured for shipment back to Rome, were small and cramped, and too short to allow a man to stand upright. But they were home for now.

One wagon held Melchior, Gaspar, and Barir; the other held Balthazar, Zoth, and the unconscious, dying Shin-shin. The guards had sensed their animosity toward Zoth and put him with the placid Balthazar as a precaution.

The trip was arduous, and they received minimal water and rations. After surviving so much, it was rather humiliating to ride the last part of the journey under such conditions. But there was at least one consolation for the Magi; they were heading in the right direction.

After they left the territory surrounding Petra, the land became more hospitable. While it was still the desert, they left the rocky highlands and entered into the outer edges of the Fertile Crescent. Away to the west, the mighty Nile gave life to the land of Egypt, and to the north, the Mediterranean blew moist breezes for hundreds of miles. Small, craggy trees appeared, and they occasionally saw tiny villages, populated by small clans of people who'd inhabited the same spot for millennia.

In their cage, Balthazar and Zoth were as still and silent as the comatose Shin-shin, but for different reasons.

Zoth was fuming and pouting simultaneously, torn between his hatred of the Magi and the infidelity of the Roman commander. He'd delivered what he'd promised... basically. They certainly wouldn't have found the hidden city without him. The Petran fighters were destroyed, for the most part. The only thing that hadn't really gone as planned was the sacking of the city, but so what? It wasn't going anywhere. With a team of a few hundred slaves and a few weeks of digging, Petra would be opened. So what was the big deal?

This cyclical argument brought him back to his original rage against Melchior and his newfound bunch of accomplices. Melchior was a weakling. That was Zoth's primary reason for hating him. Back in the mountain palace, Melchior had always ruled by council, and chosen inaction over swift reaction. He was no king. He wasn't even much of a magus; his inability to create rain in the desert or to protect his troops, proved that. But somehow, amazingly, he'd survived until now.

The child lay heavily on the floor of the cage, her lungs pressing against her ribs, desperate to inflate. A sheen of sweat, almost impossible in the dry heat, coated her brow. And her face was drawn in a death mask of pain. She couldn't last long, for saving her now was beyond even Zoth's power. He'd grudgingly done what he could and slowed her death a bit. But the poison was too deep in her body now, embedded in her flesh. Even had he wished to save her—and he didn't—only a miracle could do so now. And the day looked to be quite short of those.

Across from Zoth, sitting with his legs crossed and eyes closed, the Asian magus meditated. Deep within the recesses of his mind, he searched for answers to the many conundrums confronting him. First and foremost was his concern for Shin-shin. He still felt confusion at his companions' surprise that Shin-shin was a female, and really, what did it matter? But her sudden fall at Zoth's hand had caught him off-guard, as had so many other things on this peculiar journey.

He knew without asking that the girl was past his aid, or Zoth's. He saw without opening his eyes that her spirit fought to survive against the venomous coil tightening around it. The snake-like dart had worked its way into her inner chest and was slinking slowly towards her heart. He knew all these things, and one thing more — that he, Balthazar of the imperial line, magus, astronomer, and philosopher, had failed her utterly.

He regretted the decision to bring her, but the signs all indicated that she had a part to play in the unfolding mystery of the star. To be one of its many sacrifices, it seemed, he thought sadly. That was the only part she could play from here on.

And the star. Why had he and Shin-shin been chosen to witness, and follow, its power? That a new mighty being, a godhead in fact, had come to earth was surprising. But it was already here, as the spirits from beyond had announced a few nights ago. Why, then, were they still being called?

Opening his eyes, he looked directly at Zoth, who sat staring at him.

"She'll die," the dark one said. "In fact, she's dead already."

"Nothing is certain, Lord Zoth," said Balthazar. "Of that, I would think, even you are now aware. But the fact that she's beyond my power or yours or that of any mortal man, I do know. That you would choose to strike down a child, however — that I can't understand."

Zoth was caught without a response for a moment, then said with astonishing honesty, "It wasn't intended for her. The dart was for Melchior alone. But that fool Barir diverted its path and it struck the child. She's a casualty of war, no more, no less."

Balthazar nodded coolly, sensing the truth in Zoth's words. "Ah, but your words betray you. I think you feel guilt for this. And the rage you direct against your cousin and the world is now in question, because nothing is as it seems anymore. The truth is hidden from all of us, and you've found yourself as much a pawn in this game as any of us. I think you're...afraid." Balthazar looked deep into Zoth's eyes for a moment, then closed his own and resumed his meditation.

Zoth wanted to react with terrible fury to Balthazar's words, but found he couldn't. The little man had cut him closer to the bone than anyone else ever had. He looked down at the lifeless body of the girl and felt, for the first time in such a long time, regret.

The Roman column marched on. The Romans were feared and loathed wherever they went, and rightly so. They took whatever they wished, slaughtering cattle and draining precious wells to keep the troops moving. Fortunately for those they encountered, Pilate and his men had had enough of the desert, and even the small comforts a city like Jerusalem could offer dangled before them in the burning sun, leading them on and giving them purpose.

They had entered Judaea, officially a Roman province, but still very much a raw and untamed land. The Magi gathered what they could from their guards and the occasional native who brought them water when they stopped. They came to understand that, while Rome was in charge of judicial, martial, and pecuniary matters, they left bothersome details like the actual governing and day to day living to King Herod and the local officials and high priests, the Sanhedrin.

The legion marched long and hard, stopping infrequently for rest and nourishment. Yet it was during one such brief halt that Melchior learned a great deal about the strange land they'd entered at such a dear cost, and the people who lived there.

Dragged from their cages to stretch their legs, relieve themselves, and get their small portions of food and water, the prisoners were kept in separate groups under heavy guard. Pilate knew the dark deeds Zoth was capable of, and correctly assumed that his companions were just as dangerous. Their belongings had been taken, including the horses, packs, and supplies left on the plateau above the battle, so all they had were the clothes on their backs. Pilate had not had time to search the plunder, so the gifts of Petra remained a secret.

Standing by a stonewalled well in the center of a few shabby huts, Melchior worked the hard knots from the muscles in his legs. A young native woman walked about with a large earthenware jug, pouring out water to the thirsty travelers. The soldiers had already drunk two or three times; now sated, they allowed the prisoners a drink.

The woman approached Melchior meekly and, knowing that he was no friend of the Romans, gave him a quiet, sympathetic smile. She splashed water into the small bowl tied to the jug. Melchior slurped it down, and since his guard's gaze was elsewhere, he held the bowl out again, and she poured.

Gasping in relief as his throat loosened, he said, "Thank you. We haven't had a drink since yesterday."

She nodded and went to give water to Gaspar and Barir. But she returned to Melchior and offered him more. He smiled at her and nodded.

"What's your name?" he asked.

She was slender and lovely in a simple, unpretentious, and rugged way. Her arms and face were tanned a dark mahogany brown by the Judaean sun. Her thick, curly, dark hair reached her shoulders, and she wore a simple scarf tied round her head that once might have been blue, but had been bleached almost white by the sun. Yet it was her eyes that held his gaze, piercing, fierce discs of topaz-blue fire, framed by whites as pure as the sand. They're the eyes of a warrior, thought Melchior.

"I'm called Ruth, daughter of Aaron and Miriam. My husband is Simon," she replied.

"Tell me, Ruth, where are we? What is this place?" Melchior inquired.

"This place? It's nowhere. It has no real name; we just call it the watering hole. But this land, the land the Roman swine trample with their unclean boots, is Judaea. And it's the land of my people," she said with a proud shake of her head and raven hair.

"So," said Melchior softly, "the prophecy comes true. We've come to Judaea at last." Pouring him some more water, she kept her eyes averted, but continued to speak. "My people are called the Hebrews, and we've survived many such insults as these Romans. Long ago, the Egyptians enslaved us. The Philistines killed us. Yet we've survived, and we'll survive this, too."

Her pride is a thing of beauty, Melchior noted. It was their love of freedom, of the land they lived on, that made people like these and the Petrans unconquerable by the Romans. *Their cities might fall, their armies might perish, but their spirits will never diminish.*

"How?" asked Melchior honestly.

"Our God," she answered simply. "He's saved us before. He'll save us again. He's the one true God, Yahweh. And he's sending us a Messiah."

Melchior frowned, puzzled. "A — ?"

"Messiah. Our deliverer. With a flaming sword, he'll strike down our enemies and lift the chosen people of Judaea to freedom from the tyranny of Rome. As he delivered us from the chains of Egypt. And Babylon."

The legion began to creak back to life, goaded by the centurions. Melchior drank the last of the water and looked at Ruth with admiration.

"When will he come? Is he here?" he asked, suspecting the answer already, but probing for how wide the news had spread.

"No, not yet. Perhaps not even in my lifetime, but maybe in my son's. Yes, he'll be there to welcome the Messiah and march with him to destroy the very city of Rome itself."

Melchior heard this with astonishment. The revelation of the celestial beings suddenly took on a new context. Was this the king who'd come? A mighty liberator come to break the strangling choke of Rome? Choosing his words carefully, he said, "I hope so. I'll look for your son, and your Messiah, for they're needed here by many people in many places. Tell me, Ruth, what's your son's name, so that one day I may meet him and call him friend?"

She laughed and smiled kindly. "He's but a babe, so I think we all may have to wait for a while. But his name is Judas, son of Simon, and Yahweh has chosen him for great things, I'm sure."

A shadow passed over Melchior's heart, another like all three Magi had felt since seeing the star. He knew not its meaning and could perceive nothing in his mind, but the hair on the back of his neck rose and a sinister premonition chilled him, then passed.

"Come on, you dogs," shouted the guard, shoving Gaspar toward the cage with his spear, a move that earned him a dark glance from the black magus.

"Farewell, Ruth, mother of Judas. May the light of the blessed star shine on you and your family," Melchior called back as he was led away.

The army bivouacked by night, but the prisoners rested tied sitting upright with their backs to the outside of their cage. Barir's head had slumped down to his chest in an uneasy sleep. Gaspar and Melchior remained awake.

Too much time had passed since the revelation by the spirits in the night sky. So much had come to pass; yet Gaspar still felt that the most important part of the journey lay before them.

Sensing his thoughts, Melchior concurred. "The path before us is dark to me. Yet I feel its peril, too."

Gaspar beheld the star through the fronds of a tall palm tree, its brilliance backlighting the tree beautifully, its intense glitter beckoning them maddeningly. "It wavers not in strength, location, or call. It hangs there, leading us on. Even now, helpless, tied like cattle and led for slaughter at the butcher's house, we follow its path."

"Yes," agreed Melchior.

220

"We've—we've given so much. So much blood spilled. And our lives, stolen from us like a whispered word in the wind...Will I ever know peace again?" Gaspar wondered aloud. His spoken thoughts said enough for all of them. "I'm glad for the brief time we had in Petra, when, if only for a moment, the burden of our task was lifted from our hearts." He looked directly at Melchior, showing again the new warmth that still coursed beneath his hardened features. "And I'm glad to have found such friends as you and Balthazar. You're my brothers."

He looked up again at the star and said nothing more, for there was nothing more to say. Only the star itself knew what lay ahead.

Chapter Thirty

The legion continued to move steadily north and west. After their trials in the desert, the Magi had been taken south to Petra, a bit out of their way. They now were back on track, albeit the long way.

They traveled for another two days, seeing more and more people and habitations as they journeyed up through Judaea. The star still shone, but its majesty remained secret, hidden from the Romans and others who weren't called. The Magi heard it, pulled at their bars, and tugged at their bonds, but they couldn't free themselves. Whether due to their weakened condition, or simply that the star wanted them there was a moot point. They were going to Jerusalem in cages, like it or not.

This bothered Melchior, for many reasons. The star's song had increased in its urgency, as if time itself was now the greatest hurdle to overcome. And he knew that their ultimate destination wasn't Jerusalem, but someplace called the City of David. Casual questions to the Romans revealed nothing of its location, for they'd never heard of it. Melchior wished he'd thought to ask Ruth about it.

The Roman presence in the landscape they passed through steadily increased, and Melchior assumed, seeing the Roman statues, standards, and signs peppering the roadsides, that they were nearing Jerusalem. The prisoners had also seen more soldiers. Balthazar calculated from the number of troops passing by that there were probably three or four legions of Roman troops in the vicinity of Jerusalem. The king apparently liked to keep his muscle nearby.

Then, far away, a city appeared, glistening white in the glancing rays of the sun. And it was just then that fortune, or the star, or simply sheer boredom, brought a grizzled, sand-worn soldier alongside Melchior's iron-barred confines.

On most long journeys, the final stretch of the trip seems the slowest and the longest, and this one was no exception. Noting how the old soldier kept looking sidelong at the bizarre captive, and sensing the man's impatience with the slowing pace of the march, Melchior decided to glean crucial information on their imminent destination.

Melchior struck up the conversation casually, or as casually as a beaten, dehydrated man dressed in torn blue silk and bound within a steel box could. Not making eye contact, he feigned awe and said, "By the gods! What place is this? I've never seen the like! Surely, this Judaea is the greatest, most powerful kingdom in all the world!"

No well-traveled man of war could resist such ignorant praise. A point of pride for any warrior was the amazing lands and faraway cities he'd seen with his own eyes, and he paraded this pride in the voice of authority such vast experience gave him in any conversation. This veteran of Rome took the bait.

"Bah! Jews! They're no more responsible for this than I am for the warts on Caesar's arse," barked out the soldier.

Once again, the star's gift of tongues served Melchior well, for he was able to easily understand the patois of Aramaic, Greek, Latin, and Hebrew that flowed in a mish-mash from the soldier's mouth. Curiously, the soldier took it for granted that he could be understood and didn't find it odd that the strange man in the cage could converse so effortlessly with him.

Melchior sized up the curious man. The passage of time

and the challenges of life had been hard for the soldier. Rough-hewn wrinkles creased his suntanned brow and face, but a flush to his cheeks betrayed the vestiges of a fair complexion. That, and the soldier's light blue eyes, lighter than Melchior's own, indicated that he came from a land other than these, where the people were so dark of skin and hair. A scraggly beard and receding, thinning hairline were both graying, and the skin on his hands, arms, and throat looked as though it had stretched taut in a vain attempt to halt the escape of life from within its confines.

His carriage, while still proud, as a soldier's should be, was bent by the weight of his years. His breastplate, simple and relatively unadorned, also bore the stamp of experience in its many dents, stains, and scrapes. His scarlet under tunic had been bled pink by the sun, and knotted and spliced thongs held his sandals, mere flats of old leather, to his legs.

The sword that flapped at his side looked as though it hadn't been used in over a decade and even then, sparingly. In all, he presented a rather pathetic portrait of the Roman guard, yet it was far more realistic than Rome or Caesar would have liked. The life of the legionary was hard, and here was the proof.

Start slow, Melchior thought. *Point, then let him lead.*

"Forgive me," said Melchior in the humble voice of a novice at the knee of his master. "I've never left the boundaries of my own lands before, and this is all so new to me. Are you from here? What's the name of 'here'?"

"Jerusalem," spat the soldier, shuffling closer to the cage as it moved tediously toward the city walls. The two could now speak inconspicuously; in fact, the normally quiet queue of soldiers had grown noticeably louder, with even the usually gruff officers chatting about their plans and the loved ones, chores, troubles, and comforts that awaited them.

"Pray, tell me your name, commander," Melchior urged.

"Commander! I damn well wish. Cambrius. Just plain

Cambrius. I've been a slave in Caesar's army since I was captured as a boy and taken from me dead father's side. Nigh on sixty years, now." A shadow crossed his face as he thought of the green hills and lush highlands of his home far away.

"Like you, the dagger of Rome was pointed at my throat. But I was just a boy. So they made me a soldier. Gave me a wooden *gladius* and taught me to fight. I've killed men in so many lands and spilled blood on so many city steps that I've lost count. Now I'm just an old man who's almost run out of things to do for mighty Caesar Augustus. Second Caesar I've had to deal with, in fact. I feed the beasts and clean their muck. When I'm released or killed, and I don't care which, I know one thing for sure — I'll turn my gray-haired backside on this desert and never look at sand again!" He spat precious moisture from his mouth onto the sandy road, where it gobbed up and began sizzling away in the baking sun.

"Jerusalem, you say..." redirected Melchior, wondering whether he'd have time to learn anything of value from the man before they reached their final destination.

"Aye, Jerusalem — one of the farthest, most godforsaken cities on the edge of the so-called 'Roman Empire.' This place, like everywhere else I've marched for Caesar, is nothing more than a dump, an outpost and breeding ground for Caesar's purse. Gold, grain, and greed — that's all Rome cares about."

Cambrius rambled on, and from his diatribe, Melchior sifted out the information he needed to understand the fortress he was only a mile from entering.

It turned out that once Cambrius had expelled his disdain for all things Roman from his heart, as efficiently as he expelled his saliva, noted Melchior with grim mirth, he was quite knowledgeable, especially for a foot soldier. His gruff manner and style of speech belied a cunning mind and a deep reservoir of information on the Roman world and its inner workings.

Cambrius said that Judaea, and Jerusalem in particular, was a tributary of Rome. Judaea wasn't officially a province yet, but well on its way. Oddly enough, explained Cambrius, the Hebrews themselves had actually invited Rome within its borders, to help quell an internal war between its twelve tribes.

"And like the rude dinner guest, the Romans made themselves comfortable and never left!" commented Cambrius with sardonic glee. He went on to imply that, within just a few years, they'd imposed Roman rule and lifestyle on the city, a handprint of culture that would never fully be washed away by the tides of time.

When Melchior asked how old the city was, Cambrius explained that Jerusalem was at this time already an ancient city built generations ago by men whose names were forgotten. Built, razed, cleansed, and rebuilt a couple of times, the city's streets, bazaars, and temples had been home to many people and many religions.

Cambrius squinted to measure the distance to the walls and said, "The Roman emperor, Caesar Augustus, and the Roman Senate are no fools, prisoner. You'll learn that soon enough for yourself. But a while ago, they set their own handpicked man, a pig named Herod, on the throne here as the King of the Jews. Everyone knew he wasn't even really a Jew, barely half. Didn't matter; Herod the Great rules in Caesar's stead, collecting gold, dispensing justice, and carving a Roman face on the stone walls of this poor city."

Melchior was surprised to hear the hint of pity in Cambrius' voice. Clearly, the man had seen many cultures smashed by the fist of Rome.

"Aye, Herod. You see, Herod the Great has been busy as Herod the Builder, although he never gets his own precious hands dirty. Gaw, I'd like to see that!" Cambrius laughed, a mangled sound that transformed into the rough cough of man who'd marched too many campaigns.

When the fit subsided, he went on. "Herod 'enlisted' thousands of Jews at sword point in his grand scheme, building palaces, temples, and garrisons throughout Jerusalem. Slaves. Couldn't tell you how many of them died. Most, probably. He didn't care. Caesar wants, and Herod delivers. I'm not sure what he's going to get out of all this, maybe some seat in the Senate back in Rome. Maybe some lands somewhere with a nice villa and no sand. That'd be nice..." Cambrius' mind wandered for a moment, contemplating a life as Herod.

After a while Cambrius resumed the dialogue, with little to no prodding from Melchior. The magus noted that he described Herod's brutal accomplishments with a bit of pride, betraying just how much of Rome had seeped into his foreign bloodstream.

Cambrius extrapolated on Herod's municipal accomplishments. He'd straightened the winding cattle paths of the ancient city into a paved Roman matrix of roads and avenues. Even the gates in the walls had been altered with Roman arches and columns.

"Love him or loathe him, the man has a flair for decorating," said Cambrius with genuine admiration.

It seemed that the spread of the Roman Empire was as much economic as it was military, and often the former preceded the latter. Roman entrepreneurs, in search of exotic merchandise to sell in the "civilized" world, came to Judaea, and in doing so made Jerusalem a bustling metropolis. Cambrius cynically presumed that the always-scheming Herod had actually planned it so. By building a New Jerusalem on the model of a Roman city, he encouraged travel and commerce from afar and thereby kept an open link to Rome. And thus stayed in the emperor's good graces.

Cambrius continued to lecture, and Melchior drank in the steady stream of information, even as the distance to the fortress-city shrank. At last, they were paces away from the ancient city walls.

As the dusty, thirsty Roman legion marched through a newly crafted Roman gateway in the old wall, Roman and Hebrew citizens alike came to watch them, anxious for news from afar and curious about what the legion had been doing.

Noting the look on their faces, Gaspar said, "They can count. They know that the legion left with many more men than have returned. And few spoils from afar. I would guess that they consider us a paltry tribute for their dead soldiers."

"Indeed," replied Melchior.

Some people laughed when they saw the caged men and jeered at them. A few bold children threw rocks, missing mostly, but getting a few through the bars. The legion had slowed its march since entering the confines of the city, which in turn made the prisoners sitting targets. Then the army staggered to a halt for a moment due to some hindrance ahead. Seizing the opportunity, the children continued the pelting for a minute or so until one hit Balthazar squarely in the chest.

The wise man picked up the fallen stone and gave it a look of annoyance. Then, eyeing the child who'd thrown it, Balthazar placed the stone on the palm of his hand and flicked it with the index finger of his other. The stone rocketed through the air, made two graceful loops, and nailed the boy squarely between his eyes on the bridge of his nose, knocking the former assailant, now the assailed, backward.

Disheartened, the boy and his band of rogues dispersed. Balthazar looked at Zoth, who grudgingly nodded his approval.

The crowd around them, however, wasn't so easily dismissed. The spectators looked with a mixture of fear, anger, and resentment at the caged men. They mumbled to each other, gesturing toward the prisoners.

Taking advantage of the opportunity afforded by the pause, Balthazar knelt and addressed the crowd. "Tell me, where is the newborn king of the Jews? We saw his star at its rising, and we have come to pay him respect."

A look of horror washed over the faces closest to them. All they could make out were the words "Herod," "blasphemer," and "executed."

"I've traveled far to honor your new king, to offer him praise and tribute. Will you not tell me where he is?" Balthazar asked again.

Still, he got no response. People looked away; the crowd hushed. Balthazar looked over and lifted a brow at Melchior, who understood. He, too, got the distinct impression that they didn't want to look a dead man in the eyes.

"Yer friend should keep his mouth shut," Cambrius muttered to Melchior after the one-sided exchange. "The Jews here, while they've no love for Herod, fear him just the same."

The army lurched into a slow shuffle, and they soon left the people Balthazar had addressed far behind. But the Magi were troubled. The spectators' response was altogether odd for a people who had just been told that their new king had arrived. They took the news like a child rejecting spoiled milk, as if they wished no part of it.

The Magi had set in motion a chain reaction of fear with their questions about the newborn king. Like a wave of water, the news of the strangers, their odd skins and clothing, and their inquiries about a "new king" swept along the busy streets. The wave gathered strength as it rolled along.

Finally, it crashed ashore on the plaza before Herod's palace, turning the heads of the guards and ultimately reaching the ears of Herod's high advisor. Soon the news was presented on bent knee to the king himself. The seed of paranoia, already sown in Herod's heart, received the water to make it blossom again.

Melchior was taken with the city he saw from his cage; it was unlike any in his own kingdom. The scale of it alone was staggering. Buildings and roads were crafted from huge blocks of cut limestone. Elegant arches graced doorways. Smoke wafted from the cooking of street vendors to mingle with the dust and scents churned up by thousands of pedestrians. Canopies snapped in the breeze, guarding precious wares and their hawkers from the intruding rays of the sun. The bleats of animals, the calls of merchants, and the babble of discussion created an unexpected symphony of noise. Everywhere he looked, the cosmopolitan atmosphere of a world unlike any he'd ever seen pressed in upon his senses.

As the legion made its way northward, Cambrius gave a tour of the city. They were marching up the Cardo, the main avenue, through the heart of Jerusalem, he explained, adding that it passed through the Lower City, a neighborhood of middle-class people, then into the wealthier Upper City. As the column reached the Upper City, Melchior noted a few buildings of palatial stature. When asked, Cambrius told him that the palaces housed people of importance, including priests and well-heeled Romans.

As the legion turned a corner, now heading northeast, a breathtaking structure swung into Melchior's view. He leaned forward to peer through his prison bars at the massive building with its gilt dome shimmering in the sun, demanding the respect of anyone who gazed upon it. Melchior estimated that it could hold thousands of people.

"This, now, is called the Temple," Cambrius announced, sounding as if he'd designed and built the magnificent edifice himself. "Very holy place—the holiest, in fact, for the Jews. The actual Temple itself, as you can see, rests on that huge platform they call the Temple Mount. You have to admit, Herod does have a way of getting your attention," commented Cambrius.

As Melchior observed the scores of men, women, children, robed priests, and armed soldiers swarming like busy ants up and down the two sets of stairs leading to the platform, his guide explained that the Temple, too, was the handiwork of Herod. Though still unfinished, it was a masterstroke of the ruthless king's cunning and pride. In all of Cambrius' travels, he'd seen nothing to rival it, because Herod had wanted it so. Cambrius surmised that Herod had wished to trump the Temple of old built by Solomon the Wise.

"But the Temple's a nod to his people, too," Cambrius went on. "Herod is, after all, the so-called King of the Jews. So to keep everyone happy, or as happy as they can be while they're building the damn thing, he creates a Temple for Jehovah, the Hebrew god. Of course, it's a pretty fine place for the high priests to hold prayer, drink wine, sleep with women or young boys, and hold sacrifices. They're all in the palm of Herod's dirty hand. He's got it all figured out, that one."

Cambrius explained that the Temple was more than an ambitious creation. It was a wealth generator. Herod taxed the people to build it and kept half for himself, and then he created a mandate that all Jews must visit the Temple once a year, and pay to do so. Merchants sold their wares and trade right in front of it, and, of course, a generous portion of each sale went to the palace. Even non-Jews, called Gentiles, were welcome in some parts of the grand building. If you had money to spend, Herod wanted the Temple to be your destination. It was, in effect, a magnificent religious front for a moneymaking machine.

Gazing at its splendor, Melchior took note of its Roman style of architecture; the bold stones as long as a man, the noble columns, and the ornate doorways. The Temple dwarfed the memory of Melchior's mountain palace, trebling it in size and stature. As he passed, he regretted once more his prison and longed for the opportunity to explore the halls of the Temple.

As the orange sun sank into the west, the legion halted deep within the city at its barracks, which Cambrius called the Antonia. He said that it was named after Marc Antony, a former patron of Herod, and a Roman of some note.

A centurion bellowed an order, and the soldiers fell out of formation and went their separate ways. Cambrius looked at Melchior with a surprisingly soft look of pity, such as one would give a calf on the way to the slaughter.

"You're not so bad. Good listener, I guess. Well. I hope it's quick." And with that, he turned heel and scuffed off down a dark alleyway. Melchior watched him go, grateful for the knowledge he'd bestowed on the magus but twice as grateful that the angry lecture was over.

The small force guarding the prisoners wasn't as lucky as Cambrius. They stood their ground and held watch, waiting for their orders.

After an hour or so, Pilate and his retinue arrived. Looking with disgust at the dirty prisoners, he sneered, "Well, well. Let's see how Herod likes his new pets. Seems he's become interested in you, and the news you bear. I think the runners I sent on ahead were a good idea after all. I wouldn't want to be in your place. Herod gets what he wants, and I advise you to give it to him. He can be generous...or ruthless. My, what a difference a few words can make."

Turning to the guards, he snapped, "Clean them up and chain them inside. Tomorrow morning, we take them to see Herod when we make our report."

Looking directly at Melchior, he said, "Enjoy your evening. It's likely to be your last."

As the bound Magi were led in, Balthazar could see that the Antonia was a state-of-the-art garrison. He guessed that it could house a few thousand soldiers simultaneously.

It seemed that Herod and his architects hadn't forgotten a strong prison, either. A few rooms were beneath ground level, with little ventilation and only one staircase in or out. The room into which Balthazar, Zoth, and Shin-shin were tossed was small and uncomfortable, with a dirt floor and only a small, rectangular, barred window to the outside world high up on the outer wall.

The promised "cleansing" was nothing more than buckets of fetid water tossed cruelly into their faces and backs. Crusts of bread followed, landing on the soggy floor to the accompaniment of threats of dismemberment. Then the guards slammed their cell door shut and took positions at the top of the prison's only stairwell.

The cell door was a massive olive wood barrier held together with bands of iron. Eyeing it, Balthazar knew Gaspar, even in his best condition, would have had difficulty breaking it down.

But Gaspar wasn't in his best condition. Their long travels, their setbacks, and the exertion of the battle had all taken their toll on the Magi. Gaspar, who utilized his brute strength most, bore a few slashes and wounds, and the cramped conditions of their captivity, with little food or rest, had given him no opportunity to replenish his reservoir of strength.

Melchior, who in combat relied most on his powers, had been sapped dry in saving Petra from the advancing army. And Balthazar himself, who would normally apply wisdom and logic to find a solution to their problem, was paralyzed by his failure to protect his charge, successfully complete the quest, and help his friends.

As the oily black of night crept in, Balthazar felt true despair. Cradling Shin-shin's damp, sweat-soaked head in his hands, watching as she crept ever closer to death as the wicked poison worked its way through her body, he bowed his head and prayed for help from the power exerting its will over them. He prayed for mercy or a quick end.

CHAPTER THIRTY-ONE

Herod was the quintessential man of ironies. Herod built a Temple to honor the Jewish God, but made it in the pagan Roman style. He built theaters, harbors, and hippodromes, yet he held ghastly chariot races and cheered loudest when drivers were crushed to death beneath charging hooves. He married ten wives, but had most of them executed along with many of his own children. He vainly pursued a dream that he would be honored for the ages, only to be remembered as a cruel and heartless man, one of the most heinous villains of all time.

On this night, as the Magi sat imprisoned in the bowels of the Antonia, he set in motion the series of events that would earn him his place in the shameful halls of history.

Herod held council in the anteroom of his palace, accessible only by a hidden doorway behind his throne. It was a private place, dark but luxurious, where he met with his advisors and plotted his most atrocious crimes and audacious acts. Like a Roman salon, the anteroom was adorned with long, pillowed couches and low wooden tables on which stood jugs of wine, some already drained and others well on their way, and plates of savory food. Tall candles flickered and snapped quietly in their wrought iron stands.

A servant stood erect against one wall. Years before,

Herod had chosen him to serve in this most secret of sanctuaries and had had his ears pierced with sharp reeds to render him deaf and his tongue cut out to leave him mute.

Herod's reputation for cruelty was known within his lands and as far away as Rome, as was his cunning and his ability to ingratiate himself with the powers above him. But the man himself was yet another irony.

He was...beautiful. His chiseled countenance rivaled the face on any Roman coin. His form, strong and muscular, still retained its fluid grace. He was stately. A man of presence. And yet within this gorgeous assemblage of flesh beat a heart as cold as a crocodile's.

The King of the Jews sat slumped sideways in a padded chair upholstered in royal purple, his arms resting lazily on the gilt armrests, his legs crossed, one silver-sandaled foot flopping back and forth with overstated boredom. A circlet of silver bound his thick, dark auburn hair curled in the Roman fashion. The simple garments he wore, a white linen shift loosely draped over a single sculpted shoulder and cinched with a modest leather belt, accentuated the healthy glow of his rich brown skin.

To see him thus, it would be difficult to appreciate his fears, his dark side, his paranoid delusions. But he knew first-hand that treachery could unseat a king, as he had done so himself, and he knew in his heart that he was more Idumaean than Jew, and that one with purer blood could make a claim to his throne and receive the support of the people. Underestimating Herod's paranoia had cost many rivals their lives.

"And so? What of it?" he demanded with childlike impudence of his servants in the room.

"Well, there is more, my lord Herod," responded Herod's high advisor Ze'ev, pausing in his nervous pacing of the room. He turned in a swirl of dark green robes to address the king. "The prisoners Pilate brings from the desert are more than mere . . . stragglers. My source informs me that they're foreigners unlike any we've ever seen in Jerusalem. They understand other tongues. They wear odd garments. And their skins are strange…colors."

Ze'ev, a man in the waning half of his years, possessed a dark strength that only increased as time passed. He was tall, lean, and mean. A long, dark beard streaked with gray guarded his face and mouth, and bushy black brows shingled his dark, brooding eyes. He bore no arms, for he was a Pharisee, a leader of the high priests of Judaea. His heart, however, was anything but holy.

His words got Herod's attention, or at least, aroused his amusement. "Really? You don't say. Flavinius, I think we've found some interesting sport for the games, don't you?"

The man Herod addressed lounged on one of the sofas, a goblet of wine and a bunch of grapes in his paws. His hair was close-cropped in the military style, his jaw line darkened by two days of stubble, his dull blue eyes evidence of his Germanian heritage. He wore only a white linen loincloth secured by a leather belt and straps that ran down his bare chest and boots that wrapped around massive calves to tie at the knee. His fair skin, burned by the sun to an angry reddish brown that glinted in the candlelight, rippled with the play of muscles whenever he moved. Bronze gauntlets braced his forearms. His broadsword, the blade longer and wider than a Roman *gladius*, lay sheathed and cast haphazardly on the floor.

The Roman warrior chuckled through a mouthful of the grapes. Spitting out some seeds, he said, "They wouldn't last five minutes in there — not even two, if they were facing me. Bring them on. I need the exercise."

Herod laughed, but Ze'ev didn't share in the merriment. He resumed his pacing, hands clasped behind his back, capped head lowered, debating with himself whether to share what he knew. This unexpected arrival threatened the balancing game he'd been playing with Rome and the Jews. Finally, he strode to stand a few feet from Herod and address him head-on. "They asked questions of the mob in the street." He paused, and said quietly, "They asked about a star. A sign in the skies. They asked about...the newborn King of the Jews."

Herod's head snapped back as if slapped. He sat up straight and leaned forward, nostrils flared and honey-brown eyes flashing with anger. He glared at Ze'ev as if the Pharisee had committed treason. His knuckles whitened as he gripped the arms of the chair. But before he could speak, a raspy voice floated out from the darkness in the back of the secret chamber.

"I believe..."

Turning, the three men looked at a fourth, a crouching, bald, nut-brown man rocking slowly back and forth on his haunches. His brow bore a painted yellow circle, for the Egyptian god Ra, and black runes were tattooed upon his drawn cheeks. His irises were black as the Nile at midnight against the startling whites of his eyes. Two gold armlets, fashioned as snakes and covered with hieroglyphic symbols, writhed around his upper arms. He wore a tunic in the Roman style around one lean shoulder, but it was dyed a ruddy brown instead of the Roman white or crimson. He was unarmed and unshod. His lithe frame looked capable of terrific flexibility, and he was known for his unrivaled ability to withstand pain. A sinister energy radiated from his very presence.

The dark Egyptian spoke again. "I believe...I've heard someone else go by that name, King of the Jews," he said softly and cynically. "Let me think. Who was that?"

Ammon-Kek was a direct descendent of the pharaohs and a worshipper of Osiris, the Egyptian god of the dead. Ze'ev knew that the Egyptian was trying to draw Herod's anger in another direction from the affront. The effort failed, however. Herod was not amused. "Quiet, you!" Herod hissed, shooting a dark glance at the man on the floor, and Ammon-Kek nodded in submission, the placid look on his face never changing.

Hatred laced Herod's words. "This… is…treason."

"Not entirely, good king," replied the Egyptian, "for they are not your subjects."

"That doesn't matter. What does is that the mob heard them. It's why you should have listened to me —" Ze'ev didn't complete the thought. "This is what I've been telling you all along. *This is the prophecy!*"

Herod looked at Ze'ev as if hearing him for the first time.

"My — ah, *our* people have known since the time of Moses, through the writings of the prophets, that a liberator, a Messiah, would come. This could be the sign!" warned Ze'ev, waving his hand wildly in the air.

"We, in the Temple, perform calculations," he said softly, almost to himself. He stared off into the vacant space before his eyes. "We see things…"

Ze'ev served many masters, from Jehovah to the emperor of Rome. His role here in Herod's palace was simple; to maintain the delicate balance between Judaea and Rome by whatever means necessary. He had encouraged Herod's vain empire-building spree, the new Temple in particular. In doing so, he gave his flock a mighty new place of worship and indebted them to Herod, despite their uneasiness with its Roman style and lax rules allowing Gentiles inside. The thousands of innocent Hebrew lives lost in Herod's exploits, well, they were lamentable, but the price for peace. Saving his neck, and the necks of his other Pharisees, was what Jehovah, the Jewish god, would have wanted.

Most important, in Jerusalem he gave Herod a trophy to boast of to the Roman Senate and gave himself and the other Pharisees a headquarters from which they could rule the Jews and enrich their sacred coffers. By cutting his deal with Herod, he'd ensured his own place high atop the ladder of Jewish society and the ruling body of the Sanhedrin. However, this news of kings was unsettling. And the cold sweat that trickled down the back of his spine warned Ze'ev that everything he'd done, every scheme hatched and every plan laid, was now in jeopardy.

"It was foretold that seventy-seven generations would pass…from the day of Abraham, our father, seventy-seven generations would live and die, then the anointed one would come to free his people…" His voice trailed off into a whisper.

He regained himself, looked Herod in the eye, and said flatly, "This is the seventy-seventh generation in the line of Abraham."

This, Herod thought, is *dangerous.*

This was fuel for a fire that could rage out of control. The zealots who opposed Rome prayed for this every day. This was the kind of fanatical bluster that could feed the flames of insurrection until he was thrown down, perhaps even murdered like Julius Caesar, and cause everything he'd built to be destroyed. And it would only take a single match to ignite the fury.

But Herod was too shrewd to allow that. He was already two mental steps ahead of Ze'ev, at least one in front of Ammon-Kek and a league ahead of the muscle-bound lunk on the couch who continued to feast as if he'd heard nothing but a forecast for rain on the morrow.

"This news…this rumor of a new 'king' won't go over well in Rome, or with the Senate. This could destabilize everything. And give the zealots courage," stated Herod.

"Indeed," ventured Ammon-Kek, rising with liquid ease to his feet, yet remaining in place. "Judaea is fortunate to have self-rule under your guiding hand, my king. But the hand of Rome is heavy, and his grip is tight. A new leader would become a rallying point for an…unhappy people," he concluded.

Herod heard the menace in his master assassin's voice. Ammon-Kek was a traveler, a doer of evil deeds, and a master of the deadly arts. He was easily the rival of Ze'ev, but applied his power with a more clandestine purpose.

More than one enemy or family member had died quite horribly at the hands of the Egyptian. As Herod listened to him, he thought Ammon-Kek's cold, clinical analysis of the current situation a perfect foil to the dire and prophetic warnings of his other, more emotional advisor.

"Tell me again. The prophecy," Herod said solemnly to Ze'ev.

"Many have foretold of his coming," Ze'ev said almost dreamily as he recalled the words of his forefathers. "'*And you, Bethlehem, land of Judah, are by no means least among the rulers of Judah; since from you shall come a ruler, who is to shepherd my people, Israel.*'" He finished softly and looked down.

Silence followed. The tapers whispered and snapped in the void of conversation.

"Bethlehem? That little dirty village? The one with all the shepherds and filthy animals?" asked Flavinius, who sometimes journeyed the land enforcing Herod's will on unwilling subjects. "And who's this Judah?"

Herod ignored him. "The mob," he inquired, "what do they think?"

Ze'ev answered, "They're troubled, King Herod. They fear that the shadows of war and bloodshed have crept once again to the doorstep of Jerusalem. But there are some zealots who…well, welcome the news. They wish to take up arms against Rome. The arrival of the strangers, and their words, has stirred them."

Herod stood with an angry, regal flourish that diminished the others' presence in the room. He bent his proud face downward, the play of shadows hiding the fury that creased his face and clenched the muscles in this hands and forearms. He strode about like a trapped leopard, frustrated by a snare he couldn't see, hear, or smell, yet sensed nonetheless.

"These…ingrates," he fumed. "I build them a city that rivals the marble-pillared grandeur of Rome. I give them the races, the games. I build walls to protect them. I bring trade from across the deserts to this godforsaken piece of sand—*arrrrr!*" he roared in anger. "I even rebuilt their damned Temple! I made it twice what it was—thrice! It was a hovel, before me. Now there's none like it in the entire empire! Why, I bring stability, prosperity! And they want a new king? Ingrates!"

"Well," offered Ammon-Kek, fearing little the royal rage, "you *have* killed quite a few of these ingrates. In the mines. In the streets. Even in their precious Temple. Not to mention anyone who looked like a rival. You killed quite a few members of your own family, too. And, of course, there's a Roman garrison stationed here, ready to follow your every command. I think they have some…legitimate reasons to fear you, great one."

Herod liked it when the Egyptian was so saucy. And the commentary had its intended effect. The tempest within Herod's heart quieted to a squall. "The price of peace, dark one," he replied.

Ze'ev had stopped pacing, frozen by Herod's anger. Now he looked relieved to see Herod regain his composure. "We must act," he stressed. "Stop this before it starts. There must be no…problem."

Then Flavinius spoke in his dull, heavy voice. "So? We do what we always do. Crush them like grapes!" The ex-gladiator illustrated his point by squeezing the bunch of green fruit in his hand until the juices sluiced down his knuckles to the stone floor.

Herod looked at Flavinius with mild amusement. He'd been a gift to Herod from his Roman patron, Octavian. Flavinius had been a warrior in an army of men who had fallen beneath the swords of the Roman wedge. As the sole survivor, he'd been enslaved as a gladiator and battled his way from abject servitude to the luxury of this secret chamber through sheer savagery.

Flavinius often boasted to Herod, or to anyone who would listen, that he'd earned his freedom from the ring of gladiatorial combat by killing over one hundred men, many with his bare hands. His reward for conquering death was service as Herod's personal bodyguard. His imposing presence kept ambitious assassins and family members at bay. What the man possessed in sheer brawn, however, he more than lacked in cranial strength. Flavinius always chose death and dismemberment as his first course of action. Any plan more complex than that would have to come from someone else in the room.

"For once, he may actually be right," the amused Egyptian said.

"Perhaps, but timing...timing," said Herod, planning his next move with all the care of a haggler in the bazaar. "And we must destroy everyone. Especially this 'King of the Jews.' We must learn more. And deal with this immediately." He sat down deliberately on his chair.

"Yes, my liege," Ze'ev responded.

"Bring the strangers to me tomorrow. I wish to speak with them. Then," he looked at Flavinius with a grim smile, "we'll dispose of them."

His advisors took the cue and left. Herod, however, stayed in the chair far into the night, calculating and pondering coming events. He had to play this just right.

CHAPTER THIRTY-TWO

In the dank, smothering air of the dark cell, Barir had nodded off. He'd managed to position himself next to the guard who carried Shin-shin's limp form slumped over his shoulder as they descended the prison stairs. When he'd taken the girl's body in his arms at the foot of the stairs, he was put in a cell with her and Balthazar.

For many hours, Balthazar had held the child's head in his lap, meditating and looking toward the ceiling, mouthing silent words to what Barir assumed were the magus' strange gods. Barir had slept, only to awake a short while later to find Balthazar asleep, with Shin-shin laid out beside him. Her blood-drained, waxen skin glowed eerily in the gloom. She looked dead.

Fearing the worst, he went to her and put his ear to her chest. It moved ever so faintly, and he breathed his own sigh of relief. She hadn't yet given up the fight. And as any soldier knows, where there was fight, there was hope.

Balthazar was motionless, but the soldier had learned not to underestimate the man. Only the slight movement of his long moustache indicated that he breathed. Barir studied the man for a moment, still amazed at the collection of personalities the star had gathered together.

The magus wore the dress of his homeland. Balthazar's and the entire party's clothing had been lovingly repaired by the Petrans and returned at their departure from the hidden city. The soft, green silken shirt and pants had curious designs embroidered on the edges, and little wooden toggles held them together. His feet were still shod in simple black slippers more appropriate for the bedroom than the battlefield. Despite his gray hair, Barir correctly presumed that he was younger than he appeared. And certainly stronger. Barir had seen Balthazar and Shin-shin deploy their formidable skills on the battlefield before the hidden city and knew that more lay beneath the odd clothing than just an odd man.

He leaned back against the stone wall and slid to a seated position on the floor, his back grinding and sloughing against the rough surface of the wall. After a few moments, he wasn't surprised to see Balthazar rise quietly and approach the little girl.

Balthazar took her up, and found himself longing to see her almond eyes open and beam again with the light he'd seen within her.

Balthazar had lived a hermit's life. He had no wife, for science and philosophy were his betrothed, and he'd dedicated his life to serving them. Though it was a lonely life, he enjoyed his life of contemplative solitude.

But this child, from the start, had stirred something unknown in him. A feeling of responsibility. A different kind of dedication. And over the course of his adventure, the child — with the star as her key, no doubt — had unlocked emotions he had long ago set aside. Simply put, it was love. The love of a parent for a child, the strongest love there is. He'd not realized it until now, but there it was. And he now felt the helplessness that parents feel when the survival of their child is out of their hands. He surrendered his logic, his mind, to the power of his heart.

He scooped up the girl's body and walked to a square patch of faint blue a few feet away, made by the wan starlight shining through the barred window high in the stone wall.

Half crumpling, half genuflecting, he fell to his knees in supplication. Tears streamed down his face. He'd shed tears as a child, but not since, not even in the direst pain from a wound. They tracked thin white lines through the dirt on his face and suspended themselves at the ends of his whip-like moustache like diamonds.

When he looked up, light washed over his face—the cooling, soothing pulse of the star. The familiar song filled his ears. The starlight and the song reached out and touched the magus, deep in the bowels of the Roman garrison.

"My life," he said softly, "that which no man has had the strength to take from me, I offer to you. Spare her. She is but… a child. An innocent. Spare her."

The star pulsed as he watched it. He didn't doubt that it understood. Like the first soldier through a breached wall, he went willingly to his death here, knowing that, in doing so, another might live.

Barir looked on speechless, his warrior heart shredding with pity at the sight of such sadness and loss. He found himself hoping for a quick end for the girl and her forlorn master.

The star, however, wasn't interested in sacrifice. Its melodic voice filled his head and his soul. *Balthazar, messenger of the One God, you've come to believe. This act alone can save the child. No holocaust on earth is dear enough to save one such as this, for she is beloved by God. Many lambs will indeed perish, far too many, before this is ended. But not this one. You will indeed be called upon to sacrifice, as will all who hear the call. But your love has saved the child.*

The song subsided, but the light brightened. He squinted against the glare and angled his head away. Yet he held his place, continued holding the child in his arms before him. He felt the star's radiant heat beating against the flesh of his body. Then, with a flash, it was over.

He peered at the window. The star had returned to its original luminosity, but the song was stronger in his ears than before. He realized with humility that the hand of God touched him.

He wasn't alone. The body in his arms trembled as life returned to its frame. With a sound somewhere between a moan and a roar, Shin-shin sucked in a huge gasp of air, and her eyes snapped open.

She looked recovered; in fact, she looked completely healthy. She was the same girl he'd come to know and love, but with one difference — in her eyes danced a light, a small jet of silver fire that shone like...like the light of the star.

"Where...where am I?" she asked innocently, her wide eyes darting about with a mixture of fear and uncertainty. "Wh-why is it so dark?"

Balthazar couldn't speak. His joy over the star's gift was too strong, too powerful for words. Once again, tears streamed down the philosopher's face, but this time they were tears of grateful joy.

Another voice answered her from the darkness. "We've come at last to Jerusalem, and we're the guests of the king here. You really gave us a scare, you know."

Barir joined them in the patch of starlight. He looked at the magus, and a smile cracked his battle-worn features. Balthazar, too, smiled and nodded. Balthazar set Shin-shin on her feet, and she took a few paces around.

"Nice way to treat a guest. This place looks more like a prison than a guest's chambers. And...it stinks!" Wrinkling her nose, Shin-shin kicked at the ground with her feet in disgust.

Balthazar noted dryly, "Yes, you're back to normal, I see."

Barir looked at Balthazar and said, his voice quiet, "We've got to get her out of here."

Balthazar nodded, then walked over to look at the small window.

Barir knelt and put his hands on Shin-shin's shoulders. "We *are* prisoners here. You were hurt in the battle. You fell

246

sick and just now, well, you're better. Master Balthazar saved you. The Romans brought us here under guard. Tomorrow we're to be...executed, I think."

Shin-shin's face blanched. Barir was reminded how young and frail she was, and how vulnerable a child was in this world of war.

From the window, Balthazar spoke. Shin-shin smiled as if she knew the tone.

"This cell," he said, his hands clasped behind his arched back as he peered up at the window, "was constructed to hold even the mightiest man prisoner within its walls. Yes. Shin-shin, do you recall the lesson of the elephant and the mouse?"

"Yes, master," she replied, falling easily back into their familiar routine. "The lesson is: each is special in its own ways. The tiny mouse can accomplish great feats even the mighty elephant cannot."

"Good," replied her master.

"I don't really see . . ." started Barir, but then he paused.

"These bars would keep in an elephant. But a mouse, perhaps, could pass through them, no?" asked Balthazar, looking at Shin-shin before meeting Barir's eyes.

Barir grinned. He walked over and boosted Shin-shin up to the ledge. She squeezed, twisted, and squirmed her way through the bars in a fashion that would have made a contortionist proud, and after a few moments looked back through the barred window at them.

"I'll go around, take out the guards, and free you," she said. "Give me some time —"

Balthazar cut her off with a soft gesture of his upheld hand. "No, my pupil. Here ends the lesson. You must escape and save yourself. Our paths diverge here. You must go," he said quietly but firmly.

"But, master!" she wailed.

"He's right, Shin-shin," said Barir. "You have to leave. You have to save yourself."

Shin-shin cried, "But where will I go? I'm all alone! I'm… afraid."

Barir bowed his head for a moment, then looked up at her. She looked so small against the dark night. "Follow the star, Shin-shin, for it will never lead you astray. Its light will always be there to protect you, to guide you. Follow it. Trust it." The words sounded contrived and false in his mouth, but in his heart he knew they were true.

She looked up into the dark night and beheld the star. Her tense posture relaxed, as if she took some comfort from the sight. She turned to look back at the two men. "Master, I don't want to leave you…or you, Barir. I…I love you." Her voice broke. "I love you both."

"And we love you. And it's because we do that you have to go," said Barir solemnly.

She extended her arms through the bars, and each of the men took a hand. They stood so, frozen as if sculpted, for what seemed like an eternity. Then their hands slid apart, the fingers stretching for one last touch.

With a final wave, she turned and walked slowly off into the darkness of Jerusalem, all alone against a strange world, thousands of miles from her home. The darkness swallowed her in a moment, and she was gone.

Barir reached up and tried to pry the bars apart in vain. He grunted with the effort. He looked at Balthazar. "No chance you could bend these, eh? Maybe just one more trick up your sleeve?"

Shaking his head, Balthazar walked back to his previous spot on the floor and lay down. "To do so might have been possible at one time, but not now. We aren't meant to leave. The fact that the child did shows that she was meant to do so. No, I'm afraid we must wait and see what tomorrow brings." He settled back and said nothing else.

Barir stood looking out the window for a while, feeling an odd mixture of depression and elation at the miracle that had taken place. He glanced over at Balthazar and saw he was still awake. The thin, wet line of a tear trickled down the magus' face from the corner of his eye. Barir finally appreciated just how much the magus cared for the child, though he gave such little outward sign of it. Barir recalled Sheik Shareef's prediction about sacrifice. It looked to be true.

Within his heart and mind, Balthazar wept as well. All his life, he'd devoted himself to control and study. A life of solitude had always been attractive and logical for him.

But the child, and the journey, and the star, he guessed, had changed all that. Love and attachment had stolen upon and transformed him, much as the brush with dry death in the desert had transformed Gaspar from solitary warrior to gentler giant. Balthazar pondered the change within him, realizing it even as the child who had catalyzed it walked away into the darkness. *This bears further meditation,* he mused, and slowly drifted off to sleep knowing he would never truly understand it all.

Looking out the window, Barir said contentedly to himself. "Whatever tomorrow does bring, let's get it over with."

CHAPTER THIRTY-THREE

Long after the sun rose, Melchior looked out his window at the star. Its white light still shone rebelliously in the yellow haze of the midmorning sun, staking its claim on the sky. Melchior wondered how many others could now see its magical light and how much longer it would burn.

Eventually, guards came to take the prisoners away. They questioned the absence of the sick child, but Balthazar offered an entirely plausible story about the child passing away in the night. They had shoved the disease-rotted body out the window to avoid contagion, he said. The guards were ready to accept such a story if it meant that they didn't have to touch the body.

Now bound in irons, they stepped out of the building escorted by a large squad of soldiers, no doubt to deter any attempt at escape. They entered the square before the Antonia barracks, shielding their eyes from the bright combination of sunlight and starlight. As they shuffled along blindly, Balthazar and Barir murmured the truth to the others, that Shin-shin was healed and safely on her way out of Jerusalem.

After they'd marched a few moments, Melchior's eyes acclimated to the bright light and his senses grew more alert. He asked of a guard near him, "Where are you taking us? I demand to see the king!"

The guard laughed maliciously. He said in a voice laced with scorn, "Then your wish is my command, my lord. It's to King Herod that we're taking you. I think, though, that in a short while, you'll wish to have asked to see someone else!"

They moved at a brisk pace through the streets of Jerusalem, moving toward the far western side of the city. Off to the south, Melchior glimpsed the half dome of an amphitheater and the oval track of a hippodrome where chariot races and gladiatorial games were regularly held. The streets were busy with commerce this late in the morning, but everyone paused to see the strange parade go by. The spectators' behavior indicated that word of their presence, and the inquiries they'd made, had already passed through the city like a whispering wind. Frowns wrinkled many brows, and fear rippled across the faces of many others as they watched the cordon of men pass.

At last they turned a corner and saw the colonnaded façade of Herod's sprawling Roman-style palace. A water-filled moat surrounded the structure, and ornate fountains and waterfalls spurted water, a lavish indulgence, given the scarcity of water in such a dry climate. The result was both opulent and grotesque, Melchior observed. Three massive limestone towers rose at the palace's northern end. While the palace didn't rival in size the Temple Melchior had spied the day before, it was its equal in gross excess. The mammoth building screamed vanity from every angle.

As they drew closer, he made out ornate carvings on practically every flat piece of stone. Some were just Latin inscriptions paying chest-beating tribute to Herod, the emperor, or the gods. Others bore carved figures of the Roman gods themselves, some at war, some at play, all terrible in their beauty. Sprinkled among them were eagles and other birds of prey. The standards of the different legions and their commanders hung from the eaves, their richly dyed strips of bright crimson, lavender, and gold flapping in the light breeze. They glowed in the sunlight that struck the palace's shimmering white façade. The whole effect was intimidating, as it was meant to be, Melchior suspected.

Among the pedestrians, he saw a few Hebrews and obvious outsiders, caravan traders from distant parts and foreign dignitaries come to pay tribute, but most were Roman citizens of the upper class of Jerusalem and soldiers. Obviously, Melchior realized, while Herod was technically King of the Jews, he used the long arm of Rome keep it that way.

Melchior looked up as they were marched through an impressive arch and made out the words "Glory to Herod, Friend of Rome, Builder of Cities." It appeared, he noted, that the gift of the star included the ability to read all languages, along with speaking and understanding them. But in any tongue, the point was clear. This was Herod's House, and he wasn't a man to be trifled with.

They entered an outer court, with a well and a fire pit and well-manicured shrubs. Off to the sides, Melchior glimpsed elaborate gardens where more people milled about. The gardens seemed to be waiting areas before entering the actual palace. But the prisoners were herded through two massive doors of glowing wood from the faraway forests of Lebanon.

Inside, shafts of light fell from high openings to pierce the dim interior. Torches flickered all around, providing artificial illumination. Many Roman soldiers moved about, most in the formal livery of the palace guard, making the area feel more like an armed camp than a royal meeting hall.

Their guards spoke briefly with the head of the palace guard, who indicated an area off to the right. The guards marched their prisoners there and told them to wait. And wait they did.

Zoth had been eerily silent. Everyone noticed it, but none more than Melchior. Until now, he'd been satisfied to attribute it to injured pride and plans gone awry. But this was too long for Zoth to sit idle. They were chained together, not more than a pace apart, but they hadn't spoken yet this day. As he turned to his cousin and spoke, Melchior wondered if this was indeed the last time they would have the chance to make peace.

"Well, cousin, it looks like the end. Won't you at last take the opportunity to forget the past and any wrongs, and unite, just for once? Won't you...help me?" Melchior pleaded.

Zoth looked darkly at him. "If it weren't for you and your cursed star, I wouldn't even be here. And while you may be sure that your head will soon be parting from your shoulders, I have no such intention of succumbing to that fate. You're weak, Melchior. Afraid. No vision. You deserve to die."

Such an attack once would have made Melchior recoil, but no longer. He'd grown used to such diatribes from his cousin. Yet curiosity and the lack of anything better to do made him press. "Perhaps. Maybe you're right. But why do you hate me? You know the throne was rightfully mine. Did I ever deny you anything? You wielded all the power of a king, with no quarter. Why did you choose the path of hatred? You had no cause."

Looking around with wild eyes, Zoth waved his hand in a gesture of futility. "This! This is what we needed to face! Rome won't be happy with what it holds now. It's like a swarm of locusts devouring everything in its path, then moving on to feast some more. I saw this coming; you should have seen this coming. Now it's too late. Rome will devour us!"

He paused to catch his breath, and his voice dropped in volume, but not intensity. Sweat beaded on his translucent brow, and lines of fury creased his face as he spat, "Everything I had — gone! We should have stayed there and prepared for war. Braced for the coming onslaught instead of riding out to meet it with a handful of fellow fools! No, you led us on this silly errand to follow...a damned star. You're an idiot!

And it's your idiocy that will be your end."

He seemed finished, but then added a last thought. "And as your blood spills onto the stones, I'll be heading home to take what was always rightfully mine. And defend and protect the old ways of my father. I never needed you to 'give' me anything, fool. I was always your better."

As Zoth looked away, Melchior finally felt…relief. Granted, Zoth was a bad man. But the seeds of unhappiness were planted in his heart long ago and nurtured over time by unrealized ambition until they blossomed in the light of fear cast by the past few weeks. And his accusations were not off the mark.

Melchior said, "You've seen it. You've heard it. But you haven't listened to it, have you? The star. It's telling me — telling you — that the end is already here. And that there's nothing we can do to stop it. We're unwilling participants in an event we don't even comprehend. But still, I'm not afraid. Not anymore. My heart tells me…tells me to trust it. And to follow. If this is what was meant to be, well then, so be it. I guess it's…faith. All my life I've yearned for something to believe in, to give me hope. At last I have it. Faith. I have something to believe in."

He paused, looked down at his hands, and said quietly, "Guess it did come a little late, though. Look, Zoth. There was never any question. I had to follow. As did you. We have duties to fulfill. Parts to play. Obligations greater than those back home. This is about sacrifice. And I think that, if we do, we may just save the very people you think I've abandoned. Maybe even our own lives. But the old ways? I think they're gone forever."

For a moment, a unit of time so small it was the measure of a scorpion's strike, Melchior thought he'd gotten through. But then the moment passed. Zoth said nothing and continued to scowl. Melchior gave up and turned to lean against the cool wall and rest. But his heart burned with a renewed fire to see the quest through to the end.

However, Melchior was right; Zoth had heard him, and his heart was more troubled than ever.

After an hour or so, Pilate and his commandants stalked up to eye the ragtag group of prisoners with disdain. Pilate was still dressed as a warrior, but his breastplate, weapon, and belt shone with hammered, polished gold.

"Well, I see a night at the garrison didn't do you much good. Wait—one's missing." He turned to address the soldier in charge.

"The girl. She died in the night," the guard said matter-of-factly, leaving out the detail of the missing body.

"Really? Wish she'd done that a hundred leagues ago. Well…" Pilate paused. "It's unimportant. Herod has summoned us—King Herod, I mean."

He cued his tribunes with a wicked smile, and they forced appreciative laughter. Melchior noted two things—the Romans didn't think much of Herod, and the soldiers thought their legate was an ass. Melchior found himself agreeing with them, for once.

Putting his hands on his hips, Pilate turned and looked hard at Zoth. The dark sorcerer, bent and bedraggled but not yet beaten, met the stare and held it. After their recent conversation, Melchior suspected that Zoth had one last trick up his sleeve.

Pilate said, "Separate this one from the others. But keep him chained and watch him well. He may yet have the chance to save his neck."

Zoth bowed his head in thanks and was soon shuffling along a few feet behind Pilate's retinue. The other prisoners followed amidst their guards. Pilate led the way down a long corridor, then down a much wider corridor that ended abruptly in the throne room, a cavernous hall that could hold a thousand men, Melchior judged, with room left for a few dozen of Balthazar's elephants.

Sunlight spilled into Herod's hall from open-air windows high above. The floor glistened with tiles in a beautiful mosaic of browns, blacks, and reds. Thick, rich rugs were strategically placed about the hall, with a long blue one heading straight to the throne. More fountains burbled here, and exotic animals lay here and there on the floor. Gaspar recognized a tiger and a crocodile. Wonderfully plumed birds from faraway lands shrieked on their perches.

Men huddled in small, scattered groups. Their deep-throated conversations paused as they quickly assessed the newcomers. Sensing little other than an imminent execution, they resumed their haggling and plotting.

Against the far wall stood an attractive, dark-haired woman of middle age and simple dress. A servant, a young girl, stood beside her. She looked at the Magi with pity, but said nothing.

Pilate gestured for the guards to move the prisoners forward and to the side. He walked alone up the blue carpet to a carved wooden throne, bound here and there with gold. Its back was high, its arms thick and shaped like a lion's clawed paws. It sat between two Roman standards draped from polished wooden posts

Melchior looked up at the throne on its dais of marble and beheld Herod the Great for the first time. Certainly, he'd seen his image on numerous statues and even on the coins their guards had gambled with, but they hadn't done the man justice.

The man looked like one of the Roman gods he'd seen carved in the marble and limestone outside. Noble in stature, beautiful in demeanor, he looked as if he'd stepped down from the heavens to pay the mortals a visit. He wore a purple toga over a simple white tunic and a circlet of gold upon his head. Melchior couldn't gauge his age; the man seemed timeless, young, and if he hadn't overheard otherwise from their guards, he wouldn't have known that Herod's flawless face disguised a man of more than fifty years.

Herod was engrossed in conversation with a dark, bearded man standing at his side who, by his dress, didn't look Roman to Melchior. However, he had the king's ear, so Melchior made a mental note to observe the man during their audience.

A number of scribes, the only ones sitting besides Herod, scribbled notes on curling, crusty pieces of papyrus to his left. On the right stood a giant of a Roman warrior, armed, looking somewhat haughty and pleased with himself. Melchior assumed him to be an enforcer of some sort. And he noticed another figure hidden off to the right, far back in the shadows afforded by the throne and the standards. Melchior couldn't quite make him out, but took note of him nonetheless.

Pilate stopped short a few respectful paces from the dais. He bowed his head, clapped his hand across his metal-encased breast, and saluted the king. "Hail, Herod! King of Judaea and lands beyond. Lord of Jerusalem, Caesarea, Samaria, and other cities. Hail Herod, beloved of Rome," Pilate shouted with martial emphasis.

Herod had been feigning conversation with Ze'ev, making Pilate wait so he could better judge the strangers in the legate's charge. He was sure that Ammon-Kek was lurking about somewhere, doing the same thing.

Herod felt the rush of blood in his veins. His heart pumped with vitriolic energy. This, the game, was what he enjoyed most—the wielding of power to control not just men's lives, but the very course of history. His calculating, cunning mind had attacked the problem of the strangers and their questions from over a thousand different angles in the hours leading to this moment. The board was set, the pieces laid out. And the opening move had just been played.

Of course, he revealed nothing. It was precisely this control that had enabled him to come so far, even when the odds had been hopelessly stacked against him. Roman civil wars, the ever-shifting landscape of the Senate, and the change in ownership of the throne of the Roman Empire should have taken everything from him. Yet Herod had played it carefully and coolly, shifting alliances at just the right time and succoring those when they needed it most. This, here today in his very hall, was just the next round of the overall tournament.

Herod yawned, not a small *try to conceal it for civility's sake kind of yawn*, but a real, *I'm already bored with you, you imbecile* kind of yawn.

Only a king can pull off a yawn like that, noted Melchior. No stranger to court decorum, he'd managed a few of those yawns in his time.

But more than following the royal antics, Melchior was assessing the roles, the levels, and the agendas in the room, and planning how best to use them to extricate himself and his companions from the sticky situation they were in. That one yawn cemented Pilate as the pawn and Herod as the player.

"*Legatus* Pilate. So...good to see you again," replied Herod with tedium. "Although I think you're a bit overdue, hmmm?"

Pilate's distaste for Herod and his lack of respect for the man were difficult to disguise, especially from Melchior's astute eye. Pilate's overly robust response revealed his true feelings.

"Lord Herod, we returned once our task was done. We've scoured the lands to the south and east for rebels, and slaughtered many of them in the emperor's name. And yours, of course." Pilate finished and bowed his head. *To hide that smirk*, Melchior decided. *He thinks he's won the round.*

"You return to me a few men short, I believe," said Herod, suddenly taking on a much sterner tone. He'd transformed from sleepy monarch to royal inquisitor in the blink of an eye, catching Pilate off guard. Pilate began to speak, but Herod cut him off with a sharp wave of his hand. "What tribute do you bring? What spoils, slaves? What cities have you captured and subdued? How has the empire grown in the months you've been gone?" Herod asked him.

The hapless legate kept his mouth shut.

Melchior sensed Pilate squirming. *Ah, he sees the board now and has wisely chosen to stop moving his piece.*

"I see," said Herod, sitting back to savor his intellectual victory. Herod leaned to look over at the prisoners. "So, what have you brought me?"

All acting, of course, Melchior observed appreciatively. *It's part of the game.*

"Prisoners, King. We took them many leagues from here, outside Petra. They were aiding the Nabataean rebels. I'm pleased to report that we killed many of them, and we know the location of the city. Once I refit my men, and with another legion, the city will—"

Herod cut him off again with another curt gesture. "We'll leave your rather dismal performance against a band of camel herders armed with their grandfathers' knives for later," he said with the snide tone of a parent speaking to an insolent child. "Tell me of your prisoners instead."

Pilate grimaced at the insult, but said, "They're strangers, the likes of which I've never seen. They're decent fighters and seem a step above the others we faced. But they drew swords and spilled the blood of the sons of the Rome, so they must be punished. I bring them to you for sentencing and judgment, lord."

With an impatient wave of his hand, Herod dismissed Pilate's rhetoric. "Well, let's see about that. Bring them forward. Let's have a look."

Pilate's shoulders slumped, broken at last. Turning on his heel, he waved at the guards to bring the prisoners forward.

Melchior whispered as the five prisoners shuffled along, "Play this nicely. Defer to him. Flatter. And don't let him trick you into something we'll regret!"

Balthazar nodded imperceptibly, and Gaspar grunted. Barir said nothing, and if Zoth heard, he gave no indication.

Halting next to Pilate, the prisoners gave as low a bow as their restraints allowed. The room, which had been filled with the light buzz of conversation, became eerily silent. Even the beasts seemed to sense that something important was about to take place.

Herod sized them up and was pleased with what he saw. Secretly, he'd feared that Ze'ev was worried about nothing, that the men were simply but a bunch of wild Bedouin with too little water or too much wine. Now he could see that this wasn't the case.

"Well, you certainly are an odd bunch of devils," Herod said sardonically. "Very odd indeed, to see such… diversity…in one group."

Certainly, they were dirty. Malnourished, wounded, and most probably hosts to a dozen different kinds of lice. But they possessed a dignity that Herod couldn't deny, an inner sense of pride and purpose. He knew immediately that these men could be useful.

Melchior stepped forward. "Lord Her-ugh—" The stranger grunted as Pilate jammed an elbow into his gut. He doubled over in pain and coughed to regain his breath.

Pilate, looking to earn a few points, hissed, "Prisoners do not address the king!"

The points weren't awarded. Herod said, "No, Pilate, let them speak. I want to hear what they have to say."

At this, Balthazar perked up. *He knows*, and he sent the thought telepathically to the others. *He knows.*

Melchior looked venomously at Pilate, who returned the glare. Then he straightened and said, "Lord Herod, we come in peace. We're simple travelers, waylaid many times by misfortune and mischief. The people of the fair city of Petra saved our lives. We owed them our lives and thus our arms, when they were attacked. It was our duty." He looked at Gaspar and smiled slightly.

"But we ourselves have no quarrel with Rome or the mighty kingdom of Judaea. We sue for mercy…and our freedom…to continue our journey." Melchior stopped. He hadn't planned on anything past this point. It seemed fairly clear that he was going to get one shot at this, and he took it. Now it was up to—

"I drew no sword, good king!" interrupted Zoth. "In fact, it was I who led your legate Pilate to these barbarians. I'm falsely accused!"

If looks could kill, Gaspar's would have leveled Zoth where he stood. But the dark sorcerer paid him no mind. Instead, he looked plaintively to Pilate.

Herod asked, "Is this true, Pilate?"

Grudgingly, Pilate replied, "Well, yes. To a degree. But I believe he was false with us . . . and he practiced sorcery of a nature I deem to be evil. So I took him into custody, as well. He's part of their group, Herod, and I bring him to you for judgment, too."

"*King* Herod, Roman." The king's bearded advisor spoke for the first time.

High priest or counselor, thought Melchior, quietly assigning titles to the players in this drama. *Hebrew, not Roman. Don't trust him a bit.* Aloud he said, "I'm Melchior, from the east. This is my servant Barir, and my kinsman Zoth." He sensed Zoth's discomfort with the association.

Gaspar spoke, his rich baritone filling the cavernous hall with its dark, mellifluent music. "I am called Gaspar. I've come many leagues from my home far in the south." He bowed his head slightly as he finished.

"And I," said the little man in his sweet, soft voice, bowing low, "am Balthazar, your humble servant, from the lands of Orient, far over the mountains to the northeast."

Herod looked at them hard, as if caught off guard that they were divided. "You say you're on a journey. You tell me from whence you've come. Yet you don't tell me where you're going," he said slowly.

There was an awkward silence. The Magi looked down and avoided making eye contact with the king. Melchior thoroughly expected Zoth to sell them out. But he didn't. When he risked a glance in his cousin's direction, Melchior's eyes met Zoth's, and the dark sorcerer arched his eyebrows in mock surprise. It was almost as if he enjoyed toying with Herod as he did with everyone else.

The dark-skinned man who'd been moving about in the shadows slithered into view at Herod's side. He rested a hand with surprising familiarity on the armrest of the throne. "Of course, if you choose not to answer, there are other means at my lord's disposal," he said in a thick Egyptian accent. He stroked the long, mean knife tucked into his belt.

"I don't like idle threats. They're the currency of the coward," said Gaspar, taking a bold step forward and moving his large hands forward in a gesture of defiance. "Use it or crawl back to your hole."

The other man on Herod's side spoke up. "Now, now, patience everyone." His voice was sickly-sweet and placating, the tone of a man who'd spent a lifetime playing two sides of an argument. "This is unnecessary. Just tell us why you were traveling here."

Melchior's mind was scrambling. They were certainly in a position of weakness. But their captor's insistence on learning the purpose of their journey revealed his weakness. Herod and his cohorts knew something, but not much. Perhaps they knew bits and pieces. Perhaps they'd even seen the star. And the priest, whom he took to be a Hebrew, certainly knew of the prophecies of the coming of the Messiah. They had one piece to gamble with.

As if he'd come to the same conclusion, Balthazar stepped up beside Gaspar and blurted, "The star. In the west."

The Ethiopian magus' face fell. His head swiveled to give Balthazar the full benefit of his face, frozen in disbelief.

But Balthazar paid no mind. "Where is the newborn King of the Jews? We saw his star at its rising…and we've come to pay him respect." He faltered a bit. Like Melchior, he must have wondered why he'd said the bit about paying respect. But Melchior realized that it felt…right.

Melchior stepped forward, feeling an uncontrollable

impulse to speak, and picked up the story from his friend. "King Herod, we are...we're magi. Astrologers, if you will, from faraway lands. We've seen a sign in the sky and journeyed long to go where it has led us."

Herod kept his face placid. The game had quickly changed, and the small one's gambit had suddenly doubled the stakes. And if one was a sorcerer, a magus, they probably all were. They tended to travel in packs. But they were divided; that could be used to his advantage. He savored the continuation of the game.

"I see. Astrologers. I see." He stalled for a minute, idly stroking his chin. He then made his countermove. "Tell me more about the signs. What have they told you?"

Melchior's visage changed slightly, as if something had taken hold of him. He blurted, "We believe this child to be your anointed one, the one the prophets foretold long ago. He who would come and lead your people. The Messiah."

That one caught Herod off guard, and he couldn't keep the shock from his face. He'd expected a subtle denial. Instead, he got a direct answer, the one he actually wanted. The unexpected play left him again at a loss for words. All he could mumble was, "Where?"

Gaspar felt a burning in his stomach. Adrenaline surged in his veins. An unseen force, like a strong hand, shoved him forward and controlled him. He felt his mouth open, and words formed on his lips, but they weren't his own. The voice that came from him was his, and yet not. He, like his comrades, had become the mouthpiece of a higher power.

"In Bethlehem of Judaea, for thus it has been written through your prophet: *'And you, Bethlehem, land of Judaea, are by no means least among the rulers of Judaea; since from you shall come a ruler, who is to shepherd my people Israel.'*"

The confessions of the Magi shattered the tense silence that had filled the room, and a heavy buzz of surprised dialogue erupted. Every Hebrew in the room heard the words of the ancient prophets coming to fruition. The

Romans heard outright insurrection. Visitors from afar heard disturbing predictions that could only mean trouble.

Herod had heard enough. For now. It was high time to suspend play and create a situation where he once again controlled all the moves. These men were either mad, or they were a bigger problem than he'd first thought.

Melchior saw the high priest lean in and whisper to Herod. The dark man receded a pace, but even from where he stood, Melchior could see the smile of triumph on his face. Melchior was unsure of himself. Had they given away too much?

Beside him, Balthazar nodded imperceptibly toward the dark-haired woman against the rear wall. Melchior followed his gaze. She had her hand to her mouth, but it was in surprise, not fear. Even though Herod had never acknowledged her or even her presence, Melchior felt a connection between her and the king.

Herod and the priest spoke quietly together as the buzz continued. Then he held his hand up for silence. He spoke again, his voice warm as butter. "We shall speak no more of this. You've journeyed far, been unjustly imprisoned, and treated like common criminals." He smiled and rose from his seat. "A thousand pardons. Pilate, release them."

Next to the king, Ze'ev nodded sympathetically.

His face burning in shame at the cowardly, transparent betrayal that Herod had just thrust upon him, Pilate glared at Herod. Then he barked an order to the guards, who removed the chains from the prisoners, including Zoth. They rubbed their wrists and moved their feet in relief.

Herod continued with, "You shall be my guests. After you've washed and rested, we shall meet again to discuss this further. And to see how we might...aid you in your journey." He nodded, then swept off the dais without even noting the whole room bowing to him.

The man Melchior had identified as a priest walked over to the Magi. "Welcome," he said. "I'm Ze'ev, high priest of the Temple. King Herod has instructed me to offer you the comforts of his home. Follow me, if you please."

Pilate stayed behind. Melchior overheard him telling a few guards to stay with the former prisoners to make sure they didn't escape. He saw Zoth turn to look at legate and smile a wicked grin before they passed through the hall's entrance.

Ammon-Kek appeared at Pilate's side. "Now, be a good soldier," he said. "Herod won't forget your contribution in this matter. And he won't forget Rome, either."

Pilate looked at him sideways, unsure of what to make of the Egyptian's tone.

Ammon-Kek said darkly, "There can only be one King of the Jews. And he just left the room."

He departed, following the group. Pilate stood alone in the chamber, his arms crossed, his mood foul. He'd been played for a fool. And he had a bad feeling about all of this.

CHAPTER THIRTY-FOUR

So that was Herod. Not such a bad fellow after all," Zoth said, then continued snidely, "I'm sure he'll be just as charming when he nails us to one of those crosses later."

"They only do that to the worst criminals, according to the Roman guards," replied Barir after swallowing a bite of bread. "It's special. They'll probably just hang you. Or cut your head off."

"Oh, *much more* pleasant. *Thank you*," sneered Zoth.

They were in a large lounging chamber somewhere in Herod's palace. Couches, pillows, low tables bearing busts of long-dead patricians, and other Roman accoutrements filled the room, as well as a larger table holding food and pitchers of wine and water.

The high priest Ze'ev had left them there, bidding them to take ease, clean up and dine. He'd departed quickly, telling them that he'd go to Pilate and get their belongings back. He'd bowed severely before leaving the room.

Within moments, Gaspar had checked outside the door to the chamber and found a number of sentries guarding the way out.

Although wary of the food and not inclined to take Herod or Ze'ev at their word, Balthazar sniffed and sampled the fruit, bread, and meat and declared it safe and, after a bite or two, delicious. Soon they were all gobbling it and slurping chalices of drink. They spoke little for at least half an hour.

It was already past midday. Melchior walked to the window and discovered that they were high up in the palace facing west, overlooking the outer wall of the city. No escape there, except by falling a few hundred feet to a splattering death. He saw small buildings and dwellings beyond the wall, separated from each other by more and more of the cracked, dry earth, the farther from the city he looked. The sun burned fiercely in a cloudless sky. And there the star still shone, calling to him. He looked at it for a prolonged moment, questioning himself and their actions in Herod's chambers. Then he returned to the others.

Crossing the room, he slumped onto the floor, leaning his back against a chair leg. Barir tossed him a pear, which he bit into. A thin line of the sweet juice escaped the corner of his mouth. He wiped it with his sleeve, then took another bite and rolled the grainy flesh of the fruit around in his mouth. He savored the sweet taste for a moment, suspecting that he may never enjoy such extravagance again. Swallowing, he said, "Well, we don't have much time. They're going to call us back soon, so we'd better have a plan."

Zoth, who'd been acting as if he didn't notice, couldn't hide the fact that he was indeed noticing and listening. "The food is to fatten the calves before the slaughter. Eat up," he warned.

Gaspar said, "Odd as it may seem to say, Zoth is right. We're being fattened to loosen our tongues. I don't believe this hospitality is genuine."

"No, it's not," Balthazar agreed. "You're both correct. But we have something he wants. And how we use it to our advantage will decide whether we live or die."

Balthazar added matter-of-factly, "He doesn't know where the child is." And he took a loud bite of his apple.

Melchior looked at him and nodded. "Of course. And we do. Well, sort of…"

Gaspar said, "Do we? Do we really? Point me the way!"

They all looked back at him stupidly, half-heartedly admitting that they had little idea where to go. The star had been guiding them since the beginning. And if Herod and his priests and scribes could not see it, then…

"You were downright talkative out there, my friend," Melchior chided Gaspar. "Had a sudden, ah, urge to speak, right? The bit about that place, Bethlehem, would've been useful earlier, hmmm?"

Gaspar nodded thoughtfully. "Something outside of me controlled me, forced me to say the words. But…they were true. True words. My heart tells me so."

Melchior smiled at him and said, "I know. Me, too. Once again, we're being used to fulfill a hidden agenda. I'm getting used to it, frankly. But the effect on Herod, and the people in there…well, that was—"

"It was *great*. I loved the way the color drained out of his face. Like a man who just felt the punch he never saw coming!" interrupted Barir. "Everyone else loved it, too. I don't think they like him much here." He returned to his meal, and the others digested his rather crude yet accurate reading of the room and the king.

Logical, sound Balthazar spoke next. "We must give him something to appease him, and earn our freedom. We must at least divert his attention so we can escape. We do know a few things, of course," he mused.

"That place called Bethlehem," said Gaspar, catching on to his line of thinking. "I wonder if it's far."

Melchior mused, "I don't think distance is a problem. See how far the fingers of Rome stretch to hold even this place in its grasp." He gestured about the very Roman room. "We've got to stall him. More important, we've got to get our strength back. And that means food, sleep, and," looking at the dirty Barir, "for Caesar's sake, take a bath."

The afternoon wore on. Each man took a turn standing beneath the fountain of clear, cold water that spurted from the mouth of a cherub in a recessed room. They washed their clothes and hung them to dry in the arid air on the terrace overlooking the city. Garbed in crimson robes of Roman design, they ate and drank until their bellies groaned with protest at the thought of another bite or sip.

Eventually, sleep overtook them. They set a watch, although the idea seemed somewhat ridiculous in a palace such as this. But none were under the delusion that this was any kind of safe haven. Death was only a door knock away, and the Magi collectively wanted to greet it when the door opened.

They all felt this way, of course, except Zoth. He was particularly irate, and the turmoil within him continued. He ate some, but didn't bathe as somehow, dirt and filth seemed repelled by his black wardrobe and alabaster skin, and he never looked quite as scruffy as the others. But he, too, was weaker than he should've been. And even as he stood on the terrace and surveyed the sleeping forms of the others and the bent back of Barir watching the door, he couldn't muster up the hate he'd fed on for so long. He actually felt…empty. Lost.

Evening was falling, and he turned to look out on Jerusalem, or what little of it he could see. He perceived it as a dirty place, filled with people who crawled about its streets like insects, doing the bidding and work of Rome. It was just this that he feared most, a life of servitude to a faceless master.

Herod, Augustus, what have you, they're all the same, he thought. *Politicians, not rulers.* Certainly, they yearned for power, as did he. But their ends, and their worlds, were far different. Zoth wished for the throne so he could rule a mighty land and people, where his word was law, and his will was unquestioned. Caesar and his puppets wanted something far more mundane — wealth. They measured a man or an empire by the size of its stores and vaults, not by its accomplishments or might. This money grubbing was…

sickening. What was the world coming to?

Zoth's soul wavered and tottered as if on the point of a sword. He at last had felt the desperation of loneliness, the chilling dread that everything he'd clung to had become alien in a world that was changing too fast, too fast. Then he heard it, for the first time, truly heard it.

The star called to him. Even him. The power, or force, or god that was its source called even to him. He looked up, and the ice that entombed his heart began to crack.

He was baffled. And most afraid. For when the star entered a man's soul, he was forever changed. Zoth suddenly understood the urgency the others had felt. The star was a stern master. Yet its greatest effect on him was sadness.

Unwillingly, he thought of the years he'd spent trying to usurp his cousin for his own malicious ends. He thought of the lives he'd taken. He thought of the nights on end he'd practiced the dark arts, choosing the easier, wicked, and more seductive path. He thought, and he felt. He felt — was it even possible? — regret.

Suddenly, a beam of intense light shot down from high in the heavens and punctured him like a shaft launched from a bow. It pierced him and lifted him from his feet, pulling upward from his chest as if he were hanging on a rope of light strung from above.

Intense, burning waves of energy washed over him, opening his pores, bending his bones, carbonating his blood, and shaking his flesh with the power the light shaft sent through his dangling body. His eyes bulged, his tongue lolled from his mouth, and he hung paralyzed, yet his mind was bursting.

A voice spoke to him, its tone stern, yet kind. Zoth heard it, yet was certain that the voice spoke to everyone. It was a mix of melodic music and deadly gravity, an unearthly expression with a trumpet-like quality that far surpassed those of any of the now minor entities he'd communed with in his pursuit of evil. Was this...the God?

"EVEN THE LEAST AMONG YOU ARE COUNTED AMONG MY CHILDREN. WHATSOEVER CRIME YOU HAVE COMMITTED, THY HEART HOLDS FORGIVENESS IN IT. FOLLOW ME, AND YOU SHALL FIND EVERLASTING PEACE. REPENT AND FOLLOW."

It was over in a flash. Zoth fell hard onto the floor.

The shaft of light subsided, although he sensed that the star was still there, pulsing away. The soft rumble of the city replaced the roar of the voice as Jerusalem's citizens prepared for the evening.

It took a few moments, but he slowly regained his feet. Zoth realized he had briefly lost consciousness. He looked about, expecting the others to come running to see what had taken place. Yet they slept on. Even Barir was asleep, leaning to one side like a drunken wedding guest.

Finally he summoned the courage to look up at the star. He feared another encounter, but none took place. The star simply shone as it had before, bathing his face with its beautiful white light.

His brow furrowed in concentration. What had just taken place? Had he, too, fallen asleep and dreamed the entire thing? Had the desert madness finally taken its toll on him?

As he turned to enter the chamber, his hand absently rubbed his chest. It was tender. Pulling apart his dark robes, he found a red, star-shaped burn in the center of his sternum. He looked down at it, then looked back up at the star, his mouth gaping open in astonishment.

The summons came later in the night. The waning moon hung moodily overhead, already halfway through his nightly journey in his hunt for the sun.

A guard, one of Herod's personal garrison, banged on the door with the hilt of his drawn sword as he entered. The companions, however, were already up and waiting.

Melchior felt better. He felt his strength returning, and even his aching muscles complained less than they had since their respite at Petra.

Gaspar came to him and said quietly, "I feel pretty good. Back to myself."

"I'm better as well," said Balthazar, joining them.

"Actually, I feel great. Like I could kick an entire Roman legion on their backsides, single-handedly," added Gaspar. "Should we make a try of it? There can't be too many guards here. I think we could take them with our bare hands."

"No," Melchior said, "not yet. And I can't tell you why. I've got a feeling we have to play out what we started this morning with Herod. But save your strength, my friend. I've got a feeling we'll need everything we've got soon enough."

With Barir taking the rear, they filed out into the darkened hallway. Fires murmured in wall-mounted braziers along the way, providing just enough light to walk by, but little else.

After walking a while, Gaspar looked over his shoulder and whispered to Balthazar, "We're being taken somewhere else!"

Balthazar whispered back, "Indeed. Someplace farther back. Someplace less…conspicuous, one would guess."

Melchior, too, had noticed that they weren't going back the way they'd come.

Their suspicions were confirmed when the guards nudged them through a small doorway into a dimly lit chamber of medium size. Another ugly group of guards waited at one end of the room before the only other doorway. At the other end sat a marble table with a single high-backed chair. Their guards herded the Magi, Barir, and Zoth roughly into the room's center.

The centurion in charge barked to the waiting group of soldiers, "Chain them!"

The Romans clearly considered themselves thoroughly in control. The guards who produced the oiled lengths of heavy chain with forged cuffs at either end even looked a bit baffled that five men required such secure measures.

"Orders are orders," one of them muttered with a shrug as they manacled each prisoner's hands and feet.

Gaspar scowled a warning at the guards chaining him, but they paid him little mind. "Down on your knees, dog," threatened one, slamming his fist down onto Gaspar's shoulder. The magus didn't move. The guard took a small, involuntary step backward as if rebounding from the force of his ineffectual blow and looked up with incredulity at Gaspar's thin smile.

"All you had to do was ask...dog," the warrior said with feigned kindness. He sank fluidly to his knees, still proud and erect in his bearing despite the submissiveness suggested by his posture.

The others were forced to their knees as well.

Zoth said sarcastically, "Well, things seem to have become a bit less hospitable."

The door behind them opened with a noisy fanfare, and the group turned to see Herod entering, regal and godlike as ever in flowing purple raiment. A line of attendants closely followed Herod, the scribes and Pharisees and his trio of henchmen — Ze'ev, Ammon-Kek, and the gladiator Flavinius, bearing a long spear. The guards bowed, and all voices hushed.

Herod didn't even look in their direction as he passed by the line of kneeling men. He went straight to the table, waited for Ze'ev to hold the seat for him, then settled himself and consulted a parchment unrolled before him by a scribe. He studied it intently without looking up for some time, then finally signed it with a flourish and swept it aside.

His head snapped up. He quickly took in the men before him. Then he tilted his head to the left and spoke quietly to the giant gladiator who waited to one side of the kneeling prisoners. "Right, then. First things first. That one." He pointed to Barir.

Barir knew, but never flinched. Flavinius spun and drove a spear into Barir's stomach with such ferocity that its bloody point pieced his back around an explosion of blood and gore.

The soldier who'd weathered so many blows, beaten countless foes, and witnessed a multitude of snows in his faraway home only let out a soft moan. Blood bubbled from his working mouth; his hands held the shaft protruding from his body almost tenderly.

Next to him, Melchior screamed, "Nooooo!" and threw his chained arms around his friend. "No!" he said again, softly as his murdered friend slowly slumped against him.

Looking up at him, Barir smiled against the agony. "Don't be sad, my king—"

Death cut short his words.

Tears in his eyes, trembling with rage, an unspoken scream of anger boiling within his chest, Melchior looked up at Herod.

Gaspar was halfway to his feet when Flavinius drew his sword and pressed its point against his throat. "Give me a reason," he said with a smile, his voice low and menacing.

"Why? This serves no purpose," Balthazar protested, emotion coloring his attempt to logically process the murder. His demeanor was as steely cool as ever, but the faintest tremor in the even timbre of his voice revealed his rage.

A guard struck him across the face for speaking out of turn. Balthazar turned his reddened face back to Herod and again accused, "Why?"

The guard raised his hand to strike him once more, but Herod raised his own and stopped him. "Because you won't give me what I want," he replied calmly.

"This was a good man. We've been forthright with you," Melchior shot back.

Herod squinted a bit, as if a new perspective would yield what he desired. "Where's the child? When was he born? Tell me what I want...to...know!" He thundered the last words, and pounded his fist on the table to emphasize each one.

"Why? So you can go and murder him, too?" retorted Melchior, finally relinquishing the dead form of his friend to the unsympathetic floor. "We won't do your bloody work for you, Herod!"

Herod looked at him with an expression of mild curiosity. For a moment, he almost looked as though he admired their courage. His tone softened a decibel. "You misunderstand. I, too, wish to worship the child and do him homage. I fear, however, that you would prevent me from doing my duty to him."

"You're a pathetic liar," spat Melchior, rising to his feet, his voice laced with incredulity. "You actually think we're going to believe that? From you? Please, kill me now. It's got to be less painful than listening to your lies! Better yet, be a man and come down here yourself."

A guard stepped forward to deliver a crushing blow, but once again Herod called him off. "No! No, he's upset. Of course he is. You've lost your man. But I had to show you how serious I am. And I'm very…serious…about this."

As Melchior looked at him, he finally realized that Herod was a madman. Despite a mind and body that outwardly shone with grace, inside, a demon rotted with the insidious worms of power and hate.

Ze'ev the Pharisee spoke up. "King Herod is rightful King of the Jews. He follows the Law of Moses, and the example of Abraham, our father. If this is indeed the Messiah you've spoken of, it's his duty to Yahweh to find this child. You must comply."

Balthazar replied, "We can't tell you what we don't know. We've told you that we follow the star, which signaled his birth. It appeared to us less than a fortnight ago."

He lied easily, Melchior noted, appreciating that, in doing so, the magus shrank the timeline considerably and therefore had fewer lies to construct.

"We astrologers know that such a sign heralds a great king. Since the star led us here, we've assumed him to be the new King of the Jews. Perhaps, even your son. Your own prophets have foretold the coming of just such a king, in a land called Bethlehem."

Balthazar paused for a moment to let his words sink in.

"Again I say, we can't tell you that which hasn't been revealed to us. Who can say? If we hadn't been taken prisoner, we may have come right here all on our own. We don't even know where this 'Bethlehem' is. Is it here, in your city of Jerusalem? Perhaps we would even be presenting the child to you." He finished with a slight bow, his case made, the tempers he had hoped to quell slightly cooled.

Ammon-Kek slunk up alongside Herod and said, "This star you follow, why do we not see it? I've studied the stars all my life, yet this thing I do not see. Are you lying? Is this nothing more than a clever story concocted to save your throats? Why does it not show itself to us, so that we too can follow it?"

"It doesn't appear to the likes of you," Gaspar growled.

"Rather selective star, wouldn't you say, my King?" the Egyptian said sarcastically to Herod.

Herod sized up the prisoners again as he thought for a moment. Finally he said, "I will...release you."

Ze'ev turned and looked at him in horror. Herod didn't appear to notice. "Tomorrow," Herod continued. "Go and search for the child. When you've found him, send word."

Ze'ev's eyes bulged out of his head. "My lord —"

But again Herod continued. "A few of my men will escort you, of course, to see you safely on your journey. And to make sure you get there without delay. I trust you find the terms...agreeable?"

Melchior, suffering in his helplessness, said nothing. Herod held the board now — and the swords. He glowered at Herod. "How many? We travel light," he managed to say.

"A few hundred should do the trick, I think. Perhaps a cohort or two?" Herod smiled, enjoying the final few moves of the match they'd been playing.

276

Melchior didn't say anything and hoped he disguised his despair. He didn't. Herod's smile broadened, and he leaned forward to say as if musing to himself, "And for a little insurance…hm, which one?"

He pointed at Zoth. "That one will do. He's obviously the kin of the other."

Guards stepped forward to roughly lift Zoth by the arms. They dragged him over to one side. Melchior, watching in alarm, observed the look of panic on his cousin's face with some surprise. Apparently he didn't like being apart from his companions, despite the attitude he projected to Melchior.

Herod said, "Just to make certain that you fulfill your task and return, this one will remain behind as my, ah, guest."

Zoth spat, "Hostage, you mean!"

Herod shrugged. "Call it what you will. Fail me, and he dies a death ten times uglier than that of the man on the floor. This I promise you. And then I come for the rest of you."

Melchior looked defiantly at the Roman king. Herod had won this round. But the game was far from over.

Herod rose and swept past the prisoners, again without looking at them. Addressing no one in particular, he said as he walked, "You leave at first light. Take those three below. Put the other one in a secure place. I don't care where. Flavinius, see to it." He disappeared with a flourish through the doorway.

The guards moved instantly, and the room became a bustle of confusion as the gladiator Flavinius barked commands.

Melchior watched with trepidation as the two guards holding Zoth dragged him away. As diabolical as Zoth had been, Melchior still cared for his cousin, and feared that this was the last time he would set eyes upon him. "Zoth!" he yelled as the tall, thin man was manhandled like an oversized doll made of sticks. "We'll come back for you. Don't worry."

"Wonderful!" Zoth sneered back. "That solves every-thing! Who's going to save your skins?"

And with that last sarcastic remark, he vanished through the doorway.

CHAPTER THIRTY-FIVE

The three Magi were dragged off in a similar fashion to Zoth, but in much greater company. Twenty guards moved about the chained men like a cloud of gnats. Melchior strained for a last sight of Barir. His body lay crumpled on the floor in a wide pool of its own blood, forgotten by everyone but his companions. Silently, Melchior swore to avenge the murder of his friend.

The hallways they traveled now were coarser and darker. A few of the Romans carried noisily sputtering torches aloft, lighting more ceiling than flooring, and giving the prisoners several opportunities to trip and stumble. They moved to the northeastern part of the palace, toward the tower they'd seen earlier.

They emerged from a corridor into a spacious room with large pillars made of hewn stone blocks. The floor was dirt, and unlit torches lined the walls in iron brackets. It seemed to be a staging area or combat practice room. But the detail didn't linger here, and passed through the only other door, in the far wall.

They entered another large room, but this one was perfectly round, with a stairway curving around its perimeter down through the floor. There were no openings in the walls of the limestone cylinder. The guards nudged them down the stairs, wide enough for three men to walk abreast, but the large number in their group and the Magi's chains made the going slow.

As the guards on either side of him bullied Melchior down the first few steps, he looked up. The circular room had a domed ceiling, with a small aperture five or six paces wide at the top where a few stones had fallen out. He could see the night sky through the gap and spied the beams of the star. It seemed to be watching over them, and his heart took strength from the sight. In a moment it was gone, and he was shoved through the next door. But that had been enough.

The guards led the Magi down another flight of stairs and through a labyrinth of rooms, down yet another set of stairs, and finally to a dark, dank subterranean level. Secure doors lined either side of the long hallway, reminding Melchior of the Antonia. Shuffling and moans of pain filtered through a few of the doors from the cells beyond, though no light illuminated those they imprisoned.

Even the guards were puffing after traveling so far. Their exhaustion gave way to even more brutal treatment of the prisoners, shoving them along the corridor so hard that they stumbled to the floor a few times.

They stopped at the end of the hallway, before a door that was larger than those lining its sides. It was crafted entirely from crude wrought iron, with only a small peephole in its center. Two heavy wooden beams reinforced with more hammered iron barred it from the outside. Several guards hefted the bars, grunting under their weight, and the door slowly swung open, groaning on its hinges.

Inside, a guard stuffed one of the torches in a wall mount. In its dim illumination, the Magi saw a stone wall across from the door, bare of anything but two long lengths of chain, one on the floor and one fastened securely to several points on the ceiling with eyelets of iron.

Wordlessly, the guards thrust the Magi's backs against the wall, Gaspar first on the left and Balthazar last on the right. The guards removed the pin from one of Melchior's wrist manacles, looped the short chain and manacle over the long chain at the top, and reattached the manacle around his wrist. Each of his feet they secured similarly at the ankle by running his manacle chain through stout rings set into the floor. The same procedure was performed on the other two Magi.

Several guards pulled taut the long chain at the ceiling and secured it, effectively splaying the men out with their hands pulled tightly overhead. Balthazar, the smallest of the men, was especially stretched out. Although Balthazar wouldn't give the guards the satisfaction of a whimper, Melchior saw the other magus' mouth tighten in pain.

The guards filed out without looking at them, leaving only the lieutenant to retrieve the torch. "Sleep well, pigs," he mocked. "Tomorrow will be a long day."

He left them in darkness. The door swung shut with a clang, and they heard the heavy thuds of the bars being replaced. They heard the murmured conversation of two guards stationed outside the cell, their torch providing only a thin shaft of light through the peephole.

The Magi hung there like that for an hour, silent in their pain and alone with their thoughts. The only sounds were the *chank* and *ringle* of the chains, the soft *plip* of water dripping somewhere in the darkness, and the labored breathing of the imprisoned men. As their eyes gradually adjusted to the darkness, Melchior made out the beads of sweat on Balthazar's shiny face, and the whites of Gaspar's eyes.

Finally, Gaspar spoke. "Anyone got a plan?"

A moment of silence followed, then they chuckled grimly.

Balthazar said, "I would laugh more, my friend, but I think I'd split in two."

Melchior twisted to see his friend. "Should have eaten better when you were a child. You'd be taller."

Balthazar gave him a pained smile. "My friend, your advice comes a bit late. Yet I thank you all the same."

They were quiet again for a while, then Melchior said, "You're not going to believe this, but . . . but we've got to save Zoth."

"Normally, I'd call you mad for even thinking such a thing," said Gaspar. "But you're right, if only because I don't want Herod to have the pleasure of killing another of us. I reserve the right to kill Zoth myself." A pause. "Sorry, but after crossing the desert with that vermin, he's mine."

Melchior grimaced with pain, then replied, "Well, first you'll have to save him before you can kill him."

"Presents a bit of a problem, given our current circumstances," said Balthazar.

"Anyone have enough energy to melt the chains?" asked Melchior.

"Even at my full strength, it's beyond me," replied Balthazar, his voice tight with pain.

"Me, too," said Gaspar. "I've tried to break them, but the iron's too strong."

"Well, we've got to try something. I'm...I'm going to see what I can do," Melchior announced.

He bent his head, closed his eyes, and concentrated. Nothing happened for a long moment. Then blue fingers of intense light appeared. They crackled and fried about the manacles holding his wrists. Melchior's brow contorted in concentration. But the manacles resisted and remained locked. With a puff, the blue light vanished.

Melchior let out a burst of air as the fireworks stopped. Smoke curled upward in wispy trails from the iron, the only product of his efforts. "No . . . good," he panted. His body hung limply from his trapped wrists. "Before, could do this in my sleep. But, not now, I've got no strength. Something's holding me back. I don't see any way out of this," Melchior finished breathlessly.

Gaspar said, "We'll have to make our move tomorrow

when we leave the palace. If one of us can get free, put our hands on some weapons, we can—"

Sounds from the other side of their door cut him short. Listening, the Magi made out footsteps, more than one set, coming—marching?—down the hall. The heavy, staccato rumble of men's voices accompanied the tromping.

Melchior whispered, "Can you make out what they're saying?"

Then from outside, one voice rose louder than the others. They heard the unmistakable *shhhrrring*! of a sword being drawn, a shriek, and the *clang-clang* of combat. It ended as quickly as it began, concluding with the howl of a man obviously being impaled.

Next they heard the thudding scrape as the bars on the door were removed. The door itself creaked open, and an intensely bright torch was thrust into the room. A man in light armor followed it, but he wasn't Roman.

He had dark skin and thick, long, black hair, bound back. His proud face reminded Melchior of Ruth, the woman who'd shown him kindness in the parched land beyond Jerusalem. The man had a deep cut across his forearm that bled freely, but he didn't seem to notice it. He lifted the torch a bit, swung it noisily around to see the entire room, and stood aside.

A figure wrapped in a shawl the color of sapphires stepped in. It pulled back its hood, revealing a woman's head. Melchior slowly recognized her as the woman from the morning interrogation with Herod.

As she squinted, waiting for her eyes to adjust to the darkness of the cell, the Magi studied her. Like her escort, her complexion was olive, her hair dark and swept back behind her head, secured with pins. She was beautiful, but tears and time had worn lines in her face that gave her an air of perpetual sadness. Yet her eyes, even in the dark depths of the cell, radiated something. Ferocity? Hate? Pain?

She spoke quietly to the man, who placed the torch in

the wall bracket and went outside. He returned quickly, dragging the dead body of one of their former guards. He dropped it to one side with a heavy thud and went outside to haul in the next.

The woman looked at them. A flurry of words flew from her mouth. "You haven't much time. You must flee while you can. Before he learns. You must go. You must..." She paused to catch her breath. "Must go and save this child."

She knelt, careless of her clothes or rank, and began to work the pins from the rings holding the Magi's feet.

"You're the wife of Herod, are you not?" guessed Balthazar.

She answered without looking up, still straining to remove the stubborn pins. "Herod has many wives. I just happen to have the distinction of being the first . . . and oldest. He forgot me long ago for another."

The man who accompanied her, her bodyguard, stepped in upon hearing her voice. He said almost maliciously, as if to give notice of her stature to the chained men, "She's the Lady Doris, wife of Herod. And...and a great woman." He paused and decided to say nothing more. He left the room again.

After freeing Balthazar's feet, the woman stood and opened one of the manacles holding Balthazar's wrists. He almost collapsed on her, but the relief from his pain showed on his face. After steadying him, she went to her knees and began to free Melchior.

Her man had brought in the other guard and now brought in the body of a man dressed as he was. This corpse he treated with care. He carried it instead of dragging it and laid it gently on the floor apart from the other dead men. He crossed the arms of his fallen comrade and murmured a prayer over the body.

Doris removed the manacle from one of Melchior's wrists. The chain connecting it to the other manacle slid down with a rough whirling noise and fell to the ground with a *chang*! Melchior's arms flapped down heavily to his sides. Leaning against the wall, he slid to a sitting position, resting his head on his bent knees for a moment. Then he looked up and peered hard at their rescuer.

"You'll have to pardon me...and I don't mean to seem, well, ungrateful, but...why are you doing this? You're putting yourself in great jeopardy. If Herod finds out—"

But the woman cut him off. "Oh, but I want him to find out."

She held his stare for a long moment, and Melchior could see the determination in her eyes. Then she went on to Gaspar's feet and began to work at the pins. Melchior could just make out the silhouette of her face, framed by the dim light and her loosened hair. The torchlight seemed to caress her strong features.

She spoke to no one in particular. Her words conveyed the pain she bore in her heart. "Herod is a—uhnh! This one is stuck—is a wicked man. This place, the Temple you saw, the whole city, is built on the blood and bones of innocent people. Jews. Slaves. Prisoners. Fathers. Mothers. And children. There!"

She let out a small groan as she finally loosened the stubborn pin holding the manacle shut. She put her hand to her mouth and sucked on a finger rent by the effort, slowing the trickle of blood.

"He'll kill anyone, even his own," she said after idly working the finger in her mouth and taking it out to look at it. She held it there, glistening and red in the torchlight, speaking as if in a trance.

"My son. Antipater. He was falsely accused. Lies, all lies. I begged Herod to believe him. To trust me . . . trust his own . . . son." Her voice faltered, and tears came to her eyes. "There wasn't even a trial. There was no proof he had plans against the king—none! But . . . it didn't matter. Herod had him killed."

She paused again and looked up at Gaspar's face. "He

was murdered by his own father. Rome signed the warrant for his execution. Augustus himself said, 'It's better to be Herod's pig than his son.' And so they killed him. My baby boy." She clenched her teeth on the last words. Tears streamed from her eyes.

Then she wiped the tears away roughly with the ends of her shawl, and stood. She reached to open Gaspar's wrist manacle, but she couldn't reach it. She began sobbing again, but this time, Balthazar came and took her gently to the side. Melchior freed the Ethiope, and all three knelt beside Doris.

She had calmed a bit and looked at each of them deeply, as if gazing into their souls. "I heard what you said, why you've come," she said quietly and firmly, "and whom you seek. You mustn't fail. He must not kill another child. Herod, all this, must be destroyed. The murderer of my son...of so many...must be stopped. Rome must be destroyed. You're my — our — only hope. And the child's, too."

The Magi were quiet, and Balthazar looked to Melchior to speak.

Seeing his cue, he said, "Milady, we told the truth before the throne today. We're not that, well, sure of what we're doing. Or why. But I promise you this," he said solemnly. "Along our travels, we've often found help where we least expected to find it. Friends, when enemies surrounded us. Hope . . . when we feared all was lost."

He paused and took her hand. "Your people have one great person to count on, that much is certain. You've saved us. We shall repay the debt. And you must never lose hope."

"Avenge my son," Doris replied. She rose and walked to the doorway to stand with her man. "One of my handmaidens lay with the Roman swine, Pilate, who brought you here. She was able to steal back what you came with, but it isn't much. Some boxes . . . and your weapons." She gestured to a large bundle wrapped in black cloth her bodyguard had brought in.

"We must go. There's some water and food in there, for

your journey. It should be enough. Bethlehem is a day's ride southwest of here. You must hurry. Herod will be after you with an entire legion come morning when he finds you've escaped." She turned toward the door.

"Lady Doris, wait," said Gaspar, moving toward her. "I'm, unaccustomed to being rescued. Yet, I thank you. Your courage here tonight . . . your son would have been proud."

She looked at him. A tear ran down her cheek, but she smiled. It was the only smile they would see from her. "Go then, brave one. Go and save the child. That's the thanks I demand of you. Don't fail us."

She turned and left the cell. Her man nodded at them and followed her. He lifted a torch from its brace in the hallway, and its light shrank as they walked quickly away. Soon they were swallowed by the darkness.

The three Magi squatted about the bundle. Melchior found a gourd, shook it to learn its contents, then poured a draught of water down his throat.

But Gaspar plucked out his massive scimitar, which hadn't felt his grasp since the battle of Petra. He swung it about, slicing the air with loud swooshes and swoops.

"Ahhhh," he said to the blade, "yes."

Melchior paused. Lying forgotten on the floor was Barir's sword. He bent and lifted it, holding its blade to the light and appreciating the glint of reflected flame along its nicked edge. "I think it's time we put you to work," he said to his friend's memory and slid the heavy sword into his belt.

Balthazar absentmindedly slung his slender sword across his back, its hilt pointing above his shoulder. He focused his attention instead on the other less martial contents of the bundle—a few daggers, some bread, dried meat and, surprisingly, the three gifts given them by the Petrans.

Balthazar examined the small boxes' contents, looking shocked to see that they were mostly intact. Half of the gold remained, and the frankincense and myrrh had barely been touched. "Apparently not fashionable in Rome these days," he mumbled.

Gathering the small boxes again in the cloth with the food and water, he rolled the cloth into a tube and tied both ends together. Gaspar stepped forward and slung it over his head and across his chest.

Facing the two, Melchior said, "I don't know about you two, but I'm ready for a change of scenery."

Gaspar only said, "Let's go."

Herod had underestimated the Magi, certainly, but Zoth most definitely. Brought to a simple, bare room in one of the wings of the upper palace, Zoth was left to his own devices. Only two men outside his door guarded him.

It didn't take the sorcerer long to work his hands free. For reasons he neither fathomed nor cared to, his powers were slowly returning, as well. Unlike his frustrated cousin a hundred feet below him, he easily made the manacle pins push themselves from their locks, and the manacles flapped open like empty clam shells and fell to the floor.

He rose and went to the door. He paused, crafting a plan of escape that wouldn't raise an alarm. He stepped to one side of the door so the guards couldn't see him, then bowed his head and held his hands before him as if holding a vessel. Thick, dark scarlet smoke formed in the space between his hands and spiraled about like twin serpents in a vortex. Never opening his eyes or moving his head, Zoth turned his palms upward and sent the two plumes of smoke slithering out the crack at the bottom of the cell door.

Outside, the scarlet tendrils worked their way up the guards' legs and backs, and soon snaked around their necks. The guards' throats constricted, and they opened their mouths to suck in air. The ruddy smoke crawled into their open mouths and up their noses, invading their bodies. The gagging men dropped like stones to the floor and lay there unconscious.

Back in the cell, Zoth heard his handiwork succeed.

Facing the closed door, he extended his arm and pointed at the door. Outside, the bolt securing the door melted as if made of ice, the metal dripping and sizzling on the stone floor. The door swung open silently.

"Child's play," he said to himself and strode nonchalantly from the cell without looking at the fallen guards.

The Magi dashed down the cellblock corridor and through the door into the dark maze of stone passages. Melchior soon became lost, but Gaspar took the lead, holding the torch high and choosing pathways without hesitation.

"Are you sure...you know where...you're...going?" puffed Balthazar, second in line.

"Absolutely," said Gaspar without looking over his shoulder.

They skidded to a stop in the pool of illumination under a large iron ring fitted with a lamp that hung from the ceiling of a three-way junction. Gaspar looked thoughtfully at the two unexplored archways before him.

"I thought you knew the way!" Melchior accused.

"I do, I do. Just give me a moment," Gaspar snapped. He bent and examined the dirt floor, marking the tracks of passing feet. He stood abruptly. "This way!" he said and leapt down the passage to the right.

Melchior and Balthazar hesitated for a second, then started after him. But before they'd gone even a few feet, they heard a yell and the thud of running feet. Gaspar reappeared, his torch dancing left and right as he ran full-tilt toward them. "Wrong way! Wrong way!" he bellowed.

Behind him, Balthazar and Melchior made out more bobbing torches and heard the unmistakable thumps of many running feet. It looked as if Gaspar had run head-on into a phalanx of Romans, and they were now in hot pursuit, yelling at the top of their lungs.

Gaspar whipped by the two startled Magi and ducked down the other passage. Melchior and Balthazar followed as closely as they could.

Zoth slipped silently through the palace, melting into the shadows as patrols or other nocturnal members of the court crossed his path. Using his power as an internal compass, he crept past the doorway of a dimly lit chamber, moving toward Melchior and the others, whom he felt sure were prisoners somewhere in the catacombs below him. He didn't pause to examine the chamber's contents.

The occupant of the chamber, however, felt him. A dark form lying face-down on the floor before an idol of a dog and a plate of burning incense sat up. The white orbs of the man's eyes seemed to glow in the semidarkness, as did his slow, white, toothy grin.

Ammon-Kek murmured an incantation at the small flame before him as he reached into a shallow bowl at his side and withdrew a pinch of powder. He cast the powder into the flame, which exploded into a three-foot wall of ochre fire. Gazing into it, he beheld Ze'ev's face, lined with worry.

The Jewish priest looked up, sensing the Egyptian's presence. "I know, I know," said Ze'ev. "Don't waste your time with me. Get that beast of a man moving!"

Ammon-Kek nodded and cast another dose of powder into the flame. The image of Ze'ev was replaced by an image of Flavinius *in flagrante seducto*. He appeared to be rolling around with a pair of nude young women. Normally, Ammon-Kek would have enjoyed the voyeurism, but serious matters were afoot. He cleared his throat and said softly, "Ahem. Ah, Master Flavinius?"

Flavinius rolled to his feet, instantly producing a dagger, from precisely where, the Egyptian didn't know. Crouching in a defensive stance, he looked around for the intruder. "Who dares?" snarled the semi-clad ex-gladiator.

"It is I, Ammon-Kek. Come quickly. One of the prisoners has escaped. Time for some...exercise." The words of the sorcerer echoed in the bedchamber.

A smile crept across Flavinius' face. He stood upright and

thunked his dagger into the low wooden table before him. The women and his pleasures forgotten for the moment, he swept up his white toga and dressed himself as he walked. Stopping at the doorway, he took up his sword belt from a chair and girded it about his waist. He clapped bronze gauntlets onto his meaty forearms. Then he took his heavy wood and iron shield from the wall where it had hung since his days in the arena and strapped it to his arm. Flavinius started out the door, then turned at the last moment as he remembered his guests.

"Don't fret, girls," he said with a lascivious grin. "This won't take long. Just, entertain yourselves." And he strode from the room.

The Magi now moved at a full run, trying to put distance between themselves and the bloodthirsty lot at their heels. They'd managed to lose the guards once or twice. The Magi's unfamiliarity with the tunnels made their path a little unpredictable. This gave them a chance at escape, at least for the moment. Gaspar knew that one more wrong turn would probably put them face to face with an armed horde they'd have little chance of withstanding, being outnumbered at least six to one.

They came to a door that looked familiar, and Gaspar opened it. Beyond lay the circular stairwell that followed the perimeter of the tower to another doorway near the top. It was the door to the palace level. The circular stone floor fifteen feet below this lower door had no egress. It appeared to be a pit, no doubt where prisoners were thrown to suffer their fate, whether that be stoning, starvation, or slaughter by a snarling beast. The stairs leading up were wide enough, but their spiraling nature and their number gave strained even the stoutest legs and stomachs. There had to be over three hundred steps that would take far longer to ascend than it had to descend.

Gaspar held the door open and motioned the other

two through. Melchior made his way up first, followed by Balthazar. As he closed the door, Gaspar could hear the guards approaching, not more than a few steps behind them. Gaspar barred the door, but the small wooden beam was meant simply to keep the door from swinging open. A few good shoves from the other side would easily break it open.

Leaping up two steps at a time, the Magi made decent speed. Gaspar's long legs carried him so quickly that he almost caught up with Balthazar. Peering upward, he saw the star through the break in the ceiling. Like an old friend, it still watched over them.

Ahead of them, Melchior was halfway to the top, on a landing halfway up the cylindrical room, when the door above him opened. He froze and held up his hand to halt the others. Drawing his sword, Melchior prepared to challenge the stranger.

Zoth stepped through the doorway.

"Zoth!" Melchior exclaimed.

"Melchior," Zoth replied matter-of-factly.

"We were just coming…to find you," Melchior stammered. "Really, we were."

"I know," said Zoth in a tone Melchior had never heard before. "Thought I'd save you the trouble."

Shouts suddenly erupted below them, and the door shuddered with blows. The Romans had reached the barred door.

"Trapped!" muttered Gaspar, drawing his blade and looking with pure malice at Zoth. "At least—"

"Silence, fool," commanded Zoth, holding his hand up to the black warrior.

Gaspar surprisingly obeyed, caught off guard for a moment by the power of the dark magus.

Another shoulder slam again rattled the door below them.

Melchior looked at Zoth with wonder in his eyes, not believing what he suspected. "Zoth...?"

Zoth met Melchior's gaze purposefully stepped down the stairs to stand with him. "You were right. In the end, you...were right. Finally, I listened," said Zoth softly. He turned his head and looked up through the gap in the ceiling at the star.

"You, understand?" Melchior asked in disbelief.

"No, not really," replied Zoth, "but I'm starting to. And I see at last that this truly is your destiny. Not mine. My journey ends. Here."

He warily extended his hand, and Melchior accepte4d it with equal wariness. The icy tension that had separated them for decades began to melt. Melchior stepped closer and took hold of the inside of Zoth's thin forearm, and Zoth returned the more intimate embrace.

Zoth leaned forward. "Save what you can of the old ways," Zoth whispered into his cousin's ear.

They separated just as the bar holding the door closed below them splintered in half with a resounding crack. With a roar, the first Roman slammed the door open and began to climb. His fellow troops charged after him and began the climb toward the Magi.

"Go. Now!" said Zoth, releasing Melchior and pushing him up the steps. "I'll hold them here."

Balthazar and Gaspar dashed by him, but all three paused at the landing, confused.

Gaspar asked, "You are but one man...?"

But already Zoth held his arms aloft, gazing up at the ceiling to behold the star once more. With a grating rasp, the gap in the stones shut up like the iris of an eye. Keeping his arms extended upward, Zoth turned to face the guards.

Overhead, a scarlet cloud formed and swirled about the ceiling. It grew and swelled until its spiraling disk filled the top of the tower.

The Romans paused, first to gawk in amusement at the

man in black with the outstretched hands, then in fear as the heavy, sanguine cloud formed, and a cutting wind whipped around the circular room, generating a roar and a cold that cut to the bone and made footing unsteady.

Below everyone, the door that had been barred slammed shut. Crackling, red-hot fire fused it shut.

Overhead the cloud burst, and a black rain poured down in sheets. The guards tried to ascend to Zoth, but the wind forced them back and hurled a few off the steps onto the floor far below. The dark water quickly rose at the bottom of the tower. Within seconds, several feet of it crested and sloshed against the walls and lower steps.

Zoth looked up at his companions, his brothers at last, with sadness in his eyes. Melchior realized that it was the first time since their childhood that he'd witnessed anything but malice in those eyes, and it broke his heart. Then the sardonic old Zoth returned.

"What are you waiting for? Away, you fools, away!" shouted Zoth above the roar.

Balthazar bowed to the sorcerer and dashed up the stairs and out the door. Gaspar looked at Zoth in utter amazement, but touched his scimitar to his forehead in a tribal signal of honor. Then he, too, turned and ran upward. Finally Melchior, unwilling to leave Zoth's side, but knowing he had to, simply raised his hand in farewell.

Zoth acknowledged it with a nod. "Now go," he commanded.

Melchior reached the top landing and went through the doorway, concern etching his face. Then he hesitated and turned to rejoin Zoth, but it was too late. The door slammed shut and fused with the red fire.

Unwilling to leave Zoth alone, Melchior drove his shoulder into the door, but it didn't budge. He was about to try again when Gaspar took his arm and stayed him.

"He's given his life for us—a noble deed that undoes many others. Let it not be a waste," he said, his voice stern, his expression sympathetic.

Inside, the dark, turbulent water filled the tower like a drinking vessel. Zoth backed his way up to the uppermost landing. The winds and his supernatural strength kept the guards at bay.

A few of the Romans, unable to swim and encumbered with armor, had already sunk to their fate. The remaining guards, unable to reach Zoth or escape the rising tide, huddled in fear on the steps. Even pressing themselves against the wall did no good. The terrified men clawed blindly at each other and hurled their fellows into the watery grave in their search for a safer, drier step.

Soon the black water was so high, the Romans were forced to tread water or drown. But their gear weighed them down, and waves slapped their mouths full of the evil water every time they gasped for air. The men sank beneath the roiling surface, their lifeless corpses floating downward in a macabre dance.

At last they were gone, swallowed by the waters. But Zoth didn't still the storm. The waters washed up against the hem of his robe and splashed his legs. He intensified the gale, his arms shaking with the effort. The waters rose to his chest and soaked his face and beard. He drew a last breath as the water closed over his face. Even as he closed his eyes, he beheld something hovering above the water. A light.

The light of the star. And as his life ended, he felt himself being drawn into its glorious brilliance.

Outside, the Magi rested, gathering themselves, unaware of the deadly flood rising on the other side of the door.

Melchior's shoulders slumped. He knew Gaspar was right. He put his palm to the door in a gesture of farewell.

Balthazar said from a few feet away, "We're not free yet, my friends." He turned and took a few steps.

"No, you'll never be free," a voice called from the darkness ahead. Laughter echoed off the walls of the room.

CHAPTER THIRTY-SIX

Powf! Powf! Powf! Powf!

The torches burst into flame in rapid fire around the room. Shielding eyes that for so long had been accustomed to the darkness of this underworld, Melchior tried to make out where the voice was coming from and who owned it.

Coming down the steps on the far side of the cavernous room, Ze'ev held a staff in his hand, which he swept in a large ellipse that coincided with the self-igniting torches.

Already on the floor ahead of him was the Egyptian assassin Ammon-Kek. His laughter rippled off the stone walls, proof that it had been his voice ringing throughout the chamber. Beside him stood the hulking Flavinius, flexing his hands as he eyed the Magi like squabs on the dinner table. A hideous grin split his face like a wound; Melchior thought he was actually drooling. Flavinius had two guards with him. Apparently the bodyguard had his own bodyguard.

"I guess," said Gaspar, who'd joined Melchior, "I won't be needing this." He tossed the smoking, smoldering torch he still held to the floor, its fire long extinguished by Zoth's sacrificial rainstorm.

"I've come to the conclusion," Ze'ev said loudly while descending the stairs to join his associates, "that we don't need three of you to lead us to our prey. One will do."

Ammon-Kek said, "But which one? Who dies now . . .

296

who dies later?"

Stepping beside the other Magi, Balthazar coolly replied, "Your master Herod will be displeased, I'm sure."

Ze'ev shrugged. "He knows that only one of you will see tomorrow's sunrise. It's of no consequence to him."

"You're mistaken. I mean he'll be displeased when he learns you're all dead," Balthazar deadpanned.

Gaspar looked appreciatively at the Asian magus. "Well, look who came to fight?" he murmured.

Melchior spoke quietly to the others, a grim look on his face. "Let's finish this."

"Right," Gaspar replied. "The big one's mine."

Gaspar slid the bundle from his shoulder and dropped it as the two groups advanced. They were thirty paces apart, but closing fast.

The room was spacious, but bare. Torches, a table against a far wall with a few stools nearby, and some long chains mounted in the walls were the only adornment. The floor was made of dirt, and two massive stone pillars supported the ceiling far above.

Ten paces apart in the center of the chamber, they faced off. Gaspar held the center position across from Flavinius, with Melchior on his left sizing up Ze'ev, and Balthazar to his right, regarding Ammon-Kek as calmly as one would a neighbor. The two guards held back, unsure of where to go or whether they should just run for it.

Melchior said to Ze'ev, "It doesn't have to be this way, you know. Let us leave, and Herod will be none the wiser. We'll go quietly."

"You'll go out a dead man," intoned Ze'ev, flicking back the long sleeves of his robe and brandishing his staff.

Melchior responded by drawing Barir's sword—which in turn drew a scowl from the Jewish high priest. But Melchior held the sword aloft with both hands before his chest, pointing it upwards as a challenge. It wouldn't be used as a conventional weapon today.

Ze'ev laughed in response. "Is that the best you can do? This will be quick indeed."

Gaspar had not taken his eyes off the gladiator. The Roman brute vibrated with pent-up energy, like a dog on a leash for far too long. "Blades," was all Gaspar said. He drew his scimitar with a flourish and wielded it fluidly through the air in great arcs.

Flavinius responded by drawing his sword with a shriek of steel. He pointed its tip toward Gaspar and taunted him. "Garr!"

"Very impressive," said Gaspar, sounding disappointed.

Balthazar bowed deeply to Ammon-Kek, but never took his eyes off him. He doffed his peasant's cap and laid it on the floor beside him. Then, unslinging his long slender sword, he laid it gently on the floor, resting its ivory handle on the crown of his cap.

Across from him, Ammon-Kek pressed his palms together and assumed a rigid, frozen position.

On some hidden cue, Herod's servants struck. Awesome was the sound of the onslaught.

Ze'ev loosed a bolt of crimson fire from his staff, directed right at Melchior's heart. Almost too late — almost — Melchior deflected the blast with his makeshift staff, redirecting it up to strike the ceiling. Pulverized stone showered down.

Flavinius leapt at Gaspar with a howl, driving with his blade like a battering ram. Gaspar turned the attack with a parry and a dodge, only managing to glance his scimitar against Flavinius' shield as the Roman charged by.

Balthazar still hadn't taken his eyes off Ammon-Kek, but suddenly the Egyptian was in his face, a flurry of blows sweeping by his dodging face. With a sudden thrust, Ammon-Kek shot both fists into Balthazar's chest, sending the magus flying backward across the room.

The three sets of combatants separated, falling neatly into the sections of the room created by the two massive stone pillars. Each man focused on his opponent, but whenever a brief lull occurred, each magus quickly stole a glance to assess his comrades' situation.

Magic electrified the air in the room. The torches on the walls flashed and flickered with the gusts of power coming from the battle. The two guards blanched with fear. They seemed unsure of what to do or where to commit. A menacing glare and gesture from Flavinius told them that, indeed, their help was needed.

Melchior was worried. The sorcerer he fought had skills of the highest caliber, and his own powers had been a little less than reliable of late. But he sensed a power within his murdered friend's sword, the familiar thrill of the star. Holding the blade before him, he sent a blast of blue energy at Ze'ev's feet, tumbling the priest head over heels onto his back and sending his staff spinning away into the air. Ze'ev quickly propped himself on his elbows, a look of surprise on his face.

"End it now, Ze'ev," warned Melchior, "and everyone walks away alive."

"Fool. You underestimate me," countered Ze'ev, and thrust his arm toward Melchior, driving him back against the wall with an invisible blow.

Melchior's head spun. The high priest's strength surprised him, as did the speed at which he could summon his powers. Melchior wiped a trickle of blood from the corner of his mouth with the back of his hand.

Scarlet and lavender sparks flashed from the respective blades of Gaspar and Flavinius as they traded strokes. The Roman's shield gave him the advantage, and his training in the arena served him well. His thick shield met every one of Gaspar's mighty swipes, which in turn delivered a jarring blow to Gaspar's sword arm.

Screaming a war howl in his native tongue, Gaspar advanced lightning-fast toward Flavinius. At the last second, Gaspar dropped to a crouch and swung his scimitar for the giant's legs. With surprising agility, the Roman jumped into the air, avoiding the blow. Overextended with no reward for the effort, Gaspar looked up, only to see a roundhouse blow from Flavinius' shield catch him full in the face. He spun backward and landed on the ground in a heap of black robes.

It was then that the two guards committed to the fight with the Ethiopian. The three circled Gaspar as he leapt to his feet, each thrusting, feinting, and striking at the magus in a three-pronged attack. Drawing Zoth's long dagger, Gaspar whirled about, blocking their blows with the dagger and scimitar with dizzying speed. Motes of red light spawned and spun around the dark warrior as he drew upon his inner reserves to fight back the mismatched onslaught. But he knew that he couldn't hold all three at bay forever.

Balthazar regained his feet only to find himself immediately under attack again. Ammon-Kek's style of fighting utilized both magic and combat skills. He fought using his hands and feet, but the actual strikes were blurred and staggered, out of synch with real time and almost impossible to defend against.

Balthazar wheeled, whipping his hands and forearms about to block the blows, but too many found their mark. Ammon-Kek approached with a mesmerizing, supernatural, counterclockwise windmilling of his arms, and from the center of the spiral delivered a stunning punch to Balthazar's face. A second blow almost struck, but Balthazar managed to block it by snapping his forearm up.

Again the Egyptian kicked, his blurred leg sending Balthazar backward another twenty paces to slam into one of the stone columns with near-lethal force. The supernatural blow disturbed some of the stones. Stone chunks tumbled onto Balthazar's shoulders as he slid to the ground and lost consciousness. As Balthazar shook his head to clear it, he imagined he could voices whispering in the room. But he had no time to investigate the voices as the Egyptian was on him again.

Melchior and Ze'ev faced off again in an open area. The high priest bent his head, and his staff evaporated from where it lay on the floor and reappeared in his hands. The Hebrew high priest drove the staff into the dirt floor. The weapon stood, quivering, like a lone fence post. Melchior, a few paces away, accepted the challenge. He planted Barir's sword point-first into the earth before him.

Ze'ev tilted his head back and held his palms outward. His lips twitched with incantations. The air before him and above his staff suddenly began to move and form shapes. Caught off guard by the speed of the supernatural attack, Melchior responded as quickly as he could. Folding his arms, he began conjuring in the space between himself and Ze'ev.

A score of daggers, bronze fire blazing about their edges, materialized above Ze'ev, points downward as if held in the deadly grasp of spirits. Heeding their master's call, they swung up as one and shot through the air toward Melchior with a chorus of zwing! and thwip!

Melchior's ice shield, a circular shell of cobalt crystal, materialized just in time, but it was woefully inadequate for the task. With tinny dinks it deflected most of the daggers away, but it began to crack and perforate and a few strays got through. One found Melchior's left shoulder.

Groaning with pain, Melchior fell backward. He reached to pull the blade from his shoulder, but it dissolved as soon as his hand touched it, leaving a bloody hole in his shirt and flesh. The wound was deep, painful and, Melchior knew, life-threatening. He looked up, nearly blinded by pain and rage, to see a smile of triumph on Ze'ev's face.

With a dodge and a lunge, Gaspar turned the blade of one of the guards and escaped the triangular trap of his opponents. He flipped backward to gain some distance and space to fight. The three pursued, just as Gaspar had hoped.

The guard closest to him advanced too quickly, and Gaspar extended his leg toward the man's chest, the kick sending the guard stumbling backward into the second guard. As the two men began to sort themselves out, Gaspar somersaulted across the dirt floor and flung the long, twisted dagger of Zoth at them. The wicked weapon's aim was true; it sank into the soft gut of the first man. The crooked blade was just long enough to mortally pierce the other guard behind him as well.

The pair looked in deadly astonishment at Gaspar. He shrugged and kicked them back into a heap, still connected by the bloody blade. He turned to face the giant, the odds even at last.

Ammon-Kek ran to the crumpled form of Balthazar, preparing to deliver a deathblow to the top of his head. Just as the energy for the punch left his shoulder and began to travel down his arm, the Asian came alive, sweeping Ammon-Kek's legs out from beneath him. Ammon-Kek fell.

Balthazar rolled to his side and sprang to his feet, grunting in pain as broken ribs protested the movement. Holding them gingerly with one arm, he dashed to the table and stools against the wall of the chamber to buy a precious moment.

With his foot, he flicked one of the stools into the air and into his hands. Turning, he had just enough time to put the stool between his face and Ammon-Kek's foot. The stool shattered, but it bore the brunt of the blow. Ammon-Kek's impossibly flexible leg recoiled back to his torso. Without hesitation, his arms became a blur, striking out at Balthazar again. Prepared this time, Balthazar showed his own flexibility, bending over backward just as the fists zipped over his arched form. Foiled and frustrated, Ammon-Kek took a step backwards to reassess Balthazar. The magus spun around and put the long wooden table between himself and Ammon-Kek. Balthazar leaned wearily on the table.

The Egyptian paused. Resting his palms on the edge of the table, he leaned toward Balthazar. "Give it up, little one, and I'll make it painless," he said with a snarling smile.

"Very kind. I, however, will not." replied Balthazar calmly. The overconfident Egyptian had taken the bait. Balthazar drove his fists down on the end of one of the table's boards, popping its fastenings out and viciously slamming the opposite end of the board up into Ammon-Kek's chin. Caught cleanly and off guard, the Egyptian flew up into the air and landed heavily on the ground.

The setbacks of his bodyguards stopped Flavinius in his tracks. Then in a rage, he charged at Gaspar once more. They continued to trade blows. With a wild sweep, the Roman got lucky and sliced a stripe across Gaspar's chest, cutting open his dark robes and exposing a slash in his flesh.

Gaspar stepped back, glanced down, then looked the Roman in the face. He ripped the shredded material from his chest with one hand, exposing his glistening ebony torso, which was bleeding from a number of deep gashes. Then he drove at the gladiator with renewed power, calling on the hidden forces that had always been his allies. Orbs of crimson light exploded, pure energy flared, and sparks popped and flew as the Ethiope savagely beat at the Roman.

With a huge stroke of his scimitar, Gaspar snapped the Roman's sword at the hilt. Screaming with fury, he wheeled round and brought his blade down hard on the Roman's shield, the explosive blow splitting it in half and sending pieces zinging through the air. The gladiator, beaten, fell back, his arms raised defensively against the next deadly thrust.

Gaspar raised his weapon to finish Flavinius off, but something was wrong. It lifted too easily. He looked at his sword arm to see nothing but the handle of his scimitar in his hand. The broad blade had shattered in the fury of his attack. Flavinius parted his lips in a bloody grin.

Meanwhile, Ze'ev blasted coarse plumes of orange energy at Melchior. The flames licked and pawed at the blue barrier that Melchior was pushing out from Barir's blade. The opposing streams of power battled back and forth, but neither could overwhelm the other. It was a stalemate.

The apparitions vanished with a pluff! and the two men eyed each other, searching out a weakness. Melchior's shoulder burned and throbbed with agonizing, blinding pain.

"This is pointless!" shouted Melchior, puffing with exhaustion. "Why are we fighting? Join us, and we can help you overthrow Herod!"

"You're a fool. A dreamer," shot back Ze'ev.

"But...Rome. Your people, they're slaves. Jerusalem is occupied!" said Melchior, stunned. "This is your Messiah who comes! The savior of your own people!"

Ze'ev replied in an enraged growl, "This, this Messiah, will ruin everything! Rome leaves us alone. We pay for our freedom, and that idiot upstairs calls himself a king and keeps Rome happy! A Messiah — any new power — is a threat. He would only bring revolt. War. Then Rome would crush us! We'd be drowning under their legions! There will be...no...revolution!"

"It's too late!" Melchior shouted back. "Can't you see? The world's changing, and you can't stop it!"

Ze'ev's eyes shrank to angry slits as he intoned, "No. The child dies."

He fired two blasts of pure, copper-colored heat from his hands. They caught Melchior full in the chest, slamming him to a stone column and stunning him. Ze'ev plucked his staff from the earth and came around to face Melchior with his back to the other column. He raised his hands to deliver the death blast. In a deadly monotone, he said, "The child dies. But first, you will."

Flavinius yanked one of the long chains affixed to the wall. It came free with its heavy iron plate mount and bits of rock still attached. He swung the chain in large orbits above his head, the diameter of each loop widening as he played the chain out. He advanced on Gaspar.

Gaspar dropped his useless hilt to the ground,

defenseless. Crouching, he backed up, waiting for the chain to come zinging his way. "We said blades!" he called.

"I lied!" countered the Roman, again flashing a bloody grin.

"Cheater," muttered Gaspar to himself.

Sensing his friend was in trouble, Balthazar moved across the floor and narrowly slid on his backside beneath another lethal kick from Ammon-Kek. Still on his back, he pulled free the scabbard holding his Chinese sword and flicked it into the air with his foot. The ornate, ivory-handled weapon spun toward Gaspar.

The Ethiopian caught it cleanly. With a sweet, singing ring, he released the blade from its bamboo sheath. As he looked at the long, slender blade in his hands, however, his face fell. The weapon appeared quite inadequate to the task. He shot a quick look at Balthazar, who shrugged and rolled away to avoid Ammon-Kek's slamming feet.

Still swinging the chain, the Roman sent the iron plate on its end swishing toward Gaspar's head. In desperation, Gaspar swept the trim blade up and sliced the chain in half with an explosive, jade and crimson blast.

The Roman faltered, bewildered, but only half as much as Gaspar. The magus looked at the Chinese sword with new appreciation. Then he shifted his focus back to the giant opposite him.

The two ran at each other. Still wielding a long chunk of chain, the Roman slung it with whip-like accuracy toward Gaspar's waist. Gaspar leapt into the air and flipped over it, landing right before Flavinius. With a spin, he slashed the blade across the gladiator's throat.

Clutching at the wide, gushing wound, Flavinius fell to his knees. Blood spewed from his mouth as it gaped spasmodically.

"That's for cheating," said Gaspar. Turning, he drove his sword backward with both hands into Flavinius' chest. "And that's for killing my friend," he finished. He pulled the bloody blade out and turned to see Flavinius' eyes roll up into his head. The behemoth collapsed facedown into the dirt. Gaspar gave a silent nod to Barir, whose murder was now avenged.

Meanwhile, a battered, broken, but still breathing Balthazar struck an ancient martial pose and faced Ammon-Kek. The dark priest responded by bowing his head and pressing his palms together again. With a sickly, wet, tearing noise, two more arms burst from his sides beneath his existing ones. The new limbs, covered in slick gore, flexed menacingly. With a confident smirk on his dark face, he renewed his attack on Balthazar.

The four arms moved with blinding speed, striking at Balthazar's head, torso, and lower body. Balthazar summoned all his power and met the blows with equal speed. But he failed to land any blows himself. Then, one of the Egyptian's hands caught Balthazar's outstretched arm. Another hand caught the magus' left leg, and soon all his limbs were in the vise-like grip of Ammon-Kek's hands.

The Egyptian grinned at him. "Spider's caught the fly. Time to feast," he whispered.

With nothing left to do, Balthazar drove his forehead into Ammon-Kek's face with a jade-powered blast. The blow stunned the Egyptian, and he dropped Balthazar to the ground. The Asian magus crouched and shot through Ammon-Kek's legs and snapped back to his feet. Reaching back, Balthazar locked his arms around the Egyptian's head and flipped him over his shoulder, slamming him facedown in the dirt.

The Egyptian planted his four hands on the ground and began to press his body upward. But Balthazar hadn't yet released his opponent. With a sickening grind and a crack, he twisted the Egyptian's head all the way around, snapping his neck. The body collapsed. The four hands fluttered and flapped mindlessly.

"Well," gasped Balthazar, dropping the dead head, "not

so flexible after all."

Out of the corner of his eye, Melchior spied Barir's sword, still embedded deep in the earth. Summoning the last of his strength, he stretched out his arm and called to it under his breath. "Come . . ."

The blade tugged once, twice, then snapped a few inches from the hilt. The handle and blade shard flew through the air and landed with a fwap! in Melchior's outstretched hand.

Ze'ev paused to smile snidely at him. "No weapon can save you now," he promised and pointed his staff.

"You have much to answer for, Ze'ev," Melchior said solemnly, the words coming easily to his lips from somewhere deep within him. The strength of the star flowed through his body. "The blood of thousands of innocents is on your hands. Your pact with Rome has cursed you. The murdered of Jerusalem cry out for vengeance." Melchior whispered the last words.

Still crumpled on the ground, bleeding and broken, he held aloft the broken sword's crosspiece by the blade. A soft, whispering, hissing sound arose, coming from everywhere, but nowhere.

Ze'ev stopped, confused. In frustration, he loosed a severe blast of orange energy from his staff, but Melchior's impromptu sword hilt crucifix absorbed the blast away easily. A brilliant white light began to emanate from the crosspiece in Melchior's hands: the light of the star. Ze'ev blanched.

"You cannot stop or prevent what has begun. He's coming . . . and the wicked shall pay," Melchior continued in his unearthly voice. The cross of Barir's steel and gold in Melchior's hand burned with pulsating white light and sent filaments of energy into the chamber. The whispers in the wind turned into angry murmurs.

Ze'ev, petrified, pressed back against one of the large stone columns, made of the very stone pried from the earth by the bloody hands of countless Hebrews, indentured to serve Herod and Rome by Ze'ev's decree. The murmuring voices were the thousands of his brother Hebrews who had been worked to their very deaths.

The murmurs amplified to a roar, and Ze'ev frantically turned his head to and fro, seeking the origin of the sound.

It came from the stones themselves. Hands, dead hands made of liquid stone, grew from the blocks of the walls to claw at Ze'ev's face and body. More and more of the ghoulish hands boiled out of the stone surface. Seizing his body, the rock hands, accompanied by horrific screams from beyond, began pulling Ze'ev into the stone as if it were soft sand.

Ze'ev shrieked in fear and pain. His eyes beseeched Melchior for help.

Melchior, at once horrified and amazed, looked on with morbid sympathy as Ze'ev's arms and legs were hauled into the underworld of eternal torture. The stones themselves groaned and shook with the effort.

Finally, fingers of stone stretched out and groped at Ze'ev's face, pulling it into the deadly façade until it looked like a living relief. Ze'ev released a last plaintive cry as his still contorting face was pulled into the rock wall. All that remained on this side of the wall was Ze'ev's twitching hand, still holding his staff. A final limestone hand emerged from the wall with a grainy groan and jerked Ze'ev's frantically clutching hand into the wall. The staff fell to the ground with a loud clatter.

Melchior rose and limped over to the staff. He bent, wincing, and laid Barir's broken sword against the wall. He picked up Ze'ev's staff. Without a second thought, he slammed the staff into the wall and it shattered into hundreds of wooden shards. Orange sparks sputtered and thin trails of dirty smoke wafted from the broken bits, but nothing more. He threw the remainder of the staff on the dirt floor.

Melchior stooped to take up his friend's spent weapon again, but another small hand writhed out from the stone to snatch it and draw it into the netherworld. A gut-wrenching cry shook the room as, somewhere, the jagged edge of the broken blade found its mark in Ze'ev's heart.

Melchior stepped away from the stone column, humbled by the unseen power that lived within its blocks. Finally, he turned and went to find his friends.

Blood still trickled from the corner of Melchior's mouth. His hair was singed. The deep wound in his shoulder throbbed and bled freely. But looking at his companions, he wondered if his injuries might pale in comparison with theirs.

Balthazar sat on the floor with his legs uncharacteristically splayed out before him, delicately holding and probing his broken ribcage. Listening to his friend's labored wheezing, Melchior suspected that one snapped rib had penetrated the Asian's lung.

Gaspar, kneeling beside him, bore numerous wounds. Besides the large cut across his chest, an especially savage slash in his thigh still dripped blood. As he drew closer, Melchior could see that each man's face was puffy and reddened by blows. Those would soon turn to ugly bruises, he knew. Like Melchior, their noses and lips dribbled blood, and they were all coated in perspiration.

Gaspar looked up and said, "You look terrible."

Melchior responded, "Compared to you two, I look great."

"No, really, my friend. You look terrible," affirmed Balthazar.

Slumping to the ground with a thump that made him grimace at the pain in his shoulder, Melchior confessed, "Yes, well, I feel terrible."

"We've got to keep going. Get out of here before more show up. And, well, even I could use a little break from fighting," said Gaspar without sarcasm. He looked at Balthazar and said, "Your sword?"

Balthazar smiled weakly. "Keep it. As you can see, I

don't really need it," he said wryly. The Ethiopian nodded his thanks and slung the cloth holding their belongs around his shoulder again.

Nodding toward the exit, Melchior asked Balthazar, "Can you walk?"

The Asian nodded mutely, but pain flashed across his face.

"We'll help you," said Gaspar. He rose and offered his hand.

It seemed the dead men, overconfident, had attacked the Magi without alerting anyone else. The Magi made their way up into the halls of the palace unchallenged. With their powers finally restored, they slipped past many a guard who was suddenly and inexplicably asleep or distracted. Shadows lengthened mysteriously, and eerie noises floated from faraway doorways to draw attention from the escaping men. Along the way, Gaspar appropriated a black shirt from an obligingly unconscious servant to cover his naked torso. They moved steadily toward the southeastern corner of the building.

There, they found a window that looked out onto a small, deserted courtyard. The Magi dropped from the window to the ground a few feet below, the effort eliciting a few groans and winces, and crouched in the shadow of a wall. Unseen by all but the select few, the star overhead beat back the darkness of the still night with its mighty, throbbing glow. It seemed to be reveling in the victory of the Magi, even if they themselves weren't in a celebratory mood.

The night air was cool, in fact, cold. It was a dramatic shift from the sultry nights of the past few weeks. Frosty clouds burst from their mouths as they spoke, to hang in the air for a moment before dissipating.

"Right. We're close," Melchior whispered. "I think if we can make it across here and out to the street, we'll—"

Balthazar shushed him with, "Wait, please."

"We can't wait—"

"Wait, please," the annoyingly calm astronomer interrupted again, this time with an upheld hand.

"There," said Balthazar with satisfaction, pointing across the courtyard.

A dark figure lurked in the shadow of a far doorway. It beckoned them with short waves.

"What the...?" murmured Gaspar.

They pulled Balthazar to his feet and half-carried him across the plaza. The distance was only a few hundred paces, but the trio's progress was painfully slow. Nevertheless, their journey went unnoticed.

The shadowy figure moved ahead before they arrived, leading them down a darkened, tree-lined pathway. Draped between Gaspar and Melchior, Balthazar seemed oblivious, his attention centered on controlling the pain wracking his body. Melchior and Gaspar followed the form before them with all possible speed.

They paused at a corner of the outer wall that separated the palace from the city. Their mysterious guide had vanished around the corner a moment earlier. Gaspar supported the slumping Balthazar as Melchior inched forward and peered around. Sighing his relief, he gestured them forward.

Turning the corner, they came face to face with a small group of people and beasts huddling against the wall. Standing before them, with some pride, was Shin-shin.

"Well, I'll be a . . ." stammered Gaspar.

"Ah, yes. Shin-shin. Well done. Yes . . ." said Balthazar in a strained voice.

Gaspar looked at Balthazar in amazement. "You knew he—she—would be here?"

"Of course. Her role was . . . unfulfilled," said Balthazar. "I called to her."

The girl came forward and, with uncharacteristic honesty, hugged the old man. Balthazar's moan made her step back, however, and concern showed in her eyes even in the dimness of night. "Master, you're not well," she stated flatly.

"Yes; a most worthy opponent. Your assistance would have been quite helpful," replied Balthazar, slipping his arm from around the black magus to stand shakily on his own.

The girl bowed to her master at the compliment. Assessing her, Melchior could see the change in her. She'd grown somehow, even though it'd only been a little more than a day since he'd last seen her. But there was something else, a glow, a force that lived within her that wasn't there before.

Shin-shin's brow furrowed as she mentally calculated their number. "Barir?" she began, then stopped short in dismay.

Melchior stepped forward and placed his hands on her shoulders. He bent to look into her eyes, already pooling with tears at the precognition of the warrior's fate. "He is... no more," he said softly. "And Zoth, too. They both gave their lives to save us. Yes, even Zoth finally saw the light. They died honorably," he lied, wanting to believe it himself.

"Gone?" She shook her head in denial.

Melchior felt the pain within her, but could do no more than draw the child to his chest and hold her. Silent sobs shook her for a while as she struggled to digest the fact that she'd never see Barir again.

He whispered, "He told me to tell you something. He wanted to make sure you knew it. He said, 'When you see Shin-shin, tell her I'm very proud of her. And tell her that I love her.'"

The words, their meaning, came from deep within his own heart. So Melchior knew them to be true, even if Barir hadn't had the time to utter them before he was killed. He had said as much with every look and gesture he made to the girl.

"As do we all," added Balthazar.

Melchior released her and joined the other Magi. They regarded at Shin-shin with appreciation.

"You're the pupil no more. What you must learn, only life itself can teach you. And it was," the diminutive astronomer paused as emotion cracked his voice, "an honor to be your teacher."

Shin-shin smiled and wiped her tears with the back of her hand. She bowed deeply. "You're all, and always will be, my masters. Call, and I shall come," she said solemnly.

She suddenly became all business to cover another wave of emotion. Turning, Shin-shin led them to a man and a young boy who stood holding the halters of a group of camels. "This is Ezra. He and his family have given me shelter and food. They've been kind," said Shin-shin as an introduction.

"Thank you for taking care of my apprentice. You've assumed great risk to do so. I, and my companions, are in your debt," said Balthazar with a formal bow that must have cost him dearly.

Ezra, a Hebrew man in his late thirties, nodded his head in acknowledgement, if not amazement. He looked as if he'd seen figments of his imagination come to life before his own eyes. "Yes, m-my lords. The child was lost and hungry. We took her in, as is the custom of our people. The Hebrew people of Jerusalem and Judaea, I mean," he added defiantly.

"She told us of your journey. I must admit, I didn't fully believe her. I thought her perhaps a little…well, you know, crazy, from the sun. I came tonight so she'd give up this wild story she told my wife and I. Guess she really was telling us the truth." His eyes were wide as they took in the bizarre sight before him. Melchior recognized that this was a simple man, honest yet proud, who found himself involved in events above his station.

Shaking his head, muttering that his wife and friends would never believe him, he waved the Magi to the beasts, still held by the young boy.

"This is my son, Matthew. You believed her story, didn't

you, my boy?" he asked, stroking the boy's head with pride.

"Yes. The star," the boy said quietly.

"He wants to grow up and become a soldier to drive the Romans out, right?" Ezra asked his son, mussing his son's hair roughly in appreciation. He looked directly at the Magi. "There are many here who have no love for Rome or the emperor. Don't judge us harshly by what you saw," he gestured with his head toward the palace, "in there."

"Along our journey, we've found a few like you. Those who put honor and friendship above personal risk. You are many, my friend, even if you don't know it. And I'd put a score of you against a Roman legion any day," replied Gaspar.

"It may come to that," muttered Ezra as he turned and took the camels' lead lines from the boy.

"They're not much, but they're all I have. They'll take you far. Not as fast as a horse, mind you, but they're steadier and stronger," said Ezra.

"They're worth a king's ransom to us," said Melchior, stepping forward and clapping his hand softly against a camel's neck. The beast didn't move an inch. "We have some things of value, to pay you—"

Ezra cut him off. "No, no. Just go. A gift. And hurry; the dawn approaches." He waved his hands, as if pushing the men toward the beasts.

"There's some water and foodstuffs there. Not much. But a day's worth," Ezra said.

"That's all we'll need, I'm afraid," Melchior said quietly to no one in particular.

Balthazar looked at Shin-shin. "Of course, you cannot come with us. The road divides here," he stated as if he were describing the weather. Then, a bit more tenderly, he added, "And so we part at last, Shin-shin. Gather yourself to travel home. Be safe. Be wise. Think before you act. And look after my garden, for goodness sake. And practice your lessons. And don't forget—"

"I won't, master," the girl cut in with a smile. "Thank you. For everything." She bowed a last time.

"Yes. Yes. You realize, of course, that you saved us here tonight. Without your aid, and the kindness of these strangers you found, all would have been lost. You've done well." A soft tear escaped the master's eye. "I am very proud of you. And proud to have been your teacher."

Melchior and Gaspar nodded their acknowledgement of the praise and thanks. Shin-shin took off her cap, her lustrous hair cascading down her shoulder, and shyly bowed her head.

Balthazar lifted her chin and stroked her check fondly, wiping away the tears streaming freely down the girl's face.

"Farewell, my child. Fare well," said Balthazar and relinquished a rare smile and a nod. He sensed a satisfying closure to his time with Shin-shin.

Balthazar and his companions turned to address their mounts. With some effort, they hauled Balthazar into the saddle of a kneeling camel, which rose drunkenly to its feet with the small magus clinging on for dear life. Melchior and Balthazar mounted as well.

"We must make haste. We've only got a few hours of darkness left. Soon, Herod will learn that his, ah guests, have departed," warned Gaspar.

"Take care. Get out of here, now! And tell no one that you saw us, for your own protection!" said Melchior over his shoulder as the camels began lumbering off. "And thank you!"

The girl, boy, and man watched the departing trio melt into the darkness.

Ezra put his arm around his son and said, "Remember this well, Matthew. Change is coming. Dark days, perhaps. These are indeed great men."

"Yes, father," said the boy.

"Yes, they are," agreed Shin-shin softly, a final tear tumbling down her smiling cheek as she watched her Magi go.

CHAPTER THIRTY-SEVEN

The camel-mounted Magi lumbered through the darkened city of Jerusalem, heading toward the Lion's Gate in the south wall. A few lamps burned in lonely windows, and a few faces peeped from behind modest curtains to see who would be up and about at such an hour, but all in all, they were ignored. But alarms and shouts would be ringing from Herod's palace soon enough.

They traveled in silence, each nursing his injuries, fatigue, and apprehension in solitude. The only sound was the whip of the cold wind and the heavy thumps of the camel's broad feet on the streets. And, of course, the omnipresent song of the star in their hearts and minds.

As they approached the gate, the Magi saw a small detail of Roman troops sitting around a small fire pit, warming themselves. The firelight glinted off their breastplates and helmets. By Melchior's count, there were at least six heavily armed men there, with more probably sleeping in a small hut off to the side.

"We don't have time for this," grumbled Gaspar, reaching for Balthazar's blade strapped across his back.

"Or the strength," said Balthazar painfully.

"Wait," said Melchior, formulating a plan. "Work with me. Like in the desert. Together."

Extending his arm, his fingers cupped, Melchior

focused his power on the group of men thirty paces away. Likewise, the other Magi extended their arms. Shafts of sapphire, crimson, and emerald energy shot forth, the three beams uniting as one ice-white shaft and blasting the air surrounding the guards.

With a loud splintering sound, the shaft froze the soldiers in mid-motion. They turned a sickly blue and became living statues. Frost rimmed the edges of their mouths and noses, and their eyes became icy marbles staring into the depths of the now empty fire pit that gave them no warmth.

Riding slowly up, the Magi humbly gazed at their handiwork.

"Did we...kill them?" asked Gaspar with awe.

"I don't think so. Just...slowed them. Like the frog that sleeps in winter at the bottom of the pond. I think when the sun rises, they'll thaw and return to their natural state," replied Balthazar.

Looking down at the men with pity, Melchior shook his head and looked at his hand. "I've never done anything like that before. Not from so far away. Not so...completely," he said quietly.

"Indeed. We grow stronger. What strengths we had before are now doubled, I think. Perhaps it's the star. Perhaps there are even greater challenges ahead," ventured Balthazar.

"Well, whatever it is, I don't care. Let's get out of this city," said Gaspar, goading his beast forward. Heeding his advice, the men rode unmolested through the Lion's Gate and so left Jerusalem behind.

Within the walls, Herod slept a fitful sleep, troubled by dreams that would haunt him until his death. Cities burning...palace plots and intrigue...the slaughter of children...gored soldiers...a bloody crown of thorns... and thousands upon thousands of eerie Roman crucifixes, dotting the horizon.

The escaping Magi rode west and south along the modest dirt road that led to Bethlehem. The way was well worn, for Bethlehem was a lesser town of farmers and shepherds who relied on Jerusalem for most of their supplies and commerce. The handful of miles could be easily traveled, so the Magi goaded their dromedaries to a steady pace and used the time as a respite.

The evening, though unnaturally cold, was singularly magnificent. The star's radiance, brighter than they'd yet seen it, coated everything from the riders to the stones to the road to the hillsides with a faint cerulean light. Its majestic song filled their souls, a triumphant march that seemed to keep time with the camels' heavy footfalls. Great cumulus clouds moved in the frigid sky, their dark centers contrasting with their illuminated edges. A sliver of a moon hung in a far corner of the sky, as if sulking about being left out of the evening's celestial events.

"You know, if I didn't feel so terrible, I'd be feeling pretty good," said Melchior, trying to lighten the mood.

"I'm freezing my tail off," said Gaspar, rubbing his hands briskly together and blowing into them to ward off the chill.

"Oh, this is nothing. I'm used to this. Back home, when I was a boy in the mountains, we'd get snow that would come up to a horse's neck," said Melchior. "I don't think I'll ever see that again."

On cue, wafer-like flakes of snow, iridescent in the star's light, began falling. Melchior laughed out loud, the first time he'd laughed in what seemed a lifetime.

"Did you do that?" accused Gaspar, scowling at Melchior.

"No, I swear by the star!" Melchior laughed again.

Balthazar, quiet until now, tilted his head up and let the light and the flakes caress his face. "I wonder, if all along, Zoth possessed the power to make the rain fall. It would have been helpful a few times on our trip, especially during the dry bit in the desert. I guess we'll never know," he ventured, coming as close to humor as he was capable.

"Never could manage that one," Melchior mumbled.

"I was wrong about him," said Gaspar quietly. "I never expected him to be capable of such sacrifice."

"No, you weren't amiss in your calculation of his nature," Balthazar replied. "The man who gave himself to save us was a far different man from the one who journeyed with us."

"What changed him, I wonder?" mused Gaspar.

Melchior thought for a moment about his cousin, and of his life of anger and evil. And of the dramatic turnaround that had saved the three of them. "He had what the Greeks call a catharsis. Something changed him, touched him. I think it might have been our old friend up there." Melchior looked up at the pulsating star.

"So many are gone…lost. The price for this journey has been dear, indeed," Balthazar said quietly, staring at the road passing beneath him.

They rode silently for a while, pondering the events of the last few weeks. Melchior dwelt upon the deaths of Zoth, Barir, Shafiq, and the rest of his men. His path from his mountain home could be traced by the thick trail of blood of many good men. Once again, he questioned his role, his destiny, and the seemingly senseless slaughter of so many for such a mysterious objective. Finally he thought of Nur, certain he would never see her face again.

For his own part, Gaspar thought of the Petrans. Countless lives lost and a sea of blood spilled in the defense of a city whose eventual fall seemed inevitable. He remembered Omar's undignified death under the hot sun. For what? A child?

Alone in the agony of his own feelings, Balthazar's broken ribs ached with every heave of the camel's humpy back. Yet his thoughts wandered backward as well, to Shin-shin, to his bamboo-forested homeland so far away, to the life he'd left forever. He worried about the girl, for her journey back would be a long and treacherous one. But she was strong, and smart, and resourceful. Her life-path was now hers alone to choose. Finally, he considered the irony of leaving one child behind — only to save another.

The night seemed eerily quiet — not quite silent, but filled with the soft, vacuous hiss of the falling snow. A blanket of white gradually formed on the shoulders of the Magi and covered the hard ground, softening the edges of the arid land through which they rode.

After a mile or two, as the shard of moon crept higher in the sky, they came upon two shepherds tending a flock of sheep near the narrow road. If not for a few bleats that broke the stillness of the evening, the Magi would have ridden right by them.

The men reined in their camels and paused. The sheep, sleeping like fluffy boulders on the ground with the exception of a few wandering insomniacs, were gathering snow on their backs and black heads, too. Their two tenders sat on the ground, facing a small fire pit that had no blaze. They didn't seem to notice the Magi.

Gaspar said in a soft voice, "You know, Herod's thugs are probably right behind us."

But Melchior disagreed. "Something, something isn't right here. I don't think anything has happened by chance on this journey. And a minute to rest would do us all some good. Come on, we'll be quick."

The Magi dismounted, Balthazar rather shakily, and walked the few paces off the road to where the shepherds sat. The two men didn't move or acknowledge them as they approached. Instead, they sat transfixed, staring unblinking into the cold, barren ring of rocks.

"Good evening. May we join you for a moment to rest?" asked Melchior.

One of the two men looked up and smiled at him. "Of course. We've been expecting you."

Gaspar, in the middle of sitting down, froze and looked at the men in suspicion. But Melchior joined them easily, pretending not to be surprised. "Indeed? Well, thanks for waiting up," he said. "Mind if we start a fire?"

They said nothing, so with a wave of his hand, Melchior conjured a crackling azure blaze out of thin air. He sat down with the shepherds, extending his hands to the fire. Still they said nothing, instead just watching the soft fluttering flames of the supernatural conflagration.

Once again, Melchior noticed that their powers were stronger than ever. He'd ignited the blaze without so much as a second thought, a feat that would have required severe concentration just days ago.

He peered in the dim light at the two men. They were peasants, eking out an existence from the harsh land. The younger man had a thin beard covering his dark, angular face. The other, perhaps his father or a relative, was rounder, with a thick, voluminous beard streaked with gray. They wore simple clothes, with heavy woven cloaks wrapped about them to ward off the snow. Their knotty shepherds' staves lay off to the side, forgotten in their delirium.

Balthazar crouched carefully on his haunches, keeping his hands in the folds of his tunic. He asked them, "Do you know why we've come, then? And where we go?"

The old shepherd turned his head from the fire and smiled at Balthazar. "Yes. You've come to meet the Lord and Messiah," he said matter-of-factly.

"Yes..." said an awestruck Gaspar.

The young shepherd stated cryptically, "The angels told us."

The Magi considered them. The two men seemed almost hypnotized, yet at peace and altogether...happy.

"Twelve nights ago, they came to us in the fields not far from here," the older man said, gesturing widely with his arm. His voice fell to a reverent whisper. "They said, 'For today in the city of David...a savior has been born for you who is…Messiah and Lord.' We went and saw him. It was just as they said."

Melchior regarded them solemnly and asked, "You've seen…God?"

The young shepherd nodded slowly, smiling. "Yes. He's waiting for you. You must hurry."

The two men rose as one, and the Magi followed suit. Not sure what else to do, the Magi followed them as the two shepherds walked to the waiting camels, now frosted in white.

"Go now to Bethlehem. You'll find the child wrapped in swaddling clothes, lying in a manger. Let the star be your guide. It's not far now," said the young man.

The Magi mounted again and looked down at the two shepherds. A faint glow emanated from them.

"What will you do now?" asked Gaspar.

The old shepherd said, "We shall go to share the good news. The Messiah has arrived."

They said nothing more, silent messengers of a power greater than they could comprehend.

Melchior only said, "Peace," and turned his camel back to the road.

They continued on to Bethlehem through the snowy landscape. Glancing upward, Gaspar exclaimed, "Look!" and pointed at the star.

A beam, a definable finger of light, shot from the star, touching down at some point ahead of their present location.

"It's the final guide, the last milestone. Our destination, it appears, is at last truly revealed," said Balthazar.

Inspired, they roused their mounts to a clumsy trot, which in turn became a smoother gallop. The snow waned, and the wind died as well.

The Magi, battered, gored, broken and bruised, at last came to the outskirts of David's City, Bethlehem.

Chapter Thirty-Eight

Rome had no presence in small, inconsequential Bethlehem. Simple homes huddled around informal squares surrounding a well, laundry pit, or other public landmark. Dusty and smelly, still and quiet, Bethlehem slept, its inhabitants, farmers, tradesmen, shepherds, and their flocks, unaware that a rare blanket of magical snow had scrubbed clean their shabby little village.

It was into the middle of this quiet setting that the Magi came storming, riding their camels at full speed along the sleepy streets. They entered Bethlehem from the east, following the sentinel star ever westward. They only briefly disturbed the serene stillness of the night, a plume of disturbed white snow the only evidence of their passing.

The shaft of blue-white light from the star was a beacon, fixed and unmoving, leaving no doubt of where they should go. The Magi, with Melchior in the lead, only had to navigate the twisting paths of the village, which was no small feat.

Soon, their gallop had slowed to a walk, with Melchior constantly looking up to reference the star's position. He was grateful for the moderate pace. The deep wound in his shoulder had suffered greatly with the strain of the ride, and his shirt was wet with blood. It had been untended for so long, he no longer wondered whether he would ever use the limb again. He was sure he wouldn't. Instead, judging by the throbbing agony, he wondered if he would live out the night. And he could only guess at the pain his comrades experienced.

The brilliant starlight created dark shadows between the buildings that they now clomped through. So Melchior conjured up three floating orbs of light to pace each of the Magi a few feet above their heads and provide illumination in the darkened alleys and narrow streets. His own was blue, Balthazar's was green, and Gaspar's red. Once again, even in his compromised state, Melchior marveled at the ease with which such tricks came to him. The closer they drew to their destination, the stronger they all became.

Yes, I sense it, too, came a mental message from Balthazar, riding silently behind him.

"Did they say, a manger?" Gaspar asked loudly from the rear, his voice tainted with pain.

"Indeed. It's a strange place for a king," replied Balthazar.

As they approached the spot where the shaft of light touched down, the Magi heard a loud hum in the air, a foreign sound that increased in strength, the closer they drew. Their bones vibrated with it, and the air was filled with an electric energy that made the hairs on their arms stand up straight.

Melchior moved his reluctant camel forward. Apparently, even the camel was sensitive to the paranormal atmosphere. Moving at this saturnine pace, the Magi passed a modest building that seemed to be an inn. The door was shut tight, and baggage barrows and wagons were lined up to the side.

No longer looking up, but instead simply following his internal directive, Melchior nudged the camel around the corner of the inn and down a dark, narrow passage. The air was now thick with the sound and the energy, alerting every nerve ending in their bodies that they had finally arrived.

Melchior emerged from the shadowy passage and was immediately pummeled by the raw might of the star. Vaster. Stronger. Deeper. More magnificent than he'd ever dreamed possible. Everything he'd ever seen, thought, tasted, touched, or imagined paled in comparison to the sheer power of the star.

Somehow, the star seemed to be right overhead, a massive lamp of radiance that blasted forth the shaft of pure light from its center. The song, for so long a distant voice like a call from another room, now vibrated through the air with intimate force. Amidst the music, Melchior could detect the voices of the celestial beings who'd appeared at Petra, singing in a language he couldn't fathom, but whose meaning he grasped nonetheless. The indescribable sound could be summed up in just one word — joy.

The star dazzlingly illuminated everything, creating a surreal landscape of incandescence. At the center of the shaft of light, bathed, and washed with the star's energy, was a lowly hut used for the housing of animals, barely a roof and a few walls to support it. That such a humble place should be their ultimate destination now seemed somehow fitting in Melchior's mind.

Balthazar and Gaspar joined him, similarly speechless in their appraisal of the scene. Melchior looked over at his friends and smiled at their ghostlike appearance in the phosphorescent light. "I think we're here," he said and laughed. Truly, laughed out loud.

He couldn't explain it, but he felt an inner delight, a relief, at their arrival. Half dead, mourning the loss of so many he loved, exhausted beyond belief, still he couldn't hold back a sense of…satisfaction…that they'd reached the end of the journey at last.

Gaspar laughed, too, a loud, raucous guffaw. He slapped Balthazar, who was grinning stupidly, hard on the shoulder. The man with the broken ribs barely noticed.

The Magi's fire orbs vanished, no longer needed. They slid from their camels and left them to wander. Gaspar remembered at the last moment his bundle and untied it from the beast's back before it walked away to find a comfortable place to rest.

Melchior looked at his companions; they'd never looked worse. He looked down and saw his blood-caked clothes, a large wet spot over the site of his dagger wound. They were all bent, fatigued, and filthy. But they were alive and at the place they had traveled so far to reach. And the light of the holy star seemed to make even broken bodies such as theirs things of unearthly beauty.

"Any ideas?" asked Gaspar as he dropped the bundle on the ground.

"I think we just, go in. Right?" ventured Melchior.

"It's a sound strategy," replied Balthazar.

"Here, take something with you. It's impolite to show up empty-handed," said Gaspar, opening the bundle and handing out the small boxes to the others.

Melchior looked at him with a bit of surprise.

"What? I had a mother. I know my manners," countered Gaspar.

"I think," said Balthazar, smiling sympathetically as he accepted the box of frankincense, "she'd be proud of you."

Like nervous grooms, they walked the few steps down a rocky slope to the spot where the small stable sat. As they approached, they could see a wide doorway in the side of the shed.

Gaspar whispered, "Melchior, we'll follow your lead."

Accepting once again the leadership of the trio, Melchior turned and entered the stable.

In sharp contrast with the blue-white light of the star outside, a golden glow flowed through the simple hut, its amber hues caressing the walls and stall. It made the room comfortably warm and inviting. Melchior's mind registered some animals about, a small donkey, an ox, a lamb, and a few squabs, all swathed in the buttery radiance. Some of the straw strewn about the floor had been piled in a corner as a makeshift bed, along with some small bundles of clothing. The song of the star was muted in here in deference to the child.

The child. Just as the shepherds had promised, a babe lay in a feed trough. Swaddled in a pristine white wrap, he was awake, cooing and content in the manger. The golden light emanated directly from the child, flowing out in soft, warm waves. This babe, not even two weeks old, was a source of power that Melchior couldn't even begin to reckon.

A tall, slender man dressed in simple traveling clothes stood at the babe's side. He had a close-cropped beard and an inviting face, and some of the room's energy seemed to flow from him, as well. He looked kindly at the Magi as they entered and nodded in acknowledgement of their presence, as if he'd been waiting for their arrival.

Sitting at his feet, beside the manger, was a lovely young woman. A thin, sky-blue shawl covered her auburn hair and shoulders. She was fair-skinned, petite, and delicate, almost fragile. Her attention was focused solely on the child. A portion of the golden power seemed to radiate from her as well.

Both beamed with pride, as any new parent would, but there was more.

Awe.

Each regarded the child with love, reverence, and respect. The man and woman fully understood the import of the birth, of the moment, of the presence, of such a tiny infant. They, too, knew the world had changed forever.

Melchior and the other Magi felt the change as well. The layers of the old world, the old ways, were being stripped away by the sheer presence of the babe. They could sense the fabric of everything familiar being peeled off.

Gazing at the babe, Melchior intuitively grasped that a new godhead had been revealed, a power mightier and more terrible than any the world had ever known, all captured in the innocent gurgles of a newborn baby.

Like a man made of wood, Melchior slowly inched forward, feeling the power of the god grow with each step he took. The golden energy pierced his body and reached into his soul, wringing out the fiber of his being like an overused towel, the remains of his former life dripping away. He was at once being unmade and recreated.

Reaching the manger, he dropped heavily to one knee. The mother looked at Melchior now and smiled softly. She said nothing, for no words were necessary.

He offered the small box he held and opened its lid, revealing the golden contents. Melchior bowed his head and paid homage. "I bring a gift of gold for the King. May his reign bring peace and plenty to all," he said, bowing his head again and pressing his arm across his chest in deference.

The young woman smiled and nodded, accepting the box holding the few gold coins and laying it in the manger with the baby. He cooed softly, pleased.

Rising, Melchior stepped aside, and Balthazar took his place.

As was his custom, he bowed low, his head almost grazing the straw-covered floor. His injury seemed to have vanished. Then he knelt and proffered his opened box. "For the God most high, I bring a gift of frankincense to anoint him. May all worship him and follow his example," he said reverently.

Finally, Gaspar knelt on both knees and extended the last gift to the mother and child. "I have only myrrh to offer, precious and rare. May its scent fill his days with sweetness and erase all bitterness from his life," he said firmly, his strong baritone a melodic complement to the song of the star and the harmony of the angels. Then he stepped back with his friends.

The Magi regarded the beatific scene. The angels, only heard until now, appeared in miniature in the air above the small family, hovering and paying tribute. Their ethereal forms floated in supernatural beauty, their joy unmistakable. Softly, gently, they gave praise to the glory of God.

The Magi absorbed it all, mesmerized by the magnitude

of the moment, awed by the power such a small being could possess. Time itself stood still in the stable as the world around them was born anew.

Eventually — how long had they stood there? — the Magi regained their senses and thought to depart.

Leaving the manger, Melchior stole one last glance at the mother and god-child. She had arranged the gifts tenderly about the babe and was now stroking his head. She looked up, and Melchior was struck by how clear and blue her eyes were, and how they peered into his very heart. Gazing at him thus, her face was an odd mixture of love and pity. Puzzled by her demeanor, he lingered for a last moment, nodded in farewell, and left.

The woman stared after them for a while, a tear rolling down her cheek as she foresaw a fraction of the tragic events to come. Yet her maternal side struggled against desperation and eventually won the battle for her heart. She rejected despair at the last and embraced the beauty of the moment. She looked down on the child, felt his omnipotent presence, and her soul calmed. For now.

A few paces from the stable doorway, the Magi stood in the black night. The darkness seemed harsher and thicker than ever, and they had difficulty seeing more than a few paces. The snow on the ground was melting, turning the dirt beneath into thick mud. Gone was the crisp air of before. A cold, bitter wind raked across exposed flesh, and they heard no sound above its high-pitched howl.

It had taken all their strength to leave the child, and the stable. The energy, the rapture, the peace, all was seductive. Like the crying newborn pushed from the security of the womb, they had wrenched themselves from the manger to be forced into the cold night by a command from on high.

"My," said Melchior, leaning on a fence rail. He felt drained. Whole, yet incomplete; happy, yet hollow; giddy with both elation and withdrawal, as if he'd just ridden a stallion for leagues at full gallop and suddenly found himself sitting on the ground.

Balthazar noticed it first. "The star. It's vanished."

All three Magi looked to the heavens, but couldn't detect even a hint of the star they'd followed for so long. The normal celestial field had returned, sleepy and subdued, and the thin sickle of the moon glowed dully in its ivory vestments.

Melchior shivered, chilled, as he noted how their surroundings had changed. What had been a surreal panorama of heavenly beauty just a few moments earlier had been reduced to a cruel, inhospitable plot of mud and rock. The world had become...harsher. Simpler. Darker. Harder.

Other things had changed as well.

"My chest," stammered Balthazar around his chattering teeth, probing his ribcage delicately with his hands. "It's healed. Completely."

Melchior instinctively slid his hand into his shirt to test his shoulder wound and found nothing but smooth, healthy skin. "Me too," he said with astonishment. "The knife wound is gone. As if it were never there."

Gaspar stroked his chest and thigh and found that he, too, had been cured of his cuts and bruises. "It's a miracle, nothing less," he said in an awed voice. "Not even Melchior, not even Zoth, could've done such a thing. That child is truly a god. *The* God."

There. He'd said it. Melchior looked at the black warrior whose dark skin made him look like a void in the darkness. He'd spoken solemnly, as if delivering a death sentence. And Melchior felt it, too. Why did he have this terrible sense of foreboding? What was it about the innocent babe that struck his heart with sadness...sorrow? "Yes," was all he could reply.

Still rubbing his rejuvenated shoulder, Melchior voiced his thoughts. "I should feel great. It's as if I'd never been

stabbed. But I feel...odd. Like I'm hungry, but it's not that."
He stopped, confused.

"Yes, I feel it, too. A weakness. I feel diminished," said
Gaspar softly.

"A new age has begun," Balthazar said eerily, with the
confidence of a prediction that was already true. He spread
his arms and looked around. "The old ways are . . . no more.
A new god, a singular God, has taken hold. That which was
is gone. Our world, the old world, is unmade. A new one
is born. Here. We...we're the witnesses. It's why we were
summoned."

The reality, and the truth of his words, struck Melchior
like a blow. "It's just as Zoth feared, but much more. He
thought Rome would destroy us. He had no idea that his
world—our world—would die at the hands of... an infant."

"Melchior, see if you can create a light. Anything,"
instructed Balthazar.

Melchior looked at him with a puzzled look, surprised
buy the odd request. But he obliged and held his hands
a few inches apart, his fingers arched. He concentrated
intensely. Nothing happened. No flame. No crackles of blue
electricity. Not even a spark. He tried again, concentrating
intently. Nothing.

A long silence followed, filled only with the high-pitched
howl of the wind buffeting them.

"It's as I feared. Your thoughts are closed to me now,
whereas before I could sense your mind. And you, my
friend," said Balthazar, turning to Gaspar, "I fear you're no
longer gifted with such exceptional strength."

The Ethiope bent and grasped a medium-sized, flat rock,
and struggled even to lift it. At last he hauled it clumsily
to his waist and tried unsuccessfully to break it in half,
grunting with the exertion.

Melchior spoke, the realization complete in his mind at
last. "Now there can be only one God. One source of power.
And in the face of such a God, we've become mere men."

There followed another moment of silence filled with the moan of the wind as that realization sank in. Their mourning ended, however, when Gaspar let the rock fall to the muddy ground. It split in half with an ear-splitting crack.

He laughed, loud, clear, and pure. "A man, even an everyday man, can accomplish many things," he said. "Don't let this destroy the joy of what of we've seen here and accomplished. I'm satisfied at last. Perhaps the world will be a better place without the likes of us."

"Perhaps," said Melchior with a tinge of remorse. "Perhaps." He wondered if his departed power would be the last victim of this journey

"Our job's not done yet, though," he said as the tall, slender man, the father, walked out to meet with them.

"I am—I'm Joseph. We're...honored by your visit," he said, almost shyly. Even he, it seemed, was overwhelmed by recent events.

"We were led here by the star," said Gaspar, struggling to explain their odd presence.

"Yes," said Joseph. He looked up. "It seems to have left us at last."

"You saw it, too? Wait, of course, you saw it, too," said Gaspar.

Balthazar asked Joseph, "Why are you here, outside with the beasts? It's not fitting."

Joseph smiled at him. Even here in the dark and the cold, the Magi could see and sense the golden aura of goodness that welled from him, and they instinctively drew closer to feel it, like moths to the flame.

"We were traveling, and there was no room at the inn yonder. But they kindly offered the stable for our use. And the manger turned out to be perfect for...Him," he said, awkwardly acknowledging the godhead's presence.

"Traveling?" inquired Balthazar.

"The census. Octavian has ordered a count taken in all the Roman provinces. We had to come here to Bethlehem, where my family comes from. I'm up from Nazareth. My wife Mary and I are newly betrothed," continued Joseph a bit sheepishly. "The child . . . comes from God. We didn't, you see, it's a miracle birth. It's the will of Jehovah."

Quietly, the Magi considered the divine nature of the babe within and didn't doubt for a moment the truth of Joseph's words. Given all that they'd seen and done, a miraculous birth seemed perfectly natural.

"Bethlehem . . . the City of David . . . you're a descendent of a man named David, then?" asked Melchior, remembering the prophecies.

"Yes. King David. A long time ago, he led our people to freedom," said Joseph with a touch of pride.

"I think his progeny will do so, as well," said Melchior softly, almost to himself.

Joseph looked at him, and sadness welled in his eyes. To think of the innocent child inside the manger leading revolutionaries against the might of Rome seemed a cruel vision of the future to them all.

Remembering their task, Melchior blurted, "You must flee. Take the mother and child and leave Bethlehem. Tonight. Now. You've stayed here too long. I think we came all this way to warn you. You must leave. The child is in danger."

Joseph's eyes opened wide at the warning. "Danger? From where—"

Gaspar cut him off. "Herod. King Herod. In Jerusalem. He knows about the child. Already, the child is being called a king. Herod will kill the child to preserve the throne and appease his masters in Rome."

Joseph turned away and staggered a step or two to process the news. Melchior watched in sympathy as he swayed under the weight of the threat.

Melchior came to his side and gently put an arm about the man's shoulders. "You can do this. You must. Don't go back to your home. Go where no one would look for you.

Don't even tell us where you're going. Hide. Raise the child in safety. Help him fulfill his destiny," he said quietly and encouragingly.

Looking back at his companions, he said, "We'll head another way to draw them off. And if they catch us, we can't tell them what we don't know. Most important, the child, and you, will be safe."

Joseph nodded, accepting another mantle of responsibility thrust upon him by powers he couldn't fathom. He grasped each of the Magi's hands in thanks and went back to the manger to tell Mary they had to depart.

Before he entered, however, Melchior called out to him, "His name! What's the child's name?"

Joseph paused. "Jesus. The angels told me...His name's Jesus."

Melchior smiled kindly at the man, "It's a good name. For a good man."

Repeating the name over and over again in their minds, the Magi mounted their camels and rode off, occasionally looking back with longing in their hearts.

Yet they rode on, watching for the column of troops that was surely already on its way from Jerusalem.

Within an hour, Joseph and Mary had wrapped the child warmly in a basket and loaded him onto their small cart, sparely laden with their few possessions and pulled by a donkey.

As one trio departed westward, the other was already heading north, leaving as noticeable a trail as they could. The cold, black night embraced the travelers, its covering darkness their only protection.

Soon the Magi left the village behind and rode out into the rocky hills. After a few hours, they finally found a small cave cut into the side of a steep slope. Too tired even to light a fire, they dozed where they fell, their camels outside, hunched against the cold.

"I've never been so tired in my life," said Melchior, curling into a fetal position.

"Or so cold," said Gaspar, who appeared unaccustomed to such frigid temperatures.

"Herod will be here soon," said Balthazar. "We must move at first light."

Herod. Rome. Caesar. All of it made a sick kind of sense in Melchior's mind. All were pitted against a tiny family of three, escaping in what he hoped was the nick of time. If he had to throw himself between the spear of Rome and the babe to save him, he'd do it, Melchior thought, and as exhaustion finally wrestled him into an uneasy slumber.

Chapter Thirty-Nine

The Magi slept fitfully, uncomfortable on the frigid floor of the cave, uneasy in the knowledge that at any moment a legion of Roman centurions could march up and slaughter them where they lay. They were exhausted, depleted, and helpless.

But their concerns were unwarranted, for another force came to them in their sleep. Angels of God appeared to the Magi in their dreams, speaking to them as if they were awake.

The angel who spoke to Melchior seemed familiar, like a friend long absent. A warm, embracing sensation flooded over him as he dreamt, providing some relief from the biting cold. In his dream, and in the dreams of his brother Magi, he awoke and sat up to see the angel floating in the air of the cave, lustrous with magnificent strength.

"GOOD MELCHIOR, BELOVED OF THE LORD, YOU HAVE SERVED WELL. YOU AND YOUR BRETHREN HAVE SAVED THE FAMILY YOU WERE INTENDED TO HELP, AND THE DESIGNS OF THE EVIL ONE HAVE BEEN THWARTED," said the angel in the melodious, multifaceted voice reminiscent of the star.

"The…evil one?" he asked.

"NOT ALL REJOICE AT THE ARRIVAL OF THE LORD HERE ON EARTH, AND OF THIS NEW WORLD WITH

NEW MEANING. THE MANIFESTATION OF THE ONE GOD IS A THREAT TO HE WHO DOES NOT LOVE, THE AUTHOR OF PAIN AND SUFFERING HERE ON EARTH. THE ONE WHO IS THE LORD HAS COME TO TEACH THE LESSON OF LOVE TO ALL WHO WILL LISTEN. GOD COMES NOT WITH A SWORD, BUT A SONG," intoned the angel. "THE EVIL ONE WILL BE SORELY TESTED, AS WILL THE HEARTS OF MEN. ONLY THE WORTHY SHALL EARN THE RIGHT TO SEE THE FINAL LIGHT OF SALVATION. AND EVEN THAT WILL COME AT GREAT COST TO US ALL." The angel finished the thought with a melancholy tone, foreshadowing events 33 years in the future.

"What's to become of me and my friends? What shall we do? Where shall we go?" he asked.

"THE WORLD YOU KNEW IS DEAD AND GONE, A MEMORY NOW. THIS IS THE NEW WORLD, THE WORLD OF THE ONE, JUST GOD. THE ONE GOD HAS ALWAYS BEEN HERE, AND POWER AND MAGIC WAS HERE TO BE WIELDED BY MANY. BUT LIKE ALL GOOD THINGS THE HAND OF MAN TOUCHES, THIS POWER WAS CORRUPTED AND MISUSED. SO GOD HAS TAKEN THIS POWER AND MADE IT A SPECIAL GIFT FOR THE MOST BELOVED."

"SHED NO TEARS FOR WHAT HAS BEEN LOST. WHAT HAS COME IS GREATER THAN ANY MAGIC THE ANCIENT WORLD EVER WITNESSED. ALL WILL NOW HAVE THE OPPORTUNITY TO JOIN WITH GOD."

The angel paused and waited for the promise to sink in, then continued.

"THE ONE GOD WILL CONTINUE TO MANIFEST ITSELF IN MANY FORMS FOR THE MANY PEOPLE HERE. THE ONE GOD WILL HAVE MANY NAMES, MANY FORMS, MANY PRACTICES, BUT ALL ARE TRUE AND THE FUNDAMENTAL ELEMENT OF LOVE IS THE BINDING FORCE AMONG THEM."

The angel looked directly at Melchior. "JOURNEY BACK NOT TO JERUSALEM, FOR YOUR HEART IS TRUE ON THE MATTER OF HEROD. HE, EVEN NOW, SEARCHES IN VAIN FOR THE CHILD. HEROD WILL FAIL, AS WILL ALL EVIL ONES IN THE END. YET BEFORE THE LORD'S ULTIMATE VICTORY OVER EVIL, MANY WILL PERISH. INNOCENTS WILL BE SLAUGHTERED. UNSPEAKABLE HORRORS WILL BE UNLEASHED. AND EVEN THE ONE GOD WILL SACRIFICE IN THE NAME OF LOVE FOR ALL," sang the angel sadly.

As the being spoke to him, Melchior had brief glimpses of the tragedies to come. He witnessed unspeakable atrocities, horrible crimes, and the murder of countless good people. Tears streamed down his face.

"YOUR LOAD HAS INDEED BEEN HEAVY, AND THE PRICE YOU HAVE PAID QUITE DEAR," sang the angel. "BUT GOOD MELCHIOR, THE LORD DEMANDS MORE OF YOU. YOU AND YOUR FELLOW MAGI ARE TO BE SHEPHERDS OF MEN THROUGH THE AGES."

"Shepherds...shepherds of men?" asked Melchior, thoroughly confused. Surely, he thought, he was done serving this, this power. He'd lost his abilities, almost lost his life on numerous occasions, lost so many friends, lost so much time...what more can this God want?

Answering his thoughts, the angel replied, "MUCH MORE, MELCHIOR. SO MUCH MORE. YOU ARE AMONG THE CHOSEN OF THE ONE GOD. FOR MAN IS WEAK AND WILL STRAY. THE EVIL ONE WILL NOT WAVER IN HIS WAR FOR SUPREMACY OVER MORTAL EXISTENCE. THIS WORLD IS NOW THE BATTLEFIELD, AND YOU ARE TO BE A GUIDE OF THE ONE GOD."

Melchior felt dejection creep into his heart as he began to realize the awful truth. His life was never to he his own again, and all that he was before the journey began was lost to him. Nur, his people, even his kingdom were to be sacrificed for this God.

The angel smiled at him kindly, its asexual countenance taking on the tender look of a parent with a child.

"DO NOT DESPAIR, GOOD MELCHIOR, FOR YOUR GOD IS KIND AND GENEROUS. IN RETURN FOR YOUR SERVICE, GOD GRANTS YOU IMMORTALITY. THE YEARS SHALL NOT TOUCH YOU, AND CENTURIES FROM NOW YOU WILL BE AS STRONG AS YOU ARE TODAY. BUT TAKE CARE, FOR THOUGH YOU ARE IMMORTAL, YOU MAY STILL BE SLAIN BY THE HAND OF MAN. YOU WILL NOT BE INDESTRUCTABLE, SIMPLY AGELESS. AND WISE, OF COURSE."

Melchior frowned to himself. Certainly, the fantasy of immortality was as old as man himself. But it was a fantasy Melchior had never indulged in nor wished for. It was an odd gift, one he suspected had unforeseen consequences.

The vision of the angel began to wash out and diffuse around its edges.

"AND A FINAL GIFT TO AID YOU IN YOUR JOURNEY THROUGH TIME. YOUR BENEVOLENT GOD RETURNS YOUR POWERS TO YOU. BUT USE THEM WISELY AND ALWAYS FOR THE GOOD OF OTHERS. WHILE THE ONE GOD'S PATIENCE IS INFINITE, THE GIFT OF SUPERNATURAL FORCE IS NOT, AND MUST BE USED SPARINGLY."

The angel's image continued to dissolve, and Melchior felt the pang of longing and hunger in his heart that he always experienced at their departure.

"BUT AT THE END OF YOUR JOURNEY, THE LORD WILL WELCOME YOU AND SEAT YOU AS THE SPECIAL GUEST AT THE TABLE. SLEEP NOW, WISE MAN, AND REST WHILE YE MAY."

"But how will we know whom to help? When to act? Who—what—will be our guide now?" he pleaded, hoping for another surefire sign like his old friend the star.

The space where the angel had floated was almost empty now. Only a small burning orb of light glimmered and bounced there.

"FEAR NOT, GOOD MELCHIOR. YOU ARE NEVER ALONE. YOUR FELLOW MAGI WILL BE WITH YOU. AND OTHERS WHO SERVE THE ONE GOD, THE WATCHERS, ALREADY MAKE THEIR WAY HERE TO ASSIST AND GUIDE YOU. AND THE ONE GOD WILL ALWAYS BE HERE WITH YOU. THAT IS THE VERY REASON THE ONE GOD HAS COME."

And with a wink of light, the angel departed, and in his dream, Melchior sat for a while in the dark. At last the vision left him, and he slept on peacefully, the tears on his face drying slowly in the cold night air.

Chapter Forty

Just after the Magi departed Bethlehem, mounted scouts from Jerusalem arrived, performing a perfunctory search of the village for any signs of the escaped Magi or a new king.

Not far behind the scouts, a league back, half a legion of infantry marched, making good time. The centurion in charge estimated that they would reach the tiny town sometime after daybreak.

As the sun broke over the horizon, the scouts came riding back, hard. They reined in before the centurion, the hot sweat lathering the necks of their horses steaming in the darkness. One look was all the centurion needed.

"There's no sign of the escaped prisoners. I think they're gone already. Some say three strangers left the town, heading north, a few hours ago," the lead scout reported. "As for the child...a king...what can I say? There are lots of young children there. They all look the same to me!"

The centurion frowned and looked down. Beside him, the column trudged past amidst the clank of equipment and the heavy thuds of footfalls. They weren't far from their objective. His orders were to take the city, not chase ghosts in the dark. He was at a crossroads, and he did what any good middleman does. He stalled.

"Ride back to Herod and tell him what you told me. We're moving on. Get fresh horses, and ride back here with

Herod's instructions. Go!" he barked, slapping the horse on the flank and sending it off into the night, back toward Jerusalem.

Soon the legion entered Bethlehem, the soldiers' faces grim after a forced march in the freezing cold in the dead of night. The freak snow had turned the ground soft, and hundreds of marching feet had turned it to mush. The centurion dispersed troops throughout the town to search for signs of the missing Magi.

The blistering sun had been up for an hour and some when the scout returned, ready to collapse after riding vigorously for so long. He slid wearily to the ground and saluted the centurion as best he could. An aide brought him a skin of water, which the panting man greedily accepted and sucked down noisily.

The centurion, sitting outside at a table beside the street, had been eating some spare food appropriated from a nearby inn. Wiping his greasy mouth, he barked to the scout, "Well?"

The scout gasped through a mouthful of water, "He's gone mad."

The centurion shook his head, prepared for just such a state of affairs.

Not only were Herod's prisoners gone, the scout reported, but his three advisors were either dead or missing, too. That Flavinius had met his match wasn't the worst news the centurion had heard in a while, but that some odd stranger bested him was a bit disconcerting. And no one had ever liked Ze'ev or that spooky Egyptian, so no loss there either. But add them all up, and the result was certainly enough to send Herod into a frenzy.

Herod had launched a full-scale interrogation of everyone in the palace, certain that someone had betrayed him on the inside. Fear drove him, because he'd lost his one and only lead to the child the prisoners had described.

"We're to go through the town and . . . and . . ." The scout looked down, reluctant to complete the sentence.

"Get on with it!" shouted the centurion.

"And...kill every boy under the age of two years," whispered the scout, still not looking up. "Just to be safe."

The order caught the centurion off guard. He thought long and hard for a few moments. Herod's atrocities were well known, even in Rome, but this was a new low, even for him. But the soldier in him knew that if he didn't carry out the order, his own sons would feel the cruel cut of Herod's wrath. He slammed his fist down on the table, upsetting his cup and bowl of food. He looked up at the scout, then to his lieutenants, standing about nervously.

"Mark my words, this won't go well for Herod. Or for any of us." He already felt regret eating at his conscience. "Search for the boys. Only the youngest ones. They'll try to hide them. Kill any you find. And make it quick."

The lieutenants scattered to assemble squads of soldiers to carry out the grim task. Soon, groups of armed men were kicking down doors, searching for small boys and infants. Toddlers and babies were torn from the arms of shrieking mothers. Fathers, grabbing whatever they could, tried in vain to protect their families. Many families lost both a son and a father. Many of the soldiers themselves wept as they carried out their grisly deed, sensing the damnation they were bringing down upon themselves.

Screams of dying children, mourning parents, and horrified citizens filled the air. Others simply walked the streets in a daze, confounded by the cruelty of the deed and the senselessness of it. Soon a dirty, sooty smoke filled the air, accompanied by the foul stench from the burning bodies of the innocents.

Late in the day, their grisly task complete, the legion marched north in pursuit of the missing prisoners. Curses and thrown stones followed them, but there was no reprisal from the soldiers, for they knew what they'd done. Their souls were damned for the murders, and the dead looks on their faces said as much.

They left behind Bethlehem, which just a few short hours ago had been the most jubilant place on the face of the earth. It had become a bloodbath, a scene of despicable horror. The day had dawned where man would reap the seeds of evil he sows and pay the price.

CHAPTER FORTY-ONE

The Magi rose and assembled at the mouth of the small cave. The sun was already hot in the sky, growing hotter and more inhospitable with every inch it traversed. Judaea was returning to her desert self, the snow and cold of the night before already a fading memory. The men sat on rocks just within the cave's entrance. They shared the few provisions they had left, nibbling on dried meat and sipping carefully from the last of their precious water supply. No one wanted to be the first to speak.

At last, Balthazar broke the silence. "It seems we're to remain as companions. Our task is not yet complete."

"Will it ever be? I wonder, will we ever see our homelands again?" mused Gaspar.

Melchior swallowed his bite, contemplated his friends, and thought of the journey, the star, and the babe — life, and so much death. "Why were we the ones? Why did we come?" he asked.

"The simple answer, I guess, was the birth," said Gaspar.

Another silence followed as each absorbed his response. The world around them seemed so changed, so empty, so devoid of the energy it once held. And the future, the life without end the angel had described the night before seemed just so daunting. Taking it in, Melchior considered the simple answer.

"But was it a birth? Or a death? The world, our world, it's…it's changed so. It's dead." Melchior's voice came heavy with grief. "I find this birth hard, and bitter. I feel lost." He studied the ground.

"Ah. And so you wonder, Melchior, was it all worth it?" asked Balthazar, clearly searching for resolution as desperately as his comrade.

Melchior looked up at the horizon. The unforgiving, rocky panorama seemed a harsh reminder of the new age in which he found himself. He looked back at his friends, blinking eyes gone vague and moist. "Yes. Yes. If, in the end, the world can be saved from the pain we've seen, then…" His voice trailed off as he searched for the words. "Yes. I guess our losses in this new age are but little things." He paused. "But this? I should be glad of another death," Melchior finished quietly.

"Ha! What death?" shouted Gaspar loudly with a laugh, rising with enthusiasm and addressing the world beyond the cave. The shimmering sunlight outside silhouetted his massive frame and made him appear as a dark god.

"We're alive after all this! And now, *we never shall die!*"

"And," said Balthazar with a hint of mischief to his usually calculated voice, "there will be opportunities to shape the future, to help those who need it most. And there will be many opportunities for study, as well. I, for one, am not displeased."

"And," concluded Melchior, finally starting to see a light at the end of the dark tunnel they were emerging from, "we can do this again."

He waved his hands and conjured a tiny storm over their fire, a feat he'd never been able to achieve with success. The cloud emitted a miniature rumble of thunder. A short bolt of lightning flashed out, the cloud ruptured, and a small sprinkling of rain fell and doused the fire.

The other Magi looked at him and smiled. Inside, they knew that their world, their lives, everything was a sacrifice to the new God. The ancient world was forever lost. A new day, a new era, a new world had begun.

They gathered their last belongings and stepped out from the cave. A few thousand paces away, they could see a small caravan of white-robed men making their way directly to where the Magi stood.

"Hmmm. Those would be the Watchers we heard about in the dream last night. I hope they brought some food, or I'll take it out of their hides," threatened the famished Ethiopian warlord.

The Magi slowly walked toward the caravan winding its way to them.

"In my sleep last night, I saw new horrors visited upon the good people of this land by Herod. As the angel said, our work here is far from done," Balthazar warned, giving voice to the sense of sadness and injustice that each of them had woken up with. Balthazar's newly-restored prescience allowed him to discern the facts of the story and see the dark future they foretold, images that had only been flashes of disturbing imagery to Melchior and Gaspar.

"I would welcome the chance to sever his head," grumbled Gaspar.

"Somehow, I think you'll get your chance to do justice to many evil men in the years to come, my dark friend," said Melchior grimly.

"Good," said Gaspar. "And if I'm lucky, I'll even visit Rome and clean things up there, too."

His sadness momentarily overcome, Melchior grinned, nodded, and slapped the giant on the shoulder. But not for the last time, the tall black magus surprised him. Gaspar swung each of his mighty arms around the shoulders of the other Magi.

"You're a great man, Melchior. We wouldn't have come this far without you," Gaspar said as a matter of fact.

To Balthazar, he said, "And you, my friend, will always be an enigma to me. And I like it that way. But it looks like we'll have some time on our hands to figure you out," and finished with a broad smile.

"Lord Gaspar, you've learned much, I think. Perhaps the greatest lesson of all was trust—to trust another and trust your own heart. It brings me happiness to see you thus," replied Balthazar.

"Well, you'd never know it to look at you!" Gaspar retorted with a grin.

His arms fell to his sides, and they picked their way along the rocky terrain.

Gaspar asked, "What do you think? Will they remember us and our deeds? Will they tell the story of the Magi around the fires for years to come?"

Balthazar looked sideways at the quiet Melchior and asked, "What troubles you, good Melchior? Has your troubled soul not found peace?"

Melchior thought for a moment, paused, and rested his rump on a large rock. The others turned to look at him.

Melchior responded, "It has. I'm done searching. And while what I found wasn't what I expected, it was… satisfying…nonetheless. You've been like a father to all of us, not just Shin-shin. You were the rock. I'm in your debt."

Balthazar didn't hesitate in his dry reply. "Yes, you're right in this."

Melchior and Gaspar laughed kindly at him. Melchior looked at Gaspar and said, "And you've been the brother I've never known…I'd always wished Zoth would be that for me, but it was never in his heart. Since the day I first met you in the desert Gaspar, I've known that I can count on you. Thank you, my brother."

Gaspar smiled and bowed in thanks.

They began to walk again, and Melchior continued purging his mind and heart of what had been bothering him.

"The world—it changed, right before our eyes!" he marveled. "Would you do it again?"

"Yes," answered Balthazar instantly and simply.

"Indeed!" echoed Gaspar.

"Me too," Melchior finished. "Me too," he said again softly to himself.

A line of somber men rode up, dressed in white robes, which stayed snowy white even here in the dusty desert hinterlands of Judaea. The caravan rode on horses, and they had three spare mounts tethered in the rear of the pack.

The procession came to a silent halt. Melchior wasn't sure what they were in for and readied himself for another fight. The lead rider swung down silently and approached them. He was hooded, and they couldn't discern his countenance. But he knelt smoothly before them and pulled back his hood. With his shaven head inclined, the man spoke to them in a tongue they'd never learned, yet understood all the same.

"Master Magi, we've come to serve and escort you for your much needed rest. I'm Osran, and yours to command," the man said without ever looking up.

Melchior smiled and released the inner tension he'd been holding onto. He said, "Rise, Osran. If we're among friends, then friends look each other in the eye and speak."

The man rose. His eyes were the palest blue Melchior had ever seen. His skin was like snow, his visage ageless. Studying him, Balthazar realized that the man could have been twenty years old, or 200.

"Few and far between have been the friends we've found on this journey, Osran, so you're well met," said Melchior. He extended a hand to the Watcher, who slowly took it with mild surprise.

"You'd better have food," warned the Ethiopian.

"Of course, Master Gaspar," said Osran. Gaspar's face registered mild surprise at the mention of his name, and he realized there was more to these men than strange robes.

"You shall want for nothing," assured Osran as he swung up onto his horse's back again. "Please mount, masters. We have a long way to go before you can rest."

Balthazar walked to a gray mare and began to climb into the saddle. "To where do we ride, Osran?"

Osran replied matter-of-factly, "To Vaus, our island sanctuary many leagues from here. No foot touches its shores unless invited. We've waited and watched for millennia for the star's appearance, and your arrival. It's your new home."

"Home?" asked Melchior, suspecting the worst.

"Yes," answered Osran, turning in his saddle to address the Magi on their own horses.

"Your old lives, your old kingdoms, are gone. I'm sorry for this. Were you to go there, you couldn't find them. Dust is all that would remain. You stand now *outside* of time, as Watchers, like us. And like us, when you're needed, you'll reenter the world and the flow of time to fulfill the tasks set before you by the star. This is how it has always been and always will be." He turned his steed and led the procession back the way it had come.

Gaspar shook his head and said quietly to Melchior and Balthazar, "I'm not wearing any ridiculous white robes!"

Watchers slid back and aside the Magi, offering skins of wine to drink. Melchior took a skin, squirted the strong red wine into his mouth, and savored the taste as it swirled deliciously down his throat.

He thought of Nur and his kingdom, lost to him forever. He mourned for her, for Barir and Shafiq, even for Zoth, and all the others who had perished on their pursuit of the star. And he wondered how many others would be destroyed when the star summoned them again. His heart ached.

He'd lost many, thought Melchior, certainly too many. He searched for consolation in his heart, but found none. Yet when he looked to either side of him, he found it. The men he'd found, his fellow Magi, were good men, brothers, and he realized that he loved them.

Yes, Melchior thought, he'd be glad of another death. But this new life, this one was, you may say, satisfactory

EPILOGUE

Brussels, Belgium, the 16th of June, 1815

The Duchess of Richmond moved with grace, floating across the floor in her massively skirted gown, the very picture of elegance. Her heavily powdered face didn't betray the unease that threatened her carefully planned evening.

She despaired inwardly as she looked around the ballroom. Small groups of men, some in red British military uniforms, gathered in groups and hotly debated the implications of Napoleon's escape from Elba and the new French army he'd gathered. In response, clusters of women waved fans about their faces and twittered in dismay at the lack of social engagement by the men.

Really, thought the Duchess, *this is intolerable*. The boredom in the room was almost enough to force her hand and order the orchestra to perform a piece for the latest uncouth and indecent dance, the waltz—at least that would get people's attention off The Little Colonel, or as she liked to call Bonaparte, The Mightiest of Midgets.

The Duchess approached the largest of male gatherings, the one at which stood a man with the Grand Marshall's baton tucked under his arm, the Duke of Wellington.

They bowed courteously as she approached and opened their circle to admit her. She espied her husband, the Duke of Richmond, who was at Wellington's elbow, no doubt trying to get out of the post he currently had commanding the protective garrison here in Brussels. Oh yes, she knew he wanted desperately to get in the field. Over her dead body.

"My lords, you shame me and the lovely women who grace this hall. Will you not dance, or are your hearts only bent on waging war?" the Duchess asked, staring pointedly not at her husband, but at the Duke of Wellington.

He smiled thinly, not rising to the bait. "Dear lady, you honor us with your request. But I must confess, I'm not one for the dance. My two feet don't serve me well in these matters. I prefer to have four feet beneath me. If you would allow my men to bring my horse in, perhaps I could oblige you."

The group of men laughed heartily at the jest, too heartily in fact, as the stress of what lay ahead of them was straining their humors.

One man didn't join the merriment and banter. He wore a look of mild amusement, as if he found the whole situation ludicrous. He wore the scarlet red uniform of the British officer, but it was in the uniform's sharp contrast to his face and bearing that caught your attention. Long dark hair flowed down around his shoulders, and a matching beard with flecks of gray in it lent him a distinguished look. His skin was dark, an almost olive complexion, which set him apart from his pasty-faced comrades in the group. He was striking and handsome, but with a dangerous air about him that cowed men and attracted women alike. His azure blue eyes pierced out of his dark countenance.

A lieutenant arrived and stood at attention to the side of the group, putting all conversation at an end. Wellington summoned the man forward.

"What have you to report?"

"My lord," the lieutenant said quietly, "the Prince of Orange sends his regards. His courier has arrived with news of Bonaparte." His eyes shifted nervously, not wanting to deliver the intelligence in such a setting.

"Richmond," Wellington whispered to his fellow Duke,

"do you have a good map?"

"Yes. Let us retire to my dressing room where we can speak with less...distraction," Richmond responded with a dark glance at the Duchess.

In the Duke's dressing room, ornate tables with gold leaf insets were pushed together, and a brown map of the region was spread out. Candlelight flickered about the room, casting ominous shadows on the walls. To the side of the room, the courier finished delivering the report, his thick Dutch accent coloring the language of the intelligence and betraying how loosely allied they all were against Napoleon: English, Dutch, Prussian — basically a list of every country Bonaparte had offended in his first campaign.

"Bonaparte's army moves north from Charleroi. The size of his army is large, but it moves quickly. My general, Prince William, warns that he cannot withstand the French army, as it's too large. He sends word that Bonaparte's forces greatly outnumber ours, and that my Prince of Orange is engaged in heavy fighting at Quatre Bras. He fears the outcome will not be...to your liking." He finished his reporting looking straight ahead, not daring to look at the shocked faces of the officers in the room.

"Damn. Damn! Damn! DAMN!" muttered Wellington, pounding his fist on the map. "Napoleon has humbugged me, by God. He's gained twenty-four hours' march on me!"

He stood and looked accusingly at his small assemblage of officers, speaking to no one in particular, imploring them all in general.

"Time. I need more time to get more soldiers to Orange in Quatre Bras. I need a day. If Napoleon is not slowed, he'll take Quatre Bras and divide our forces irrevocably. And if he does that . . ." His voice trailed off, Wellington almost pleading with the men, searching their faces for a miracle.

The tall dark man stepped forward from the rear of the officers gathered in the small room. The candles on the map lit his face from beneath and gave him a supernatural aura, which in turn made the other men uneasy.

"I may have a suggestion, Duke," the dark man said easily, with a confidence that seemed out of character with the mood in the room.

"Yes, Major Melchior. What do you suggest?" Wellington asked.

"Give the order to move the army to join with the Dutch. I have a feeling that the French will be slowed and unable to attack because of, ahm, inclement weather."

Sudden thunder rumbled outside. And the dark man smiled.

Napoleon Bonaparte looked at the skies in disbelief. There hadn't been a rain cloud in the sky here in Waterloo an hour ago. Now, the heavens opened and a deluge soaked the terrain for miles in every direction. He'd have to delay the deployment of his artillery and his infantry by a least a day. The delay was excruciating.

"*Merde*," he muttered and slid his hand inside his jacket to warm it against the cold wind that had mysteriously blown in as well. Why, he wondered, why were the stars always aligned against him?

— End —

About the Author

Paul Harrington has been writing professionally for over 20 years. *Epiphany* is his first novel.

Epiphany fulfills a promise he made to his mother, and he hopes she's proud up there.

Paul resides in Upstate New York with his beautiful and intelligent wife, two sons who make him laugh every day, and of this writing, a pup named Henry who needs to mend his chewing ways if he wants to continue to live with the author.